LIGHTNING DAYS
BY COLIN HARVEY

There's a mystery in the caves of Afghanistan...

British Special Agent Josh Cassidy knows there is no such thing as a routine mission when he is sent to accompany an ill-prepared band of reservists on a hastily prepared mission into the heart of Afghanistan. The mysterious heat source that showed up on the military satellites could be just about anything, but nobody is prepared to find a group of refugees from an alternate universe: a group of intelligent, **NEANDERTHAL** refugees.

Sophia and her people have shifted universes for years, trying to keep ahead of the vicious race of Sauroids that is intent on exterminating the Thals. Now the long-running battle has come to our universe, and Josh Cassidy is the only man who stands between the Sauroids and the total annihilation of everyone on the planet Earth.

Lightning Days
Swimming Kangaroo Books, July 2006
Arlington, Texas

ISBN: 1-934041-10-6

This book is a work of fiction and any resemblance to persons, living or dead, or events is purely coincidental. They are productions of the author's imagination and used fictitiously. While the some of the settings of the book are real, specific locations are fictional or are used in a fictional sense and are in no way intended to depict actual events.

Cover art by Duncan Long

Swimming
Kangaroo
Books

For Chris, who was there at the beginning,
and Bill, who was there to the end.

ACKNOWLEDGEMENTS

A huge number of people helped me over the course of writing this novel:

Bill Oullette, Chris Upson Rogers, Steve Jebson, Sheila Crosby, David Norris, Jeremy Minton, Brandon Butler, Rachel Collins, Clea, Ed Nickum, Jonathan Laden, Patrick Dilloway, Ron Parente, Jo Brooks, Stuart Malin, Clive Exner, Barbara Bates, Katrina Kidder, Jack Calvert, Gwen Veazey, Trent Waters, Tiffany Jonas, Bruce Boston, Jude Chao, and of course, for putting up with all the times my head was elsewhere, my wife Kate.

PART ONE

Now

Prologue

One Year Before Present Day

For a microsecond, reality slipped and a second Earth appeared, barely thirty thousand miles from the first, the pair orbiting the sun as close to each other as cars tailgating microns apart on a freeway. Anyone blessed with the Gods-Eye-View usually reserved for astronauts would have noticed both Earths were identical, even to the Suez Canal and Great Wall of China on each. A doppelganger moon orbited the second earth.

The titanic stresses created by the duplicates rang like a clanging chime through the planets' crusts- air, water; even the magma deep inside surged in one sudden movement.

Then the interlopers vanished.

The event was so brief that satellites missed it. The only indicators were the storms that for months afterward seemed to spring from nowhere, a surge in the Pacific that if it hadn't lost momentum as suddenly and inexplicably as it started would have dwarfed any known tsunami, and a plethora of readings inexplicable to the seismologists and oceanographers studying them.

On the remaining, original Earth, life returned to normal.

For a time.

CHAPTER ONE

Present Day

Cassidy stiffened as the shots rang out across the still Afghan morning. After several hours of nerve-shredding tension, the soldiers' discipline was momentarily fractured, and four of them scattered like quail.

Graves looked furious, but said nothing. He held up his hand until his men's training kicked in and they grew still. He murmured, "I thought the shots were in the next valley, Major."

Cassidy said equally quietly, "They were. Trust your judgment, Lieutenant." Graves' red face flushed at the implied reprimand. Cassidy continued, "You want me to stand sentry while you talk to them?"

"They're good men," Graves insisted. "Just raw. They're weekend soldiers. No one prepared them to be sent deep into bandit country with no bloody back-up, and no idea why." He glared at Cassidy.

"I know," Cassidy murmured, seeking to defuse the tension. "It's okay, Digger." He used the nickname by which Graves had introduced himself at Kandahar. He added, "At least no one fired and drew attention to us." He stretched to clap Graves on the shoulder. Cassidy was six feet tall, and few men towered over him as Graves did.

Graves nodded, his jaw still tight, and beckoned to his now immobile men. Cassidy surveyed their surroundings, turning slowly in a circle as all fourteen men huddled, the rest slowly making room for Farooq, their guide.

Not for the first time, Cassidy wished he'd bypassed the army entirely, had Iftikhar recruit a guide and set out alone, but that hadn't been an option.

The huddle broke, and the men lined up, scuffing their feet in the thick dust, their scarves wrapped round their mouths. Cassidy cursed the fools who'd planned this for not thinking of horses. That would at least have put the riders above most of the dust. The thought led to another. He tapped Graves' arm; "Do your men have night-goggles?"

Graves shook his head. "No, I've got the only pair. You?"

"Yeah. But just two pairs are no use. The men could march over a cliff in the dark." He shook his head disgustedly. *What a cock-up,* he thought. Other conflicts taking the headlines had also taken much of the budget. Resources had become increasingly stretched as little by little, cutbacks had bitten into efficiency. Cassidy sighed. "Get used to it," he muttered, too quietly for Graves to hear. "These men are all you'll get." Six of the squaddies marched in front of him, six behind, Farooq at the front, followed by Graves. High overhead, a buzzard mewed.

Soon afterwards, they entered a narrow valley, parallel to the source of the shots. "*A perfect place for an ambush,*" Graves signaled with a look, and Cassidy nodded, watching for the flash of sun on metal or glass. It was unlikely that the local bandits would be so clumsy. They had spent hundreds of years fighting the British, and the Russians, and now they fought the Americans and, once more, the British. When they weren't fighting each other.

Cresting a rise, the squad emerged into the open, walking along a narrow ridge. One side fell away, so that they walked on the side of a steep hill of dangerously unstable scree, partly covered with sparse scrub, upon which a few skeletal-ribbed goats munched. Cassidy saw no sign of any owners, so he hoped fervently that these were wild animals.

One of the men slid down the slope, turning his ankle. After a few minutes rest, he limped on, but their pace was slow. When another man twisted his ankle, Cassidy checked GPS unit again, and said quietly to Graves, "We don't have time for this. The first squad has twenty-four hours head start. We **must** catch them up. If necessary we'll leave the next man who gets injured behind to take his chances."

Graves' eyes narrowed, but like Cassidy he kept his voice low, no matter how much emotion crept in. "With respect, **sir**, I guess you're used to working alone, or with better-trained men. My boys have had basic training, but not to SAS or whatever level's needed here, and they've had no time to prepare. Meeting every Tuesday night and two weekends a month back in the UK is not enough to prepare them for being alone, in hostile territory, miles from any kind of support."

Cassidy nodded curtly.

Graves continued. "We've only been here a month. Long enough to see for ourselves how dangerous it is, but not long enough to learn how to deal with it. While you were on your way out, we had too many conflicting orders: Wait for you; get into the mountains; observe radio silence; don't involve the

Americans. Given such contradictions, we had no option but to split the platoon and send half of the men ahead. And no one has told us why we've had to hotfoot it up here from Kandahar. Sir."

Cassidy pulled a half-sympathetic, half-rueful face. "Welcome to the British Army, Lieutenant. Any army, any period in history. No one's criticizing you, but sending less than twenty men into the mountains with just a set of co-ordinates, and no instructions except, 'Look out for anything unusual' is barmy, and we're only compounding the folly of sending them in."

"Why didn't a big shot like you get us more help?" Graves asked in such a tone of wonderment that it robbed the words of their sting.

"Why do you think I spent so long in with your CO?" Cassidy asked. "We were supposed to move out at four AM, but I spent thirty minutes begging for more men. There simply aren't any. The ones who haven't been sent to the Balkans have gone to Iraq, to help the Americans fight the latest uprising in Tikrit. What's left are needed back in Kandahar. No disrespect to your men, but if there had been more experienced soldiers available, I'd have taken them." His throat irritated by the dry air and dust, Cassidy coughed, and swigged from his water bottle.

"I wondered what all the shouting was about," Graves said with a slight grin. He pointed at Cassidy's uniform, devoid of anything but a major's insignia. "Interesting regiment."

Cassidy grinned. "You mean where am I from? I wondered how long it would take you to work up the nerve to ask. I'm just a civil servant." Which was technically true. "Assistant to the Assistant to the Secretary of the Under Secretary of State. Chief tea maker."

"Bollocks are you!" Graves turned away, his color rising and his jaw set. He kicked angrily at a stone. "You're as much a civil servant as much as I'm a Martian."

"I suppose you're too young to remember Northern Ireland during the Troubles?"

Graves stared. "You served there?"

"I did," Cassidy said grimly. "It's not a memory that gives me any pleasure. Whenever we went out on patrol, it never felt like we had enough men, or were fully prepared. Anything could happen, and we knew it. Anyone who seemed friendly might have a concealed gun. You learned to look under every car, including your own. The point, Digger, is that if we survive this mission, you still won't ever feel prepared. Get used to that feeling. When it's not there, that's when you become complacent. That's when you're most likely to die. But if you survive, like me, you become a useful asset. The army seconded me to the political sections, and it's a near permanent thing, but yes, I'm a civil servant. Just like you and everyone else who works for the government." He stared at Graves. "Imply that I'm a liar again, and when we get back, I'll break your jaw."

Graves muttered, "Sorry," and looked away.

To ease the tension, Cassidy said, "This country's had every misfortune possible; occupied for centuries by British, Russians, and now the UN; internecine strife between ruling warlords. They even have drought." His laugh was sad.

Graves nodded, still stiff with resentment. "The landscape looks...what's the word? Blasted?" he said at last, when the silence threatened to become awkward.

They resumed their trek. Two more men turned ankles, but Graves, casting dark looks at Cassidy, urged them to limp on.

The silence was broken by a clatter of rocks tumbling down, and several of the men flinched. Cassidy stood statue-still, every nerve straining, listening for the sounds of men moving. When he was satisfied that the rocks had simply fallen and not been dislodged, Graves waved the squad on.

The hills shimmered in the heat. The sky was a vaulted arch, so fiercely blue that it hurt unshielded eyes. The ground rose and dropped, twisted and turned, as if determined that only the fittest and bravest would walk it.

Graves stopped panting, and drew enough breath to echo his earlier statement, "It may be blasted, but it's beautiful." Lifting his scarf, he spat. "Even if all you can smell or taste is dust."

"But it's a beauty like that of a poisonous snake," Cassidy said. "It'll kill you at any moment. Its people are as inconstant as the land." He added, "There will be less dust the higher we climb, especially as we emerge from the rain-shadow cast by the mountains."

They emerged from a long ravine into open ground, in the shadow of a rock that was vertical on one side, and a forty-five degree slope on the other. Graves said, "The men could do with a meal. They had us packing our rucksacks at three this morning." He grinned. "You probably know how much fun it is packing sixty-five kilos in the dark."

Try doing it in the snow sometime. Cassidy thought of a nasty mission in the Norwegian winter, but only nodded. "Twenty minutes." He glanced at his watch. Men on the move needed at least four meals a day to balance all the calories they burned. *All the more reason to keep the breaks short,* he thought.

Graves signaled the men to halt. They dropped to their knees in the shelter of the rock, out of the wind. Cassidy dragged air into his oxygen starved lungs. He'd trained at altitude before, but never this high. And they had still higher to climb. Although the others were probably ten years his junior, they were breathing just as heavily as he was. One man lay prone on the ground. As Graves posted guards, they unclipped their packs, stretched, and broke out their rations.

After a few minutes, Cassidy took a cautious mouthful of chemically reheated shepherd's pie. Chewing, he looked up to see Graves studying him, and raised an eyebrow in silent question.

"What happens," Graves said, "if you're buried under an avalanche?"

There was a long silence then Cassidy said, "You'd better make sure that doesn't happen."

"That's your fallback plan?" Graves asked with quiet fury. "My men are here for eight months, supposedly on police duties. The regular army sneer at them as 'weekend warriors,' yet with no warning they're marched halfway to nowhere and expected-"

"Lieutenant," Cassidy warned.

Graves fell silent, folding his now empty ration tray over and over again into an ever-smaller square. He repeated, "What happens if you're buried under an avalanche? Do we abort?"

Cassidy stared into space, thinking furiously. He said, "If you repeat any of this, you'll spend the rest of your life under house arrest." Graves looked so serious, that Cassidy almost laughed. "Where to begin?" He smiled at Graves. "At least you've been spared sitting in the August Bank Holiday traffic jams."

"One thing I don't miss," Graves said. "That where you were Monday night?"

Cassidy nodded. "I've barely slept in forty-eight hours."

Graves chuckled. "And there I was bitching about getting up at three. Sorry."

"Don't worry," Cassidy said. "I sat in a traffic jam, having a blazing row with my girlfriend over my supposed commitment phobia. My spare mobile rang." He smiled at the memory of Caitlin's incredulous, "How many bloody mobiles have you got?" His smile faded. "I was summoned to a briefing at COBRA," he continued. "The Joint HQ-"

"I know what COBRA is," Graves said harshly.

They stiffened at a muffled roar in the distance. For perhaps twenty seconds neither man spoke, then Cassidy resumed. "A satellite had photographed a large heat source. A huge number of bodies, maybe ten thousand, in the mountains northeast of Tora

Bora. On the next orbit, they'd disappeared." He sighed. "I take it you realize the...concern this caused?"

Graves smiled thinly, "Oh, yes. One of the most sensitive areas in the world, and they have a vanishing army. That's why they're panicking?"

Cassidy nodded, impressed at how quickly Graves caught on. "That, and the fact they've no idea who the bodies are. Not knowing *anything* scares our elected masters more witless than usual."

Graves smiled. "All the usual suspects are accounted for?"

Cassidy nodded. "Until we find who or what is in the mountains, no one is to know, not even the Americans. So radio silence, and absolute secrecy."

"What happens when we find them?" Graves asked.

Cassidy said, "That depends on what we find."

While the men finished their food, and lit cigarettes, Cassidy stood and loosened up with Tai Chi exercises, ignoring the other's smiles. Despite his aches, he felt alive. Anything could happen. He always felt this way at the start of a new mission. Maybe this time he wouldn't end it feeling like a slowly deflating balloon.

Turning away from the others, he took Caitlin's picture from inside his pocket. Kissing his fingers he touched them to the photo. "Bye babe," he murmured, "It was good, but it's over." He wished he'd ended it more gracefully than dumping her publicly on the motorway.

He became aware that Graves was watching him with interest. "That the ex-girlfriend?"

Cassidy nodded. He studied Graves, looking so long and hard at the young man that the Lieutenant blinked and then looked away.

Cassidy clearly came to a decision. He grinned wolfishly. "If I was Intelligence, as you think," he held up a hand, "which I'm not, of course, but if I was, I'd go mad without someone to talk to. The security services discourage Catholicism, unless the priest is vetted. Can't give confession to the unauthorized." He chuckled grimly at Graves' face.

"Is that true?" Graves whispered.

Cassidy smiled. "Of course. I never lie."

Graves laughed softly. "Which is itself a lie."

Cassidy said, still whispering, "Once an agent found out about Hitler's v-weapons, but she couldn't tell anyone without compromising security. When a V-1 killed a member of her family, her guilt caused a nervous breakdown. Unless someone is a psychopath, it's impossible to keep secrets, or assume another identity for long periods, without some kind of safety valve. It can be a mirror, or a picture. Everyone needs someone to talk to." He tore the picture up, and buried the pieces.

"Who will you talk to now?"

"You," Cassidy said. Relishing Graves' shocked look, he said, "Come on, time to move on."

Graves lifted up his backpack to muted groans from the men.

"Make sure you bury your cigarette butts, and any other rubbish," Cassidy ordered.

As they neared noon and climbed ever higher it grew colder as the biting wind that cut through their thermals gathered strength. The only sounds apart from an occasional muttered comment were the buzzard crying in the wind, and, suddenly in the distance, the high-pitched chopping of a helicopter's rotors. "Trouble, sir." Graves said, looking young, green, and very scared.

Cassidy asked, "How many choppers do the tribesmen have?"

Graves grimaced sheepishly. "It's ours."

"Don't worry," Cassidy said. "We're all a bit twitchy."

A soldier signaled, waving to the northeast. Cassidy saw smoke rising in a thin twisting stream, torn by the wind, but still holding together, so thin and slight it would have been invisible, if they hadn't been looking for it. Even so, they were lucky to have seen it. "The first patrol?" Graves said. Cassidy nodded.

They quickened their pace, and every time they slowed, Graves urged his men on. They rounded a bend, and saw bodies strewn across the defile. A small fire burning in the midst of the bodies was the source of the smoke.

Graves waved a signal and the men ducked, two of them running crouched to the bodies, while the rest dived, lying prone in a star-shape, guns pointing outward in all directions. The runners checked for identity tags, and scuttled back.

"Five men, sir," the lead soldier, a Stan Laurel-look-alike in his late twenties with horn-rimmed glasses and an oversized adam's apple said, "Ours and theirs. Weapons are gone." He looked pale, swallowed several times. "They've been shot. No mutilations."

"They don't take ears, or scalps, soldier," Cassidy said. Stan's face went blank. Cassidy said, more kindly, "Pashtuns, Uzbeks, other tribes; they're all skilled, brave warriors who fought the supposedly superior Russians to a standstill for ten years." Stan looked like he'd swallowed a wasp, but shut his mouth. *Good,* Cassidy thought. *The roasting's taken his mind off those corpses.*

"But it was locals who did it?" Graves asked.

Cassidy shrugged. "Probably. Most of them are gangsters of some type. They won't have changed their habits, even though the Taliban are no longer in power. If it was them, they'll be selling the missing weapons in Peshawar before you can say knife." The Pakistani border markets were the main channels through which goods flowed in and out of Southern Afghanistan.

"More bodies there," another soldier pointed up a defile.

Cassidy followed the soldier who scurried to check them out. He turned one over, and a young Afghan stared back with sightless eyes.

"Sir," someone hissed as the others joined them. "Looks like they took their wounded with them." He pointed to drag marks in the sand.

Graves and Cassidy exchanged looks. Graves asked, "Do we follow?" and Cassidy nodded.

"Sir," the medic called, "Take a look at this." It was another Afghan body. The orderly's finger highlighted tiny wounds, surrounded by oddly shaped burn marks.

Graves hissed an in-drawn breath. "Seen these before?" As Cassidy shook his head, Graves said, "Would you say if you had?"

Cassidy allowed him a small smile. "Maybe." He added, "How many men from the patrol?"

Graves counted the corpses, "Four bodies," he said grimly. "The guide's one of them. So nine men missing."

They should have waited, Cassidy thought. Orders or not, they should have waited and sent us all together. Thirteen men are too easily picked off.

They quickly piled rocks over the bodies, Cassidy glancing discreetly at his watch. Graves said a simple but heartfelt prayer, his voice quavering as he said, "They shall not grow old."

They moved on, the sound of their laboring breath and their boots crunching on stones the only noises in the stillness. Cassidy was aware of every passing second, and that the fate of the first group lay with his men finding them as quickly as possible. But he was also aware that he might have to abandon them, rather than endanger the mission.

***

Fourteen months earlier

MaryAnn Stanford chewed absently on a granola bar. It had grown gradually hotter throughout the day, thunderheads building from the east until the sky was an inky black. By mid-afternoon, forked lightning stabbed the ground.

"'Nother twister there, Freddy." MaryAnn peered through the windshield. "Been a lot of 'em lately," she muttered, switching the radio off.

It started to rain. In less than a minute, raindrops were bouncing three inches off the pickup's hood. "Shoot!" She jumped as a hundred yards away a lightning bolt gouged up clumps of soil. Her old black retriever lay on the front passenger seat. He whimpered, trying to bury his nose in his blanket. "It's okay, baby." She fondled his ears absently.

She swerved to avoid the shape that loomed from the curtain of rain, and wrestled with the steering wheel, fighting to keep the pickup right side up as the world tilted crazily from side to side, before ending up in a drainage ditch that ran parallel to the road. She opened the window and leaned out. "Yuh moron! Yuh coulda killed us both!"

He wandered closer, standing naked in the downpour. It took her a while to realize that he was deformed. He had too-short legs, a curved spine, and a flatter than normal skull with a bulge at the back, almost like an egg laid on its side. His forehead was almost non-existent, and his eyebrows perched on a thick shelf of bone.

Even from several feet away, she heard his hoarse little cries. She'd seen the look on his face before; it had been on a man whose arm had been sheared off in a thresher. The look of a man just before he was hit by the full enormity of the pain. The look of absolute, overwhelming shock.

MaryAnn remembered a school trip from forty years before, to the Indianapolis Children's Museum. Although she couldn't dredge up the word, "Neanderthal" from memory, she recognized that he looked just like the models of pre-humans had in the museum dioramas. She was so distracted that she never thought of the impossibility of his presence. Although she had no children, she had strong maternal instincts, and this poor creature looked as if he needed a mother badly.

She jumped out, and they both shied at the lightning bolt that blasted the ground only yards away. He bared his teeth and shouted at it.

"C'mon! We're getting soaked here!" MaryAnn yelled.

He gave her a wary look.

She yanked open the rear passenger door of the pickup. "Git in, dammit!" She waved frantically at the doorway. Edging round her, he climbed in, with little of the nervousness she would have expected from someone like him. She'd never intended the rear bench of the pickup's elongated cabin for anything but junk, but he couldn't sit in the open bay of the flatbed. Reaching round his cowering figure, she swept candy wrappers, a McDonalds® box and a pair of Freddy-chewed socks onto the floor.

She jumped in and gunned the engine. It didn't move. She tried it again; it reared and then rolled back. At the third attempt she managed to back the pickup out.

They resumed their crawl through the rain. Lifting his head, Freddy thumped his tail. She patted his head. "You like dogs?" she asked, as if her passenger understood every word.

He said something in what sounded like the drunken slur of Russian or Portuguese. At least he could talk, even if he did look like a circus act.

"His name's Freddy," she said, and remembering what she'd been trying to forget, her voice wobbled, "I'm taking him to the vet. He's old, an' he's shitting blood."

He clearly understood her tone of voice, if not the words, and spoke gently, patting her arm through the gap in the seats.

Freddy growled softly. "Hey, no jealousy," she warned the dog, pleased at the distraction. "He's not used to having a man round," she explained, "It's always been jest me an' him." They drove through the rain at a steady thirty.

"What's the smell?" She said after a while. "That you? Like wet fur and I dunno..." She paused. "Makes me think of food." She chuckled. "To be honest, everything reminds me of food. It's why I shop at outsize shops." She waved a granola bar at him. "Ya want one?" She passed it to him, and unwrapped a second one. "It ain't chocolate," she said. "Doc Hewlett warned me off chocolate, though the zits still ain't cleared up. And I dunno if it'll help my," she paused, thinking, "cholesterol." She looked in the mirror. "Y'ain't s'posed to eat the wrapper!"

After an hour or so of companionable semi-silence marked by MaryAnn's occasional muttering, they passed the windmill that marked the edge of Pocona. "We're here." Her voice was barely a whisper. "Vet's place." She wiped her nose and eyes. Walking round to the passenger side, she opened the door and stroked Freddy's square black head. He whimpered. "Okay, baby boy," she crooned. "Momma'll stay with you." She turned, said to her passenger, "Don't know how long I'll be. Stick around, or not." Grunting with the effort, she lifted the dog, blanket and all. "Okay baby," she crooned again, as Freddy started to whine. She panted, "He's only skin an' bones now, but he still weighs a ton." Pushing the door shut, she trudged through the downpour.

***

The rain had slackened to a drizzle by the time she emerged. Still holding the blanket she stood by the passenger door as if unsure what to do, trudged round to the other side, and stopped. She returned to the passenger side, and holding awkwardly onto the blanket, opened the door. "Don't know what happened there," she said, in a high tight voice, placing the empty blanket gently on the seat. Returning to the driver's side, she climbed in. Mucus ran down her nose unchecked, but she paused only to wipe her eyes.

Starting the engine, she asked, "Where ya wanna go?" He didn't answer, so she set off the way they had come. When they had driven a few miles, her grief overtook her, and she cried, "I gotta stop!" She pulled over, and her entire body shook with great, heaving sobs.

The Neanderthal reached out toward her, making soft little crooning noises, but stopping just short of touching her. When her sobs showed no sign of stopping, he reached out again, but they both flinched as his hand touched her arm.

Moments passed with her still sobbing, and then he reached out again. He half-flinched, but this time left his hand on her arm, and stroked her arm gently. "I guess," she spluttered, and he took his hand away, but she couldn't finish the sentence, and he resumed stroking her arm, still crooning gently.

"Funny," she said, with a laugh that was more a sob, "Yuh prob'ly can't understand a word I'm saying, but I can talk to yuh. Then again, Freddy couldn't understand me neither. Maybe that's why I could talk to him. He couldn't tell me what a load of cack I was spouting."

At Freddy's name, she began to sob again. The Neanderthal made a cautious half-movement toward the front seat, and hesitated. When she didn't protest, he climbed carefully into the front, making soothing noises, and stroking her arm. She groaned and he drew back, but she slumped over the steering wheel. When he stroked her lank hair, crooning, MaryAnn fell into his arms, clawing at him, howling her grief. They were so preoccupied that they never noticed the swirling clouds high above the car. The clouds coalesced into a vortex.

***

Cassidy wriggled backwards on his stomach, and when he was well away from the edge, stood and dusted down his fatigues. Below them was a village, an adobe compound with lookout towers and gun slits around a square, nestled in the valley. "No adults about," he said. "Just children and a few scrawny hens."

The squad marched on, Cassidy occasionally glancing over his shoulder, although he couldn't say why he felt so spooked.

At noon Graves checked his GPS. Farooq knelt in the direction Graves indicated, and prayed to Mecca. As Farooq stood one of the men pointed. Cassidy followed the soldier's outstretched arm.

"Looks like a dart," Graves said. It flickered in and out of sight and turned end over end. It vanished, and Graves said, "Experimental plane?"

"No idea," Cassidy said. "Nothing I've ever seen moves like that." For the first time he felt as afraid as the people in Downing Street must have. Graves waved the men onwards.

Graves leaned conspiratorially toward Cassidy, clearly wanting to talk. "How did you end up not a spook?"

"Before I joined the civil service," Cassidy stressed the last four words. "I served in the Royal Greenjackets. I made major, then took a career break to attend university. Never went back but was allowed to keep my rank in return for making myself available as an advisor." Graves looked impressed. Cassidy said, "What do you do, when you're not playing weekend warrior?"

Graves glared at him, then grinned back. "Snob," he jeered. "I'm a Phys Ed lecturer. But I've always wanted to serve my country, probably in reaction to my parents. They say we either behave like them, or behave completely the opposite."

"Your parents don't approve of your being here?"

"Ma's never forgiven me for joining the oppressive war machine, even on a part-time basis," Graves said, grinning. "She was a peace protester at Greenham Common back in '83. My partner's not exactly happy with me being here, either. I live with someone. Lived," he corrected himself. "I don't know if she'll wait eight months. Does your – oh, no partner, is there? What do your parents think of your being a..." he paused for effect, "...civil servant?"

"They don't think anything," Cassidy said. "My mother's dead." Seeing Graves was about to offer condolences, he interrupted. "I was born in a London squat, apparently, to a girl who couldn't name my father." She'd left him only her genes, and a burning desire to be more than what he had started as. Seeing Graves' shocked look, he said, "What?"

Graves shrugged. "Not the glamorous background I'd have expected for one of your lot," he said.

"My lot?" Cassidy asked, deliberately misunderstanding. "Do I look like a film star?" He added, "My eyes are too close together, my lips are too thin, and my nose is too big."

"And it's been broken," Graves said.

"Twice. Thank you for pointing that out." Cassidy said. "So you see, I'm far too ugly to be a spook."

"You're not ugly, you're just..." Graves floundered.

"Forgettable?"

"Forgettable," Graves agreed. "Which is perfect for a man in your line of work." He grinned. "And you know I don't mean a film star."

"My work is as mundane as any other civil servant's." Cassidy didn't explain that much of his work was state-sponsored petty crime. Theft, burglary and observation with some occasional violence, unpleasant but necessary.

"Why do you do it?"

Cassidy shrugged. "Not for money or glamour; there isn't much. Maybe a mix of idealism and vocation." Perhaps this mission would re-infuse him with some of what had seeped away.

"You must have broken every rule in the book, telling me all this," Graves said.

"What rule?" Cassidy asked. "You don't know how old I am, what my name really is, or anything. And I'm a good judge of character. You won't tell anyone." Graves raised an eyebrow, but Cassidy changed the subject abruptly. "The lads have done well today. There's always a danger that men will buckle in the field. No amount of training can really prepare them." He added, "It's not for me to tell them that they did well, of course."

"Thanks," Graves flushed.

Clearing the tree line, they walked again on bare, hard rock following the trail left by an occasional flattened shrub. "This is too easy," Cassidy muttered to Graves, looking up from his GPS unit. "The trail is leading us right to the coordinates where we need to go. Keep the men alert."

Dense, thick forests now lay below, in every direction. Cassidy said, "These must be the remnants of the cedar forests I was told once covered Afghanistan." He never knew what faint noise alerted him, but something did. He threw himself flat, shouting, "Down! Down!"

CHAPTER TWO

One of the others wasn't fast enough. He spun in time to the metallic rattle of an AK-47, his cry cut short. Another soldier shrieked and clutched his abdomen with bloodied fingers. Cassidy smelled the coppery tang of blood and the fetid stench of a soldier soiling himself in death. The squad returned fire in a whizzing hail of bullets. Rattling gunfire, shouted commands, and the screams of the wounded made an infernal din.

Cassidy tasted blood, and realized he'd bitten through his lip. He watched for a few moments, calculating, then trained his sights. He waited, fired, and saw a body topple sideways. He waited for another assailant to show himself, squeezed off a single shot, and waited.

No movement. *Good,* he thought. Probably four left, if he'd judged it right. He sighted the next assailant, twenty yards to the right, and picked him off. "Hey, Digger?" he called to Graves, but the lieutenant didn't reply. Cassidy looked and saw the man's body lying facedown. Cassidy rolled Graves over. He saw the open, staring eyes, the fly buzzing on Graves' ear, and hissed, "Oh shit." He called out to the scared-looking Stan Laurel-look-alike. "What's your name?"

"Davenport, sir." Although he looked as if he hardly needed to shave, Cassidy guessed Davenport was in his late twenties.

"Davenport, have the men lay down three hundred sixty-degree covering fire. Have them take a segment each, rather than all firing at random. Got it?"

"Yessir," Davenport blinked behind his glasses, but he moved quickly, passing the order along.

Cassidy lifted his head a fraction, heard the whine of a near miss. His heart bumped so fast it threatened to break free from his body; but when he saw movement, he fired steadily, and ducked back. Davenport and the others laid down covering fire, allowing him to bob up, and fire long, intense bursts.

The noise level dropped slightly. "Disengage!" Beneath the ringing in his ears from the firefight, Cassidy heard only silence. "They're finished!" The battle had lasted perhaps two minutes, but in the adrenaline maelstrom it had felt like hours.

***

They interred the dead, friend and enemy together. Cassidy led the prayers. Graves was the hardest one to bury; only hours before the lieutenant had himself led the memorial for the fallen. Cassidy wondered how Graves' mother would take the news, and thought of the partner that might not have waited for him. But he was uncomfortably aware, too, of how little time they had to mourn. At least duty obliterated the nagging feeling of abandonment that was always there when a friend died.

Davenport said, "What about the wounded, sir?" He indicated the two men propped up against the rocks. One of the men was white-faced and shaking, his teeth clenched in agony. The other one sat with his head lolling forward, blood trickling from his ear.

"We observe radio silence," Cassidy said flatly.

Davenport looked at Cassidy imploringly.

"Christ alive, we can't leave them!" someone shouted.

"The next man who questions orders," Cassidy said severely, and, looking in turn at each of the men, released his safety catch. "Will be treated as a mutineer, and face a field court-martial." The word "execution" hung unsaid in the air. "Got it?"

Davenport led the reluctant nods.

Cassidy added, to offer a little hope, "We'll call in a chopper as soon as we no longer need to observe radio silence. We'll move the wounded men there," he pointed to a flat, open area. "And provide the co-ordinates as soon as we can." Normally moving wounded men was unthinkable- if they had spinal injuries, they risked suffering paralysis- but this wasn't a normal situation. Leaving men behind to die never got any easier.

Two soldiers carried each wounded man, one by the arms, the other his legs, morphine injections easing the pain. Cassidy brought up the rear. When they reached the open area, the bearers gently deposited the wounded and propped them against a rock. "They should be partly hidden by the rock, at least from that side." He pointed to the lee side of the rock. *It's better than nothing,* he thought.

Leaving a little food and ammunition, the soldiers resumed their hike, some of the men looking back unhappily.

When they were in the next valley, Cassidy said quietly, "What's your first name, Davenport?"

"Brian." He smiled, showing rabbit-like top teeth. "They call me Bunny."

"You married, Bunny?"

"I've got a partner, sir. And a one year old. Daisy," he grinned, a fleeting smile that made him look younger still. "I didn't think what a daft name Daisy Davenport was, until after we'd named her."

Cassidy nodded at the other soldiers. "How old are these men? Twenty-five?"

Davenport nodded. "Twenty-two, twenty-three, mostly. Reed's twenty-five, with kids. Pavey's twenty. He's going to College in the autumn. Most are on the dole. Joining the TA's something to do at weekends, to break up the monotony, and give them some pin money – what isn't reclaimed by the DSS. You're unavailable for work on those days so they dock your dole money..." He shook his head at the unfairness of it. "They're good lads," he added.

Cassidy wanted to say that he'd make sure they got home but it would have been a hollow promise; the mission came first.

They said little for the next hour, concentrating on the march. They followed the continuing trail of dislodged rocks, broken shrubs, or a scrap of clothing while at the same time Cassidy kept checking the co-ordinates of the satellite photos. The trail was leading the squad inexorably toward where the heat-signatures had been. They entered a narrow valley and stood at what the photos had indicated was ground zero for the mass of bodies.

Farooq stood on the bumpy, uneven ground at the base of a cliff and pointed upwards. The tracks vanished, but the damaged bushes and occasional boot prints were clear signs that someone had climbed it recently.

Cassidy made out the mouth of a tunnel half-hidden in the shadows. He looked round at the high walls of the sheer-sided cliffs surrounding them and cursed. There was no chance of calling in air support if he needed it. He signaled, and Farooq led the line in single file, up the twisting track carved into the side of the cliff.

***

Henry Obanga whispered, "The wind at your back has blown over three thousand miles, all the way from the South Pole." But he couldn't help feeling disappointed. Separated from him by a hundred yards of steel-blue shale, the Perito Moreno glacier was dirty gray, not the crisp clean whiteness he'd expected.

"I bet they don't have nothing like this in South Africa," Jackson boomed. *Detestable oaf,* Henry thought, but said nothing. Henry was a lightly built five-foot-five, and while no coward, he saw no point in picking a fight with someone a foot taller, ninety pounds heavier and thirty years younger than he. In the middle of Argentina, as isolated and empty as it was possible for a place to be, he had to be stuck in the same tour group as this booming, mountainous boor. Determined to escape Jackson, he stalked away past Jerry, who gave him a wink.

Henry had met a kindred spirit in Jerry. Middle-aged, apparently stolid, Jerry's round frame hid a wicked sense of humor and a child-like fascination with wildlife. Whenever he spotted a bird or an animal with his binoculars, he would exclaim joyfully and pass the binoculars on to the rest of the group so they could share his delight.

Jerry and Pam Hobbs had asked Henry to join them at dinner two nights earlier. Henry wished he'd met them before. Despite, or perhaps because of their English reserve, he liked them a lot. He had booked a customized tour, so Jackson and he often only traveled with people for one or two days before he or they moved on. It had proven surprisingly lonely. After three years of widowhood, he had thought he'd grown used to solitude.

Jackson's booming voice interrupted Henry's reverie. Again. Things were always bigger, better, newer in Texas. Henry wished he had a rand for every time Jackson had said the word "Texas" that day.

If Jerry was a white English version of Henry, Jackson was a copy of the Afrikaners of Henry's youth. They had been loud, opinionated, and so insensitive to the feelings of the local people that that they had driven the mild-mannered Henry into the African National Congress, causing him to abandon his early dream of studying archeology. The nocturnal struggles against oppression as well as the duties of raising a family and cleaning the Stein Mutual office left no time for childish dreams.

The highlands beyond the glacier rose gradually toward the horizon of snow-capped dun and khaki-colored hills. Although he could not see the distant Andes, he knew they were there beyond the horizon. Behind them, an immense steel-blue alluvial flood plain shone beneath the fierce southern sun, the tracks of the previous year's floods still obvious in the piled mounds of gray slate. It was barren desert. Anything that tried to grow here was blasted out when the flash floods hit like water from a cannon.

"We've come as close as we can get to the glaciers," Esteban, their young guide said, kicking at a dirty white ice-slide, an avalanche frozen in time. He flashed the bright smile that had amused Henry for most of the last week.

Juan, their rumpled, swarthy driver, whose Zapata moustache dominated his face, spoke little English, so Esteban had done the talking, pointing out the sights while they sped along the highway across the pampas. Esteban was in his early twenties. He clearly thought he was an international playboy, with his toothy smile, shirt open halfway down his chest, gold medallion glinting, and exaggerated charm toward every woman he met. Even so, Henry liked him. Beneath the comic predator was a nice kid.

"We're not going to walk on it?" Henry was surprised at how disappointed he was. Grace, his wife, had always wanted to walk in the snow, and Henry was making this little pilgrimage in her memory.

Esteban shook his head, with a grimace, either of regret, or at the thought of walking. "I'm sorry, no, is not possible."

"Just as well," Pam said to Jerry. "You'd probably turn an ankle." She was a small, red-faced woman who spent most of her time fretting, mostly about Juan's driving.

Nearby, a stream ran toward the melt-waters on the plain. Cables in the water led to a small box and a panel facing the sun. Henry mused at the incongruity of finding something man-made in the middle of nowhere. "What does it do?" he asked.

"It measures the flow of water and the temperature." Esteban lit another of his incessant cigarettes. The solitude was illusory; as they tramped round a bend in the stream, their feet working the shale as if it were sand, they came upon three heavy-duty wooden tables and benches bolted to the ground. Beyond the benches, footprints arrowed toward the glacier: "Tourists?" Henry asked, wondering how old the prints were. No one answered.

In the midst of such immensity, beneath a surprisingly warm sun and a blazing blue sky, Henry felt euphoric. He wanted so much to walk on the glacier. Grace had never had the chance- she had died of cancer before they could take this trip- and here he was, so close. He couldn't see any reason why he couldn't take one little step outward onto the snow. As the wind blew at his back, he slipped away from the group, determined to fulfill this part of his and Grace's dream.

It was heavy going on the shale, which continually slid beneath his feet. Jerry had joined him, as much, he suspected, to stop his suddenly obsessed friend from plunging into a sinkhole, as from any urge to walk on the snow, but the other man soon fell behind.

As soon as he broached the top of a hill, another reared up in front of him. Henry's shoes were soon coated in gray dust. Apparently solid, the dunes sat atop the glacier, the snow, rock and gravel layered like the raw mix of marble cake. The landscape reminded him of that of the moon, he decided, complete with craters. He tossed a stone into the melt-water filling one of the small basins, and dipped his hand in. Instantly he pulled it out with a startled hiss. The water was cold enough to freeze his fingers off!

He came to one of several fast-flowing streamlets running from the glacier base. Picking the narrowest channel, he stepped carefully over it and climbed yet another shale hill.

Jerry's voice startled him. "I think Esteban's terrified you'll drop down a hole," the other man called. "They've followed us," He pointed to the figures of Esteban and Juan trudging behind them. "Think how it'd look if they lost a tourist."

Henry smiled. He could see Jerry's point, but he still wanted to walk on the glacier.

They were nearly at the base of the glacier. Just as Henry could smell the snow, could almost stretch across and squeeze it in his hands, he saw a large lake of melt-water in front of them. He stared at it, dismayed. "If I'd only brought my waders," he called to Jerry.

"I think you'd need more than waders to get across that," Jerry came up beside him, wiping sweat off his brow. "There's no telling how deep that is at it gets further out. You'd need a boat."

Henry sighed, and took a deep breath. "Time to go back," He said, finally defeated. To ease the sudden ache of longing that would never be fulfilled, he swept the skyline with Jerry's binoculars. He wasn't expecting to see anything but hill and sky, but he was wrong. He clutched Jerry's arm. "Look!" he said, passing the glasses back to his friend. He pointed to a nearby slope. There was a group of men sliding down the dun-colored hill.

There were about twenty, all masked and wearing goggles. There was something odd about them, but Henry couldn't quite work out what it was. They moved quickly, but with an eerie silence; the only noise Henry could hear was the swishing of the shale as they slid down the steep bank. "Where the heck did they come from?" he wondered aloud.

Time seemed to slow. Esteban and Juan ran toward the men, shouting and waving handguns. Henry had never dreamed that the guides carried guns, but perhaps he'd been naïve. They were, after all, in a country where the number of people who had disappeared at the hands of the secret police ran into the tens of thousands.

Juan stopped, took aim, and fired. *He's got no chance of hitting them at that distance,* Henry thought.

As the newcomers came nearer, Henry heard them calling to each other in a strange, harsh, guttural language. One of them halted, and aimed a rifle-like weapon at Esteban and Juan. There was a thud, and Juan stopped and then toppled backward down the slope. Esteban stopped as if paralyzed.

"We'd better get out of here," Jerry whispered tersely.

"No point," Henry said grimly. "They'll out-run us easily."

"Please God, don't let them hurt Pam," Jerry said in a low voice. As the group skidded to a halt around them, Henry and Jerry raised their hands slowly.

The uniforms were unfamiliar, dark green overalls with bulging pockets. Their helmets were flatter than normal, and oddly egg-shaped. They wore bandanas wrapped round their lower faces. The wind blew one bandana up for a moment, revealing an almost chinless face.

Everything Henry had ever believed possible fell away beneath him. He felt as though his legs could no longer hold his weight. "I thought they were bandits, Jerry," Henry said. "But they're not. They may wear modern uniforms, but these are Neanderthals, or I'm an Afrikaner."

***

Cassidy had never felt so exposed as when the squad crept down the stygian gloom of the tunnel. The men's shuffling footsteps echoed in the silence. Their torches, filtered to minimize disruption to their vision, shone red on the tunnel walls. Cassidy wore night gasses so he could see beyond the pitifully narrow circles of light cast by the torches.

He steadied his ragged breaths, wanting to sound calm for the benefit of his men. "Shine the lights on the floor!" he hissed. "Or I'll be half-blinded in these things!"

He heard whispered "Sorry's" from behind him and the beams moved to the floor of the tunnel. Suddenly he heard one of the men say in a loud whisper, "Don't move, sir!"

Cassidy froze. He lifted his goggles, looked down and saw a body in the red light of his torch-beam. He knelt and touched its neck. It was cold to his touch. "One of the first patrol," he said. There was no trace of steam on the small mirror Cassidy held to the dead man's mouth. "There's nothing we can do for him. But at least we know we're on the right trail." Night gasses on again, Cassidy saw a faint light ahead of them, coming from round the next corner.

"It's warm in here," one of the men behind him whispered.

"Maintain silence!" Cassidy hissed. It *was* warm. With their stuffy heat and poor ventilation, the tunnels reminded him of the depths of the nearby Tora Bora

Cassidy wondered if he was out of his depth. Maybe he should retreat and call for back up. He dismissed the thought almost instantly. There was nowhere for any support to land. "Come on," he said, stepping carefully around the body on the ground.

Seconds later, he heard a rumble. The ground bucked and heaved beneath his feet, like a wet animal shaking itself. He could hear the men behind him scrabbling to keep their footing. He placed his hand on the wall for support. The quake passed, leaving behind clouds of dust dancing in the torchlight. Several of the men sneezed. "Cover your mouths!" Cassidy hissed, "Or we'll announce our arrival." He considered sending those who were sneezing back, but decided that he didn't have any men to spare. He hadn't left a guard at the tunnel's mouth for the same reason.

They waited while the dust subsided, and then resumed a slow, careful, steady march down the tunnel, toward the faint light, until they reached a bend in the corridor. Davenport waved a trooper forward, but Cassidy ordered, "Stay!" and the man froze.

Davenport stared and whispered, "What are you doing?"

Cassidy ignored him and stepped forward. It was a breach of protocol, he knew. As senior officer, he shouldn't unnecessarily expose himself to risk, but he felt he needed to take this one. Leaving the wounded men behind still stuck in his throat.

He turned the corner into a wide, open cavern. Half of the walls were lined with air conditioning pumps, while cupboards and racks containing tins of food, medical supplies and ammunition ran from floor to ceiling on whatever space was left. Several other tunnels led away from the cavern.

In the middle of the cave sat a group of people. All but one of the group wore British uniforms. They sat cross-legged on the floor with heads bowed, as if meditating. Only one of them was not manacled.

She wore no uniform, only briefs, and a top wrapped round her small breasts. She reminded Cassidy of an extra from Metropolis or Flash Gordon. Her hair, a streaked shoulder-length mixture of blonde and ash-gray, hung forward, obscuring her face. She too appeared to be asleep.

Then she lifted her head, and he saw with a shock that her chin was almost non-existent. Her forehead sloped back, and above her eyes was a bony shelf that thrust outward. Cassidy stared at her, stunned. *Ohmigod, I'm looking at a Neanderthal,* he thought. Her skin was blotchy, as though she suffered from a bad case of eczema or vitiligo, and her face was a harlequin patchwork of brown, pink, vanilla white and black skin. But when she opened her eyes and spoke in flawless English, her voice was as warm and rich as honey. "Welcome, Major Cassidy."

CHAPTER THREE

Cassidy's first thought was that someone was playing a huge joke on him. He felt waves of shock, disbelief and anger sweeping over him in quick succession. Had he walked into a trap, he wondered. He took a step backward, hoping his men behind hadn't shown themselves. He forced himself to take deep breaths to ease the adrenaline surge, to calm down, and to get a chance to think.

The woman stood up in one flowing movement that almost took his breath away, and he automatically clicked off his semi's safety. She froze, opened her palms, and held them up. He put his hand out sideways, palm out, signaling his men to hold fire.

"No need for that, I'm weaponless." Her voice was half soothing, half scornful. "If we wanted you dead we could've killed you long ago." She was stocky, and seemed too heavily muscled to move so gracefully. She gestured to her skimpy clothes. "Do you want me to remove these, to prove I'm unarmed?" Her chuckle was a liquid bubble. "Do you think I'd dress so luridly without good reason? I had to show you I carried no concealed weapons."

Cassidy said, his voice harsh. "Who are you and why are you holding these men prisoner?"

"My name's Sophia," she said. "I'm willing to release these men. I don't have the key; if I'd held onto it you might have thought it was a weapon. I'll call the man who has it out of the tunnel to my left, if you promise not to harm him."

Cassidy edged to one side, so his men could see the second tunnel. He pointed to it and said loudly, "Only the man with the key comes out of that tunnel. If he's armed, he'll be shot." He sneaked a look behind himself and saw one of his men positioned behind him, gun at the ready.

"Agreed," she said. "While he's bringing the key, would you humor me?"

"Possibly," he said.

"If I speak to you in my tongue, will you tell me what you call my people?" She uttered a series of guttural barks unlike any language he'd ever heard and looked at him expectantly.

"Neanderthal," Cassidy said, watching a second Neanderthal shuffle clumsily around the prisoners, and unlock their manacles, one by one, stepping back from each freed man faster than if he was freeing rattlesnakes from a cage. None of the captives spoke, though most of them glared at him. One of them nodded an acknowledgement to Cassidy.

The sheer intensity of her smile almost knocked him backwards, as she shot him a puzzling look of relief, and hopped a little on one foot, capering with joy.

His peripheral vision caught the second Neanderthal scuttling out of sight, as several of the men stretched, and they all rubbed circulation back into their arms and legs.

Despite the situation, he couldn't help smiling at her obvious, almost child-like glee. "As far as we know, Neanderthals are extinct," he said.

"Do I look extinct?" She pirouetted slowly, arms outstretched, as if modeling a new dress.

"No, you don't," he admitted. "So what's the story? Are you a lost tribe that has hidden here for millennia? Is this Shangri-La? Are you what's behind the Yeti legend?" She shook her head, and he replied, "I didn't think so. Are you time travelers from the past?" Seeing her puzzled look, he added, "One of my past bosses said I was able to mix realism with an almost limitless capacity to accept the impossible." He laughed. "I don't think it was a compliment."

"So you can accept the impossible?" she asked.

"We-ell," he drawled, and then grinned. "I draw the line at more than three impossible things before breakfast." She looked bemused, and he realized she'd passed a test he hadn't consciously set. Recognizing Alice in Wonderland would have shown her to be too familiar with the world outside, and shown she was a fake. Part of him didn't want her to be a fake. "History books state that Neanderthals no longer exist. It appears to me that they got it wrong."

The first captive passed him and he said, "Walk round the corner. Our men are there."

She nodded and said, "I'm sorry about taking your men prisoner, but they followed our patrol back into the tunnel from out in the valley, and fired on us. We had to defend ourselves. We could have easily killed them. We chose to keep them alive."

Cassidy turned to the ranking officer of the survivors, a copper-skinned, lithe soldier whose pelt of hair on his forearms was so black it was almost blue. "What's your name, Corporal?"

"Tandala, sir." Despite his fatigue, he snapped off the sharpest salute Cassidy had seen in Afghanistan.

"Is what she says true?"

Tandala opened his mouth, hesitated and reluctantly nodded. "Pretty much, Sir. We didn't know-"

"Relax," Cassidy clapped him gently on the back. "You've done nothing wrong."

Sophia cocked her head sideways, a faint smile round the corners of her mouth. "So at last we meet."

He half listened to his troops greeting the first patrol with shouts and whoops. "You talk as if we know one another."

"We haven't met before, but we were always going to."

"Destiny?"

"Yes."

"That's why you were so relieved when I said Neanderthal?"

She smiled. "Don't you get nervous at important moments?"

"And it's destiny that you speak flawless English?"

Another hint of a smile. "You still don't trust us?"

"Would you, in my position? How long have you been here?"

She thought, pushing her full lips out, then in. "Maybe a week. You lose track of time in the tunnels."

"You've made yourselves at home."

"Do you want a tour?" When he hesitated, she said, "You can choose the route – that way, we can't hide anything."

He pondered. The prisoners seemed unharmed. The men could report back without him if he was captured. "Davenport?"

"Yes, sir?"

"I'm going for a walk. If I'm not back within an hour, take the men back to Base." He turned to Sophia, "Let's take a walk."

***

Habib was uneasy. Most of the eight hundred people of Baidur had stood in the village square through the day, scanning the sky for signs of the monsoon, which was now two months late. As the local policeman, Habib was often concerned, but rarely uneasy.

He fiddled with the pointed tips of the thick, luxuriant moustache covering his lower face. He oiled his mustache each morning. Those familiar with him knew that he rarely showed emotion, except by stroking the tips of his mustache. A dapper, dark, wood-carved block of a man, he stood impassively while sorting out traffic jams, or while merchants, ferrymen or other disputants shouted at one another that they were a sodomite, thief, or whore's son.

By this time of year Habib should have been working on the flood defenses that kept the number of deaths in Bangladesh to comparatively low levels. Normally he'd be cursing wet feet, wrinkled skin, and the summer chill that always followed standing too long in wet shoes and trousers.

But this year the rains had failed to sweep through the Bay of Bengal, depositing their life-giving payload. Many river-taxis sat idle on the banks of the rivers, their drivers reduced to spitting out betel-nuts, and wondering if the driver whose turn it was to make the run would ground his shallow-keeled boat. With travelers hesitating to leave their homes before the rains came, and so few crossing the rivers, the drivers had banded together and forced up their prices as 'insurance'.

Habib had hoped that the clammy wind that licked his face the night before with a moist, slightly salty tongue had been a harbinger of the rains, but that hope had died today with the same still, electric air they'd had all year.

The electricity wasn't just in the air. Today the villagers had gathered, ever more fearful that they'd angered gods they didn't publicly acknowledge but privately propitiated. All day the tension had built, and several times Habib had had to step in and act as peacemaker, which wasn't unusual. Today, however, the raw hate in the fighters' eyes, and the ferocity with which they'd traded punches had been frightening. The men knew what drought would do their families. They'd seen their children's distended bellies before, knew that nursing mothers would be unable to lactate, that eyes would glaze and that life fade from them.

Habib tugged the tip of his moustache. He couldn't quite put his finger on why the crowd worried him. Normally the people in the marketplace were mostly men. Today, however, it was mostly women and children thronging the streets. He finally decided it was their body language that worried him. The women were anxious and shuffled to the edge of the square as if to escape; the men were angry and bewildered, and kept looking to the skies, as if to bring the rains by desire alone.

To the south, thunderheads piled atop one another, roiling like swirling dervishes in the un-seasonal blue sky. Thunderheads were common in the summer, but they were usually lost in the gray backdrop of the total cloud. Today green-blue curds swirled through the piercing white clouds, sweeping them up and fuelling the growth of the thunderheads by the minute.

Vikram Khan strode into the square, carrying a bundle, and Habib's heart sank. A tall, wizened twig of a man, Khan's hair stood out from his head in a halo. Self-proclaimed village elder, rabble-rouser, parasite; those were some of the more polite descriptions of Khan that Habib had heard. He thrived on argument, conflict and anger. Perhaps that was why he'd never stood for the Village Council – joining those he despised would have deprived him of intrigue. Habib thought, however, that it was more likely that Khan knew he'd never be elected.

"Listen to me, everyone!" Khan threw out his arms at shoulder height, opening his hands as if casting doves into the sky. "We are in desperate straits! You know this! I know this!" The crowd murmured like distant bees. "Even those fools of councilors on the Parishad know this! So what do they do?" He glared around him, as if hoping someone would answer him. "I will tell you what they do for you! Exactly nothing!"

The murmuring increased, and Habib stepped closer.

"You know this! I know this!" Khan slapped his chest. "We have angered the Old Gods whose names we dare not speak!"

Habib drew his breath in sharply as the crowd shrank back. Only Shoab Tharkrar had the courage to shout out, his face mottled with anger, "Allah strike you down for your blasphemy!"

"He will not!" Khan passed his bundle to a woman who stood nearby, Rena, his neighbor, and strode to Tharkrar, thrusting his face into that of the other man. He said, loudly enough that they all heard, "You know I speak the truth! Allah has forsaken us! We have been good Muslims, we have observed the Koran, we have prayed faithfully at the Mosque, and what good has it done us?"

Shoab stepped back, and Khan moved forward, keeping them nose-to-nose, his bully's instinct choosing the one person he needed to silence. "Shoab, we must appease the gods," Khan was reasonable, almost pleading. The crowd's buzzing grew.

"You should not speak of false gods," Shoab said so quietly that Habib had to strain to hear what he said. "It's blasphemy," he added without conviction.

Khan turned away, his victory won. "Now we will put things right." His voice was harsh.

In the distance, lightning speared the ground. Khan took the bundle from Rena and unwrapped a baby. Habib stepped closer, waiting. He would give Khan enough rope to hang himself.

"This should have been my niece," Khan shouted, his voice ragged, his eyes wild. "But my sister died last night, giving birth to this stillborn demon!" Khan held up the body. The crowd fell silent. "I am telling you that this is a sign!" Khan spat. "Allah has abandoned us!"

Even from Habib's position, the child was clearly deformed. Habib had attended college in Chittagong. One of the lecturers, an American, had spoken of pesticides leaking into the water table, and the consequential dangers, such as increased infant deformities. Somehow, though, Habib doubted whether this was the time to ask whether the baby was deformed because the old gods were angry, or because of invisible particles in the water.

Khan took a knife and slit the baby's throat. A woman shrieked, while other women shielded their children from the sight. One woman forced her child to watch the gruesome ceremony, holding his head still in her clenched hands.

Khan chanted above a descant of gasps, as blood dripped onto the ground. Dipping his finger into the wound he'd opened, Khan daubed the dead child's blood, on his own forehead; "Nameless ones, forgive us for turning away from you." Then he daubed it onto the forehead of the man next to him. "Forgive us for doubting you," and then to the next. "Forgive us for forgetting you. Forgive us." One after the other, he wiped his finger on the foreheads of those around him. "Show us your forgiveness by sending the rains. Show us your compassion." He took his bloody bundle and walked round the square, daubing the forehead of each person, until he came to Shoab. Locking eyes with him, Khan reached out with a red forefinger. Shoab flinched, but Khan said something Habib couldn't hear and daubed the mark on Shoab.

Finally, Khan stood in front of Habib, and reached out, but stopped when Habib said, "You've had your little game. But if you touch me, I'll arrest you for assault."

"As you wish, Officer," Khan said. "Though I am thinking rather, that you will regret this."

Thunder boomed, still in the distance, but louder now.

***

The barracks of the 504th Parachute Infantry Regiment were an oasis of calm in the noise and bustle of Baghram Air Base. They'd spent the morning cleaning kit until they could see their faces reflected in their boots and metal fittings. Then they cleaned their guns.

"The Brits have been having problems with their rifles jamming," Kaminski said. "Their government says the guns aren't being cleaned properly. That's crock of course," he added. "When the findings were challenged, they back-tracked, said it was because," he adopted a falsetto voice, "the training regimen changed, requiring that the rifles be cleaned slightly differently."

The troops roared at that, and Garcia said, "Jesus Christ, their troops take shit like that?"

"That'll do, Corporal," Adler's voice was quiet, but it cut through the hubbub like a cheese-wire. Sergeant Adler's men didn't take the Lord's name in vain in front of him.

"Sorry, Sarge," Garcia muttered, rolling his eyes.

"So, gentlemen," Kaminski said. "There's no way we're going to let anyone hang that one on us. I want cleaner than clean. I want those guns so you can eat off the stock. Got that?"

"Sir!" they roared.

It was mid-morning before Kaminski was satisfied. Then they started their physical training beneath the fierce Afghan sun. After charging through the assault course, they started their shooting drills. It was an ordinary day, until three o'clock, when Kaminski was summoned to the Commanding Officer's office.

CHAPTER FOUR

"This place is a maze!" Cassidy said. "How far down does it go?" They had been ambling for a while, but it was hard to tell how long, as he had forgotten to check his watch. *Next time dummy,* he thought, *check your watch. Time's slipping away.*

"We don't know," Sophia replied, "The tunnels blend into each other. They cover more than thirty levels and are connected by ramps. Their builders obviously expected a lengthy siege."

"Thank God they never got a chance to test them out. I assume it was Al-Quaida who built them- what?" Sophia was staring at a pillar, running her fingers over a crescent moon-shaped carving in the stone. *I thought the Taliban were vehemently against icons,* Cassidy thought, *unless someone was showing his defiance by secretly carving this.*

Sophia was silent for a moment. Then she said: "When I next talk to you, will you say your name?" She uttered what might have been a question in her harsh language.

He said, "Josh Cassidy."

"Thank you." She fell silent, then said, "The circle squared." Paused. "A prophecy completed." She gave him that radiant smile again.

She is quite a plain looking woman, he thought, *apart from her eyes. But she has so much personality!* Despite her ordinary looks, he felt so attracted to her that it made him edgy. He worried that it might cloud his judgment. "What do you mean?" he asked. His words sounded more suspicious than he had intended, but he pressed on. "Ever since we've met, you've talked in riddles. I need some straight answers."

When she answered, her voice was serious, but her eyes were amused. "I'm sorry; this must be frustrating for you. But surely you see how few we are, how little threat we pose?" They rounded a corner into a cave, and he stopped in his tracks. While they had walked, the temperature had grown steadily colder, and here a small fire burned in one corner, smoke fluttering up a ventilation shaft cut into the rock. In the shadows cast on the cavern walls by the dancing flames, the pathetic group huddled round the fire seemed faintly sinister, like a group of refugee imps.

"So what do your people want?" Cassidy broke the silence.

She nodded at him. "You, of course. You are the one who will deliver your people, and mine."

"And you speak English so well, because...?" He still wondered if this was all an elaborate hoax.

"We...borrowed someone about a year ago. There was an accident, and we lost one of our patients. When we found him, he had company." A human woman clutching a baby emerged from the shadows in response to Sophia's wave. "This," Sophia said, "is MaryAnn Stanford." MaryAnn nodded, a swift bob of the head, and Cassidy smiled back as Sophia continued, "Once she calmed down, we taught each other our languages. It was very hard at first."

"Borrowed? Sounds more like kidnapping." Cassidy said with a glare.

Sophia's smile faded. "We prefer to call it protective internment." She looked uneasy, and Cassidy wondered how many other humans had been "borrowed" by Sophia and her people.

MaryAnn nodded, "They bin good to me," she said. "They said we should come git you," she added. "So we came." She was obese, with lank hair and an acne-scarred face. *But someone wanted her enough to father a child by her,* Cassidy thought.

***

Marriott barked, "Come!"

As Kaminski entered his office, Marriott looked up from his huge desk, and said, "At ease, Captain," in response to Kaminski's crisp salute.

The 504th's new Commanding Officer had taken over only two months before, and Kaminski was still trying to figure him out. He was a hard man to get to know. He seemed okay, but Kaminski wasn't entirely sure about him.

Kaminski nodded to the new Intel Officer, Gross. A suitable name, Kaminski thought, viewing the man's thick-lipped arrogant sneer with distaste.

Unusually, Marriott wasted no time on small talk, "Stuart, got a job for you." Marriott nodded to Gross, who swiveled a laptop on the desk around for Kaminski to see.

"A few days ago, the Brits asked us to flyby," Gross said, calling up recon photographs. "Since then, they been pretty close-mouthed 'bout why. We think that's a bit off, seeing they asked us for the favor in the first place."

Kaminski studied the night-shots, which were little more than red and yellow blobs against the white background of the terrain. "Where are these?"

"On the Northern edge of the Jalfreya Hills," Gross said, "Near the Tora Bora Mountains."

"Who are they?"

"We don't know," Gross said with a shrug.

Kaminski speared Marriott with a startled look. Marriott lifted a non-committal eyebrow. For someone from Intel to admit ignorance was unique.

"Could be any one of a half-dozen possibilities," Gross added.

"Sir?"

Marriott cleared his throat and looked uneasy. "You're taking a platoon on a training exercise, Stuart, down at the edge of our area. You'll get a little lost."

"Won't the Brits be pissed, sir?"

"I'm sure they will," Marriott said.

"Bottom line is," Gross said, "we own the fucking operation round here. If they wanna play games, they'll find out who calls the shots."

"What Captain Gross means," Marriott said dryly, "is that we play a major role in keeping the peace. We're sure our allies appreciate that."

"And if they don't, they can kiss our asses," Gross added.

***

Henry had no idea of how long they had been marching. Days, perhaps. But his watch had stopped, and time seemed disjointed- the days here were abnormally long. In the place where they had started from, the days had been shorter. The dreary slate-gray sky gave no clues as to the time, but mirrored the bleak land through which they marched.

They had been caught by twenty, maybe twenty-five Neanderthals, led by one who was massive and muscle-bound even by the standards of his comrades, and who had stayed almost completely silent throughout their march. It was, Henry decided, the silence of soldiers deep in hostile territory.

"There's something wrong," Henry murmured to Jerry, when they stopped for one of their increasingly infrequent rests. Jerry said nothing. He'd become withdrawn in the days since their capture, and Henry wondered whether the others blamed his insistence on walking on the glacier for their capture. If he hadn't been so adamant that he wanted to walk up there...

Esteban said, "Why you say that?"

"Look at their body language," Henry said. "Their heads are drooping. The Fuhrer's biting– oof!" He staggered as a rifle butt caught him in the ribs. He didn't understand Neanderthal, but the message was clear.

When they'd been captured, Jackson had tried to run. A Neanderthal had taken aim as casually as if he'd been wiping his nose. They had left Jackson where he fell, to be disposed of by the local scavengers. After that, any thoughts the captives may have had of escape had evaporated like early morning fog.

Then the Neanderthals had herded the captives together, and, looping a length of chain round each prisoner's wrist, marched them up the glacier. "I finally get to see it," Henry whispered sadly, "but not the way I'd have liked."

After an hour of trudging across the snowfield, they had halted. The Neanderthals formed a ring round the captives. At the leader's pantomimed urgings, captives linked hands to the sound of Pam's muttered, "I don't like this, Jerry." A Neanderthal placed his hands on Esteban's shoulders, while another chanted something. Henry felt a momentary sensation of stomach-churning nausea, and then his head felt turned inside out. He bent over double, his eyes squeezed shut, fighting the urge to vomit.

The urge passed, and when he recovered, he gaped, like the others.

They'd been standing halfway up a glacier, with a glorious blue firmament above them. Now they stood beneath a sullen gray sky on a monotonous plain, littered with rocks peeking through scrubby grass. From the frantic mutterings, head scratching, and shouts between The Shaman, as they had christened the invocation-chanter, and The Leader (or Fuhrer, as Jerry dubbed him), things hadn't gone as they should have.

One of the Neanderthals studied something that looked like a feather duster, as he turned around and around. "It must be a map, or compass of some sort," Henry whispered, but Esteban hushed him. The Navigator nodded across the plain, away from the jungle. The Fuhrer barked a question, and the Navigator nodded hesitantly.

They rested for a few minutes, passing round water and what Henry guessed were strips of dried meat that were almost too tough to chew, before the Neanderthals signaled they were to move on. Henry's stomach growled and he realized it was the first food they'd had since breakfast. Later he pantomimed that he needed a toilet stop. The Fuhrer signaled he was to go where he stood.

Apart from occasional breaks and to sleep, they'd been marching ever since they'd undergone that weird, gut-wrenching dislocation. Their feet bled into their boots, but there was no respite. The others were phlegmatic, but Pam grew increasingly unable to cope with the punishing schedule. Finally, after two days, she sat down on the ground, refusing to budge despite Jerry's pleas, and the Fuhrer's shouts. The argument ended with a sharp crack, and without warning, Pam pitched forward, the back of her head a bloody mess. Jerry was silent for a moment, and then leapt screaming for their captors, only to be yanked back by the weight of Pam's lifeless body on the chain. While Henry and Esteban held him back, their captors stared blankly at him, until he broke down, sobbing and cradling Pam's body in his arms.

The Fuhrer spoke to Jerry again, gentler than before but his tone implacable. Henry and Esteban pulled Jerry to his feet, and hauled him with them. They had left Pam's body where it lay for the carrion eaters. Since then, Jerry had barely spoken, and his eyes were dull and lifeless.

Now they slowed, the navigator peering anxiously at his device. "They don't seem to be able to find what they're looking for, whatever, or wherever it is," Henry whispered, eyeing their captor's rifle butts warily. He wondered how long it would be before their captors took their frustrations out on them.

***

"Before we go any further," Cassidy said, "I need to debrief my men."

Sophia led him to a tunnel. "We can detour up a level," Sophia said.

Cassidy checked his watch surreptitiously, as he had every few minutes. He had a deadline weighing on his shoulders. Every minute he was down here, the possibility increased that the Neanderthals might encounter one of the other peacekeeping forces or worse, run into the local tribesmen. Cassidy couldn't see the locals tolerating the presence of an almost alien race.

Cassidy and Sophia climbed back up to where they'd started. The British troops were camped in the outermost corridor. Cassidy beckoned to Davenport. "Have you talked to the men?"

Davenport nodded. "Informally, of course." He pointed at the non-commisioned officer with the dark-blue hair. "I suggest that you talk to Tandala, sir. He can bring you up to date."

"Okay," Cassidy said, and puffed out his cheeks. "Tandala," he called.

The young corporal approached him nervously.

"At ease," Cassidy said, "I don't bite."

Tandala smiled hesitantly, but relaxed a little.

"Tell me about the journey up here," Cassidy said, leading the corporal away.

Tandala's journey had roughly paralleled Cassidy's, although they had lacked a clear trail to follow. They had meandered toward the target co-ordinates, their path blocked by natural obstacles, until they blundered into a firefight with Afghan tribesmen. Still reeling from the brief battle, they'd then had shock of their lives when they had encountered the Neanderthals. Despite their shock, they had then pursued the Neanderthals to the tunnels.

"We never had a chance in that fight with the tribesmen. There just weren't enough of us!" Tandala snarled. "What kind of cretin sends out a dozen lightly armed men into this area?"

"A cretin who's under enormous pressure to do something, no matter how stupid, just to show he's not sitting on his hands," Cassidy said, with a wry smile.

"When we met the Neanderthals," Tandala said, "we assumed they were the tribesmen's allies, because they were in such close proximity." He added, "I'm not so sure, now."

"Understandable," Cassidy reassured Tandala and dismissed the corporal before rejoining Sophia.

"Care to continue the tour?" she asked mischievously.

The ground shook, and dust fell from the roof of the cave. Cassidy seized Sophia's arm. "This is earthquake territory. It's unsafe down here." The ground shook again. "Come on, let's move. We can talk more later on."

"Can I show you something?" At Cassidy's nod, Sophia called forward one of the other Neanderthals who carried a small device, which he offered to Cassidy, saying something in Neanderthal.

"I don't understand," Cassidy said.

The Neanderthal again offered it to him; it was a black metal band, with an arm on one side, and something that looked like an optometrist's apparatus for testing eyesight at the end of the arm. "It's a projector." Sophia explained. "We insert a ghost-crystal here." She pointed at the eyeglass.

Cassidy tensed again, even as he took the device, and held it gingerly. She sighed in exasperation. "What do I have to do to get you to trust us?" She spoke to the other Neanderthal, and he pressed something into her hand. Then he retreated, bowing to them both. "Do you want me to demonstrate it for you? Am I really such a threat?" She motioned at her skimpy outfit, and he noticed that her flesh goose-pimpled. "You want to search me?" she snapped, although he thought he saw the ghost of a smile, quickly suppressed. "Go ahead. All I have I hold in my hands. Here, I'll prove it to you." Reaching behind her, she unclasped her top, her breasts spilling free, her brown nipples pointing in the cold.

Cassidy snapped his eyes up to meet hers with an effort of will. Quickly, he said, "It's okay. I believe you."

She replaced her top and held out the objects, a half dozen crystalline disks, the size and shape of casino chips. "The answers are here, if you have the courage to trust me." Somehow, she'd regained the initiative.

She said something else in her language. Cassidy understood his name at the end of whatever she said. She cocked her head and looked at him. "Well?"

The ground shook again, and he seized hold of her. Somehow, she ended up closer than he intended, actually in his arms. She looked up at him, and there was no fear in her eyes. "Let's get out of here," Cassidy said. "It really isn't safe."

She shrugged. "Nowhere is safe," she said, moving away when he released her. "Will you take a look at the crystals?"

"Maybe," he agreed cautiously.

Davenport rounded the corner. The relief on his face when he saw them was comical. "I thought you might have been caught by the quakes," he said.

"You okay?" Cassidy clapped him on the shoulder, and the young man nodded, still tight-lipped. Cassidy could tell that Davenport had been subjected to far greater pressure than his training had been intended to cover. He looked as taut as a drawn bow. Cassidy took him to one side. "I'm going to test one of their devices."

"Sir?"

"Our brief is to obtain answers. So that's what I'm going to do. That a problem?"

Davenport shook his head reluctantly. "No, sir."

Two of the Neanderthals placed the frame on Cassidy's head, and tightened it until it fitted snugly. "We've configured the crystals so you'll understand them. You'll think they're talking English. Just don't watch their lips," Sophia grinned. Seeing Cassidy lick his lips nervously, she squeezed his arm. "Don't worry. If we'd wanted to harm you, we'd have already done so."

She slotted one of the crystalline chips into the eyepiece, and Cassidy felt a sharp pain in his temple, as if a needle had been plunged into it. For a long time nothing seemed to happen, but just as he was about to suggest that the device wasn't working, he seemed for a split second to fall toward the cavern walls. Just as he was about to hit them, the world turned black and silent. Then the others reappeared, still standing round him, but now they were ghostly, almost wraith-like. He blinked and-

PART TWO

Now And Then

CHAPTER FIVE

34,000 Years Before Present Day

Cassidy soared above a burning city, a part of him aware, beneath the turmoil of his confusion, of another presence. He shouted, "Who's there!" but heard only shrill shrieks. He looked at his right arm, and nearly fell out of the sky in shock. He was looking at a wing! He looked left and saw another. Somehow, he could hear, feel and see through the eyes of an eagle.

Below him, thousands of panicked Neanderthals fled from the city, pursued by an invading horde of barbarians who'd swept across the plain. The invaders slaughtered thousands more in only hours. The brave Neanderthals who stayed were butchered where they stood, while the rest were hunted down like rats. Before long the stench of death spread for miles, and corpses jostled in the river by Janipur's southern wall.

Cassidy wondered briefly how he could know so much, and at the idea of Neanderthals living in a city, which contradicted every textbook he'd ever read. Then he remembered the technology he'd already seen. In the rational part of his mind, he knew that he was standing on a cold stone floor in a cave, wearing a headband and eyepiece. However, despite that knowledge, he could feel the wind against his wings (That he had wings was itself a revelation. *How do they do it*, he wondered.) and could see the tiny animals scuttling across the ground from under the horse's hooves. He decided to stop fretting and simply accept what was going on, at least for the moment.

Meanwhile, sated at last with murder and rape, the horde below raided the cattle yards containing the city's winter food-stocks, and lit fires to roast the lowing, screaming beasts. The fires soon swept out of control; the city was mostly constructed of wooden buildings that burnt furiously. The mud houses followed, and last the few stone dwellings of the wealthy merchants and city elders ignited. Pillars of black smoke mushroomed into the sky.

Above the city the eagle/Cassidy circled, soaring in the day's last thermals, as the sun sank towards the Evening Sea.

Then – Flick! He huddled trembling in a doorway within Janipur's walls. He knew somehow that he was Pagoter, a young man barely past adolescence. His eyebrow ridge bled from a sword cut, and his tunic was filthy. The boy's memories were an open book- his comrades' shameful desertion when the slaughter started, and the hellish hours of roaming the city, trying in vain to sneak through enemy lines.

He watched drunken carousers lift a tattooed giant onto their shoulders. Pagoter barely reached the shoulder of most of the invaders; amongst even them, this man was huge. Cassidy thought, *My God, beneath all the hair, that thug's Homo Sapiens!* The man's hooked nose had healed crookedly from a break, and his face was a scarred ruin on one side. The giants who'd butchered the Neanderthals were ordinary men, savage, but still men of his own kind.

Gripping a bloody haunch of beef, the giant lifted a wineskin in a toast, "My heroes! Let's send the scum we've slain off!" A huge roar erupted from the crowd. "Here's to the not-men who waited, shaking to be slaughtered, or ran like chickens! Another nest flushed clean! They'll learn to live like men, or die like vermin!" The crowd roared. The giant took a huge slug from the wineskin and continued, "We'll celebrate with a few days rest in the clean open air, before marching on their den on the Eastern Grasslands. By summer, we'll have kicked over that termite's nest, leaving only one last stronghold." More cheers echoed around the courtyard. "They'll bend their necks in fealty," he roared, "or join their ancestors!"

Cassidy/Pagoter had heard enough. For hours his shame had been greater than his terror- until now. His parents had fled to Centola, the horde's next target.

Desperate to do something, he headed for the granaries. The savage's skills didn't extend to baking, so maybe they'd left them undisturbed. He concentrated, and the lock, meant to deter only children and casual passersby, opened. *Psychokinesis,* Cassidy thought. *This goes beyond belief. It's too much like a 1950's sci-fi film!*

Filling his pockets with grain, Pagoter strode outside to be greeted by an invader's shout. He ran, cursing, wishing he were adept enough to cloud their minds and become invisible.

He dodged through a labyrinth of alleyways and finally lost his pursuers. He took several deep breaths, trying not to cough from the all pervading smoke, and gathered his wits. He crept into a courtyard and emptied his mind in readiness. He looked skyward. *"Come little ones,"* he thought, casting his mind upwards and outwards. *"Come to dinner."*

There was no response. He breathed deeply, hurling his thoughts again, and then heard beating wings, as the messenger birds released blindly in the initial panic returned. He scattered grain on the ground and searched for the healthiest one amongst them.

Projecting feelings of calmness, he gently picked the bird up. It flapped its wings, but he hushed it, and after a couple of beats it stopped fluttering, its panting the only outward sign of its turmoil. *"Be calm,"* he thought. *"Be tranquil, listen, and remember my message."* He concentrated, pressing images on the bird's mind. This time there would be no panicked casting of the birds to the winds. He threw it skyward and watched it weave through the maze of alleys, out over the city walls, its stubby wings flapping furiously. He relaxed, and then spun round at a noise behind.

A barbarian stood leering in the doorway. "Look boys," he said to his comrades behind him. "Another playmate."

Pagoter's death was slower and more agonizing than any torture training Cassidy had ever undergone. As darkness claimed him at last, Pagoter prayed with his last breath that his death wouldn't be in vain, and his parents would escape.

One moment Cassidy was sharing Pagoter's death agonies then flick! He flew over the ground, his wings beating rhythmically. He felt a shadow. This pain- as the swooping eagle plucked it from the air- was sharper and shorter. He flicked again, to a second bird that Pagoter had released, which flew on as the eagle ate the first.

The bird flew until its wings felt as though they were weighted down with lead and until the breath rasped in its lungs. Then it rested in one of the vast steppe's few trees. At daybreak it resumed its flight, ignoring the hunger pangs that gnawed at its vitals. Delivering that message was all that mattered to the bird.

When it reached Centola, with another flick! Cassidy found himself in the mind of Centola's dispatcher. By this time, Cassidy was so caught up in the drama that he barely noticed the transition from one point of view to another. The old man listened to the bird's message and then sent an explosion of birds flying in all directions, to outlying villages, towns and the last city, all carrying the news, "Janipur has fallen; the Longlegs march on Centola next."

***

Halfway around the world, on the edge of the Morning Sea, Holma/Cassidy battled to keep a six-foot length of tree trunk upright, while paddling with a branch, until the trunk rolled and dumped him, cursing, into the icy water.

Even someone as lacking in self-awareness as Holma knew that his tribe had always thought him a little strange, but that they shrugged his oddness off as the price of his talent. Since his wife, Waleen's, death he'd lived away from his tribe. Living near women and children brought him too much pain, too many reminders of what might have been. Living alone, there was nothing to curb his strangeness. He ate odd foods like grubs, fruit and vegetables or talked to the spirits that only he saw. He wore a leaf-and-mud waistcoat held together with magic, to keep out the cold. Sometimes he seemed to go completely mad and huddled in his strange coat, babbling in tongues. Next spring, if the erratic weather held, he planned to paddle through the maze of channels to the nearby islands.

Out to sea, a pod of whales were migrating south for the winter, their tall black back fins slicing the air. The calves leapt from the water, their mothers sedately blowing great columns of water. He searched with his mind, found feelings of contentment mixed with anxiety for the calves. He wished he could read thoughts as well, but that was beyond his talent. Greater minds might be able to do so, though he suspected there was a price.

Soon winter ice would crust the ocean and he'd need to look for shelter. He sighed, longing to follow the whales to warmer climes. That would solve the problem of staying warm, but he would doubtless find other problems if he left. The lands to the south were said to be even less hospitable than those northwards. In the south, he had heard that the earth shook, fire belched from the ground, and hostile tribes dwelt, both his own kind and tribes of long-limbed strangers.

His stomach growled. Playtime was over. Finding food was a fulltime preoccupation for the whole tribe. It was time to go home. There was no point in taking risks by lingering. At this time of year storms out to sea often whipped inland with lightning speed.

Beaching his canoe, he looked up at the ridge with the lightning blasted tree from which he'd carved the canoe.

Two hundred yards down the beach were rock pools with sea otters frolicking in the high tide. Two played, while a third lay on its back, tearing at a fish. The sight gave Holma an idea. Tucking his over tunic into his loincloth, he waded thigh-deep into the shallows. He murmured thanks to the spirits and the life that would sustain his own so as not to desecrate the kill. Kneeling, he cast his mind, further and further outward, until he felt a dim awareness. He chanted the Spell of Summoning,

"Ehh...ukali... leyen...ah...kuali. Little sister, heed my call, my need is great, and I will revere your memory."

He waited, re-sending the spell, and then, sensing the exact moment, he grasped and arose with a thrashing fish as long as his arm. He tightened his grip and concentrated, and the fish's heart stilled.

He waded to the shore, and lit a fire, using tinder until the sparks flew, wishing he had energy left to just rub with his mind, but catching the fish had exhausted him. When he was younger, he'd dreamed of just snapping his fingers to use magic. As he grew older he realized that magic was harder than its physical equivalent.

Eventually the fish was mostly cooked, and, offering a brief prayer of thanks to the appropriate gods and spirits, he gnawed the blackened parts, and left the others, where blood still oozed. He ate until he thought he'd burst, then wrapped as much as he could carry in leaves, burying the rest for later.

A moment later, it seemed, he stood on a hill several miles away, facing the setting sun with no memory of how he got there. He'd been Summoned. Caught in the same manner as he'd snared the fish. Someone with great power had great need. Still under the compulsion of the Summons, though it had weakened slightly, Holma/Cassidy trudged westward until he could walk no further. As Holma fell asleep, Cassidy wondered how he could be so phlegmatic in the face of such power.

***

Flick!

Cassidy/Tand watched the sun setting at the top of pink sandstone cliffs. Down in the canyons, the autumn gloom had been deepening for over two hours, and the villagers were lighting the torches. The fires comforted the villagers, and extended the daylight hours. Tand sat cross-legged, waiting. The visitor wouldn't arrive until dark, but he should prepare properly, so he burned the appropriate herbs. He rubbed his eye socket. He'd lost the eye years ago, but it still itched occasionally. He decided against soothing it with ointment. His visitor might smell it.

In their cliffside chambers, the villagers of Djebela were eating their evening meal, followed by games for the children and lovemaking for the younger couples. All their sacrifices and petitions to the local spirits had failed, and they must have wondered why the gods had visited their punishment upon them. Their situation must have been appalling for them to ignore their hetman's wishes and ask an itinerant warlock for help. Tand hoped he would not let them down. *Enough,* he thought. *It was time to clear the mind.*

Hours passed. Or perhaps only minutes. Time was suspended in the moonlight over the canyons. The only noise breaking the silence was that of the crickets chirping. Except, very faintly, Tand heard a cough in the night, a muffled grumble as the big cat approached. The leopard's eyes shone in the night like beacons.

Tand stared at the beast, awed at its beauty, refusing to let fear dominate him. How should he proceed? He could kill it by projecting his will and gripping it round the heart in an iron fist, but he recoiled at such waste.

He willed it to come closer. The leopard slunk nearer. Perhaps it thought that Tand was an easy meal just sitting there for the taking so it wouldn't have to raid the village for dinner. Tand peered at it. Was it his imagination, or did the animal favor one foot? If it were lame, the consequent inability to hunt would explain why the leopard had first attacked livestock, and then in desperation, started to kill people.

Tand crooned, softly, "Sleep, brave warrior. Rest your tired eyes, your head is heavy and sleep is calling...sleep is calling...sleep..." The leopard's ears flicked at the sound of his voice, but his crooning soothed it, and soon, when its brain was starved of oxygen, it slumped. It snarled once, as if realizing unseen hands were at work, but soon it was snoring heavily.

Tand examined its paw, which was crusted with dried pus and blood. He cleaned the wound and sat back, waiting. When the leopard awoke Tand conjured an image of a wolf pack and the big cat fled, yowling with terror.

The next morning the villagers bombarded him with questions. Tand waved them away. "It'll return tonight," He said.

"But you promised to kill it," the hetman said. He'd lost face; seeing Tand fail would salve his pride.

"No. *You* asked me to kill it. I agreed to rid you of a problem, which I'll do in my own way. I made no promises. Nor have I finished yet."

The villages retreated, muttering amongst themselves, and he descended to the guestroom at the base of the cliffs to sleep.

The leopard returned that evening. He'd guessed it would. Its injury would heal, but it had grown lazy.

Tand waited until it was near, and chanted a spell. The dust whirled and formed a man-shaped giant. Tand's amplified shout echoed, off the cliff. As nearby bushes burst into flames, the leopard fled. Tand's dust-giant lumbered after the fleeing cat. The whole act had taken barely a minute.

Tand slumped forward, exhausted. When he got to his feet, he staggered down the path to the first cave. "It's gone," he said to the family inside, then collapsed.

Word spread like wildfire. They carried him to his room, where he slept as though he were dead.

The next morning the chief visited him. "You have our heartfelt thanks," he said, "Stay as our guest for as long as you wish. Whatever you want is yours."

He stared in silence as Tand walked out of the room, and kept going, out past the edge of the village. To Cassidy, who still shared Tand's consciousness, it was as if an unseen hand had reached inside Tand's head and detached his brain from his body. The warlock's muscles acted independently, his body compelled to follow the call, wherever it led. Tand cried out, "I'll save you, Father!"

It was hours before Tand regained control of his body. By then the village was miles behind. He'd brought his belongings with him, but was only half-dressed. Whoever or whatever had Summoned him was enormously powerful, but it wasn't his father, who'd been dead for years. Tand strode northward, toward the Great Eastern Road.

Cassidy skipped again.

***

This late in the year it was often dark before the men returned from the hunt. The women spent their days cooking the previous day's kill, together with whatever they could spare from their stocks.

Even in summer a bitter wind blew across the steppes, but now it cut like a knife through the yak-fat with which they all coated themselves. Cassidy/Danor shivered and drew her furs closer round her. She wished it were summer. She winced when the chief wife slapped her. "Enough daydreaming! Get on with your work!"

She resumed grinding the herbs. They'd add them to the communal stewpot to hide the taste of partly putrefied meat. *Sour old hag,* Danor thought. *You're just bitter because the chief has younger wives, and your juices have dried up.* As Danor's would, if she didn't get a man soon. Bad enough that she was taller than most men, but she had to be strange as well. Everyone knew it was unnatural for a woman to have such powers as she. She was lucky she hadn't been sacrificed the first time she showed Talent. Only her father's popularity had saved her. He'd beaten her so thoroughly, in public where everyone could see, that she'd never openly use her powers again. Even so, the men in the village would sooner share a bed with one of their yaks than with her.

Somehow she finished her chores without being cuffed again when a cry went up from lame Garimak, who was on watch. "A stranger! On his own!"

The stranger's long strides ate the distance. He was unusually tall and his long legs had none of the People's distinctive bow. There was more than a hint of the *other* about him. She reached out with her mind, hoping that her murmured spells would go unnoticed amongst the hubbub caused by the interloper.

Shocked, she pulled her thoughts back. There was such a blaze of power in him! She looked up, registering the women's voices. "Why did he stop like that?" someone asked.

"It was just like he walked into a cliff-face," another voice muttered.

The stranger resumed his walk. When he reached the edge of the camp, the women funneled him to the elders. At a safe distance, he stopped and bowed. "I'm Lorkett," he said loudly. "I travel eastwards. May I ask shelter for the night, in return for whatever I can offer?"

Close up he looked very odd, with long spider like limbs, no chignon, and his eyes were sunk deep compared to theirs, with their shelf-like eyebrow ridges. Everything about him shrieked of strangeness. Cassidy felt but did not share Danor's bemusement. He recognized that Lorkett was at least part Homo sapiens.

For the first time in many moons, Danor felt a surge of attraction. She couldn't read his walled-off mind so she sent another sliver of thought toward him. Eyes widening, Lorkett looked around, slowly studying his hosts. Danor caught his eye and nodded slightly. She wasn't sure, but she thought she saw a faint smile.

"How can you pay for our food, and the warmth of our fire?" The question was ceremonial; lone travelers were almost unknown and refusing to provide hospitality would've been an act of appalling rudeness.

The traveler said, "I can sing and do a few paltry tricks to amuse you."

The elders waved him to their tent. "Come." The crowd dispersed, some urged by the head wife to resume work.

That night they feasted better than they had for many months. This was Lorkett's due; anything less would have shamed the tribe. They ladled out large helpings of meat and vegetables; whatever small animals they'd been able to catch, the vegetables they'd dug up, and unleavened bread made from the grain, from seeds scattered the last time they'd migrated this way, all of which supplemented their staple diet of yak.

When Lorkett sang about the cities, the elders hushed him. "It's not our way to discuss such things in front of the youngsters," the elders said. "Such talk disturbs them. The tribe has lived this way for generations; they're better off without such nonsense."

Instead they urged Lorkett to perform cute little tricks such as pulling eggs from behind children's ears, or Summoning small animals. The shaman watched with barely disguised contempt, from beneath his yak headdress. Danor wondered why Lorkett didn't show the power she'd felt within him. She stared at him, drinking in his exotic looks, until he caught her gaze, and smiled. She looked away, her heart hammering and her cheeks flaming. Throughout the evening they repeated this dance. She'd study him until he noticed, and then she would look away.

The youngsters sang, or did small tricks under the shaman's guidance. At the end of the evening, Lorkett bowed to the chief and the shaman, and then stood near Tanibah, her father.

Danor's pulse quickened.

"I have a boon to ask, my Lord," Lorkett said. "Your daughter's beauty does you great honor," he pointedly ignored the sniggering. "And I suspect her devotion to you has led her to decline all marriage proposals."

"Fair words," Tanibah replied.

The chief interrupted, "It's unseemly to discuss this here. We'll retire to my tent, after Lorkett petitions Danor."

Lorkett stood in front of her, and began the betrothal dance. Spinning, hands cutting through the air like knives, he whirled through the air like a dust devil, faster than she'd ever seen it danced. All too soon, he finished.

Now it was her turn. Her dance would give her answer. She took a deep breath, stepped forward.

Afterwards, the men talked for hours, in the tent. Danor lay in her blankets, struggling to stay awake but she succumbed to sleep before she could hear the outcome of the talks.

***

Cassidy/Acharya awoke with a jolt. He sat at the top of the world, a meter above the ground, motionless in the blizzard that swirled round him. Cassidy was starting to feel as if he was on a treadmill, and wondered when he'd understand what was going on, or if he ever would. There was no guarantee that Neanderthals thought stories should have beginnings, middles or ends.

Acharya had raised his body temperature, and felt quite cozy. It had taken the village shaman two years to teach him the technique. When he could no longer sustain the spell, he dropped gently to the ground, and then walked a short distance, back to his cave.

He stayed there until he needed companionship more than he needed to be alone, and when that happened, he slid down the mountainside. Below him in the watery sunshine lay a village of a dozen huts with an area to one side for the cattle, surrounded by a low fence, holding several goats. He'd been born here. His mother had died giving birth to him, and his father had drowned in a flash flood that had swept down a gorge when Acharya was three.

He frowned. He saw people who normally would be out with their herds, or working in the rice fields. Acharya quickened his pace. The village was eerily silent. He heard none of the faint sounds he'd normally expect to drift on the breeze. A crowd had gathered outside the shaman's hut, and Acharya searched the crowd vainly for Stejona's ceremonial headpiece. He vaulted a fence. "What happened?" he asked the village hetman.

Fidetra looked away, a tic in his cheek pulsing. "The shaman's dead. His powers didn't save him from the avalanche." He spoke bitterly, as if by dying, Stejona had betrayed him.

"When?"

"Yesterday morning. The village is in mourning."

"Then we should prepare him to join the gods."

"Mesimak is already doing that." Fidetra licked his lips nervously. "Stejona named him successor before he died."

"But he'd already named me the next shaman!" Acharya said.

"He changed his mind," Fidetra said, avoiding Acharya's eyes.

"Were there witnesses to this sudden change of heart?" Acharya asked.

"Sarl and Glams."

Acharya stared at Fidetra. Sarl and Glams were distant kin to Mesimak. "How convenient. And you accepted their story without question?"

Fidetra was obviously unhappy about the situation, but he looked downwards. "It's not my place-"

"-to interfere in spiritual matters," Mesimak said from the doorway. "Is it, goatherd?" He stared at Acharya coolly.

"It is when years of preparation are changed in a moment." Acharya wondered where Mesimak's cronies were.

"You question our shaman's will?" Mesimak stood straight and with confidence. Acharya paused to choose his words, and Mesimak, thinking the other man's silence meant he had won, grinned.

The grin vanished as Acharya said, "I question your version of it. I think you're lying."

"You whoreson! I'll-"

"You challenge me?" Acharya asked.

"Yes! I challenge you!"

"Very well," Acharya said.

***

Whilst mourning Stejona, he felt a call from his dead master. The summons plucked at him, making every nerve and fiber with him want to head north. It almost worked, but Acharya had just enough talent, stubbornness, and above all, enough need to avenge the old man who'd been friend, father figure and teacher to hold out against it. Knowing the message was a fake, he didn't move. Instead, he sent a reply. *"Who are you?"*

Again, Stejona's image appeared in his mind.

"You lie. Who are you?"

"Mogrun." Acharya saw an image of an old, tired wizard, albeit still with enormous power. The wizard sent a plea to Acharya. *"Help."*

There is something I must do first, Acharya replied.

***

The duel took place next day, after they sent Stejona on his journey to the spirit world. Acharya's grief was overwhelmed by rage. He'd warned Stejona about his nephew. Acharya had the talent to make him the shaman's obvious successor but Mesimak had kinship.

As the one who was challenged, Acharya had the right to choose the weapons, place and time of combat. He chose magic as the weapon and insisted that Fidetra confine Sarl and Glams.

Acharya walked naked, so that Mesimak couldn't use his robes as a weapon, up the valley, into a blizzard so sudden it was clearly Mesimak's work.

Acharya peeled the clouds back. Then he counterattacked, so that Mesimak stood knee deep in the shitting grounds. Acharya felt Mesimak's fury, and braced himself for the next attack.

Mesimak transformed him into a rock, but Acharya changed back before the spell could set permanently. Mesimak hadn't followed up properly, but Acharya wouldn't make that mistake. He thrust quickly twice with his mind, first using the same spell Mesimak had used, and then while Mesimak counteracted being made a rock, Acharya set the his opponent's robes on fire. Whilst Mesimak screamed and tried to douse the flames, Acharya, his nose bleeding from the immense drain on his energy reserves, shifted his opponent again, this time dumping Mesimak into a swift flowing river.

Mesimak was now so disoriented he was still fighting the fire he'd already doused. He tried to shift himself out of the river, but Acharya held him there, battling his own fatigue as well as Mesimak's power.

Acharya questioned with his mind, *"Submit?"*

Mesimak struggled but Acharya's power was greater. Mesimak finally had no choice but to concede. Acharya left him alone to struggle to shore, while he staggered back to the village.

The battle should have been to the death, but Acharya had other plans. He'd felt the greatness of Mogrun's power, and knew that he could learn a lot from such a wizard.

While the bedraggled Mesimak limped back to the village, Acharya cleaned up, rested, and ate a meal of cold rice and vegetables. He called upon Fidetra. "I'm going away."

The hetman's face clouded with outrage, but Acharya ignored him. He summoned Mesimak. "I appoint you shaman. You will exile Glams and Sarl. If you perform well I won't need to return. If not..."

Mesimak licked his lips. "And if I refuse?"

"I've beaten you once, I can do it again." Acharya waited for Mesimak's response, sending him a momentary image of the rising river from their battle.

Mesimak thought for a moment, then nodded curtly.

***

The Great Eastern Road wound past mountains that were like huge black mounds of folded sourdough. In their shadow, isolated villages dotted the seared plain, dwarfed by the mountains' rolling majesty. Tand thought that the wasteland was the most awesome, beautiful and terrifying thing he had ever seen. Cassidy, who again shared Tand's mind, had seen the Pamir Mountains before, but was still awed by the sight.

Tand's epic journey had taken him through steep defiles, past a semi-desert plain fringed by mountains that seemed like ghosts in the mist that shrouded them. The plains villages, although walled and guarded, were hospitable to a lone traveler, for to refuse was bad luck. "This is bandit country," one villager warned him. "Be careful."

Fortunately, he met none of the gangs who periodically swept down from the North, but he did see animals that had grown huge and hairy enough to counter the biting cold that seeped into his body and his bones. There were giant sheep, with horns as big as his arms. He considered hunting them but decided against it as he had no weapons, and the magic he would need to bring one of the giant beasts down would unnecessarily exhaust him.

The semi-desert grew even drier. Sometimes he saw shining spires and wondered if it was the legendary Invisible City. The villagers had warned him of spirits in the dunes who cast illusions of the City, beautiful women, or shaded waterholes to lure the unwary. "Ignore them," they had warned. "Or you'll die where you fall."

His rations dwindled by the day. He was always hungry. His flesh seemed to evaporate; his muscles corded like rope. To Cassidy, who was used to leaping into a car or onto a plane, the world he'd always crisscrossed so casually seemed to have grown incomprehensibly immense. So must it have seemed to Tand's generation, he thought. Tand walked in a half trance, almost missing the village at the far end of the plain.

He approached the open gates where two men stood alongside the guards, the younger one dressed in rare finery, the other, like Tand, wearing only ragged skins. Tand recognized a half-breed with a flare of suspicion. The last halfling he'd met had cost him an eye. The well-dressed young man stepped forward with a broad smile. "Hello Tand," he said. "Welcome to Pamirat. I'm Neza." He held up open palms and Tand hesitantly returned the gesture. Cassidy, seeing him through Tand's eyes, guessed that Neza was about twenty, but his guess could have been five years out either way; even in this comparatively sophisticated version of prehistory, people aged hard, with boys becoming fathers almost as soon as their balls dropped, and girls becoming mothers within a year of starting to bleed, unless like Danor, they used caring for their fathers as a way of eluding the parent trap. That brought Cassidy up short. Most of the men whose minds he shared were single. Did sexual abstinence go hand in hand with their talents?

Neza waved at the halfling and added, "This is Lorkett." Lorkett held up his palms and stared back levelly, ignoring Tand's obvious animosity, and said, "The others are resting inside. We'll stay here tonight, and move on tomorrow." He added to Neza, his face grave. "Centola fell three days ago."

Neza cursed. Though his features were patrician, they had been affable enough until now. He said, "What about the people there?"

"Dead. Or enslaved."

Cassidy wanted to ask them who they were and why had Tand been called to this lonely village? How did they know Tand's name? But exhausted, with his mouth and throat parched, and his tongue swollen, Tand only nodded. The three of them passed the watchful guards into the citadel.

***

The sun was at its zenith, and the tent was like a furnace. The desert heat grew daily as they slowly moved further south. Holma still didn't know what was going on. He slept as near the flaps of the tent as possible, his skin crawling from the other's nearness.

He'd walked for months to get to Pamirat. When he arrived, he'd collapsed onto a bed and slept for two days. Four days later, Tand had arrived from Djebela, and Lorkett and Danor from the steppes to the northwest. Neza was from Shalimar, the Invisible City.

They had started traveling as a group the evening after Tand's arrival. "We'll set out at nightfall," Neza had said, "and rest up by day. I'll carry the water bottles. Tand, you carry the food. Lorkett, you'll carry shelter skins."

Southeast of Pamirat, they walked through an avenue of scrawny trees whose branches pointed straight up, as if molded that way. Then they passed through a narrow ravine, into a valley with sides stretching up into gaunt cliffs. Three days later, they entered The Sea of Sand, which Cassidy recognized as the Takla Makan Shamo. He could see why travelers called it a sea; the sand stretched endlessly like the water on the ocean.

Cassidy could feel the compulsion that pulled Holma onwards, despite his obvious reluctance, and wondered at the power of this Mogrun.

Danor groaned. She was heavily pregnant and suffered in the baking heat. Lorkett wiped her face with a damp cloth. "How much further must we go?" he asked between gritted teeth.

Cassidy noticed that whenever Lorkett looked up, Tand would watch the halfling as if he was a scorpion. Tand looked away at last, studying the hair on his arms and picking at a scab. "You could always go back to where you came from."

Lorkett leaned forward, and the air in the tent crackled with tension. The towering Lorkett dwarfed Tand, but the halfling was reed-thin so Tand was a little heavier.

Danor slapped Lorkett's arm. "Stop it! Both of you!"

Lorkett smiled at Tand, a baring of teeth. "No. If you can stand it, so can I."

Neza turned from contemplating a sandstorm on the horizon. "Not much further. Tomorrow, maybe the day after." He sounded positive, but he'd already admitted that they could easily get lost and wander in circles until they ran out of water. He looked from Lorkett to Tand, and asked idly, "Tell us about yourself, Lorkett."

Lorkett scratched his armpit, thinking. "I'm a wanderer," he said at last. "My ma looked like you, but my father was one of a band of Longlegs who ran into my mother's tribe. Her people welcomed them as they would all guests. They raped her in the night, and threatened to kill her if she told anybody what they had done before they left.

"When my talents showed, the shaman trained me, but the tribe used my talents as a reason for me not to marry. When the old man died, they cast me out rather than make me shaman in his place. They said they'd rather live without magic than with a shaman who turned their stomach." Lorkett couldn't keep a grim satisfaction from his voice. "I heard after I left that Longleg raiders had massacred them."

Danor reached out and stroked his arm. Lorkett resumed. "One night last year I dreamed of a girl I'd once loved. She told me to go east, where I'd find her again. As she now dwells in the spirit world, I took it as a sign my days were numbered," he laughed. "Then I met Danor. Whenever we stopped, I would dream of the girl again."

"We knew," Danor interrupted in a way that would have earned her a beating in many villages, "that these dreams wouldn't cease until we followed the spirits orders and traveled east. But now you tell us that they weren't messages from the spirit world at all."

"Why are we called like this?" Tand demanded.

The same question was asked every day. Neza always ignored it. "Don't you think it strange," he said now as he drew circles in the sand, "that though only one in ten of us has power, and almost none," he nodded at Lorkett, "of your father's race has such abilities, that you and many other halflings have talents?"

"I hadn't really thought about it," Lorkett said.

"Why do you think that is?" Tand asked.

Neza said, "I think it's like adding water to flour; you make dough. It's the same with halflings."

The conversation died. Then Tand said, "I thought halflings were just like Longlegs. I never thought halflings might suffer 'cause of them, too."

"A Longleg saved my life," Holma mused. "Pulled me from a river. They're not all bad."

They all fell silent, lost in thought. They resumed their trek at sunset, although the sand was still so hot it burnt through their hide shoes. They trudged through the night, resting only for Danor's benefit.

"We must keep going," Neza urged, as the sky lightened to the East, "we can't afford to lose another day."

"Why?" Tand asked.

Neza said, "We're not far now from Shalimar." He added, "Let me tell you now, why Mogrun has called us." He licked his lips. "Last year Janipur in the Far West fell to the Longleg hordes, who then marched eastwards. A demagogue called Stral has used their fear and distrust of us to unite their warring factions. Early this year, they annihilated the great tribe of the grasslands. We believe they won't rest until we're enslaved or hunted to extinction."

There was a collective gasp as the others took in his words.

Neza ignored them. "Shalimar is next," he said. "Mogrun has a plan, but it involves using magic in a completely new way, and he's not certain it will work." He fell silent, letting the others gather their thoughts.

Lorkett broke the silence, "I've no reason to go back."

"I felt life was pointless," Danor said. "Until I met Lorkett. Where he goes, I go."

Tand said, "I'll keep going, but I'm not sure I trust this Mogrun."

Neza nodded. "I can understand that." He added with a chuckle, "Though as he's my uncle, family honor should demand that I be mortally offended. But we're all friends here, so I'm not."

There was an uneasy silence as they all looked at each other. Then without a word, they continued onward.

They were close to exhaustion several hours later when they crested a dune and saw a city perched on a rocky island that rose from the sea of sand. "Can you see it?" Neza asked them. They all nodded, and Neza said, "If you can see Shalimar, so will Stral's tame halflings."

***

"It looks impressive." Lorkett watched the looming thunderheads. "But why bother? Surely we've enough water in the reservoirs?"

"We decided once as an experiment to not harvest the clouds," Mogrun said, "It was high summer, granted, but it took only nine days to drain the underground reservoirs dry, and nine weeks of constant downpour to refill them. How much water do you think these orange and lemon trees need? Or our gardens, and these date and palm trees that guzzle water? Some think them a luxury, but they're vital to our wellbeing. And how much water do the tens of thousands of people who live here drink? The two hours of rain from cloud-gathering every day keeps us stocked."

They walked round Fountain Square, the only large flat area in Shalimar, and a favorite walk for Mogrun. Acharya and Holma worked together under the supervision of wall-eyed Secheray, Mogrun's assistant. "Each of you concentrate on your part." Secheray was a big florid woman, who preferred the tree-shaded plazas to the heat of the open. "Holma, make the air below rise. Acharya, drop your section. Easy does it."

Cassidy/ Lorkett noticed the way she put a hand on Tand's shoulder, and the smile Tand sneaked her. "They look at ease."

"It's not easy for them," Mogrun said. "They're not used to working as a team. Holma has lived alone so long he's frightened of even small crowds." He fiddled with one of his four remaining teeth. Seeing Lorkett stare, he said, "One of the problems with living more than forty years, is that one starts to fall apart."

Cassidy was surprised. He had thought Mogrun was at least eighty years old. But Lorkett simply said, "Is he scared of halflings too?"

"You noticed," Mogrun said. "His fear almost overwhelms him, yet he stays to fight."

"You shouldn't have Summoned him," Lorkett said in gentle reproach.

"Tcha!" Mogrun snorted. "You know how great our peril is. If we fail, they'll hunt Holma down with the rest of his tribe."

They ducked as a vase careened and wobbled across the square. "Sorry!" Acharya bellowed in its wake.

"He's like a bear pup," Lorkett laughed. "And probably as dangerous. His pranks will kill someone."

"We need some youth round here." Mogrun said. "Compared to the Longlegs, we breed too slowly. Their families have four, five, six children. We'd be swamped if they weren't so fragile."

They circled the square. A cloth covered the old man's head to protect it from the sun, and what hair peeked out was as dirty white as the beard hiding his sunken mouth. He leaned on a stout stick, his breathing labored. Lorkett wondered why the great man didn't look after himself better.

He'd asked Neza, who'd said with a shrug, "He's too busy worrying about the city to think of himself. The city's so old we've wormed our way into every nook and cranny, and filled every crevice with plants to break down the rocks, but still my uncle thinks he's tending a frail old woman."

Lorkett reached out, but Mogrun shrugged his hand away, tapping a hole in the dry stone wall with his stick. "That needs blocking up, or the next heavy rain will wash the soil out." He shot Lorkett an amused look, and added thoughtfully, "It doesn't hurt to remind people how fragile the city is, and who protects them. It's the reason they heed my warnings. Many are so complacent that they think my wits addled."

They continued walking until Mogrun said, "Well! Fancy seeing my fellow council members!" His surprise was so fake that Lorkett almost burst out laughing. He guessed this was the real reason for his unexpected break from the relentless training.

"Untimar. Ceerlan. Zayed," Mogrun said.

They greeted Mogrun in return. The corpulent Zayed scowled.

Untimar, the oldest of the council asked. "Lorkett, how are Danor and your new daughter? They're well?"

"Very well, thank you. My daughter's the image of her mother. Just as beautiful." His words answered the unspoken question of whether his daughter was, like him, a freak.

"Have you decided what you'll call her?"

"Nesta. It means "a raindrop," in my native tongue."

Ceerlan said, "I hear that Mogrun has you playing with sticks and swords. Do you enjoy such games?"

"Spears and swords, Ceerlan, as you know," Mogrun said.

Ceerlan shrugged. "I find it odd that we waste time playing soldiers when we have such fine wizards."

"That's exactly the reason," Lorkett said. "What happens if our wizards are killed by sheer weight of numbers? It happened at Janipur. One day we may have to rely on spears and swords, rather than our powers."

"We have to able to defend ourselves physically, as well as by magic, when the time comes," Mogrun agreed.

"If the time comes," Zayed's gravelly rasp interrupted. "I'm not as convinced by your dark tales as the others, Mogrun."

"They will come," Mogrun was firm. "And when they do, we'll need warriors as well as mages."

"But why would they bother with us?" Ceerlan asked.

"They've always feared us," Mogrun said. "We're different from them, and they fear our abilities. Because they have no talents, they think us unnatural." He speared the others with his glare. "Now they use slave halflings like Lorkett to sniff us out. They'll find us in the end, even if they have to circle the world five times. When they do..." he let his words sink in and then bowed his head. "Sirs, excuse me; I grow weary."

They parted, mouthing pleasantries. As Lorkett and Mogrun continued walking, Lorkett said, "Ceerlan seemed very uncertain about all this."

Mogrun chuckled, "Ceerlan knows what's needed. He plays the fool to help me. It's Untimar who's unsure. Zayed thinks me a lunatic, or worse. And you're a great help."

"Is that why I'm here? To frighten them?"

"You are useful," Mogrun said. "You've brought yours and Danor's talents."

"You have foresight. Will we survive?"

Mogrun was silent, then said, "I don't know." At Lorkett's raised eyebrow, he added. "The future's unclear; the weeks ahead are full of dark spaces, and shrouded with ghosts. There are many possible outcomes." He paused. "You'll come for dinner tonight, an hour after we light the street lamps." They returned to where the others worked at gathering the storm clouds.

"Look how well they work together!" Mogrun's voice rang with pride. He added quietly, "Holma had a month's head start, but Acharya has the greater ability. I worry for Holma. He hasn't the strength of the others. But we must use what we have. Once you, Tand, and Danor complete your physical training, you'll join them. When two of us work together, it's as if we are four. When three of us team up, it's like nine." He pointed upwards. "Look!" Gently at first, then with growing violence, big fat raindrops pelted the square. Thunder rumbled, and lightning flashed overhead. Mogrun smiled and clasped Lorkett's arm in a surprisingly strong grip.

***

Late in the evening, they all gathered in Mogrun's chambers, which were little more than a kitchen, and linked cells, one with a stone slab for a bed, one with a basin for washing.

Acharya was the last to arrive. He stood a little apart from the rest, as he always did. Perhaps the fact that he was some years younger than the rest of them added to his isolation.

Mogrun served them wine, poured from an amphora into clay beakers. Lorkett savored the wine, which was sweet, yet harsh, and nibbled at a biscuit smeared with a bitter paste.

"Perhaps you know," Mogrun began after they had all been served, "that cities usually spring up on trade routes. By rights, Shalimar should be a ghost town. Centuries ago, when the climate was milder, and before the Longlegs spread so wide that we jostled each other's elbows wherever we went, long before we needed to hide from them, the city was at the crossroads for every route the camel trains took. Even then, there were so few oases that travelers always stopped. A few of them stayed and found life good. In time, our forefathers learned how to make the rains come, and grow food here." His eyes clouded over as he took a sip of wine, before saying, "Success brings enemies, as surely as day follows night. Now we pay for our forefather's success, one way or another." He passed a plate of sweetmeats around, and each of them took a couple.

"Our people think," Mogrun continued, "that big men who carry swords can't use magic. That mages can't lift anything heavier than a stick. That they should work alone; and that we shouldn't teach magic to women," Mogrun nodded to Danor, who smiled, and bobbed her head. "But the Longlegs have taught us something; if we're to survive, we have to do things differently, and to work together. We have to have warriors who can wield a sword in the times when there isn't time to weave a complex spell, but only time to hack your opponent's head off. So I summoned you." He bowed. "My warriors. Today you gathered a big cloud. Tomorrow you will work together as one, and gather the biggest one yet."

Mogrun's voice seemed to speed up to a chitter, then slow to a long drawn out drone, before returning to normal. A cold wind blew through the room, and the shadows moved in ways that didn't match the people who cast them. *Something in the wine?* Cassidy wondered.

"Almost twenty years ago," Mogrun said, "I came here as a young man, and realized that my destiny was here. One night I brushed one of your minds, in a dream. When I knew the storm was gathering, I drew on those memories." His voice seemed to be coming from a long way away. "My younger self heard me talking to you like this, and of our need to see into the future. You all have a touch of foresight, and now I must stand on your shoulders to see if there's hope for us!"

Lorkett concentrated, as did the others, on pushing Mogrun's mind. In the middle of the room a tiny flickering shape appeared. Outside, the wind grew stronger. Lorkett smelt incense on the breeze. The vortex in the room grew larger as strange shapes flickered in it. Cassidy recognized some as images of things and people to come. Other shapes were unfamiliar to him.

Lorkett had no such knowledge, and quailed inside, though the drugs in the food and drink calmed him. He shook with the effort of boosting Mogrun's talent. Blood flowed from Neza's nose, and Holma's forehead was slick with sweat.

Images flashed by like a pack of cards being dealt. Lorkett watched a man walk into a cave, and heard a woman say, "Welcome, Major Cassidy." Shocked, Cassidy recognized it as the scene where he had met Sophia. He was surprised to see how impossibly tall he looked from the viewpoint of the Neanderthals. And ugly.

Flick. Flick. Flick. More images passed by, a deck of cards of the future. The woman asked, "What's your name for us?"

Cassidy answered, "Neanderthal."

More images flicked by; he lay beside Sophia. A city burned. Another was scoured by a vast wave. Flick, flick, flick, so fast Cassidy couldn't keep up, until they blurred.

Lorkett's head felt as if it would split open.

With a cry, Mogrun toppled forward. He lay unmoving.

They all stood, stupefied, for several minutes. Then Danor moved. She listened to Mogrun's heart, waving for silence. At last she said, "He lives. Help me carry him to his bed!"

Each of the group took it in turns to keep vigil beside Mogrun's bed. Days passed into weeks, until one day Mogrun's eyelids fluttered weakly, and he sat up.

Their joy at his revival was short lived, however. The next day they learned that the Longlegs were camped outside the city.

***

"They've been out there ten days." Neza tapped his thigh impatiently, and looked at the steps carved out of the rock. There were stairs at each corner of the city, descending from the gates to the sand. "What are they waiting for? An invitation?"

"The stragglers are still gathering," Mogrun said. They'd had this conversation many times. In the three months since the horde stumbled across the city, they'd spread like an ink stain over the dunes, for miles around. Since then there'd been a phony war of sporadic skirmishes, as the invaders tested the defenders' resolve on the steps.

They were perched on the high wall that surrounded the city. The attackers' camp spread over the rocks of the escarpment's lower level, a two-hundred-man-deep ring encircling Shalimar. Camp followers, prisoners and, slouched miserably in neck braces attached to iron chains, the halfling adepts used to sniff out the city, all swelled the horde.

"They'll force their way in," Mogrun said. "Even if they have to form a human pyramid, and crush those on the bottom to death. Don't underestimate them, boy."

Neza scowled at the last word. Cassidy could see it suited Mogrun to keep him on edge. The boy knew that he'd succeed Mogrun. He'd grown even more sure of his succession with the arrival of the other mages. But now, with the arrival of the horde, he had lost some of his assuredness. He compensated by talking even louder than he had before.

Cassidy liked most of the Thals- Holma, despite his eccentricity and demophobia, Acharya, with his scholar's thirst for knowledge, Danor, an untypical woman in this man's world, and Lorkett, who would cut off his arms and legs to protect his wife and child. He even liked Tand, who had battled to overcome his distrust of halflings and to work with Lorkett. They all tolerated one another as best they could.

But Cassidy didn't particularly like Neza. From sharing the youth's thoughts, Cassidy could see Neza wasn't the slightly puppyish young man he presented to the others. Only Mogrun sensed his impatience and arrogant ambition, but had no idea that his nephew considered his uncle a doting fool, and the others as provincials with no place in his city. As for the idea that they should play at soldiers, when all adepts knew that magic was the true vocation, that was lunacy. "Why are you ignoring the council? Attack them now!" he urged, ignoring the fact that the council was split, and that the Primate, the city's ruler, supported Mogrun.

"Not until they're all here," Mogrun said, "We mustn't just defeat these, or the ones who have yet to come will try again. We must crush them so badly they'll never return." He limped away, leaving Neza fuming.

***

That evening Cassidy flicked again. He looked down at Mogrun's trembling liver spotted hands. Oddly enough, few of Mogrun's memories were open to Cassidy in the way that the others had been. There was, however, an enormous sensation of latent power, even though it was now dimmed by time's ravages.

Holma, Secheray, Acharya and Lorkett had crept down the steps, tiptoed through the lines until they were well clear, and pitched their tents beyond the enemy lines in a giant diamond formation.

Danor asked the question none of the others had thought of, or perhaps dared not ask, "What happens if one of the enemy's scouts stumble over them?"

Mogrun said bleakly, "We had best hope that that does not happen."

Mogrun and Neza met with the councilors in their chambers for a dinner of chicken, vegetables and fruit. They prayed to their grandfathers and the spirit world for success. "We lost so much when the other cities fell." Mogrun gazed out into the twilight. "One in a thousand of our people have the talent. As few again become mages. We lost most of them at Janipur and Centola. We can't allow this city to fall. Shalimar is our pinnacle, a beacon of light in the darkness. It must not fall."

"I agree," the Primate said. He agreed with Mogrun a lot. It was a sure way to stay in charge, though no one ever actually said so. Cassidy noticed that Mogrun regarded the man with wry amusement, instead of the contempt with which Neza viewed him.

A young man knocked at their door and bowed. "The enemy's envoy calls under a badge of truce." Mogrun looked at the others, who nodded, and said to the soldier, "Bring him."

The envoy was young, and Mogrun thought it difficult to tell who was more frightened, he or the councilors. The youth's forehead was beaded with sweat, his sunken eyes wide, and the nostrils of his long narrow nose flared.

It was the first time Mogrun had actually met one of them. He was struck by how truly alien the boy was. Old and frail though he was, Mogrun could still have snapped the youth's spine like a twig. He watched the Longleg study their heavy physiques, wide shoulders, short arms and legs. Cassidy/ Mogrun saw the pictures of hate in his mind, visions of smashing their faces in, until there was only a bloody mass left. The boy emanated hate and fear like the stench from a corpse. When he spoke, his voice broke and still squeaked at times. "My liege urges you to surrender. He says you'll be treated fairly."

"As the people of Janipur were?" Mogrun's voice was silky.

"Yes."

"You were there?"

The youth's head lifted slightly; he blushed. "Yes."

"So. Women raped, children butchered, houses burnt to the ground." Mogrun held up his hand, silencing the envoy. "This is treating us fairly?"

"No more than you deserve! You and your kind's vile sorcery! Lurking in your lairs-"

"Show him out," Mogrun waved him away. "Gently. We'll not sink to their level." The old man looked at the councilors, his face ashen. "The war has begun," he said solemnly.

***

That night, the enemy drums started beating an incessant booming to fray the defender's nerves. The dull pounding was more like a churning in their guts than an actual noise. The drummers continued into the next day, and by noon the defenders were snapping at one another.

"I could take a break from cloud building," Neza said. "If we can spy out the drummers, we can stop their hearts."

Mogrun nodded. "Do it."

So began a duel that lasted for hours. One by one, the drummers fell clutching their chests, or scrabbling at their throats as they turned blue. Those around them shook their fists in impotent fury at the city, as others took up the drums.

After an hour Neza was sweating, and a pulse throbbed at his temple. He brushed aside Mogrun's suggestion that he stop. "I'll kill them all if need be," he snarled. But as dusk neared, he conceded defeat. "There are simply too many."

"Which is why I've not killed Stral," Mogrun said. "This mob has taken on a life of its own. If we simply kill Stral, another man will take over. We need to absolutely smash them." Cassidy couldn't read Mogrun's thoughts, but even so, he could feel that the wizard wasn't as confident as he pretended to be.

To protect the women and children, Mogrun had them smash chairs, tables, and anything else they could carry, and use the pieces to build barricades at crossings and behind the city walls. Now the women and children huddled between the barricades, the women armed to the teeth, their children subdued, unsure what was going on.

Mogrun gathered the older women together and said, "I don't believe that the city will fall, but if it does, we must kill the children ourselves rather than allow them to be captured." The women nodded grimly at his words, remembering the fate of the women and children captured in the other battles.

Danor and Tand chanted their mantras in the square all day, continuing to build the stacks of clouds. Little by little the clouds to the far west thickened, but it was slow work as they fought the wind, which kept pushing the clouds away from them. They had worked together so much, so intensely, they could feel each other's emotions. Consequently, they all knew when a Longleg scout fell over Acharya. All of the erstwhile companions felt the flash of agony from Archarya's wound, felt the energy drain from his body as blood poured from his side.

Mogrun shouted, "You can't help him! Save your strength!"

Flick! Cassidy saw through Acharya's eyes. Out in the desert, the youngster wielded his sword like a madman as he fought for survival. He'd been caught by surprise, the wound weakening him just enough that he couldn't gather his thoughts enough to Shift. There was no time to cast a spell; in despair he redoubled his sword thrusts. It was a gallant effort, but against overwhelming odds the end was inevitable. As his blood stained the sand, and his life ebbed away like the tide, Cassidy felt Acharya's last thoughts as the youth wondered why he had been left to die alone.

Flick! Cassidy looked down at Neza's hands. Horrified, the young man whispered to his uncle, "You could have helped him! Why didn't you?"

"Think, boy!" Mogrun drew himself up. "All our attacks on the drummers have been made from here, while the others lie low until their moment comes. If they thought they had killed anything but a lone scout, all that preparation would have been for nothing! If we had helped him, we'd have drawn even more of them to the area, and risked making him seem important." He summoned a soldier. "Take a squad, attack their northern end. Only stay out as long as you need, to get their attention." The soldier wheeled away.

"Tand!" Mogrun called. "Go and replace Acharya at the Southern end of the diamond. Our attack will draw them northward." He was racked by a spasm of coughing. "Danor!" he gasped when the coughing fit had passed. "You and Neza divert them. Use fire, thunderbolts, anything you can think of! Lob some snake's nests amongst them!"

They nodded, Neza shaking. Cassidy wondered what the youngster had expected a battle to be like.

Mogrun's mind followed Tand as he crept past the enemy lines. When he was in place, Mogrun told Neza and Danor to halt their attack.

They relaxed with a sigh. "How can we do this without Tand?" Danor gasped, panting with the effort she had put into the attack, while Neza, desperate for something – anything – to eat, munched on some fruit.

"We'll manage," Mogrun said. "We've done all we can. Now we wait."

An hour later the deep moan of a horn came from the enemy camp. "That's the signal. They're fully gathered," Mogrun said, turning to the anxious pair. Cassidy/ Neza watched him cast his thoughts like a fisherman casting his net. He found Stral as the enemy walked silently through the invader's camp.

"Stral!" Mogrun's amplified voice boomed. "I could squeeze your heart!" Stral convulsed for a long, painful moment before Mogrun eased the pressure. "But I want you to see this." Mogrun spread his arms wide theatrically, then waved his hands, signaling the diamond of warrior-mages hidden beyond the enemy lines, their formation magnifying their power.

Neza waited, the blood roaring in his ears. The enemy fell silent. An eerie hush hung over their camp, and the city.

The first sign was an ominous rumble, deep underground. The ground began to shake and heave, like a wild horse needing to be broken. Some of the attackers fell to their knees.

Neza watched the quartet of warrior-mages beyond the enemy lines walk steadily toward Shalimar, felt them pour everything into their efforts; Secheray slowed for a moment, shaking as if she were lifting a vast weight and struggling to hold it up, but just as she risked distorting the formation out of shape, she marched on.

With a mighty heave, the ground bucked once more, and with a scream, a ring of rock around the city broke free, lifting the enemy camp. Stral stood openmouthed in horror, as stones and scree, animals, men and women dropped from the camp. The ring climbed higher, rising twice a man's height with every heartbeat, and drifting toward the north.

When the camp was no more than a dot in the sky, and had cleared the city, the group relaxed. The ring disintegrated, and rocks, rubble and survivors fell screaming back to earth. From each corner of the diamond, the warrior-mages walked toward the remnants of the enemy camp, which were swirling and bubbling in panic. A few brave individuals charged toward the city, but their tenuous discipline was broken, and as individuals rather than a unit, they were an easy target for the defenders. Some of Stral's tame Halflings worked individual spells against the few defenders that they could see over the ramparts, but although Neanderthals on the city walls fell in places, the Halflings fell faster, the defenders firing rocks at them with catapult spells.

Danor and Neza locked a wall of air around the city, while Mogrun cast a similar bubble round Stral. The Warrior-mages outside rubbed the air over the western escarpment with their minds again and again, heating it until it rose so quickly that despite the protective wall of air, it ripped a few roofs from the buildings nearest the edge.

The vacuum created by the rising air sucked air from the west, bringing with it the storm. Turning toward it the warriors outside agitated the air still further, until it reached critical mass. Lightning flashed, and thunder rolled.

"Find some shelter!" Mogrun sent the frantic thought. His efforts had cost him a nosebleed, and a red tear trickled from one eye.

From the west came a rumbling roar like a colossal avalanche. The warrior-mages hurled themselves to the ground. Moments later, a hurricane of sand hit the remnants of the attacker's western flank, scouring skin from flesh, flesh from bone, catapulting packhorses into their men, slamming survivors against the city walls and mashing them into a bloody pulp. Only Stral stood, still protected by Mogrun.

When the storm passed, Stral stood in the desolation, as if wondering where the next blow would come from. He seemed to remain immobile forever, even after Mogrun released him, his only movement a drunken swaying in the breeze, like a fighter who has taken one punch too many. It took the sight of Lorkett, walking back to Shalimar, to rouse him. "A halfling?" Stral's voice dripped disgust, and he signaled the last of his men standing nearby.

Whether the man was inspired by Stral, or equally enraged by the presence of what looked like one of his own kind, the enemy soldier lurched toward Lorkett.

Either Lorkett didn't see him or he thought the enemy was no longer a threat. Some of the others who were still linked to him were quicker. *"Change direction!"* Cassidy/ Neza caught the warning thought from Secheray, who managed to summon one last burst of energy and with the others' help, muttered a spell to stop the enemy soldier's heart just as he reached Lorkett, before she fell to the sand with exhaustion.

To avoid the enemy soldier, Lorkett lurched toward Stral. Shaking with rage, Stral reached down and grabbed a spear. Bracing himself, he let out a howl and stabbed the surprised halfling, puncturing his lung.

Watching from the walls Danor screamed "Lorkett!" and clutched her chest- her mind locked with his. Lorkett staggered, and frowned in concentration; Stral slumped to the ground, coughing blood.

Danor reached out to Lorkett, but even as she tried to pull the edges of the wound together, she felt the connection with him fade. She looked at Mogrun's slowly shaking head and beat her fists on his shoulder in frustration.

Minutes later the defenders burst from the city to attack what little was left of the attackers, most of whom had been swept miles away, to fall broken on the ground, or had been buried beneath a wall of sand. A few of the enemy fought on, and Cassidy felt Neza's reluctant admiration for the bravery and tenacity of his foes, who fought and died where they stood.

Danor staggered across the sand to where Lorkett lay. Kneeling, she cradled his head and whispered endearments, before singing songs to send him on his way to the spirit world.

Later that day they buried Acharya and Lorkett together. Danor wept as she cradled Nesta.

Tand laid a hand on Nesta's head. "I'll look after you, little halfling."

"As will I," Mogrun said, but Danor looked away.

***

A year passed. To most citizens of Shalimar, life was good. They knew nothing of the gradually spiraling cycle of clashes between Longleg and Neanderthal to the North that had started four months earlier. "What we did bought us a year," Neza said, but sooner or later another Stral will float to the surface; they always do."

Mogrun lay in his rooms, pneumonia clogging his lungs, a mere shadow of the Mogrun from the year before, kept alive only by his sheer stubbornness. He summoned the Warrior-Mages to his rooms. Propped up on pillows, his face was pale and lined with exhaustion.

"I tell you, there'll be no peace while we and the Longlegs are on this earth together. They'll not rest while even one of us lives."

"We can't go through another battle," Secheray said.

"There is one other choice," Mogrun said "You all know it's possible for a man to Shift from one place to another. We must make a longer leap than anyone has ever made before. To the spirit world if need be."

"Have you lost your wits?" Danor asked. Then seeing the others' shocked looks, she added in a more moderate tone, "We fought the Longlegs before, we can beat them again."

"To do it, we must tear a hole in the very fabric of the world." Mogrun coughed. "I'll be the lens through which you shine your light," he said. "Focus your powers through me." He broke off into another coughing fit, and when he removed his hand, there was blood on it.

"It'll kill you, you fool!" Danor said.

"I'm dying anyway. If I could cure myself, I'd have done it long ago. My death can at least serve a purpose. Come, gather round, link hands and focus."

"But-" Tand said, but Mogrun swept his objections aside.

"Would you argue me to death? Come now," he barked. "Enough. Gather round."

The sky began to flicker and whirl, to change color, black to red to green, while the stars became lines, then back to points. Outside, the shadowy landscape round the city shimmered, and flowed as the sky continued its multi-colored dance. With a cry, Tand pitched forward, catapulting Cassidy into Neza's viewpoint as Mogrun murmured, "My brave warriors," and with a final racking cough that stained his tunic with blood, died.

***

Danor stood beside Holma, cuddling Nesta. She shivered in the new morning's chill. The city now nestled in a meadow. From its highest tower they could see mountains to the north. To the south a stream flowed westwards to the sea. The smell of ozone overlaid that of the nearby cedars.

Secheray joined them, her breathing labored, her smile brittle. "It's beautiful. I hope it was worth the price."

"Is Tand no better?"

"He cannot move on his right side. I still can't say if he will live or die."

As Neza said, "Now at least we can stop running," Cassidy heard a great, hollow chiming vibration. He plummeted in endless, silent, absolute blackness.

CHAPTER SIX

Present Day

Cassidy/Neza heard no sound, felt nothing, saw nothing. Then he saw ghosts standing round him, watching him hungrily, like birds of prey gathering round a carcass.

This last jolt was one sensation too many; he'd been many different men, a woman, a child, a bird of prey, even the small, furry creatures it hunted. He could take no more. He couldn't remember who he really was.

One of the ghosts was a woman, and when she reached out to touch his head, he shied away, before memory started to edge back, and he remembered that he was no prehistoric Neanderthal warrior, but a twenty-first century Homo Sapiens. He read her lips as she mouthed at him in the gloom, "Remove the headband."

He touched the band, and for a moment again there was that absolute black silence. Then he could see again. The walls rushed first towards, then away from him. "Are you okay?" the woman asked, as he climbed to his feet from where he'd been sitting propped up. He rubbed the numbness from his buttocks.

His heart beat as fast as a machine gun, and he felt light-headed, with a deep hollowness in his stomach. When he looked at his hand, it trembled like a leaf in an autumn gale. His legs gave way beneath him, and he crumpled to the floor.

"Help me!" Sophia called to one of Cassidy's troops. *Davenport, that's his name,* Cassidy thought. "I'm okay, just a little disoriented," he said. His bladder felt full to bursting. He made a wry mental note to himself not to drink too much water before using the headband again.

"The crystals do that to you the first time you use them. They seem so real; it's overpowering."

Cassidy noticed Davenport standing to one side, his face bloodless, his eyes fixed on Cassidy, as if searching for something.

For the first time, Cassidy noticed the tension in the air; his men and the Thals watched each other warily, guns pointing at each other, safety catches off. "What's happening?"

Davenport ignored the question, instead asked Cassidy, "You okay? That thing didn't do anything to you?"

"If it had," Cassidy said with a feral grin, "I'm unlikely to admit it to you, am I? So if I say it didn't, are you going to believe me?"

"I'd have to," Davenport grumbled. "No alien tech could do that good an impersonation of a civil servant."

Cassidy grinned. "At ease, gentlemen." Sophia said something to her people, who slowly, almost reluctantly holstered their weapons.

Cassidy turned to Sophia. "Pretty realistic, that," he said. "Good story."

Sophia's eyes narrowed. Cassidy was unsure whether she was angry, or laughing at him. "You thought it was just a story?"

"Yes." He frowned, but said no more, wanting her to make her point.

"Why?"

"Well," he said, aware that by making him answer, she'd beaten him at his own game. "There's no evidence that your people could have had cities as long ago as those in the crystal."

"No? What sort of evidence? No buildings? No remains?"

Cassidy thought for a moment, and said, "While some aboriginal remains may date back to even before Shalimar, back some forty or even fifty thousand years, we've never found anything like the level of sophistication that I saw on the crystal."

"So you know absolutely everything there is to know?" She stared at him bright-eyed, daring him to make such a claim. "You know every feature of the Earth? There isn't a single thing you've missed?"

"No, of course not," he said at last.

"So why couldn't it have happened this way?" She leaned forward.

"Some of the remains, where there are remains, are open to different interpretations." It sounded feeble, even to him.

"Exactly!" She slapped his arm. "Stone crumbles. Wood rots. Bodies decay. A vengeful army scatters the remains to the world's four corners."

"So all that happened?" he mocked her. "We've missed all the evidence of it?"

"Maybe. Or maybe not here," she agreed reluctantly. "But why not in other realities? If every action creates a different possible world, until there become an infinite number of alternate Earths, why shouldn't it have been an enterprising Neanderthal who first herded a bunch of goats together thirty thousand years before one of your people?"

"Oh, come on," Cassidy laughed, "Even if I bought all that, what about this supposed magic?"

"Why not? Magic. Talents. Call it whatever you want."

"Show me," he demanded. "Prove it."

"What am I, an exhibit?"

"Show me."

"I can't—" she held up her hand to cut off his crowing laugh, "—just like that. What weight are you?"

"Um, thirteen stone, eighty-three kilograms." He watched her work something out in her head. She was probably converting his weight into her own numbering system, he guessed. He continued, "An old man who can see into the future? A prophecy about a savior?"

"One who quoted precisely the conversation we had when we met," Sophia pointed out.

"You must have had a reasonable expectation that I'd give those answers."

"And if you answered differently?" Her scorn was palpable. "Perhaps we had a cunning master plan? An alternate crystal?"

He changed tack. "So how did I understand everything? It was as if they all spoke English."

"You didn't try to lip-read, did you?" She chuckled, her good humor returning as quickly as it had fled. *She really is a mercurial woman*, Cassidy thought. It only added to her appeal.

"No."

"Just as well. As I said before, we don't recommend it. The headset fed directly into your brain. They were talking Thal."

"Is that how I knew it was thirty-four thousand years ago?"

"Yes."

Everything he knew and had learned insisted that what he'd seen was only a fantasy, but it had felt so real.

But that probably meant nothing. These people, whatever they looked like, weren't savages; they had technology as advanced as any he'd ever seen. "The headset fed directly into your brain," she had said. The implications sent tiny millipedes of fear tickling up and down his spine. Did that mean they could have brainwashed him?

The problem with such thoughts was that the resulting paranoia could paralyze him. He had to trust his instincts, which told him that the Thals weren't hostile. Whether their presence posed an unintentional threat was a question he couldn't yet answer. "How do you capture the memories?" he asked.

"Another machine scans the brain, and records the memories onto a crystal. We scan as many people as we can and put them on the same crystal, so you get the different viewpoints."

"How do they enter the memories of people who died thousands of years ago?"

Sophia looked shifty when she answered, "It's a little hard to explain. It'd be easier if you viewed the later crystals."

Cassidy felt a flare of suspicion, but he ignored it, for the moment. Sophia frowned, and bit her lip, before saying, "It's a little like asking MaryAnn how her car's engine worked. She could probably talk generally, but if you wanted detail, you would be better asking a specialist. We have such a person, if you want a detailed technical explanation."

"Not me," he held up his hands and laughed, "I'm no more an expert than MaryAnn. It's way over my head. But we may want him to talk to our technicians later." He fell silent, realizing that he had just stated implicitly his acceptance that the Neanderthals would be around for some time. He studied the tattoos on her arms and legs, so tiny he hadn't noticed them before, and the dangling teeth-like earrings, normally hidden by her long hair, but revealed when she swept it back. He wanted so much to stroke her hair, to hold her, and he couldn't help feeling compromised by his emotions. And if he were completely honest with himself, shocked. He suspected that if he had simply seen her photograph, he would have said that she was ugly. It was life that gave her beauty. She caught his look and returned it, and the white parts of her face flushed.

"So why are you here?" he asked. "Assuming I accept the crystal as fact, there you were in your bright new world. What happened?"

"It's a long story." Sophia exhaled a deep breath. "I could tell you, or you could get it firsthand from another crystal."

"Okay," he said cautiously. "Let's start, after I've had something to eat. I'm ravenous."

"I bet you feel as if you've run round the world." Sophia patted his arm, and he felt a thrill run through him.

"Yeah," he ran his hands through his hair, "Who'd think that watching TV for a few minutes would be so exhausting?"

"Not a few minutes, sir," Davenport interrupted. Cassidy realized that he'd forgotten the man was even there. "It was ten minutes short of three hours."

"What?" Cassidy stared, yet deep down, he wasn't surprised. It felt like he'd lived in that world for almost two years.

Sophia smiled. "You don't just watch – you participate. If you watch someone experiencing a crystal, you see their arms twitch, their legs spasm, and hear them mutter to themselves."

She broke off in a fit of laughter, and when she recovered, added, "You should have seen the look on your face just then."

"Thanks," he said dryly. He said, "Davenport. What have the men been doing for the last three hours? Asleep?"

Davenport smiled. "Those of us who weren't here watching you like hawks have been taking a look around. You would not *believe* how far these caves extend."

"Tell me about it while I eat," Cassidy said, and turned back to Sophia. "Now, where's that food?"

"Hold on," she said. "Stand still. Don't move a muscle."

"Why?" He asked, but she shushed him.

Then invisible hands gripped him round his legs. He rose into the air, and hovered about two feet off the ground. His stomach lurched in denial of what he knew to be impossible. He'd flown often in an airplane, but that was something he understood. This was completely different. "Is that," his voice was a squeak and he forced it down, "you doing that?"

"Yes," Sophia panted, as if she'd been running up stairs. "I didn't need you to stand still – that was just for effect. I thought I'd wait until you were least expecting it."

Gently he sank to the ground. It had never felt so good to stand on solid earth. "I apologize for doubting you."

She bowed, and took his arm. "Thank you for the apology. Let's eat."

***

"Looks like they find what they looking for," Esteban whispered.

"They look happier," Henry agreed. He asked one of their captors, "You want us to link arms again?" He pantomimed the action with Esteban.

The Neanderthal nodded.

The captives linked arms, the Neanderthals encircling them again, one placing a hand on Esteban's shoulder. Henry thought of a wagon train forming a circle in an old western.

As the Shaman started chanting, Jerry said, "What they've done is wrong." Henry recognized the look in Jerry's eyes; he'd seen it before when he was a young man, in the eyes of men whose children had been killed by the Afrikaner security forces. Jerry was still alive in a purely functional sense, but that was all. There was no emotion left, apart from hatred and despair.

"Jerry," Henry whispered a warning.

"They shouldn't have killed Pam," Jerry said, and pulled his arms out of the circle as they went through the same stomach turning inside-out process as before, even as the Neanderthals howled a protest.

***

The scouts dropped the last few feet from the Chinook, and fanned out, checking the Demilitarized Zone. When they signaled the area was clear, the chopper landed, and the remaining soldiers leapt out, carrying the squad's supplies. Few orders were needed- this was only a training exercise, as far as the men of the 504th knew.

There were four squads altogether, two columns of twenty men each. Watching them set off, Kaminski felt a surge of pride at the way they moved like a well-oiled machine. He turned to Adler who grinned, sharing his pride. The Chinook lifted off, the high-pitched whack of its blades fading into the distance.

"I still can't believe we're really on the edge of the Tora Bora," Adler said. "This is all happening too fast. A week ago I kissed Pen goodbye at Fort Bragg. Today-" He shook his head.

Kaminski knew what Adler meant. He felt the same air of unreality. "You spoken to Pen?"

"Last night." Adler's voice was wistful. "Dylan will have had his third birthday before we go back."

"But at least you'll be home before she comes to term," Kaminski said. Adler's wife was expecting their second child. She had company. Kaminski's wife was also pregnant. He felt a pang of homesickness and wished he were back with Barbara.

"You wanna lead, sir?" Adler's voice, soft yet insistent, cut through Kaminksi's reverie.

Kaminski shook his head, taking midpoint between the squads, with Garcia at the rear, and Adler leading. The men set off at a brisk pace, eager to get as far into the hills as possible before the day grew too hot. After ten minutes of marching, Adler nodded Kaminski away from the line, while still watching for Hostiles. Kaminski studied the small dark figure at the rear of the line. "What do you make of Garcia?"

Adler passed him a stick of gum. "Seems okay. A bit mouthy sometimes, but that's gang-banger machismo." Adler added, "Most of his family are dead. If he hadn't joined up, he'd a probably been shot in some liquor store holdup, too. But he's got what it takes. Even officer material, if he can keep his trap shut."

"That good, huh?" Kaminski valued Adler's judgment. After all, Adler had picked Kaminski to be his son's godfather. Kaminski grinned at the thought.

***

The Thals led Cassidy's men through brightly lit corridors, to another cavern, deeper in the complex, where the light was much murkier. If there ever had been lights, they had been broken or the Thals had removed them. A huge metal pot hung from a tripod frame over the fire.

"Shall we send food to your men on guard?" Sophia asked.

"Why not?" Cassidy said.

Two of the women ladled bowlfuls of vegetable stew, and passed them around. "Bread?" Sophia passed him an uncut loaf, and he ripped a lump out of the end.

"This is good," he said between mouthfuls, running the bread round the rim of the metal bowl. "Where'd it come from?"

Sophia finished her mouthful, said, "We brought ten days worth of vegetables with us, and bread. We raided the stores, and found tins of vegetables and meat, and frozen bread that we left out to warm. When we run low, we'll eat those."

"Sir," Davenport interrupted, "What's going on? What happened while you were under that...thing?"

"I'm not sure yet," Cassidy admitted. He told Davenport what he had experienced with the crystals. "Do you believe it?" Davenport asked incredulously when Cassidy finished his story. "Medieval, even Renaissance-level technology?"

"Well, I've always thought it odd how Neanderthals just vanished," Cassidy said. "We've always assumed it was due to climatic changes, or their being absorbed by Homo Sapiens. But those are all just theories, as solid as a house of cards." He leaned toward Davenport, "Give me a debrief on what the men have found." He leaned back and listened to Davenport rattle off what they had learned so far, the depths of the caves, the tunnels filled with supplies, equipment – some of it familiar, some of it strange – that they had found. He realized that Davenport had finished. He looked up.

"Shouldn't we send someone to report back since we can't get a radio signal?" Davenport pulled at his collar.

Cassidy nodded and said, "We'll send two men with a holding message. 'Have made contact. Believed not hostile.' They guard each other. If they make it back to base, they can send help for the injured men we left behind. If they don't return, we send no one else. We can't afford to have our men shaved off. Got it?"

Davenport nodded, and removed his glasses to blearily wipe at his face. Cassidy ordered Davenport to get some rest and turned back to Sophia. "I want to see the next crystal," he said.

"The experience of the crystals is so intense," Sophia said, "We normally allow a day to recover. You should wait till tomorrow before you do it again."

"I don't have the time," he said. "It has to be now." He didn't like to think of how complicated things could get if the Americans, the rest of the United Nations, or worst of all, the Taliban found out about the Thals before he could secure the situation – and to do that, he needed to know exactly *what* he was securing.

She opened her mouth, saw the set of his jaw, and shrugged. "Don't say I didn't warn you." She refastened the band around his head, and slotted another crystal into the eyepiece. After another long pause, he felt again the sensation of falling toward the onrushing walls, and the pitch-black silence.

CHAPTER SEVEN

3500 Years Before Present Day

It happened in mere moments, neatly dividing Palo's life into Before and After the End of the World. Palo was matching glares with Tinto when Cassidy entered her mind, and before he could get oriented, the Death-Screams echoed through her head and...

Palo/Cassidy was a sailor on a grain barge in the Middle Sea checking his position; he wasn't caught looking directly at the flash, but the world turned briefly red-gold-red, and the agony of perforated eardrums nearly blew his head apart...

They were a shepherd boy, high on a stony hillside near Inner Sea, watching a distant pillar of fire rising to the heavens...

They were men, women and children caught by the river of fire from the collapsing volcano, or boiled alive in the waters around the island. Palo/Cassidy nearly passed out with the agony, which cut through them like lightning.

The visions faded.

"What is it?" Tinto's voice falsettoed with fear. He cleared his throat. "What did you do?" Wide-set eyes beneath his eyebrow shelf narrowed suspiciously.

Reading the tattoo that extended halfway down her right arm from her elbow, she invoked the spell to mind-link with Dytas. But before she could send a question she staggered, knocked backwards by thousands of Death-screams, so powerful they eclipsed the earlier ones with their teeth-grinding, head-ripping, eyeball-melting pain. She covered her head with her hands, but the screams reverberated so that she thought her brain would burst. She had no idea how long she stood, unable to move. Only when she managed to mumble the end-spell and sever the link did the screams stop, though their echoes rang like a chiming bell.

"What's wrong?" For the first time in the two weeks since she'd come to the island, Tinto had lost his normal dark color, and was white with fear. Layman or no, even he'd felt something.

Looking around wildly, he took her arm. She felt suddenly giddy at the physical contact, and snatched it away. "Where are the children?" he cried.

Even as he asked, D'Nor and Chessel ran to them. "Papa! Palo! Are the Gods angry with us?"

Palo tried to speak, but the aftershock from the death-screams was too great, and her knees gave way. With Tinto still clutching her arm, she slumped, her teeth chattering.

The children hugged them tight in terror. Even if the adults had tried to let go they couldn't have. Tinto moaned with fear; then his voice was drowned out by the loudest noise Palo had ever heard. It was as if the gods had used a hammer to strike a gong the size of the world. It roared and echoed and overwhelmed them completely. If the children screamed, she couldn't hear them. They all clutched one another as the ground shook and heaved.

The noise and tremors finally passed, and they held one another, temporarily deaf, terrified, and exhausted. When her mind finally returned to something near normality, Palo thought about how the day had started so ordinarily.

***

Six hours earlier she'd dabbed at the cuts on her jawbone with a sponge and water. *One day we'll have decent razors,* she thought, *not these blunt iron lumps that leave you needing to smear the cuts with lotion.* She thought it every week, when she shaved her light covering of facial hair to keep her tattoos clearly visible.

It was harder to spot the blood on the black patches of her skin than the white ones, so she took a little while to cover all the cuts with the clotting ointment.

She picked up a bigger pot with another lotion from beside the stone slab that was her bed, and she smeared it all over herself, as she did first thing every morning and last thing at night. The pots weighed more than the rest of her minimal belongings combined. It smelt rank, like fish left in the sun for a week, which wasn't surprising, since that was its base, but Dytas had promised it would help stop insect bites from turning bad. "It made our family fortune, so don't moan about it," her uncle had said cheerfully. She wondered how much that fortune had overcome any objections from the church about her joining.

Ever since Dytas had first shown her how to nudge things with her mind, she'd honed her skills. Her parents disapproved; they'd rather she didn't stand out from normal people at all, but if she had to practice magic, she should find a nice, safe little job until she met the right man and started a family. They'd never understood that she wanted more than that. They'd underestimated her determination, and a quiet war had raged between them, Palo and her uncle, until Palo's view that the Church was the best place to develop her talents prevailed.

Smearing cream on her face, she studied her reflection in the tiny wall mirror. Her eyes were bloodshot from too little sleep; her eyebrows needed plucking soon, or the tattoos would be obscured and the spells impaired. If her green eyes were her best feature, her weak jaw was her worst. She looked like a Longlegs, she thought as she worked lotion into her jaw.

Then she smeared it down her body. *At least my breasts are small enough not to sag,* she decided. She looked at her triangle of hair below, and because such thoughts reminded her of filthy dreams about a certain married man, she quickly uncupped her hands.

"Are you practicing your spells?" The girl's voice startled her, but she managed not to jump.

"Something like that," She turned to look at the little girl. "D'Nor, you should bang on the door before entering someone's dwelling."

"You don't have a door." D'Nor said with the six-year-old's inexorable logic.

"Then you should call out."

"Why?"

"Because." Palo fastened her shell necklace, her parent's grudging initiation gift, slipped her functional robe on, and shook her moccasins free of insect lodgers. "Do you want something?" She bound her black-and-white streaked hair with a clasp.

"I brought you this," D'Nor held out a cooked lizard. "For your breakfast."

"Thank you." Palo was touched. "Does your papa know you're here?"

D'Nor shrugged. "He says you're a meddling bitch who should have children and not play with magic. He said so to Chessel." She added, "Why doesn't he like you, Palo?"

Palo couldn't resist asking, "Did he like the last priest?"

D'Nor shrugged again, and called back as she left the cave, "The last priest was a man!"

Palo hoped D'Nor wouldn't get into trouble, sneaking over to visit, but she would know later, when she visited Tinto, for she would visit him whether he wanted a visit from the island's priest or not.

She swallowed two of the mineral tablets she'd brought with her to stave off heat-sickness and remembered to ask Dytas for more. Then she ate the lizard, which was stringy and partly raw, but D'Nor's thought had been kind, so Palo savored it as best she could. At least she wouldn't have to hunt her own breakfast. While she finished eating, she visited the dew-still outside the cave. Scooping the dew with a half-coconut she kept there, she drank it thirstily. Water was always a problem on the island. Despite the tablets and water, she'd often wake in the night, haunted by cramps that lurked like a hungry predator.

Finally she meditated and practiced her spells. When she'd finished, she felt a tug on her mind, as if she'd just remembered something. It was a mild Summoning from Dytas, who wanted to speak to her. "*I'm here Uncle,*" she thought. "*How are you?*"

"*A little achy this morning, child. I still feel like a young man, but my body keeps letting me down.*"

"*Your body has many years left,*" Palo teased. "*But you did not Summon me to complain about your aches.*"

"*There is much happening, which no one will explain. People disappearing without reason, the ground shivering and strange portents like dead fish floating up to the surface of pools. When I ask those with Foresight, I get half answers, or evasions and denials. Be careful; call me if anything unusual happens.*"

"*Such as?*"

"*Something in the earth, but I know not what.*"

He vanished from her mind, and she set out on her morning rounds. The island was on the margin of habitability for her people, who preferred the cold. Although early, it was already warm. The air smelt of pinesap, sage and hibiscus. Her moccasins slapped on damp stones; it had drizzled in the night. Around her, small birds cackled defiance at one another. Apart from stinging insects, the only harmful creatures on the island were water-vipers that swam over from the other islands, an occasional venomous spider, and nasty little ants that hunted in swarms. One of her tattoos was a protective charm to ward them all off.

As the newest arrival, the priest, and a woman, she was triply guaranteed the worst dwelling on Thalke, though she actually liked the cave. It didn't need the constant repairs required by a hut, and it was cool, even at midday. But it was a very long way from the huts, and she begrudged the time she wasted each day clambering over tree roots, though she no longer stumbled as she had when she'd first arrived. Her progress was steady, but slow.

The island could barely support its score of inhabitants. A few more children, and the eldest would leave, as the islanders had left their parents. This diaspora had continued since prehistory, each new generation forced further south by slowly increasing numbers, until they had reached this marginal foothold on the very edges of the habitable world. The island was only bearable because of the surrounding water. Few journeyed further south to the blistering furnaces of the desert Hot lands. Fewer still returned.

She was surefooted enough now to look away from the ground while she walked, and with a quick *clip* of her mind, she twisted an orange from a tree, nearly hitting a passing monkey. She caught the fruit and peeled it, pulling a face at the bitterness of its flesh. She picked another dozen, and carried her booty in her arms.

She came to Gotn's hut, the first on her circuit, still clutching her spoils. The old man kept a handful of goats and grew a few vegetables. Palo believed that he mainly existed on the charity of his neighbors. Like all the islanders, he smelled of stale sweat; she suspected she did too, under the stench of Dytas' vile insect repellant.

Gotn had a cut that had turned nasty and oozed pus. She washed the area round it with water from one of the many salt-springs on the island. While they exchanged small talk, she changed the poultice, and performed a healing spell, reading the swirls of the tattoo on her left hand for guidance. She had a nasty feeling that her art wasn't yet equal to the old man's wound, but she could only do her best.

Her tutor hadn't really expected her to save lives when this island had been allocated as her parish. "A priest must accept the same work as other novitiates, Palo," he had told her. "Practical work to help lay people, not just the glories available to magicians."

She felt her temper rise at the thought of the fat old hypocrite and how, resentful of her because she was a woman, he'd tried to label her as a shallow glory-hunter. He'd made sure her post was here at the hot, far edge of the known world.

"I beg your pardon?" She realized with a guilty start that Gotn was talking to her.

"Said, you'm a brave girl," he pointed to her tattoos. "Must've hurt like buggery, heh?" The old man had few teeth and his words were almost incomprehensible, unless she concentrated.

"The tattoos?" She pointed to her hand, and the old man nodded. In fact the paint-coated bone needles with which they'd pierced her skin had caused the worst agony she'd ever experienced. The tattoos still hurt, but without them, she'd never be able to recite the spells that focused her mind.

She laughed and said, "They do hurt. But pain and sickness are tests from the Gods to show our worth." She'd heard it said that the tattooing in some way caused the lockjaw that killed many priests, but that was widely dismissed as nonsense.

She finished tending his wound, and stood up to go.

"You," suddenly grown shy, Gotn stammered, "want summat to eat?"

She shook her head. "I've just eaten." The islanders normally fed their priests, in return for working spells and the teaching they did, but she guessed that of anyone, Gotn could least spare food. She handed him an orange to distract him, and he took it with an awkward diffidence, that she knew was a mask for embarrassment at needing her help.

She pointed to Jarol's boat, bobbing on the water like a cork. "I see our ferryman has gone back to fishing."

"No beggar wants to come here." Gotn smiled toothlessly. "Except you, so he might as well take up fishing again."

"True," she grinned. "Maybe he can spare you some fish."

She could ask. But while Jarol was a fine sailor, he was the only link between Thalke and the other islands, something he knew, and exploited. And there was something about him, although she couldn't say what, that set her teeth on edge. Maybe it was the too familiar way in which he had looked at her when she had climbed into his little boat.

"No need," Gotn lied airily.

She spent the rest of the morning on easy, low level work. Visiting those other islanders who were at home, swapping gossip, working routine spells. Then she went down to the water's edge, encouraging fish to leap into the islanders' nets. As the morning passed the ground shook occasionally, which happened often, but there were more tremors than usual, and today the very air seemed charged.

Her last call of the morning before her noontime devotions was to Tinto's hut, which overlooked the islands to the north.

Tinto crouched in the vegetable patch, immobile, as if deep in thought. Palo was about to call out when she realized he was mumbling to himself. As she walked nearer, she noticed the stone cairn, and slightly apart, two smaller ones. His wife, and two of his children were buried there.

He was thick set, and she tried not to notice his corded muscles, and how his black hair covered his arms like fur. She didn't want to interrupt him, but she must have made a noise, because he suddenly looked up, his black eyes unreadable in his dusky face. "What do you want?"

"I was passing by." When he didn't answer, she added, "Are the children fishing?"

He nodded. "They've work to do. As do I." He turned away.

She wasn't ready to be so dismissed, but instead of chiding him, she asked something that surprised even her, "Who are your friends?"

He stopped, looking puzzled. "I've no time for friends." His voice was level. "That's a luxury for city dwellers."

She blushed at the rebuke. "Have you time for enemies?"

His laugh was a humorless bark. "I suppose my neighbors count as enemies, in hard times." He squinted. "Why? Or is this just aimless chatter?"

She shook her head. "I have very few friends myself, apart from my uncle. And my only enemies are in the church. I just wondered why," she hesitated, "why you so dislike me."

His face went blank, and he turned away. "Who says I do?" He said it as if he'd had to carve the words from stone. Cassidy felt Palo's heart leap.

"Can I help the children with their fishing?" she asked.

"Please yourself," he didn't turn round. "Just keep your God-bothering to yourself."

"If you so dislike God-botherers," Palo said, "why is D'Nor named after the Goddess?"

When he strode toward her, she thought he would hit her, and she shrank away from him. His mouth and eyes were clenched so tightly they were nearly invisible. "'Twere my wife's choice of names. Much good it did her! Your precious gods didn't help when the plague struck, did they?" He turned his back on her in dismissal.

The children stood waist deep in the shallows in the next inlet, clad only in loincloths, heads bowed, spears in hand, two dark brown stains in the water. Palo mumbled a simple spell, guiding a fish toward Chessel's spear. He stabbed, and as he straightened up, Palo guided another fish to D'Nor. She shrieked gleefully. "I've got one!"

"Baby!" Chessel scornfully threw his fish onto the sand. "I've got three!"

They soon had eight small fish between them. D'Nor being less experienced lost two more in her excitement.

Meanwhile, Palo built a sand-statue away from the water, holding it in shape with her mind as well as her hands. When she finished, she strode to the water's edge. "You've done well."

"Palo! Palo! I caught three fish!" D'Nor jumped up and down in the water, and Palo wondered how it felt to grow up with brothers and sisters. It sometimes seemed a mixed blessing, but still she had to suppress a pang of envy.

"Did you help us?" Chessel sounded as surly and suspicious as his father did.

"Of course not." Her smile felt false in the face of his scowl. "You'll eat well today."

"Don't mind him." D'Nor said loftily. "He's just a boy." She looked at Palo's arms. "Can only piebalds work magic, Palo?"

Sitting on the sand, Chessel felt around and triumphantly dug up a sharp stone, with which he gutted the fish. "Course not," he muttered. "Stupid."

"I'm not stupid!"

"Almost anyone can work magic, D'Nor, whatever their skin color." The effort of holding the statue in shape while talking made Palo shake. *I need more practice at working spells while doing other tasks,* she thought as she crouched, facing D'Nor. "I built a model of the statue of the goddess D'Nor in Sartonin. Would you like to see it?"

"Oh yes!" D'Nor shrieked.

Palo led her by the hand to the replica. D'Nor walked around the statue, which towered over them. "How does it stay up?" she breathed. In the original, the goddess's brother gods Lorkit and Mogrun stood beside her as she peered into the distance while holding her baby, but Palo had omitted the brothers from the sand sculpture.

"Magic," Palo said. The original was three times bigger, but she felt she'd caught the likeness. "You'll be able to do this when you get older. Let's do some spells now."

"Dad'll be mad." Chessel appeared like a conjured sprite.

As though he had heard them, Tinto called at just that moment. The children each impaled four fish with their spears and turned and ran home, holding their spears with the points outward.

Palo strolled after them, shielding her eyes against the noonday sun. When she looked back, the statue had already collapsed, and would soon be nibbled away by the waves.

Tinto lit a feeble, sputtering little fire, and was gutting the last fish. "You'll be going, then," he nodded at Palo in dismissal.

His rudeness infuriated Palo. She hadn't planned to stay, but manners dictated that he ask. Chessel smirked, and she knew that in the time it had taken her to get there, the boy had painted a picture of her corruption of D'Nor. "Children, go and play," she said to them. Chessel looked as if he wanted to argue, but Tinto waved him away.

"They need more than daily drudgery," she said, "They need to know about the world." It wasn't the first time they'd had this conversation.

"They don't have time for *learning*," he sneered. "They've work to do. We live in the real world. We have to find food."

"I live in it too!" she snapped. "Making things, casting spells, healing people. And, yes, telling stories about our ancestors. The real world is all the worlds, yours and mine, spirit and flesh. They're all as real as gutting fish. The children don't have time not to learn,"

His jaw set in mulish defiance and she added slyly, "Learning some spells would at least help them catch more fish."

He looked away. She guessed he'd never had time as a child for anything but work.

"Why do you hate the church so much?" she asked.

"Nonsense," he snorted, breathing heavily. She was unsure if he meant her question, or what he thought of the church.

"I'm sorry my predecessor couldn't save your wife, but don't blame me for it." She'd wanted to hurt him, in return for his rudeness, and shake him out of his complacency, but she saw such pain in his eyes that she regretted her words the moment she said them.

Before he could reply, or she could apologize, the world as they knew it came to a sudden, shocking end.

***

Even when the roaring had faded, and the shaking ground stilled, the four of them still crouched, holding each other. It was Palo who stood first, her calves aching. She stretched, and gingerly reached out with her mind. *"Uncle?"* There was nothing but silence in her mind.

The quiet frightened her, though it was better than the endless living nightmare of the death-scream. She cast her mind out again. "I can't hear anything," she whispered, staring eastwards, where evil looking clouds swirled and billowed in an angry red sky.

"The Gods must be furious," Tinto said, and Palo shot him a sharp look, expecting irony, but he seemed serious. She decided that like many who were cynical when times were good, he suddenly believed in Gods when things got a little tough. *"Palo?"* Dytas' thought was cobweb-gentle at the edge of her mind.

"Uncle? Where are you?" She squeezed her eyes shut to help her concentration. *"Are you safe?"*

"I've made it to Sartonin – oh Gods, there's nothing left that isn't covered in ash and soot! Did you hear the screams?"

"How could I not?" She barely noticed Tinto and the children staring at her. *"Where are Mama and Papa? Are they safe? What's happening? Is this the end of the world?"*

After a long pause, Dytas answered, "I'm sorry, dear. Raba and Pepperdin are dead. They were nearer the blast." In her mind Palo saw again the giant eruption, the river of boiling mud, hurtling as fast as a brush fire in the dry season, burning everything in its path. Dytas added, *"Those who died quickly were lucky; others weren't so fortunate; they died by suffocation, or were cooked in rivers of lava."*

"I'll take the ferry. It'll take weeks, but I'll-"

"NO!" His mental roar almost broke the fragile link between them. When he continued, he did so gently, as if speaking to a child. *"The city is deserted. Those who could, fled already. I suspect they could only move a few, and abandoned the rest of us. They've Shifted, child. Gone to the next world. When I look to tomorrow, I see only darkness and endless winter. Either we Shift, or we die. Take as many as you can with you."*

"I can't! I don't have the Talent for this."

"You must! I can't help you from here. You'll have to do it on your own." Dytas paused and then said gently, *"I'm sorry child. Time to face your duty. Our tasks are not always pleasant."* His voice faded, and she was left alone on the beach, staring at nothing.

"Palo?" Tinto said gently. "What's happening?"

She took his forearm, her hand barely reaching halfway round, and she saw from his wince how tight her grip was. The chill in her heart must have shown in her bleak gaze.

Tinto licked his lips. "You're frightening the children."

The wind was refreshing, blowing steadily from the northeast, a blessed relief after the noonday heat. But the cool salt tang seemed to carry the stench of disaster; she could almost smell the burnt flesh, and feel the heat. "They're gone."

"Who are?" Tinto tried to pull away from her grasp.

"My parents are dead. Sartonin's empty; the buildings buried beneath a rain of ash, streets full of bodies, like a charnel house." She tried to paint with mere words the horrific scenes she'd witnessed.

"Sartonin? The 'golden city?'" Tinto said derisively.

"Yes. Sartonin. The hub of our world." Palo spoke bleakly. "It and all the cities and towns around it, are gone. Do you know what that means? Those left will have nothing but what they can scratch from the land." She laughed bitterly. "Suddenly you're the New Rich, Tinto. You don't need money, or possessions, or knowledge. You can hunt and cook. Unlike me."

"Can't you mind-speak to others, get together, rebuild?"

She shook her head. "I can only mindspeak to Dytas. Mindspeakers are very limited. We can usually only link to one, or at most a couple of relatives. Those who can talk with anyone are the elite."

He nodded in understanding. "What now?"

Palo seemed to ignore him. She looked down at the children. "D'Nor, you know the story of the Goddess?" she asked.

The child nodded, pleased to be the center of attention. "D'Nor was handmaiden to the chief God, Mogrun," she recited in a singsong voice. "Mogrun led our people from the Devil Lands, where the Longlegs hunted them, to our world."

"That's right," Palo said.

D'Nor smiled toothily.

Palo turned to Tinto. "What if I told you that the stories are true? Thousands of years ago we came from another world? That almost all our people have Shifted again, not from the Longlegs this time, but away from that eruption, which we all felt?"

Tinto looked blank, but Palo continued, "Dytas wants me to Shift as well, taking as many people as I can. But I can't do it! I've never been able to work such spells!"

"Leave all this?" Tinto waved his hands. Palo knew he was alarmed at the thought of leaving the graves he'd made into shrines.

"I can't do it," Palo said. "Shifting as many people as they did is a huge undertaking- the Church must have been preparing for months to abandon us." She had to hold back tears. The scale of their betrayal left her exhausted. She slumped on the sand, sifting it through her fingers. What should she do now? Should she stay with the islanders and make a life for herself here, or should she go to Sartonin, despite Dytas' pleas?

"Why can't you Shift?" Crouching on his haunches, Tinto patted her shoulder, concern warping his weather-beaten face.

"Why can't you fly?" she sneered. "Just flap your arms!" It seemed unreal that he was suddenly so worried for her, when only hours before he could barely speak civilly to her. *Maybe he thinks he can talk me into going away,* she thought sourly.

He nodded. "Like that, is it?"

"It is," She sighed. "I'm hungry. Can you spare a fish?"

"Yes," He rose and helped her up. "Let's see if they're cooked."

"What's that?" Chessel shouted. "There!" Palo and Tinto froze, followed his pointing finger.

The air seemed to shiver and then turn sideways. Someone, or something, fell to the ground and staggered to its feet; it froze, staring at them from a few feet away.

It was quite manlike, Palo noted. It was shorter than she, but probably weighed as much as squat, stocky Tinto. It walked on two legs, had a large, domed head, and leathery green skin. Its eyes were yellow and reptilian, and instead of hair, its head sported tufts of feathers that shifted through the colors of the rainbow with dazzling speed. Where its ears should have been were gill-like slits down the side of its head. Beneath its rough blue overall, its chest rose and fell as it panted. The three-clawed hand that clutched a long, curving knife had an opposable thumb. Its teeth were sharp and pointed, and looked as if they were meant to eat only one thing. Flesh. Afterwards the others claimed they could feel hatred radiating from it, but Palo dismissed that as hindsight.

Time stretched. They all looked at one another for a few heartbeats that seemed to last forever. Then the creature jumped at Tinto, slashing at him with the knife. Tinto leapt back, the blade missing his stomach by a hairsbreadth.

The children ran screaming into the water, while Palo ducked the slashing knife, and threw sand into the creature's eyes. As she leapt backwards, she clipped an orange from a nearby tree with her mind, and thunked it into the side of its head. It hissed and she reached out mentally, stopping its next knife thrust, saw its eyes widen in amazement.

Tinto stabbed it in the throat with a spear, so hard it broke the shaft. The creature let out a whistling shriek.

Palo concentrated. She made it swing the knife into its own leg. Blue-colored blood fountained from a severed artery, and covered Tinto, who stabbed the creature with another spear. It screamed again, flopping around on the sand; then it stilled and died.

Palo peered at it, ignoring Tinto's warning bark of "Be careful!"

"Blue blood?" she asked.

Tinto kicked it to check it was dead, and when it didn't move, he kicked it again.

"Enough!" Palo said.

"It could've killed us!" He spun, his fists clenched and his eyes wide open. For a moment, Palo thought he might hit her.

"It's dead now, it can't harm us."

"How do you know?" Tinto said. "What is that thing? Where did it come from? What's it-"

"Hush." She put her fingers to his lips. "Enough questions that I can't answer."

Tinto nodded slowly and took several deep breaths. He called the children out of the water, and filling a bowl with seawater, Palo bathed their various scratches and cuts, and they all walked to Tinto's hut.

"Chessel, fill a cup with spring water," Tinto said.

"It's okay, I have some oranges!" Palo protested.

"No, we've earned this." When Chessel returned, Tinto passed her the cup. As their guest, she took three sips appreciatively. "Thank you," she said, licking her lips to make sure she got every precious drop. She returned the cup to Tinto, who then passed it to the children.

"I'm going to talk to my uncle. Maybe he will have more information," Palo said. *"Dytas? Are you there?"*

It took several attempts, before Dytas answered, *"Here."*

"Can't you join us?" she asked. *"Can't a boatman bring you?"*

"I'm too weak. I can barely breathe with all the ash that is in the air." She felt his coughing fit as staccato interruptions to his thoughts.

When she told him about the strange creature, he was especially interested in its reaction when she'd fought back. *"It didn't expect your Talent, Palo. You did well not to let it escape. It's either a scout or a refugee. If it's a scout, keeping our powers a surprise could work to our advantage. If it's just a refugee, that's even more worrying in some ways."*

"Why? How much worse can things get?"

"Think girl! It sounds more like a two-legged reptile than a man, even if it does walk upright. The few realms we've lived in have all been similar to each other. There are no Longlegs here, but other than that, it's like all the others. How different would a realm have to be to spawn something like that? If it's a refugee, then volcanoes must have erupted in other realms as well as ours. And if it's a scout, then it can shift realms like we can. In that case, our people need to know about it. You HAVE to warn the others!"

"I can't!" Palo cried in her head. *"What do I have to say to convince you? I've tried, but all I get are headaches, like my head's splitting apart."* She hammered out each word. *"I. Cannot. Do. It!"* Muttering the end-spell, she burst into tears.

The others watched her, D'Nor chewing her lip and Chessel wiping his nose. Tinto passed her a fish with a ghost of a smile that was only there for a half-second, but it was there, and her heart surged.

"Thank you," she mumbled round a mouthful.

"What now?" Tinto said.

"Well," she said, "We're far enough away to be safe from the volcano." She thought of Dytas' warnings of an endless winter and decided that he was just trying to scare her into shifting with the others. *Well, damn him to the Devil Lands,* she thought. Her family was dead. She owed the Order nothing now.

Tinto squeezed her hand. She snatched it away, and at his surprised look she said, "I'm sorry; you startled me."

"Sorry."

"I should go home," she said. "It's late. Walking in the dark, I'm likely to break something, or get bitten by a nasty."

Tinto said, looking away, "You could stay here if you wanted." He looked up, and she saw fear in his eyes, but wasn't sure of what. "The children would be happier having you round."

She swallowed, mouth suddenly dry. She was overwhelmingly aware of his nearness. Although she dreamed of him every night, she wasn't sure she was ready to make her dreams real.

"Palo!" Dytas' mental shout broke the tension of the moment. *"Get into a boat, quickly! With as many people as you can!"*

"You want us to come to you?" Palo asked, puzzled.

"There's no time! Get as many as you can into a boat!" He fell silent then. He'd sounded faint, as if his strength was failing.

"Palo!" Dytas' mind voice was feeble. *"What happens when you drop a pebble in a pond?"*

Was he losing his mind, she wondered. *"You get ripples,"* she said patiently.

"And if you're an insect on the edge of the pond?"

She shrugged mentally. *"You get swamped."*

"The volcano's like a stone in the pond. There's a wave coming, as high as a mountain. Your little island will be swamped. In an hour or two, the wave will come, and scour the island bare. You need to get out to sea before it is too late!" The sending ended as abruptly as it had begun.

Palo bit her lip, wondering what she should do. It seemed crazy, but her uncle knew things she didn't. She made up her mind. "We're going for a boat trip," she told Tinto. He started to argue, and she cut him short.

"Come on!" Palo grabbed D'Nor and yanked her along. They raced round the island to Jarol's hut; several times the children stumbled, and Palo turned an ankle, but she was quickly able to run it off. On the way, she gasped an explanation. She wasn't sure Tinto believed her, but he stayed with her.

"We need your boat," Palo told Jarol, wasting no time on pleasantries.

"Oh?" They'd spoken little since she'd arrived; their paths rarely crossed. Jarol folded his arms. "I don't sail this late. The open sea's no place to be at night." He was shorter than Tinto or Palo, though he was almost twice as broad as Palo. His long hair curled to his shoulders, and beneath his pelt of hair, he was burnt black from working on his boat. He'd festooned himself with fish bones, coral bracelets and necklaces, as if worshipping the Sea-Gods.

"You'll take her, or I'll cut your throat," Tinto held his knife to Jarol's neck.

"You'll take *us*," Palo said.

"We'll not get three adults and the children in my boat," Jarol said impassively. "Maybe the children and two adults. Or will you steal my livelihood, as well as threaten me?"

Palo looked down, ashamed, realizing she'd miscalculated.

"I'll stay," Tinto lowered his knife. "I'll push you out."

Jarol didn't acknowledge him, but instead nodded at bare sand. "Tide shouldn't be out that far."

"Then we'll carry it," Palo said.

"What's my payment?" Jarol stood motionless.

Tinto tensed but Palo waved him away, "Give me a moment," she said and took Jarol's arm. "What's your fee?"

"What can you give me?" He licked fat lips. "I'm healthy, and I have enough to eat." He edged closer, leaning into her.

Palo shut the small, terrified part of her mind down, and thrust her breasts out. "Whatever you want," she whispered. She had to get the children to safety. "Get us off this island."

"It's been so very long since I had a woman," he said hoarsely. His hand brushed her breast; she wanted to slap him, but held still.

"Whatever you want," she said again.

Jarol studied her and then nodded. "All right," he said.

It took all three of them to lift the boat. "What does he want?" Tinto gasped.

"Long life and health," she panted. "Just carry the boat!"

It took ages, and her arms burned with fatigue, but finally the boat bumped in the shallows. Jarol checked the ropes and unfurled the sail. "Who stays behind?"

"Me." Tinto took Palo to one side, and put a forefinger to her lips. "I hoped things could be different." He stroked her arm and added quietly. "Look after Chessel."

She hugged him fiercely. "He'll be fine! And I'm coming back for you!" She hoped he didn't realize how unlikely it was that she would be able to. He kissed her, and she knew he did.

"Come on!" Jarol ordered.

She jumped in and joined D'Nor at the back, while Jarol and Chessel sat at the front. The boat was so low in the water that water spilled over the sides.

"Oh, Mother Goddess," Palo whispered, staring out to sea. Ahead reared a thunderhead like a moving mountain. Black, blue, and gray, and in places even green, it heaved and roiled. Lightning scampered up and down it, a nervous whiplash of light, and then, in quick succession, three rapid massive strokes of devilry spewed fiery light into the storm's heart.

The tide surged out faster than ever. Palo looked back and waved at Tinto, already only a smudge on the beach. She blinked back tears.

"I don't like this," Jarol said. "I've never seen an ebb tide this far out."

Palo called Dytas, but got no answer. She tried again, and again. No answer. *He must be dead,* she thought and slumped with despair.

She felt a faint tickle. Her heart leapt. "*Dytas?*"

"*Here.*" His thoughts were barely whisper-loud.

"The tide's going out, not in," she said. *"Where's this wave?"*

"It'll return, bigger than ever, and wipe the island clean. I'm dying, Palo. But I have to tell you how to Shift before-"

"Dytas!"

"Palo Janosdot'r! WILL you listen!" His voice blasted into her mind and made her head spin. After a while, he sent faintly, *"Think of where you want to go. Describe it to the others. Put them into a deep trance. It's a slim chance, but if you all think of the same point, it may just work."* The silence stretched. Then he said *"Goodbye, sweet girl,"* and was gone.

Palo wiped tears from her eyes, and croaked, "D'Nor, have I told you about the lands we came from? Big and empty and cold?" She talked on, describing the far off land, shouting to make herself heard above wind and waves.

D'Nor fell into a trance. "Chessel, come back here!" Palo called.

He snorted but came back. She described again their destination, and when he could recite it perfectly, she sent him to sleep, his head slumping forward and hitting the gunwale.

"Jarol!" she shouted, and clambered forward, drenched to the skin. They were way out to sea now with only water around them. The boat moved so quickly, it seemed as though they were flying. "I want you to listen while I describe a place to you."

"Are you mad?" Jarol shouted. "This is no time for tricks, girl!" The boat caught a wave and shuddered. Jarol started to turn it side on.

"Do you want to live?" she screamed. "Listen!" She dared not put him in a trance lest he lose control of the boat but shouted the description instead.

Ahead of them the sea was rising, blotting out the sky. The still raging storm roared down on them like an aerial avalanche. She realized the wave was coming, just as her uncle had said. She shut her eyes in concentration. She felt no more than a faint flicker of awareness from the children. She hoped it would be enough.

She reached out with her mind and gathered the children's feather-faint consciousness to her. "Think!" she screamed at Jarol, placing their presence in the world; working outwards from Sartonin at the center, through all the landmarks on her journey to the island. Then thinking again of cold, blessed open steppes, she twisted with her mind, like turning a key in a lock, and felt the world turn sideways.

CHAPTER EIGHT

The world around Cassidy chimed again, and turned to silent blackness; then faster than before, the ghosts became familiar faces. "How long was I under this time?" he asked.

One of the soldiers said, "A bit under two hours, sir. Corporal Davenport is with the men, exploring the tunnels." He added, slightly sheepishly, "He asked me to keep an eye on you."

"So what happened to Tinto?" Cassidy asked Sophia. "Is he on the next crystal? Why didn't she insist he go in the boat?"

Sophia held her hands up with a smile. "We don't have any other crystals mentioning Tinto. Palo survived, but precise details are unclear. And you know why she didn't take Tinto. There simply wasn't room, and expecting him to leave the children would have been unfair."

"But there's no way he'd have sent his children off with someone else," Cassidy said.

"Wouldn't he?" Sophia asked, and Cassidy, thinking of the British families who shipped their children to Canada at the start of World War II, only to lose those children, the ships torpedoed from beneath them, nodded in understanding.

"It just seems, so..." he struggled for the word. "Messy."

"Isn't that how life is?"

He saw the glint in her eye, and nodded ruefully.

It was then that he stopped thinking of the crystals as stories, and began to see them as factual.

"How do you feel?" Sophia said with a worried look beneath her smile.

"I'm okay," he assured her. "I need food, though." He stared hungrily at the pot that had hung over the fire. "I don't suppose..."

"There's nothing left in the pot," Sophia said, "but we can open some tins."

***

The platoon crested the ridge, and Kaminski stared across the valley, into the shadows. The sun had just dropped behind the hills, and in dusk's soft light, the valley held a stark breathtaking beauty.

"Seems peaceful," Adler said.

"Yeah, that always worries me," Kaminski said.

"Why'd the Brits take such a cockamamie route, rather than coming the way we did?"

Kaminski grinned. "Because they'd have had to ask us for permission to cross our zone, and we'd have asked them why. We may be allies, but they'll only tell us what they want us to know."

"Sir!" one of the men called. "Down there! I see bodies! They're in uniform!"

Kaminski searched the valley through his field glasses until he found the bodies. They wore British uniforms. He saw movement; they were alive.

He worried he was leading the men into more than territorial problems with the Brits. He had a bad feeling about this whole mission, and over the years he'd learned to trust his feelings.

***

"Somehow," Henry said, "I don't think we're in Kansas, Toto." Part of him felt bad about joking with Jerry's bullet-riddled corpse lying nearby, but it was either that, or break down and cry like a baby. He would be damned before he'd give these bastards that satisfaction.

"Que?" Esteban said, his face a frozen mask.

"We're not in Kansas," Henry repeated deadpan, knowing the joke had fallen flat, but unwilling to let it go.

"No." Esteban sent him a look as if to say, "I know we're not in Kansas, you moron." Wherever they were, the land was a desolate plain of peat marshes, dotted by rocky crags. An occasional scraggy tree perched atop the rocks, leaning in the direction of the prevailing wind. The air was dank, and eerily quiet.

"From our friend's behavior, I don't think they know where we are," Henry said.

"No, I don' think so," Esteban looked nervously at their captors. "I think they kill us soon."

"Not unless we force their hand like Jerry and Pam did," Henry said. "I think they're frightened witless." He wasn't really sure he and Esteban were safe, but suspected they had been spared only because they had so clearly tried to control Jerry. Their captors were growing more brittle by the hour, and he had no illusions about how trigger-happy panicked soldiers could be. He didn't want to rattle Esteban any further, however. The kid was already scared stiff.

"This situation has all the hallmarks of a major cock-up. Wherever they were meant to be, and whatever they were doing, I don't think they expected to encounter us in Patagonia. I think they were as surprised by us as we were by them," Henry continued talking to Esteban in a low voice. "They took us with them as the least worst alternative to killing us, or leaving us behind. They're lost, and scared, but they've not abused us as long as we've done as we've told."

He fell silent as the Fuhrer swung round and glared at them. The Thal hissed at his troops, who dived for cover, two of them pulling on their captives' chains.

Something chattered like oversized woodpeckers, and a row of tiny explosions ran along the ground in a daisy chain as spurts of soil were thrown up into the air. One of the Neanderthals cried out and clutched his side.

***

"One dead, one badly wounded, sir," Garcia said to Adler. Garcia dribbled water on the survivor's lips. It had taken them well over an hour to get down to the bodies, and the valley was pitch black at night. Fortunately they wore night glasses, and what heat there was from the survivor had guided them in. The other two squads were about four hundred yards away in the darkness, close enough to assist if needed, but far enough away not to be caught in crossfire, if they were ambushed. "He's already showing signs of hypothermia, and wouldn't have survived the night."

He added, "The other one's not been dead too long." The tightness of his voice echoed Adler's thoughts.

They had just been a little too late, Adler thought. He felt anger burn through him like indigestion at the callousness of leaving wounded men to die alone. "Can we move him?" he whispered.

"Negative, sir," the medic said, equally softly.

"Hey there, soldier." Adler leaned over the wounded man and touched his shoulder gently.

"Yank?" came the whispered reply, the soldier's disbelief evident.

"The cavalry's here, buddy." Adler softly patted the wounded man's shoulder. The soldier tried to move, and groaned. "No, lie still. What's your name?"

"Key, sir. Private First Class Michael Key."

"Where are the rest of your men, Mike?"

"Gone on ahead, to the northeast."

That explains how we missed them, Adler thought. He and his men had approached from the northwest. Still, they must have been close.

Kaminski appeared djinn-like, and tugged at his sleeve. They moved further away, and Adler said, "The one that's alive only has a few hours left. I'd like to stay with him. It won't be long. We need to rest up, anyway." That wasn't strictly true, the men could keep going for several hours yet.

Kaminski appreciated Adler's request. "Yeah, the trail will probably be cold by now, so the infrared imaging won't work," he said. "We'll need to track them the old-fashioned way in the morning, when we can see. Let's rest up."

The other squads came down and joined them. Adler took Kaminski to one side. "The..." he searched for a word strong enough to show his feelings without blasphemy and then gave up. "The bastards left them to die as if they were unwanted animals to be slaughtered."

"Yes," Kaminski said, voice studiedly neutral.

Adler lowered his voice. "You think that's right?"

"I don't think it's good, but sometimes you have to do something that's wrong in order to do something right at a higher level. I hope I never have to do it," Kaminski said.

They fell silent, and watched the stars in the night sky.

Key died just after midnight.

***

"Your men seem anxious," Sophia said quietly, as Cassidy ate. "Is that because of us?"

Cassidy chomped on some unleavened bread before answering. "Your presence in this area would worry anyone. You're in one of the most politically unstable areas in the world, in the midst of a long-running conflict. Our enemies sometimes seem like will-o'-the-wisps. They strike without warning, and then people die. We knew of the caves nearby, but not about these caves."

"And that bothers you?"

"Not me personally," he said with a chuckle. "But it bothers the people I work for." He paused for thought, "They think knowledge equals security, if not power. Plus, if they don't know about these caves, what else don't they know about? That's what is worrying to my people. Your turning up right here and now is as though you had wandered into an ammunition depot holding a live bomb."

Sophia sighed deeply. "I'm very sorry if we've caused a problem." Her mouth twitched.

"Don't be," he said around another mouthful of bread. He wiped his mouth, and suppressed a small belch. "I'd never have thought cold tinned frankfurters could taste so good." He pondered and said, "I suppose the third crystal is what happened to Palo?"

"No." Sophia said, "In the back of MaryAnn's vehicle were some pictures and the thing that takes them-" she paused, searching for the word.

"Camera," he offered, and she nodded her thanks.

"The crystals are like the camera; they take only, not pictures," she muttered to herself and then looked up with a grin of triumph, "snapshots!" She waved her hands again, muttering to herself.

Every time Cassidy started to think of Sophia as human, she did something to remind him of how alien she really was. This was no twenty-first century woman. He told himself that he would do well to remember that she was a member of another species.

"The crystals are snapshots of a period in time. They're not an overall history. Does that make sense?"

He nodded slowly, broke off another piece of the bread, and said, chewing slowly, "I'm surprised by how simple life was there. I mean, Palo's memories included Sartonin, but even so, that city was little more advanced than Shalimar. Did your people advance so little in almost thirty thousand years?"

Sophia shook her head. "Palo's world was not the same as the world at the end of the Warriors' crystal. Thal civilization has been up and down the ladder of progress many times as we've moved. Don't be fooled by our cities. We're nomads at heart." She puckered her lips. "We'll take any excuse to shift worlds. Invasion? Shift. Volcano? Shift."

Cassidy stared thoughtfully at his plate. "The island looked vaguely Mediterranean. I suppose it'd be hellishly hot for your people?"

Sophia said. "We prefer cold to heat, but we've learned to adapt."

Cassidy had been working something out in his mind. "I wonder," he said thoughtfully, "if Palo's volcano was the one that wiped out the Minoan civilization on this world."

"Perhaps," Sophia said. "The worlds have been fairly alike so far. But don't expect things to stay that way," she added.

Cassidy nodded toward a woman who stood in the nearby shadows, "Is that MaryAnn over there?"

"Yes. Why?"

Cassidy climbed to his feet, still holding the loaf of bread. "I just want a quick chat with her." He sauntered over, smiling to reassure the woman, but she looked anxious anyway, so he asked, "How's your baby doing?"

"He's okay." She looked down at the child.

As if their words had prompted him, the baby wriggled for a moment, burbled, then settled down.

"What's he called?"

"Raoul." MaryAnn relaxed slightly. "You wanna see him?"

Cassidy nodded. MaryAnn seemed a little slow. "Is his dad around?" he asked, as MaryAnn opened the blanket and showed him the young baby. He was covered with hair and his eyebrow ridge and stubby limbs hinted at his father's ancestry.

"Aulth was taken by the Sauroids bout six months ago." MaryAnn's expression showed how much she missed him.

"Sauroids?" Cassidy narrowed his eyes at her. "A lizard-man?"

"Yup."

Cassidy realized that he did not need to worry about the Thals treating her well. Even if they had treated her like a dog; she would stay with them in the hope that Aulth would come back.

"You miss Aulth?"

MaryAnn nodded. "He weren't the brightest." She laughed. "He was subnormal, made me look bright compared to him. Oh don't worry," she added, "I know I ain't dealing with as good a deck of cards as you are."

"I was just thinking how well you've adapted after what must have been a terrifying experience." He felt ashamed. He'd thought her a dimwit because of her accent, and she'd noticed it.

"It weren't too bad," MaryAnn said, "Aulth escaped from a hospice after a Sauroid attack on Prime. When they got him back, they got a bonus." She laughed. "If you can call me a bonus."

"Prime?"

"Their Earth, sort of."

She'd relaxed enough for him to make his suggestion. He was pretty sure what her answer would be, but he had to ask. "You don't have to stay with them, you know. We'll be going back to report. We can take you and Raul with us." He was stretching the truth a little. He had little intention of taking them back anywhere until he knew what was going on, and had the situation totally locked down, but he had to know how free she was. There was the possibility that she was being manipulated.

She looked at him pityingly. "You really haven't got it, have you, Mister? These people have been better to me than my own kind ever was." She turned her back on him, and he returned to Sophia.

It's possible that she has the Stockholm Syndrome, or been brainwashed, he thought, but there was no reason for him to think so.

"Okay?" Sophia tilted her head to one side.

"Yeah."

"Maryann's a simple soul." Sophia laughed. "She once said to me," Sophia deepened her voice like MaryAnn's, "What yuh see is what yuh get with me." She added, "I liked that."

"And you?" Cassidy said.

"Me?" The corner of Sophia's mouth lifted.

"Is what I see what I get, with you?"

"Maybe." Her smile faded, "But I'm not sure you've seen everything yet."

He nodded. "Time for another crystal. I can manage one more tonight."

She shook her head. "It's too soon. You'll burn yourself out. It's like you've run a long race, what did MaryAnn call it?" She tapped her forehead to remember.

"A marathon."

"That's it! You burn up so much energy, it's like you've run a marathon. You've run two marathons in one day, and now you want to run a third?"

"I don't have time to wait for tomorrow," he said, fastening the headpiece around his forehead. "You've got four or five crystals here?" He took her little pouch, prying it open, and the crystals in it from her fingers.

"Seven."

"So that would be a week I'd need to spend learning what's going on, when you could tell me in what, a day? Two days"

"It's better that you learn this through living it rather than me just telling you about it."

"Maybe," he agreed, "Or maybe this is a way to keep us occupied us for a week, and I'm cutting two days off your schedule."

"Oh! For-" She broke off, and turning on her heel, she stormed off, shaking her head.

Cassidy's head hurt with the clamped-vise-pain of a tension headache. The weight of her expectations, the demands of his superiors back in London, and the need to try to keep the raw recruits safe acted together as a physical weight pressing down on his shoulders. He'd thought himself good at handling pressure, but this was a whole new magnitude of stress.

He didn't know why, but he knew that what was happening here was important. That knowledge only added to the pressure. He slotted the crystal into the eyepiece. He was getting used to it now, but he was still clumsy compared to Sophia. There was the usual long pause, before the falling sensation kicked in, and-

CHAPTER NINE

310 Years before Present Day

In darkness lit only by the spectators' flaming brands, the Inquisition piled wood round the huge cross to which Cassidy/Felipe was tied. A priest stepped forward, lifting a crucifix to his lips. "Instrument of Satan, your presence offends Our Lord, God Almighty. Retro Me, Satanas!" He spat at Felipe's feet.

Those who'd watched when the Inquisition took him sang a *Kyrie Elision*, their voices as ragged as the torchlight. Felipe looked up at the stars above the crucifix, which had suddenly turned into the Dreaming Tree as the Thals called it.

It was then, in what he now realized was a dream, that Felipe recognized the priest's eyebrow ridges, and the bandy, short-legged walk of the Thals. The priest was Sergeant Jonas.

The kindling lit and flames licked at his flesh. Pain seared through his nerve endings. The ape-men sang, "Your pain is your flavor." The whole choir was made up of Thals. They'd betrayed him. When the pain grew too great, he fainted. He awoke bathed in sweat.

He lay in the cool dark, amid empty hammocks outlined in the gloom. He realized he was in his quarters. The room was quiet, apart from the whirring fan.

Laughter echoed down the corridor, and he heard Jonas's shout. "You! What are the protocols concerning Talents here?" There was a pause, and then a reply Felipe couldn't hear. "What?" Another pause, another reply. "So why're you showing off? You could spark a riot if the Skinnies see you! Thirty days latrine cleaning!"

As it grew quiet, he heard murmurs in another room. It was those that had roused him. They forgot his hearing was better than that of any Thals. He heard a new voice that he didn't recognize. It sounded agitated. "If we withdraw from this world, what happens to the Friendlies?"

The second voice was that of the Base Commander. "We didn't know when we first Shifted to this world that we'd arrived in the middle of a religious war. The Protestants are as bad as the Catholics. Each thinks we're allied with their enemy. This base is the only one not besieged, because it's so isolated, and Spain is even more primitive than its neighbors. Even that may end. Spies have warned us of a Papal army marching through France."

The first voice sighed. "If only we'd arrived two centuries ago, before this Martin Luther stirred things up. Perhaps they'd be more civilized."

The commander snorted, "You're a fool, if you think this lot will ever be civilized. They're like all their kind, not even remotely sapient." The voices drifted away, and Felipe shut his eyes and slept.

***

In the morning a new doctor called instead of Lang. All Thals were hairy; this one even more so. Under his protruding eyebrow ridge eyes as black as his hair shone through a thicket. It was like looking at a picture of the Barbary Apes that lived on the rock at Jebel Tarik, at the southern end of the coast. Like all the other Thals, parts of his body were shaven, revealing intricate, multicolored tattoos.

"It's all right." His Spanish was barbarous, but his voice was gentle, not the rumble Felipe had expected would come from one with such a face. He recognized it as the first voice he had heard talking in the night. "I Doctor Rynarsson. How you feel?"

Curiosity eclipsed Felipe's shyness. "Where's Doctor Lang?"

"He around." Rynarsson sat on a stool, studying a clipboard. "You fell during yesterday's test. A healer help you while you sleep. More Dark Arts." He flashed a grin, mocking the stories about the ape-men. "I ask you questions to check your head injury."

"You think I'm mad?"

"No," Rynarsson smiled, "Unique, not mad."

"*D'Acuerdo,*" Felipe nodded.

"Name?"

"Felipe Prieto Iniguez."

"Where are we?"

"Reklavarik Base. In Spain."

"Who is the King?"

"Felipe the Fifth." Felipe said with a smile, "I was named after him."

Rynarsson made notes, and asked, "How old are you?"

"Fourteen."

Rynarsson tapped his teeth. "Why you want to join the Tourlemaine Guards?"

Lying back, Felipe thought of long, hot days out with the fishermen, or tending the goats alone. He thought of his mother, who had no choice but to lie with any man who'd pay her. He wanted to tell Rynarsson that he wanted more than that kind of life, but he knew the Thal wouldn't understand. Instead, he asked, "Are you from Home?" He'd often heard them talk about Home.

"Yes," Rynarsson said. "A long way from here."

"Farther than Roossya? Or Cathay?" They were the furthest places Felipe knew of. He'd like to have read more of the books in the library, but with so much to learn, he'd had no time.

"Much farther." Rynarsson smiled, through his beard.

"I'd like to go there," Felipe said, as explanation.

***

Felipe squinted as the sun bounced fiercely off the scrub-covered rocks. No sane man would venture out at midday, but these soldiers took a fierce pride in showing their toughness.

"You sure you're ready?" Rynarsson looked worried. "It's not worth killing yourself."

"I'm okay." Felipe wriggled, his pack already chafing. It wasn't designed to fit someone like him. "I have no illusions now. They want me to fail. I probably will, but I have to keep going."

"Master Sergeant Jonas, he's ready," Rynarsson said.

Jonas scowled, "Very good, Doctor." From his sleeveless tunic to each pleat on his skirt, Jonas was immaculate. A network of scars showed through his hairy knees. His boots shone. Under his helmet, unlike most other Thals, he was as bald as an egg apart from a ring of brown curls round the side of his head.

"No cheering troops?" Rynarsson said. Unlike the previous tests, when the whole regiment had watched, there were only a few men present today.

"No." Jonas jerked a thumb upwards; "There's a seer above. They can watch from indoors." He lowered his voice, but Felipe could still hear. "The men have few enough pleasures in this dustbowl. Why shouldn't they have some fun?" He glared at the doctor.

"If he must run in full combat gear," Rynarsson ducked the implicit challenge, "Let him use water-gel like other recruits."

"Valdesson, throw me a gel-tube." Jonas caught it, and his callused hands applied the lotion to Felipe's neck, face, and other areas of exposed skin. "This forms an uneven surface," Jonas explained. "Allowing cooling through both radiation and convection. There's a much greater surface to air contact with all the ridges." Jonas could've been talking Greek to Felipe, who decided he'd look it up in the library later. "The only way to get the gel off is to apply an anti-gel, which peels it off."

Jonas handed Felipe two cylinders each holding ten metal discs. One cylinder contained red discs, the other green. "You take a red disc," Jonas said, "and attach it to the marker on the far hill. On your return, you attach a green disc to this marker. That's a lap. When you complete ten laps, you've finished." He paused and then said, "You can start whenever you're ready." He offered what was meant to be a friendly grin. "Good luck."

Felipe knew he was insincere, and hated him for it. It only made him more determined.

He set off.

The other hill was a half league away, so small no one had even named it. There he took bottle of water, this time from the table at that end, drank it straight down, and ran back.

Before there had always been chanting troops, but this time Felipe ran alone. Early on boredom was a worse enemy than fatigue. He counted paces, which took him through four laps, but when he reached the tens of thousands, it disturbed his rhythm, so he stopped.

Instead, he thought of when the troops had swaggered through the village, ignoring the locals, who peered from the doorways of their white-walled shacks, making evil-eye gestures against the demons. The Thals had behaved as if they owned the place. Felipe wanted to be able to swagger like that.

Coastal villages like Los Tres Arroyos had sprung up to provide a respite for the caravans linking the Frankish North, with what had once been the Moors' domain in the South. When the Thals appeared from nowhere, one bright spring morning when Felipe was a baby, like djinns summoned from the lamp of *Al Adin*, the villager's lives had changed forever. The Thals gave them better fishing nets, winter feed for their flocks, and even rich, fertile soil conjured from nowhere. In return the villagers provided their new neighbors with valuable supplies of fish and any surpluses of fresh produce from the rare bumper harvests, and some of the villagers cooked and cleaned for them. A few 'lost' souls like Felipe's mother even lay with those the King's Men called 'Agents of the Antichrist,' who treated Maisa and her small son, Felipe, better than any Spaniard ever had.

The price for the village's prosperity was the curses of the 'respectable' folk in the neighboring villages. Lately, youths from those villages had taken to lurking on isolated tracks, waiting to throw stones at lone travelers.

One morning, herding Mama's goats toward their summer feeding of scrub and almost inedible acacia, Felipe took a detour, and had peered at the ape-men through the fence surrounding their base. He loved watching their tame demons, especially the silent behemoths that lifted from the ground, lurching ungainly at first, but then climbing higher and faster, until they flew as tiny arrows across the sky.

Now he had reached the end of his seventh lap. His stomach was cramping, and sweat squelched in his boots. He still had to run to the hill and back three more times. His knees started to buckle, but he gritted his teeth, lifting his feet higher. This was tougher than the earlier trials had been. He almost longed for the icy water he'd had to swim through, or the sand fly nest in which they'd buried him. While in the infirmary recovering from sand fly bites, he'd heard an orderly say, "Gods, he almost made it this time. I thought he'd fold, but the little sod toughed it out."

"Don't matter how close he gets, they ain't gone let no Skinny into The Guards," the second Thal had said scornfully. When Felipe had asked Lang what the Thal had meant, the doctor had looked away.

He completed another lap. Two more to go. His feet grew more leaden with each step.

The murmurs grew louder, so he could no longer block them out. He kept hearing "Skinny," and "Longlegs," but couldn't understand why they mocked him.

He reached the hill again and placed another red disc on the marker. "Blank out the fierce noon sun," he told himself. "Blank out thoughts of water. Blank out everything."

Felipe had been told he'd be allowed four attempts to join the Tourlemaine Guards. In the infirmary after the second trial, Lang had finally told him the truth, "They'll never let you join. Even if you pass the tests, they'll find a reason to keep you out."

His answer had almost broken Felipe's heart. Grief slowly turned to rage. Without fully realizing it he gathered that rage inside himself to use as an aid in completing the tests.

He wondered if his mother would be proud of him if she could see him now, or if she would think that this was just another one of her son's stupid dreams. He slapped down the penultimate green disc and turned for the final lap back.

Rynarsson watched him at the other end, his chin cradled on his palm. When Felipe wobbled, Rynarsson threw him a water bottle. Felipe drank some and poured the rest over himself.

"No helping the runner!" Jonas bellowed at Rynarsson.

"The Gods man, if I don't, he'll kill himself!"

"He's allowed a water bottle each time he reaches the other hill. That's what everyone gets," Jonas shouted.

Felipe shut them out, and started back to the hill. He counted the twisty little thorn bushes that dotted the way, to distract him from the soreness where the pack rubbed, and from the blisters that formed where his boots chafed. "If I get through this, I'll have to get them to provide aerated ones," he croaked, and then reminded himself not to waste precious water or energy in talking. He placed the last disc on the marker, drank deeply from a bottle in the box beside it, and poured the dregs over his head.

On the way back, he veered from side to side. He had maybe two furlongs to go, he thought. It seemed so far away, it might as well have been two leagues. He weaved slowly toward the line. One more furlong. He nearly toppled over. With just a few chains to go his foot snagged, and he sprawled. He beat at the sand in frustration. "Get up, dammit!" he told himself. His legs knotting with cramps, he crawled on his hands and knees to the line.

Jonas and Rynarsson ran toward him, but he waved them away. One hand. One foot. The other hand. The other foot. "Come on Felipe!" Rynarsson screamed. "Come on, you can do it! Come ON!"

One hand. One foot. The other hand. The other foot. He climbed to his knees at the finish, slapped the last disc on the marker, and toppled backward. He lay on his back, savoring the moment, daydreaming of being known as Felipe of the Tourlemaine Guards.

He looked up at Jonas, who stood nose to bulbous nose with Rynarsson. "What's the matter with you?" Jonas' face was brick red, the tendons stood out on his thick, heavily muscled neck, and his eyes threatened to pop out of his head. "You *want* to ruin centuries of tradition? You *want* Skinnies in the Guards?"

"That'll do, gentlemen," the Commander interrupted.

Felipe climbed back to his feet, swaying to attention.

The Commander was a red-haired, thin-faced Thal, who turned pink when angry, as he was now. He turned to Jonas. "Did the candidate complete the course?"

"Yes, sir."

"Did he comply with the requirements?"

Jonas head lifted hopefully. "No, sir. The Doctor helped him."

"I'm sorry." The Commander didn't sound sorry; he only sounded bored.

"Sir, permission to speak." Felipe stood erect.

"Proceed."

Felipe stayed calm, despite his frustration. "I'd like to take a retest."

The Commander glanced at the impassive Jonas.

"Or am I only good for latrine cleaning?"

"I'll think about it," the Commander agreed reluctantly.

***

The ornithopter flight home was silent. As Felipe's adrenaline ebbed, depression set in. He wanted to just walk away from the camp, the Thals, the tests, but pride stopped him. He slumped in the webbing, sucking a moisture tube, watching his companions.

Jonas looked furious. The Commander looked pensive, his mouth a thin line, and he drummed his fingers on his legs. Rynarsson caught Felipe's eye and winked, but looked worried.

Upon landing, they sent Felipe to the infirmary. Rynarsson asked, "May I examine the candidate, sir?"

"Permission denied," the Commander said. "Lang will monitor him."

Rynarsson stiffened. "Very good, sir," he said and saluted.

The Commander waved him away.

The infirmary was becoming depressingly familiar. That evening Doctor Lang examined Felipe. He had never gotten to know the Thal, who spoke in monosyllables, in contrast to Rynarsson, who told Felipe everything he did, and why. Felipe had learned more in two weeks with Rynarsson than in two months with his predecessor. Tonight, Lang was as close mouthed as ever.

Shortly before lights out, Rynarsson popped his head around the doorway. "You okay?" His voice was low.

Felipe nodded.

"I can't stay long. Just wanted to check." Rynarsson added, "I was wrong earlier. Doctors should be concerned about their patients, but they need to keep it in perspective; patients can easily return as corpses."

"Will they let me try again?"

"I don't know. Depends if my report Home stirs them up." Rynarsson checked Felipe's charts, unable to stop being a doctor, even though Felipe was no longer his patient.

"Why did you help me?" Felipe asked.

Silence. Rynarsson eventually said, "Your species chased us from our homeworld. But it's time we stopped blaming you for that. I don't like their using you as amusement, and I admire your persistence." Voices came from the next room. Rynarsson's smile was a momentary flash. "I'd better go."

***

Dull days dragged by. Sergeant Jonas visited one morning, warier than before. "Seems you've got another chance," he said resentfully.

"I'll be ready," Felipe said. When he wasn't exercising, he pored over the musty leather-bound encyclopedias in the library. When he'd first been allowed onto the base, a soldier had taught him to read. "Read everything you can, boy," the Thal had said. "Knowledge is power. How do you think officers get to be officers?"

The Thals collected knowledge like jays collected baubles. They seemed to know everything about his world, its people, and its history. However, there was little about the Thals themselves in the books Felipe read.

There were ghost crystals. The first time the librarian stroked one to summon its ghost, it took all of Felipe's self control not to flee the library. The crystals were alarmingly close to sorcery in Felipe's eyes. He never felt entirely comfortable around the ghosts, though in time he learned to control his fear.

The crystals answered his actual questions, rather than the bare facts presented in the encyclopedias. And while there were few books about the Thals, longer ghost crystals included story versions, such as *The Lost Colonies*, which he'd have viewed if he'd had the time, and the intriguingly titled *A Sea Of Grass*.

The base had grown eerily deserted. "Peacekeeping," the librarian explained. "The troops have moved north. The locals are getting restive." The librarian looked uneasy when Felipe asked about Rynarsson.

One morning Jonas entered the dormitory, and Felipe leapt to attention. "At ease," Jonas said. "You got another chance to prove what a great addition you'll be to the Guards. You're going back into the desert. This'll be a test of patience and endurance." His smile broadened, full of malice. "You're gonna sit under a tree. Most soldiers love a chance to sit and do nothing." Felipe shivered, despite himself. There was only one tree that would make Jonas smirk so. The Dreaming Tree.

***

The bat-winged ornithopter was the oldest, most battered on the base. It flew at a stable altitude for a while; then it dropped back as if tired by the effort, and then climbed again.

"Most have Shifted to another world," someone said. "We've had another run-in with the Lizards," he added cryptically.

The ride was bumpy, and Felipe kept clumping his head against the wall, but he took the pain stoically. He couldn't show weakness in front of Jonas, Nurn, Valdesson, or any of the four others. The journey dragged. No matter how far Felipe's thoughts drifted, they always circled back to the test.

At one point, Jonas said, "The one thing you ain't been tested on is your killing instinct. A cook, a truck driver or any other Guardsman has to kill when the time comes. If you can't do that, all yer running and parallel bars ain't worth dog-spit."

For the rest of the lumpy, bumpy flight, Felipe's thoughts gnawed at that thought like a dog at a bone. To pass the last test, he'd have to kill.

The ornithopter landed close to the Dreaming Tree, its wake blowing the tree's tendrils back, revealing the pink, flesh like trunk. The craft squatted so they could clamber down.

Over the years, traveling caravans had cut inland beyond the twisting ravines into a wilderness of boulders that were scattered like marbles. Beyond that was open desert, and beyond that, an oasis fringed with palm trees. They called it *El Poner De Los Viajares* – The Traveler's Rest. According to legend, a strange tree was seen there one day. Those who ventured too close were stung, sickened and died. The tree spread until its tendrils choked the other trees, and soon the oasis was abandoned. Those few who passed nearby spoke of ape-men performing occult rituals to summon demons.

Over the years, travelers had gradually come to avoid the oasis. Now a whole new cult had sprung up, started, it was said, by the Thals. Now the only travelers to the oasis were those who worshipped death. They came to cast their dead into the tree's penumbra.

Nurn saw him staring at the tree and said, "There's no need to worry. Honestly." He leaned closer, "Okay. Some facts. Its roots tap into water reservoirs deep below the surface. It takes its mineral needs from its occasional prey. Anything that wanders within reach of that cascade of branches is stung to death. When its victim's flesh decomposes, the needles on the end of the branches drill into the corpse to draw nourishment."

"Where does it come from?" Felipe whispered.

"We discovered them several millennia ago," Nurn said. "Each world we settle, we seed with one. The Order of Talents have kept it a closely guarded secret for centuries. When we administer the antidote to the tree's stings, it boosts our Talents, so we can Shift bigger groups." He nodded toward the pakula, cowering in its cage. "That came with us too."

"Will I dream if I take the antidote?" Felipe asked. "Or will I die?"

"That's what Home wants to know," Jonas interrupted. "We've never tried it on a Skinny before. Your friend Rynarsson really stirred things up." He grinned evilly. "Shame he ain't gonna see what happens. He's been transferred Home. C'mon."

Nurn was one of the nicest soldiers on the base. He'd often encouraged Felipe, and shown him pictures of his family on Newhome. Now he doubled as shaman. "Foremothers, Grandfathers, give this youth courage, wisdom, and your guidance." He opened a small jar. "Eat this," he said. When Felipe hesitated, he said, "Do it for Rynarsson's sake. He asked that you have the ceremony." The transparent jelly was tasteless. "His grandfather's. The highest honor Rynarsson could pay you."

Felipe fought the urge to be sick.

They sedated the pakula. Its six legs hung limply, and a blue tongue poked from the side of its mouth. They tied it to a stake.

Jonas and Nurn wrapped a robe around Felipe, uniform and all, and led him into a storm of branches, ignoring the branches' rustling frenzy. The stings that did penetrate Felipe's skin made him gasp.

They propped him against the tree trunk and removed the robe. "Okay boy." Jonas injected something into him. "This will knock you out for two hours, long enough to let the tree calm down. When you wake up, you have to get outta there. The antidote to the venom is in the pakula's pouch, where it's carrying a young one. It's up to you how you get it. Maybe you should just ask it real nice."

"Tut," Felipe tried to sound brave. "Sarcasm."

"We'll be back in two days," Jonas said.

Soon after, the ornithopter lifted off, and Felipe slept.

***

He awoke in silence. He was sitting with his legs straight out in front, and propped against the trunk in the same position in which they'd left him. The flesh like bark of the tree felt warm against his back.

The air was cooler in the shade. When the temperature fell after dusk, he would shiver so much that his movements would drive the tree frantic. Though he had to get clear of the branches before then, he dared not move until he was ready. As long as he kept still, he was fairly safe. They'd sedated him to slow his metabolism, allowing the tree to relax.

He inhaled, slowly. Exhaled, steadily. Carefully, so as not to disturb the tree, he felt in his pockets. In one was a small bottle of water. In another was a small, sharp knife. He held his breath as he nicked his thumb with it. Even that small bit of activity made the tree quiver.

"Don't think of the toxins working round your system. That'll speed the pumping of your heart," Lang had told him. "Just relax until you're ready to move."

His breathing quickened. Soon he would start to ache. Then would come cramps and vomiting, before death came as a release. "Concentrate on the antidote," he told himself. Without it, he'd die. He had to take it from the pakula's abdominal pouch, where Jonas had placed it when the animal was sedated. But he would have to kill the pakula to do so. He remembered reading that pakulas fight to the death to protect their young.

The leaves of the tree rustled, as Felipe moved. *Stay calm,* he thought, breathing deeper. The branches rustled some more as he pulled his knees up very, very slowly, and braced his feet against the ground.

As he leapt to his feet and ran, the branches lashed at him. It was only ninety feet to the tree's edge, but it felt like leagues. The branches punctured his flesh with their stings, looking for veins, eyes, and any other weak spots.

Clearing the tree's branches, he rolled on the ground till he was completely out of its reach. The branches hissed and thrashed, but couldn't quite reach him. He lay still for a moment, assessing his wounds. Burning welts covered his body where he had been stung.

The pakula hissed a nervous warning. It was a bat-eared, fox-like scavenger from one of the worlds the Thals had passed through, the local equivalent of a jackal. It was evil-tempered, but semi-domesticated. Its tether limited its movement; the pup in its pouch made it nervous.

Felipe only wanted the little pouch with the syringe full of antidote. But he'd never convince the skittish pakula of that. He'd have to take it forcibly, killing it in the process. He pulled the knife from his pocket, and strode toward the now terrified pakula. It bared its teeth and hissed, retreating as far as its tether allowed. It raked at him with its talons, and he stepped back. The beast relaxed slightly.

Felipe leapt, planning to hurdle it and attack it from behind. He almost cleared it, but his leg caught its head, and he fell in a heap on top of the beast. He now found himself wrestling a hairy demon that squealed and hissed, scrabbled with its front paws, and snapped at his ear with its teeth. Its fetid breath sprayed into Felipe's face as they fought.

He wrapped his right arm around its throat, forcing its wriggling head back, and slashed with the knife in his left. Blood spurted. It snapped at his arm, but didn't connect, and bucked further, almost dislodging him. He carved again with the now-slippery knife. It squealed in agony. The next few seconds seemed to last forever; it bit through his sleeve in its death throes, as he slashed again at the yowling creature.

When it finally lay still, he climbed to his feet. It twitched once, its eyes dull, and then died.

Felipe was a sticky mass of blood. He hurt all over, both from where he'd been stung, and from where the pakula had bitten him. Blood ran from his earlobe, and his arm and leg. But he was alive. Filled with hormone driven fury, he stood just beyond the tree's branches, and bawled defiance in the direction of the ornithopter's flight; "It's a shame you weren't here to see this!"

He saw a smudge of smoke in the distance. *No one sets a fire in the desert,* he thought. *It must be the ornithopter.* If the others were hurt, he'd have to make his own way back.

He slumped, forever it seemed, with his head in his hands, not knowing what to do. Finally, he straightened and forced his hand into the dead pakula's pouch. The cub stirred and he snatched back his hand, clasping the wallet holding the antidote.

After he'd injected it into his leg, he rinsed the blood out of his eyes with a little of his precious water and drank the rest. Fighting nausea, he sliced open the pakula, draining its blood into the empty bottle. A lot missed, but he still managed to fill it; he needed all the liquid he could get. Then he cut the animal's flesh into strips, and slapped his thigh rhythmically, to give himself courage, "Our forefathers ate food raw. Come on, *hijo de puta*, you can do it!"

When he'd eaten as much as he could, he tore the legs off of his fatigues and cut them into strips. He wrapped the remains of the meat in one leg and wrapped the other strip round his head in a robe as he'd seen travelers in the caravans do.

He'd have to walk ten times as far as the last test, without water-gel. This time, if he failed, carrion-crows would pick his bones clean.

Then without warning, his world went black. He screamed. Instead of looking over bare desert, he saw mile after mile of grassland, covered by a mist that moved like windblown smoke.

The breeze strengthened, blowing the smoke-mist faster. The sky darkened by the moment, turning from light to dark blue, then to purple. Shooting stars crossed the heavens.

Shuddering, he closed his eyes. When he opened them, the world was normal. He stood near the Dreaming Tree again. *Was that a daydream? Was I magicked elsewhere? Or am I going mad?* he wondered.

He shrugged. He wouldn't learn anything by standing still. He started walking. The burning ornithopter would be his beacon.

***

The sun beat down through his headgear, and his feet felt as if someone had tied a brick under each boot, but he never took his eyes off the smoke. When he grew too thirsty, he forced down some of the pakula blood.

When the smoke finally faded away, he guessed the fire had burnt itself out and hoped he would keep his sense of direction.

Just before nightfall, he found the wreckage – scattered pieces of burnt metal, twisted out of all recognition. There was one particularly large piece of wreckage. The hopter's nose had broken clear from the body. Everything was smashed, including the pilot.

By the main body, Felipe found Nurn's corpse. Next to him lay Jonas. He was the only survivor, but he was badly hurt. Felipe listened to his bubbling breath, and wondered how long the Thal would live. Bones protruded through his skin at one of his elbows; his legs were badly burnt, and he was smeared with dried blood. He still gripped the douser he'd used to put out the fire.

Felipe found more water bottles and poured a trickle onto Jonas's brow, cleaning him up so he could examine him. Jonas's skin was clammy and cold, his eyes half-focused. "Skinny," he whispered. "Am I dead?"

"No," Felipe said. "I won't let you die." *Even though I hate your guts,* he thought. "Will they send a search party?"

"Maybe," Jonas mumbled, "If they can spare the men."

"Can you stand?"

Jonas tried, but his legs buckled. "Search the wreckage," he said, between fits of coughing. "See if anyone's comm is intact. I took a blow to the head, so mine's broken. There's a Homer in my pocket. It's set to Base. If you're on the right course, it stays green."

Felipe ransacked the wreckage. "Water-gel. Rations. No comm." He stared at Jonas, sighed. "I don't know what your injuries are, so I don't know what to do."

"I have no spinal injuries," Jonas said. "I can still feel, although Suppressers in my blood dampen the pain."

"Neat," Felipe said, awed. He'd read about the tiny creatures that ate pain.

"So are the coagulants in my blood," Jonas smiled weakly. "When exposed to the air, they form a second skin. For minor wounds, they work fine. Probably halved my blood loss." Jonas smiled again. "That was the good news. If we don't get back to base, I'll still die. They just buy time. If I don't get a transfusion quickly, they become a liability. They affect my circulation. Now, check my pulse periodically. Like this- take my wrist. If it goes over a hundred, inject me with this syringe. But it's the only one, so don't use it if you don't have to."

"What if it doesn't work?"

"My blood pressure will fall, and my pulse–rate will climb. If it goes over a hundred and twenty after you've injected me, you can bury me." Jonas grinned. "That was a joke. Laugh skinny. We're gonna be fine."

"Ha. Ha."

In the gathering gloom Felipe made a travois and a harness to loop round his shoulders. He loaded guns and ammo, and as much water and gel as he could carry.

"If you piss," Jonas said, "bottle it."

The sky turned a bilious green, rent by lightning flashes. Thunder rumbled in a single endless groan. The lightning lit massed ranks of uniformed skeletons, marching in perfect time at right angles to him. He shut his eyes. When he opened them, he was again kneeling by the wreckage.

He wondered whether to say anything to Jonas, but decided against it, instead hoisting the Thal onto the travois as gently as he could. When Felipe paused, alarmed by the Thal's groans, Jonas urged through gritted teeth, "Keep going." Felipe threw in a couple of spare guns, just in case they needed them.

Felipe set off, hauling the travois through the still night. Jonas fell into a labored sleep, leaving Felipe alone with his thoughts.

Then he saw his Mama walking beside him. She was much older than when he'd last seen her. Dressed in her widow's weeds, she looked insubstantial and wraithlike. *"So these Thals will look after you? Many will call you a traitor, Felipe. Will they protect you from the mob that will howl for your blood?"*

A jolt to the travois and a groan from Jonas brought him out of his daydream, but it was dull, trudging alone as the harness dragged at his shoulders. Again, he dropped into a quiet reverie of his solitary childhood in Los Tres Arroyos. Born out of wedlock, poison tongues had whispered, he'd learned to be comfortable with his own company, until the Guards offered him something to belong to.

He wondered if moving Jonas was worsening the Thal's wounds. He'd dressed them, but Jonas' burnt flesh and wet breathing worried him. "Talk to me," he said to Jonas, to fill the silence. "Why are your people really here?"

"Acclimatization," Jonas croaked. "We've wandered world after world, and been attacked on so many, mostly by the lizard-men. So we've set up bases to keep them at arms length. To provide early warning and shelters if needed. Some worlds we find too hot, so we only spend short times there, adjusting to the heat."

"Worlds?" Felipe said. "Are these like kingdoms?"

"Something like that. We can shift between worlds as easily as you step from land to river." He added, "Though I've heard that it's harder than it used to be."

Felipe thought for a while. "So, now you're going Home?"

"Probably," Jonas admitted. "They've recalled us."

"Where does that leave those who've helped you?"

"I don't know," Jonas admitted. "In dire peril, I suspect."

Felipe blurted, "Why do you hate me so much?"

The silence lasted so long Felipe thought the Thal had fallen asleep, but at last Jonas said, "I don't hate you."

"Really?" Felipe didn't bother to hide his skepticism.

"Really," Jonas said flatly. "I treated you the same as every other recruit. Some need encouragement. Most, especially the keen ones, respond better to obstacles than encouragement. Admit it, your hate for me drove you on, didn't it? But it wasn't personal, Felipe. I'm just the grit that turned you into a pearl..." Jonas grew quiet, exhausted with talking.

Felipe didn't mind. He had a lot to think about.

They stopped at dawn, and Felipe erected a makeshift shelter. Jonas was feverish, so Felipe held him when he was cold, released him when he grew hot, and wondered if the Thal would last the day. But toward dusk Jonas' fever broke. They resumed that evening. As the Suppressers wore off, Jonas' whimpers grew increasingly frequent. Their progress was slow, and as the night wore on, Felipe had to stop more often. Each break lasted longer.

When the morning star rose over the horizon they slept fitfully, resuming the trek at dusk. They were nearly out of water, and completely out of food. Felipe was soon exhausted and close to tears. He could move faster alone, he knew, but quashed the thought. Instead, he escaped again into memory.

Felipe summoned all his nerve and approached the mesh fence carefully. When Juan Lago had touched it the week before, he'd been bitten by invisible eels. Felipe said, "Buenas Dias, Señor."

"You shouldn't be here, son," the gate guard said.

"Por favor, Señor, I want to join the Tourlemaine Guard."

For a moment the soldier looked as if he'd laugh, but he merely nodded gravely. Only afterwards did Felipe realise the soldier was mocking him with his solemnity. Pretending to take the crazy Skinny-kid seriously made the situation even funnier.

Pausing, Felipe trickled water into Jonas' mouth. Jonas' breathing had eased, but he slept constantly. Waking him to drink seemed increasingly cruel.

"Well, Niño," Sergeant Jonas had said, and Felipe smiled back, thinking how friendly they all were. "We don't normally let just anyone join. People lose interest when things get tough. If you're sure you want to join, we'll test whether you're intelligent, which we're sure you are, and test to make sure you don't have criminal tendencies. Then we'll give you some physical tests. None of that should put you off, if you really want to join."

"Oh, I really want to join, Sergeant," Felipe said.

"What's that?" Jonas said with a moan.

"Talking to myself." Felipe trickled another mouthful of water into Jonas' mouth; most of it spilled down the side of his face. Felipe said, "These other worlds. Do any have green or purple skies?"

Jonas took so long to answer; Felipe thought he'd fallen asleep. Then the Thal said, "I can't think of any. Why?"

Felipe described his visions. "They felt so real," he added.

"You've been dreaming," Jonas said, "They're hallucinations caused by the Tree's venom." He slept again. Sighing, Felipe restarted his weary journey. The terrain grew bumpy and Felipe stumbled often.

"What is it?" Jonas said a few hours later. "Why have you stopped?"

"Banditos," Felipe said. "Nearly a score of them." They were dirty ruffians, missing eyes, hands, or arms. Most carried swords and knives, but three or four brandished flintlocks. A gray horse stood at the back of the group. Furtively, Felipe undid the string holding the rifle onto the travois.

"What's this?" One man swaggered forward, spitting a stream of black saliva and tobacco juice. "A demon and his slave? Step out of that harness, boy." His voice was kind, but his eyes were hard as pebbles. His grin showed that there were very few teeth left in his mouth.

Jonas had shown Felipe little kindness. The Thal had ridiculed and done all he could to hinder Felipe. But it wasn't just the harness that bound him to Jonas. He'd saved Jonas' life; their fates were bound together. If he walked away, the men would probably kill him anyway once they'd finished with Jonas. "I'm taking him home," Felipe said.

The brigand shook his head, his smile fading. "*Mal paso, niño.*" Bad move, boy.

"Are you boy, or are you demon in disguise?" A second voice whiplashed. An old, stooped man in cleric's robes pushed his way through the ruffians. Felipe recognized the Inquisition's sigil, but the fanatical gleam in the cleric's eyes would have given him away even without it. "Well, are you Satan's imp, or Catamite?"

"I'm nobody's bum boy," Felipe stepped from the harness. As the men relaxed he quietly slid the rifle's safety catch off, signaling Jonas. Felipe had fired a rifle before, but this was different. He swallowed hard. What he did now would determine who'd go home to their families and whose blood would stain the hot sand.

"When I shout 'now'," Jonas hissed. "Shoot the riflemen, and dive for cover."

"See how it hisses like the serpent!" the priest cried. He was pallid, and if once he'd been handsome, years of fanaticism had corroded him from within. He called to the men, "Kill the creature! Save the boy for examination!"

"Now!" Jonas shouted. Yelling with pain from his injured arm, he rolled off the sled, his first shot taking one rifleman in the throat, his second hitting another's shoulder.

Felipe dived behind a head-high rock. Without Jonas' years of practice, his shot at the third man's chest missed entirely.

Their opponents scattered.

"They were careless," Jonas said from behind another rock. "A boy and a cripple. They didn't see any need to surround us." He squeezed off a shot at someone who was circling round, and the man dived back under cover.

"Be silent, demon!" the priest shouted. "In the name of the Holy Trinity!" He stopped talking abruptly when Felipe shot round the rock at him.

"My talking bothers them," Jonas said loudly. "I'll cover our left side, you take our right."

"*De acuerdo*." Felipe fired at a man sneaking round to his right. With a puff of dust, the man vanished. "They think you're cursing them." He saw a movement, and took careful aim; this time his precision was rewarded with a choked scream.

He counted his refills and the number of cartridges on the gun's display. The last bullets were for Jonas and him, Felipe decided. He knew there would be no restraint from the *Consejo Supremo*. It would be better to die quickly from his own bullet than to suffer a painful, slow death on the rack. He had heard about the tortuous methods of the Inquisition- limbs amputated one by one, or a hot poker shoved up the anus. He shivered at the thought.

"Do you trust me?" Jonas said.

"What?"

"I'm going to do something that will look like sorcery. It isn't, any more than breathing or walking."

Felipe popped his head up to fire another shot, heard a whine, and the crack of a bullet's impact.

"The effort may kill me, but we're dead anyway while the priest's there. He may talk the men into charging us, however suicidal that may be."

"Go on!" Felipe felt a small flare of hope.

"You sure? It's not sorcery, I promise."

"Do it!" Felipe urged.

Jonas laboriously pulled himself upright, the fingers on his good arm scrabbling for purchase. "Must make a shield first," he muttered. The air by his skin darkened, as he stood upright. Two rifle-balls thudded into the inky barrier and then just stopped. Glowing red-hot, they fell to the ground, battered out of shape, as if they'd thudded into a cliff-face. The hairs on the back of Felipe's neck lifted. He wanted to run screaming; his bowels felt as if they'd turned to jelly.

"I've pulled the air together," Jonas gasped, "If you fold wool over and over it becomes stronger. It is the same with the air."

The terrified priest shrieked, white-faced, "Christ is with us! Stand your ground!" He chattered something, so fast it was unintelligible. The sunlight glinted on his crucifix. Its chain twisted abruptly, as if turned by invisible hands, and tightened against his throat. His face slowly turned purple, and his fingers scrabbled at the makeshift garrote.

Two men fled screaming in terror, one clambering aboard the priest's horse. Felipe rested his rifle on the rock and, aiming carefully, fired in rapid, steady succession. The rider flung up his arms to embrace the sky, and fell from the horse.

Two things happened almost simultaneously. Jonas groaned and slumped, and the chain round the priest's neck snapped, giving him precious air. The priest screamed, then Felipe's bullets thudded into his chest, and blood darkened his soiled carmine robes further, as he toppled backwards.

As the remaining bandits fled, Felipe ran to Jonas. He was shocked at Jonas' eyes; so many blood vessels had burst, they were red ruins.

Jonas chuckled at Felipe's expression, and spat blood. A steady stream ran from his nose. "That's why we don't have Skinnies in the Guards; no Talents." Then he stiffened. "Stay still."

The air between them and the departing bandits twisted, and something man-shaped appeared, as if it had stepped through a door, but this man's skin was the color and texture of a lizard's. "*Madre*!" Felipe whispered. Five more lizard-men followed.

The nearest bandit was alerted by the shouts of his terrified friends. He looked around as the first lizard-man grabbed him. The air twisted again, and both of them vanished. The other bandits fled. The lizard-men knelt over something that made a clattering sound, and the bandits dropped as they fled, as though a great scythe had taken their heads off. "No witnesses," Jonas whispered. The lizard-men checked the corpses and vanished as suddenly as they'd come.

"Gone," Jonas breathed. He swayed, and then pitched forward.

Felipe checked Jonas' pulse, plunged the needle into his neck, and checked it again several times, as it slowly dropped. He heard a whinny, and looked up. The bandit's horse, now riderless, stood watching them with a puzzled expression, its ears flicking.

Felipe ran around and grabbed every canteen he could find. He led the horse to Jonas' prone body. Somehow, although it was like lifting a heavy sack with arms and legs that kept popping out at awkward moments, he got Jonas up and across the horse's back. Climbing on behind him, Felipe pulled Jonas upright, leaning the inert Thal back against him. Wrapping his arms round Jonas, he grasped the reins, and dug his heels in. The gray ambled off.

Every few minutes Felipe checked Jonas' pulse. He sighed with relief as it gradually dropped.

They rode through the morning. The sun felt as if it was frying Felipe's brains- his head hurt, and he had to keep his eyes shut much of the time. When he saw the patrol, he thought it was a mirage.

But as the sand-colored cruiser neared, he allowed himself to hope, just a little. The orderlies off-loaded Jonas into the cruiser. "Easy now," their lieutenant said, helping Felipe up. "Leave the horse. We'll fetch it later."

"Will he live?" Felipe pointed to Jonas. Medics surrounded the Thal.

"I don't know," the Lieutenant said. "Maybe, maybe not. You did good, bringing him in." He patted Felipe's shoulder; "Well done, Guardsman."

CHAPTER TEN

Cassidy emerged from the now-familiar blackness to find Sophia staring back at him. There were other Thals around, but no sign of Cassidy's men. "You've colonized worlds occupied by Homo Sapiens?" he said, wasting no time on small talk. "I'm no historian, but that looked like sixteenth century Spain."

Sophia nodded.

"How did your presence affect their history?"

"I don't know," Sophia said. "We withdrew from that world."

"But by then, you'd already affected it!"

"We affect the Multiverse every time we breathe. We can't waste time worrying about it. We were just another point of divergence for that world-line."

Cassidy said, "Those books in that library, were the first ones I've noticed. For such an advanced society as yours, that's unusual."

Sophia nodded. "Maybe it was our nomadic culture. Always having to move onwards, we had to keep restarting civilization. Or maybe writing wasn't something we found easy."

"Do you think it held you back? Gave your enemies an advantage?"

She stared at him, surprised. "You mean, that's how they stayed ahead of us?" She thought for a while, and nodded, "You could be right. Without writing, we may have found it difficult to develop your kinds of technology." She grinned, "But you've already seen we have our own ways."

Cassidy yawned so wide his jaw cracked. "That last crystal wore me out," he said, sheepishly. "I think I need a nap."

"Is the interrogation over?" Sophia asked, smiling.

"Sorry," Cassidy said, "I get a little intense sometimes." He wondered where his men were, if they were still exploring the tunnels. He sat down against a wall, and before he could think any more, sleep claimed him.

***

Daybreak over Antarctica.

Twenty minutes out of Mawson Base, the Sikorsky S76 cast a dragonfly shadow over the blinding whiteness of the Antarctic snowfield, which stretched monotonously to the horizon. Almost fifty kilometers away, four parallel ranges of what newcomers often called 'toy' mountains- short, stumpy and rugged – struggled up into an intensely blue sky. A faint smudge on the horizon was the only sign of the violent eruptions on the other side of the Pole. Erebus had spewed millions of tons of ash and dust into the stratosphere. Pollution, natural rather than man-made, had come to Antarctica.

The sky out to sea beyond the ice field, by contrast, was a dull gray, the border of the clouds directly over the ragged edge. Spring was only a month away, but the ice was at its thickest, reaching farther out to sea than at any other time during the year.

The ice was one vast sheet laced with snaking tide cracks, the only dissonance being the red hull and white superstructure of the *Aurora Australis*. It battled through the sheet ice, pushing up onto the floes, using its weight to break through.

"Beautiful, isn't it?" Phyl shouted said from the co-pilot's seat over the raucous clatter in the cockpit, so constant that they simply raised the decibel level of their voices. "Cocooned in here, you can't feel how bitingly cold it is."

Turner grunted assent. He was better with machines than people, better with people than with words. He could take machinery apart while blindfolded, but squirmed if he was asked to talk to strangers.

"Reports are that it's two point three degrees lower than usual at this time of year," Phyl prattled. "Clouds and ash from the eruptions are offsetting the worst effects of global warming." She sighed into the quiet. "But all the submarine vents are melting the ice shelves; we could end up with icebergs in Sydney Harbor." Pause. "I'm looking forward to Cairns, and getting some sun on my bones." In the face of his silence, she gave up.

On the ice floes, Adelie penguins brayed their defiance at the strange interlopers. Penguins sometimes lay in the path of icebreakers, and the AA was so unwieldy that it inevitably crushed some birds where they lay.

"Mawson Fly, this is AA, you're green to land," Heather's Kiwi-accented voice crackled in Turner's ear. One of these days, he promised himself, he was going to meet her and see if she looked as good as she sounded. He often thought about it, but he was always too busy unloading the outbound freight from Mawson Base, and loading the replenishments. This was the first time on its current voyage that the AA had come into range, and that was only because he was landing on deck. Without re-fuelling, the Sikorsky's range dropped from 400 to 200 miles.

He'd have no time to look her up. He told himself that if he did, he'd only be disappointed.

He took the Sikorsky over the heli-deck at the stern. "The wind's swung round to the west, and dropped to five knots. Landing should be a piece of cake."

"I thought you could do it blindfolded, George," Phyl said.

Turner looked nothing like George Clooney- well, maybe vaguely. She knew he didn't like the nickname; her use of it had been deliberate. He was halfway through a five-year contract, and could fly the helicopter in his sleep. For company, and as a treat for someone, he always let someone going home sit in the co-pilot's seat on the outbound leg, and a new arrival do the same on the return leg. Phyl was today's leaver. The 'George' crack made him wonder if he'd made a mistake letting her sit in.

He decided it was best to ignore her. "Yesterday, the wind blew from the north, and gusted to forty knots, so we couldn't fly. The boat's out of range unless we refuel." He landed easily, the machine settling like an old woman after a long walk.

He switched everything off, unbuckled the webbing, and rose, stretching his legs. "All done?" He kept his tone brusque, to stop her from getting emotional; he'd noticed her eyes glinting, and knew she was struggling not to cry, as she had at last night's leaving party.

"Yep. All switches off Cap'n," she half-mocked, flicking long red dreadlocks back. Except for the George dig, he didn't mind her teasing. If it got her through the next hour, she could mock him as much as she wanted. He'd miss her sense of humor as well as her abysmal cooking.

Relationships at Mawson were inevitably transient. People came, often for a year, sometimes two. Rarely did anyone sign on for as long as Turner. They were isolated, thousands of miles from loved ones, and with the camp so cramped in the winter, people drifted in and out of what were essentially holiday romances. He'd had such a "romance" with Phyl and assumed that she understood the transient nature of their affair. If she'd thought otherwise, she'd picked the wrong man.

Out on deck, he heard a low rumble, and wondered if Erebus had erupted again. He drew his parka more tightly around him. It was thirty degrees below zero Celsius, without the wind chill factor, which dropped the air temperature by another five degrees. "Hey, Ethan!" a deckhand shouted, "Captain wants you up on bridge, now!"

Turner gave a rueful grimace to Phyl, who smiled thinly and waved him away. He was secretly relieved and annoyed that he felt that way. "Must dash, m'dear," He kissed her perfunctorily, and quickly climbed the ladder to the bridge.

Captain Bazoukis snapped, "G'day. You're late."

"G'day Captain. Nice to see you, too." Turner wasn't going to let an old fart like Bazoukis intimidate him. "You wanted to see me?"

"Yeah. We're getting readings off the aft sonar. Submarine disturbances." Bazoukis sighed. "I don't like asking, but can you take the chopper for a look?"

"How far?" Turner didn't want to refuse, but wasn't keen on the idea.

"The readings are coming from the Shackleton Ice Shelf."

"Bloody hell, I'll never make it there! I'd need to re-fuel on the shelf to get there and back." He stared suspiciously, "There isn't someone there who could re-fuel me, is there?"

Bazoukis shook his head, "Nah."

"Why couldn't your chopper have gone?" They'd crossed half way, and the AA Fly would now be re-fuelling at Mawson Base. When they confirmed readiness, they'd take off simultaneously, ensuring they crossed mid-way again.

"Because they're at bloody Mawson, yer mongrel!" Bazoukis growled, losing patience. "We only got Hobart's request an hour ago. The AA Fly'd already left." He took a deep breath. "Sorry mate, desk jockeys always cheese me off." He pondered, squinting into space. "If you fly with spare tanks instead of cargo, how far can you go?" He paused, and added, "Hobart are putting a lot of pressure on us to turn back and take a look."

"Okay," Turner nodded slowly, doing the math in his head. "She should be right for an extra hundred and fifty miles. If we use the safety margin, another, maybe forty. Almost two hundred extra miles. Soon as she's refueled, I'll take her up." The sooner he left, the sooner he'd be back, he thought.

Normally, re-loading the Sikorsky took thirty minutes, but today the AA's mechanics re-fuelled it in twenty. "You coming?" Turner asked Phyl. She could fly the Sikorsky while he changed the hoses to the emergency tanks. He was lucky she had shown an interest in learning to fly the craft. Or maybe it wasn't so much luck as the consequences of mutual attraction. He had wanted to be with her, and she had wanted to be with him, and if that meant she had needed an excuse, learning to fly was a convenient pretext.

"Where?" She studied him. She had already said her good-byes.

"If you don't want-"

"No, I'd like to," she said quickly. She added with a grin, "You know me. Risk is my middle name." He grinned at that. She'd been the one who'd tried every lunatic stunt available at Mawson, reminiscing about how she missed the extreme sports. When she'd been 'jailed' for a week for tobogganing on a tea tray down the 'ski-slope' on the nearest hill and warned that any more stunts would see her on the next boat home, she'd channeled her energy into learning to fly the helicopter.

"We're headed east. Hobart wants us to check out some weird readings on the Shackleton Shelf."

Five minutes later they took off and climbed to a thousand feet. For a long time they said little until Turner said to make conversation, "You posted your penguin photos?"

"Yeah," Phyl's smile was wintry, but it was a smile. "I'll miss the little buggers. All I had to do was put up a tripod near a roost, and I'd be completely surrounded within minutes."

"They probably thought you were food."

"Oh, I've no illusions," she laughed. After another long silence, she said, "Why are we doing this? What's happening?"

He said, "Something's put a bug up Hobart's arse. They wanted Bazoukis to turn around. The AA Fly's stuck at Mawson while we look."

She sighed, "I didn't want to see Paul just yet anyway."

"You haven't seen him for eighteen months," Turner said. "I know it's hard. But as soon as we're done, you can be back on your way."

"Don't you ever get tired of being so right?" Phyl laughed. She added, "Do you miss your wife and kids?"

"Sometimes," he said. "Belinda knew it'd be tough, but I don't think anyone knows how really tough it is." He paused and added, "The divorce comes through next week."

Phyl laid a hand on his arm. "Sorry, mate."

He shrugged. "It's okay."

"Is it?"

He laughed, ruefully, "No, it hurts like buggery."

"Is that why you've been acting like a prick all morning?" He saw her smile out of the corner of his eye.

"Yeah. Sorry."

"It's okay," she said. They flew on.

Phyl said, "That's the ice-shelf in the distance."

"You take the con while I get the binoculars." Turner rummaged behind the seat

"What we looking for?"

"Something that's a sign of underwater seismic activity." He snorted. "Bloody wild goose chase, but poor Bazoukis is under pressure to be seen doing something, however useless." He stiffened, like a hound dog scenting game. "Jesus Christ!"

"What is it?" Phyl tried to grab the glasses but he shrugged her off.

"Put the radio on hands-free!" he said, reaching for his camcorder. Moments passed while he filmed, muttering, "Jesus Christ," occasionally.

"Mawson Fly, this is AA." Heather's voice crackled in the cabin. "I hope this is worth us sitting here in the ice, playing with ourselves."

"Heather, get Bazoukis on!"

After a moment, Bazoukis' voice echoed as if from a deep bowl. "Go ahead, Turner."

"Looks like all that seismic activity at Erebus and Terror is affecting the sheet." Turner struggled to keep his voice level. "Your seismo readings are the ice sheet calving."

The helicopter bucked in a sudden draft. "Sorry," Phyl muttered.

"How big?" Bazoukis said.

"The entire sheet looks as if it's shearing off. There are lumps the size of Melbourne crashing into the water. I'm guessing that it's worsening; if this had happened hours ago, you'd know about it by now."

Bazoukis said, "Can you get a closer look?"

The helicopter bucked again. Turner asked, "Can you keep her steady?"

Phyl shook her head, "But I can film, if you take the con."

"Let's try." He slid into his seat and took the controls while she reset the camcorder. "AA, we're encountering extreme turbulence but going down to five hundred feet. Those slabs must weigh over a million tons each. If they fall just a few feet, that's a shitload of water they're chucking up, pardon my Kiwi."

"Pardoned," Heather drawled wryly over the com. "You okay?"

"Yeah, but those slabs are generating some awesome waves – Holy Motherfucking Christ! That's the biggest yet! That's-"

"AA," Phyl interrupted, still standing up while she held the camcorder, "The Shackleton Ice Sheet is breaking up. I'll transmit pictures. You guys need to batten down against some extreme waves. When this lot hits land the tides are going to be bigger than anything we've ever seen. Sumatra's due north of here. Perth, Adelaide and Melbourne will also face severe flooding, but it'll devastate the sub-continent. Bangladesh will be swept away. You'd better issue warnings." Her calm broke. "Ohmigod the things breaking off it must be the size of

Queensland! The shockwave's nearly as high as we are! Turner take the thing up we're shaaaaakiing! Ohmigoood!"

Turner wrenched the Sikorsky up violently. Still the tip of the wave brushed their undercarriage, an evil green wall that flashed by in seconds. The helicopter tumbled, an autumn leaf in a crystal blue sky. Turner worked the pitch, collective and yaw controls, shutting everything else from his mind. *Come on, sweetheart,* he thought. Fortunately, they were in the lee of the wave.

Four hundred feet. Three hundred. Two hundred. One hundred.

They were barely sixty feet above the boiling, heaving water when he managed to stop their headlong plummet. Then they started to climb.

After a long pause, Turner said, "That was scary. Y'okay?"

Phyl nodded, holding a tissue to her nose. She was shaking, and gasping for breath. She started to laugh, half-hysterically. "No more bungee jumps for me," she gasped. "Not for a while, anyway."

"Take the controls," Turner insisted, despite her frantic head shaking, "Take her straight up, nice and steady. I've set our course to two-sixty degrees." He said sharply, "Take her, Phyl!"

As she slid into her seat, he stood up and said gently, "Let go of the tissue." His breath hissed, but he smiled at her white staring eyes, and said, "It's messier than it looks, but I don't think your nose is broken."

"I must look a right sight," she said, but she'd lost the gasp from her voice. The panic attack had faded in the face of his bullying and her trying to concentrate on flying.

"You look beautiful." He stretched the last word to four syllables, as he opened the medikit. "What's our altitude?"

"Two thousand feet."

"Okay, level off. We haven't got much fuel left."

Turner dabbed at the blood with a moisturizing tissue, responding to her hiss of in-drawn breath with a soft, "Sorry, I'll try to be more gentle."

As the craft settled, they became aware of Heather's frantic call, "Mawson Fly, do you copy?"

"AA, this is Mawson Fly."

"Shit, Ethan, we were worried!" Heather shouted, panic turning to anger.

Turner grinned at Phyl, pulling his lower-lip under his top teeth, "Sorry, things got a little tight there for a while. How's the weather there?"

"Lumpy," Heather said. "I'm gonna sign off for a while. We've sent the pictures of the ice-shelf, now we need to batten down."

"Yeah," Turner agreed, "Copy that." He said to Phyl, "I've left the channel open. It'll hit the AA any minute now."

"What happens then?"

"She'll be all right," he said with a confidence he didn't feel. "Bazoukis'll turn her, bow to wave."

Heather's voice crackled over the intercom, "AA Fly, confirm your position, please." Her voice was high, breathless.

"AA, we should be with you in just over an hour."

"AA Fly, prepare to render urgent assistance," Heather said. "All shipping, this is the MV *Aurora Australis*." Turner could tell by her voice that she was fighting to keep from panicking. "Mayday. Mayday. Our position is Seventy degrees forty inches East, Fifty degrees Thirty-one inches South. We're taking on water badly. Repeat. Mayday. Mayday. This is the MV *Aurora Australis*. Our position is Seventy degrees, forty inches East, Fifty degrees, thirty-one inches South. We're taking on water badly. Repeat-" A burst of static was followed by silence.

"Are there any other vessels in the area?" Phyl whispered, the blood draining from her face.

Turner shook his head. "It's down to Mawson."

"AA, this is AA Fly," the voice burst over the intercom, "We're proceeding to your last position."

"AA, Mawson Base here, we're scrambling all available helicopters to your aid."

Phyl voiced his own thoughts. "We can't help them. We need help ourselves, don't we?"

"If they've sunk, yeah."

"Could the AA Fly re-fuel us?"

"Only if we land on the ice. I don't think they'll have any spare fuel. Neither of us might make it back to Mawson." Turner spoke into the radio, "AA, this is Mawson Fly, we're headed to your last position. All units, this is Mawson Fly; we're low on fuel. We can make it as far as the AA, but no further. We'll not be able to reach Mawson Base without emergency re-fuel from AA. Repeat, we will need emergency re-fuel. AA, can you confirm you're able to re-fuel?" He repeated it. There was no response from the *Aurora Australis*, only crackling static.

***

Cassidy awoke in near darkness, with a blanket draped over him. The minimal lighting that marked 'daytime' had been turned down. He felt a weight on his left shoulder. The weight was warm, and her hair smelt nice.

"Good morning," Sophia whispered. "Sharing a blanket seemed the best way to keep warm."

"Morning," he whispered back. "Sleep well?"

"Like a baby."

"So you dribbled a lot, and wet yourself in the night?" He was rewarded with a giggle and an elbow in his ribs. "What time is it?" He lifted his arm clear of her and lifting the cover, stared at the glowing dials of his watch face. "Oh, bloody hell. Why didn't Davenport wake me?"

"I said you'd left him strict instructions not to."

"And he believed you?" *I'll have words with young Davenport about accepting only direct orders from me,* he thought grimly.

"If you slept that long, then you must have needed it. Don't be too hard on him. Come on, breakfast."

"Okay, okay." He held up his hands in mock surrender.

"I don't want you accusing me of delaying you."

They wolfed down bread, dried meat and tinned fruit in juice, stolen from the stores.

Sophia fastened the headband and inserted the crystal.

Hello darkness, my old friend, he thought, as it returned.

CHAPTER ELEVEN

280 Years before Present Day

The old Thal woman impaled Lessus/Cassidy with her gaze. "If this mob gets in, they'll tear us apart," she said. Her stringy arms and legs were festooned with tattoos, some of which actually seemed to move. She crouched rather than sat on the ornately carved and gilded high-backed chair.

Lessus heard the crackle of small-arms fire and dived for cover, the thick water-bison hide carpet saving him from bruises. He dug his fingers into it, enjoying the softness. Cassidy noticed that his host's fingers were green; he longed for a mirror.

"You should stay back," the old woman added, so quietly he had to strain to hear her. "Or you'll go home in a shroud."

Home. Half a world away. An evening's drinking in his suite at Kmera University seemed a long way from Lessus' present predicament, but it was probably going to get him killed. Stupid, stupid, to have let Shortime goad him into such rash actions. His climate-conditioned rooms in the Western Highlands seemed infinitely preferable to this brawling, eastern madhouse of a city, where heat, hate and passion hung as heavy in the air as the near-total humidity. With the windows broken, the room was open to the outside, and the temperature had soared, as usual, down here at sea level. The yeasty tang of the body odors of six million people mixed with the rich dankness of the world-forest.

Lessus had snapped at Shortime, "I'll show you we can still do fieldwork!" Four days later he'd left on the great snaking road train that was the Trans-Isthmus Express, with six hundred other people and assorted cargo. On a journey that rattled his bones with every pothole the iron wheels hit.

Three months of slowly descending the long, narrow, mid-world isthmus, plotting how he would enter The Zealot's Sacred Temple, gathering skin dye and clothing at the occasional stops. Every day reading the telegrams from Shortime, then composing his answers to his friend's pleas to reconsider their wager, even as his own conviction wavered.

Until the day when he ran out of answers and didn't bother to send a message through the signal-tower on the next hilltop.

A crash brought him back to the present, and he started.

"It's only a rock," the crone said.

Lessus sneaked a look out of the window and squeaked in fear. Outside, the mob climbed over the walls and hung from the branch of every tree round the Embassy, a sea of bodies lapping at the inner gates. They sang, slapping their right hands furiously on their left forearms. "We will skin you; we will boil you alive! Death to the unbeliever! Death to those who shelter him!"

Cassidy noticed that their skins were also green. It might have been his imagination, such was the gloom beneath the cloud cover, but they all looked slightly darker than Lessus.

A dull thud echoed over the hubbub. The Midday Drum, Lessus thought. It sounded like a death knell.

The woman took a bauble from her gaudy, voluminous robes, turning her back to him. Gazing at the murky gray skies, she repeated an incantation. Lessus couldn't make out the words.

A man scuttled into the cavernous room. Another Outsider, Lessus thought. "The Tourlemaine Guards are here," the Thal said.

"Good," she replied. "I've no faith in the Embassy Guards. They're fine for demanding passes but not for keeping order."

This second Thal was as stocky as the woman was lean. His hair was shaven back from his forehead in a triangle. Like all Outsiders, he walked slightly stooped. His nose was big and fleshy, his thin lips pressed tight together. His face shone with sweat, and he plucked at the collar of his ceremonial ruff. He sighed. "You seem to have upset your fellow Jaya." His voice was mild but the rebuke clear. He straightened his gray cloth trousers, the same color and material as his tunic.

Lessus winced. "We aren't one homogenous people," he said. "The Easterners are more-" he searched for the word, "-emotional than we Westerners." His sketched smile died at the look of barely contained fury on the Outsider's face.

His anger is hardly surprising, Lessus thought. The mob wouldn't believe that he had only chosen the nearest haven. They would blame the embassy for what he had done.

"So it seems," the Thal said, ducking another rock crashing through a window, spraying broken glass. "Your militia is as bad as the rest; they're firing on us too. What did you do?"

"It was safe here," Lessus ignored the question, wondering how much more miserable he could feel. "When a mob of screaming fanatics are yelling for your blood, safe is a very appealing prospect." When he had fled the temple, surprise had got him clear before the guards could react, but by the time he was dashing through the wide tunnel in the trees, his pursuers were in full cry. Some had dropped full, ripe seedpods from the trees that would have brained him if they'd hit him, but instead they had splattered harmlessly on the pathways. Surprise had also carried him through the rear Embassy Gates ahead of the mob. He'd lost valuable seconds arguing with the Thal guards at the back entrance, but when Lessus' pursuers had rounded the corner, the head guard had taken him inside, saying, "We'll worry about legalities later."

The Thal had led him through corridors where the tree limbs pushed out of the walls before saying flatly, "Wait here," and spinning on his heel. A moment later Lessus had noticed the Thal crone in the corner.

He peeked out over the city again. Nazandl was a sea of greenery stretching to the horizon, while the forest-city's center grew high and thick. Outside the inner gates, the forest opened out; the desirable marshland, the preserve of the rich, in one direction, in the other, the comparatively open spaces of the trunk routes beyond the Eastgate. Around the embassy walls the Jaya government had thinned the trees at the Outsiders' request. Lessus wondered if the Thals had foreseen a situation like this, and planned accordingly. The embassy was separate, unlike most buildings in the forest where the crowds could swing easily from tree to tree.

"So what started this?" the male Thal repeated, ducking another rock and the spray of glass that scattered in its wake. His red face got redder, and he bellowed, "Will you stop that!"

The watching Cassidy guessed that despite his sang-froid, the Thal was scared witless but would never admit it.

Lessus looked down at his arm, which had bubbled and blistered when he'd dipped it in the Water of Life, probably a reaction of the water to his slightly different skin, he thought in the rational part of his mind. The baser part gibbered, "*Blasphemy! Blasphemy!*"

"I did something very stupid," Lessus admitted. "I showed contempt for their God."

When the guards saw his blistered arm, Lessus' fragile courage had shattered like glass, and he'd fled. The guard's alarm spread like an epidemic, as did Lessus' assumed intent. Within minutes he'd become an infidel or a spy. "I only wanted to watch a religious ceremony," he said, aghast at the result of his actions.

"Oh, Gods," the Outsider said. "I might've guessed there would be something religious behind this." He glanced at the woman, who was still chanting and fingering her bauble. "No offence, Hilga."

"You're an academic," Shortime had said, trying to soothe his feelings. His words had only served to inflame them, however. "There's nothing wrong with never having done fieldwork. It's not like medicine," Shortime had continued. Now Lessus wondered if that apparent concern had actually been meant to have the opposite effect. Shortime was the nearest thing Lessus had to a friend. Who would know better how to provoke him?

"Not religion," Lessus said. "Disrespect." How could the Outsider understand? Lessus had immersed his hand in the Mother-pond. To these simple people he might as well have spat on the picture of Mondrian III on the wall. Of course they were angry.

The howling mob swayed forward like a single organism. Their advance was halted by the Embassy Guards, who linked arms and held their ground despite the fear etched on their faces.

"How long until the Tourlemaine Guards are here?" For the first time the man's voice quavered.

The woman paused. "About forty minutes." She resumed chanting.

"What's your name?" Lessus asked the man.

"What?" he replied. "Oh, sorry. Raph Skandakar."

"Lessus ne Arak-Tor," Lessus bowed and continued plaintively, "I never really understood. I'd argued with a friend who said I lived an isolated life with no contact with reality. I thought studying their ceremonies wouldn't hurt. I just wanted to show I could improve our understanding of the Easterners." He trailed off.

"There's been trouble building for two years," Raph admitted grudgingly. "Little idiocies. Water shortages in Ibara Province. Rabble-rousers claim the East gets a raw deal. It only needed one more thing for it to boil over."

"I didn't know."

"You wouldn't. It's not something the Council advertises."

"And I've made things worse," Lessus said.

"No, you've made them impossible," Raph said. "They say we're taking over Jaya. Nonsense. But once the Tourlemaine Guards intervene, the gullible will rush to believe them."

Peering out, Lessus gasped. The mob had grown, like a death-cape that had dropped from the tree, gorging on its prey. Across the square and into the trees, massed ranks of Easterners formed a sea of anger, shouting and gesticulating furiously.

There was another crash, and flames whooshed up the brocades. "They're throwing firebombs!" Raph shouted, ushering them out. "Into my office!"

As they left, a mist descended from the ceiling. *More Outsider tricks,* Lessus thought, his moccasins skittering off the polished floorboards of the dark corridor. The door slammed shut, and he was shepherded into a small room.

It was quiet, set further back in the building, which, like many others, had been built around one of the giant trees that made up the world-forest, one of its branches forming part of a wall.

In the shadows was a man-sized box whose lid rested against its side. A huge Outsider, towering over the Jaya, stood beside it. Visibly startled, he dropped something on the floor.

Raph lit a corner-lamp; in its light the giant's chin was unusually strong, his forehead flatter than most Outsiders. "What the-" his voice was deep. He said in Outsider tongue, "Have you lost your mind?" Glaring at Raph, he groped and found what he'd dropped, a tube, which he put into the box. "I'll give it the next injection when you've got rid of **that**," the giant nodded at Lessus.

Hilga sat on the floor and resumed chanting.

"There was nowhere else to go," Raph snapped back, glancing at Lessus who looked bored and wandered around as if he didn't understand a word they said. Raph exhaled a long, shaking breath and reverted to Jaya. "It's getting nastier by the minute. Where are the troops?"

"Nastier?" Lessus cackled at the understatement. A glare from Raph stopped him.

Lessus said to the stranger, "You should be able to protect us." The stranger stared at him blankly.

"Antonio doesn't speak Jaya," Raph said. "He's a cross; his mother's a Thal, his father's what we call a Skinny, or Longlegs." He chuckled. "His Papa's even taller than he is."

"Sounds interesting," Lessus leaned forward, studying the giant. "I'd love to meet Papa." He added, "You can't imagine what it's like to be an anthropologist in one homogenous society. Two, if you argue as some do, that our West and East are different enough to be two societies. Our experts argue over trivia like that. They've nothing else to do."

"I can't help noticing your passion when you find something that interests you," Raph said.

Lessus smiled, feeling as though he'd gained some slight approval. "Everywhere we go, we're following someone else's trail," Lessus said, thinking to himself that Raph **understood.** "Every little thing is analyzed to death. When a movement like the Zealots starts, of course we want to study it." He paused, continuing in slower, calmer tones. "That's why you're so fascinating; you're so completely different. When you appeared, as if you'd dropped out of the sky, we'd only recently started to study the heavens. It's not easy, star-gazing through blankets of clouds. Then you told us that we were looking in the wrong direction, that Jaya was just one of a multitude of worlds alike and less like, side by side."

"This one's unique, as far as we know. We've never found another Earth," Raph used the Outsider name for Jaya, "with so much surface water. And where the sky is always so overcast."

"You can't imagine what a revelation your first appearance was!" Lessus continued, as if Raph hadn't spoken. "We went wild with fascination for a while. All the things you brought us. History for the historians. Physics, chemistry-" Realizing he was babbling, he stopped.

"It's ironic, that some of your people now claim we're making you our puppets," Raph said.

"Maybe it was a reaction to offset our earlier eagerness, a sort of over-compensation. Don't you have people like that?" Lessus asked. "No matter what benefits there are, they only see the cost? No matter what you do for them, they complain?"

"We do," Raph said. "But lately the complainers have gained support. They revived an old religion to lend them legitimacy, and conveniently accused us of consorting with demons. Now they have fresh ammunition. They'll claim you're our spy."

"I'll tell them I'm not!" Indignation overwhelmed Lessus' natural diffidence.

"The more you deny," Raph said, "the less they'll believe."

"Why did you come if not to conquer?" Lessus grinned slyly.

Cassidy knew the history of the Thals well enough by now, but Raph said, "We keep running, and still they hunt us like vermin. We found more and more such worlds already settled, enough for our seer Majkular to coin his Theory of Evolution. Some were enough like us they could've been kin. Others were as unlike us as you are. We try to ally with as many as we can. If we're much more advanced than the indigents, we risk inadvertent domination, of becoming an empire by default." He saw Lessus' shocked look, said, "We worry about it as much as your zealots."

"So how do you avoid creating an empire?"

"Good question," Raph said. "If you find out, tell us."

Lessus finally gave into the mental itch that had plagued him since entering the room. "What's in there?" He sauntered toward the box. Antonio went to block him, but not before Lessus saw what lay inside.

It slept. Bipedal, upright, like Jaya or Outsider. Only gray-green scales and hairless head marked it as truly alien. A head with only a crest of multi-colored feathers along the crown. His nose was barely a gash, and slits on either side of his neck pulsed in time with his breathing. His mouth hung open, a thread of spittle bridging two razor-sharp canines set in the midst of wicked little needles.

"Oh," said Lessus. "This must be your enemy."

"Raph," Antonio growled.

"It is," Raph ignored him. "The first captive we've managed to keep alive for any length of time. And," he added, "the basis of the demon accusation. A local cleaner stumbled over it, and the story spread like wildfire."

From one side of the box a catheter ran to the creature's pendulous penis, while from the other, another ran into his arm.

Raph said, "One tube drains wastes and the other provides nutrients." He asked Lessus, "What do you see when you look at it?"

"Large skull, so he must be fairly intelligent. With those sharp teeth, he's a predator." Lessus pinched him. "His flesh is cool."

"Cold-blooded," Raph said.

"I assume you're taking him home to study him?"

Raph nodded. "We'll keep him sedated until then."

"Wait a moment." Lessus pondered. "You shift between worlds; you brought things with you. Why is he here?"

"It's taken us several days to ready a transport. We were about to move him, when you blundered in."

"Raph," Antonio growled. "Enough." He glared at Lessus, said in Thal, "This isn't your concern."

Lessus heart pounded, but, acting as if he hadn't understood what Antonio had said, he kept his voice steady. "Where did you capture him? Here? The West?"

"Many worlds over," Raph said. "In an isolated skirmish."

"So why haven't you moved him?"

"We're unsure why, but there's something about Jaya that disrupts our abilities. There are weak spots in the fabric of existence that we can exploit, Portals. We need to get our friend up into the air to one of those portals." He laughed nervously, "Don't ask me how it all works. I'm just a junior diplomat."

"So how are you-"

"Enough!" Antonio said, moving threateningly toward Lessus with hands clenched, his eyes like a wild animal's.

Uh-oh, I'm dead, Lessus thought. *Just as it's getting exciting.* His stomach roiled, but he was pinned to the spot, like a small animal caught in the nightlight eye of a land-train.

"If you hadn't brought it here, we wouldn't have a problem!" Raph snapped, distracting Antonio.

"I told you, there was no choice!" Antonio snapped. "We didn't even intend to come to Jaya. The Shift just went completely wrong. Once we were here, we had no option but to bring it to the Embassy. What should we have done, parade it through the streets?"

"Quiet!" Listening, Raph held up a hand.

Lessus strained to hear. He felt rather than heard a heavy drone.

"The Tourlemaine Guards are here," Raph said with relief.

There was a crash, some screams and orders shouted in Thal.

Three men dressed in camouflage entered the room. One of them, to Lessus' surprise, was a Jaya, with an Easterner's darker skin. Another was an older soldier, even taller than the crossbreed, gray-haired, with an eye-patch over one eye, a pointed chin, flat forehead, and whose scarred features bore a remarkable resemblance to Antonio. "*Hola*, son!" he said.

"Hey, Papa." Antonio's grin lit up the room. They touched hands. Antonio turned to Raph. "I present my father, Master Sergeant Felipe Prieto Iniguez. Señor Raph Skandakar."

"Sir," Felipe nodded, glanced at Lessus.

"A guest," Raph said. "Sheltering from the disturbance outside."

Lessus was grateful Raph hadn't said why he'd had to seek shelter, but felt his color rise in shame nonetheless.

"Idios, check the rooms," Felipe instructed the third soldier, and turned to the uniformed Jaya. "Azdal, you lead." He said to Raph, "Please follow Azdal. We've got twenty men and thirty Soljas waiting for us. We'll have you out of here in no time."

"This way, please," Azdal invited them calmly in Thal. His glare at Lessus left no doubt that he knew who was to blame for the riot. Lessus had to force himself not to shrink from the searing contempt in that look.

"I didn't know you had Jaya in the Guards, Sergeant," Raph said.

Felipe said, "Six months now, sir. A trial, to see if Jaya are suitable." He added, "He's not here as a token, though, he's one of the best we've got. Lead on, Azdal."

"Sir!" Azdal said.

Lessus watched him. Most Jaya were fatter than Outsiders, their bodies holding higher water content. Azdal was an exception, as lean as an Outsider, his muscles threatening to burst through his clothes. He stood erect, watching, listening as they walked, every fiber, muscle and sinew ready. He was clearly a proud young man.

Lessus felt very old, and very inadequate.

Two more Guards entered the room. They lifted and carried the box that held the reptilian creature. They trod softly down the corridor. Lessus fought to quiet his breathing, which rasped in the sudden silence. Other Outsiders and a few Jaya embassy staff caught in the siege joined their little procession.

"Take the stairs, Azdal," Felipe called from the back. "No sense getting caught in the lift-shaft."

"May I suggest, sir?" Azdal asked.

"Yes?"

"We could be caught on the stairs," Azdal said. "Let's use the balconies."

"Abseil?"

"Abseil."

"We'll be exposed."

"For a few seconds," Azdal agreed in a voice so calm that he might just as well have been discussing the weather. "But we'll be in position much faster."

"Good idea," Felipe said. He interrogated Raph as they walked; Felipe would murmur as though to himself and then listen further. Lessus overheard some of their discussions, their preparations for escape.

Antonio joined Raph and Felipe, lowering his voice. "The test results from Home are conclusive. All the signs are that fewer Thals with Talents are being born."

Felipe sighed deeply. "So the problem isn't Jaya?"

Antonio shook his head. "Apparently not. What we thought was a problem local to Jaya is fairly widespread."

"Many less?" Raph murmured.

"Enough," Antonio said. "We're already finding it harder to Shift between worlds. Each generation has fewer possessing Talents, and those that do are less adept than previous generations. If our research is correct, in ten, maybe twenty generations, none of our children will have Talents. We'll have no means of Shifting. The clock is ticking for our people."

The sergeant clapped his hands for their attention.

A patrician Outsider spoke. "We will remain, sergeant. No rabble is going to chase us away."

"Understood, sir." Felipe issued orders; they all split into three groups. One group, which included a half-dozen troops, stayed in place. Azdal's men led Lessus, Hilga and others to an open balcony on one side of the floor, while a third group carried the box to the balcony on the other side.

At the sight of them, a roar went up from the mob, a surging, bubbling, animal noise that chilled Lessus' blood.

"It's time." Hilga clasped her hands.

"Look," someone said.

It had started to rain. The rain grew heavier until it became a downpour. White drops pinged onto the balcony. "Hailstones," Lessus marveled. Hail was almost unknown this close to sea level. Some of the crowd cowered, others dashed for cover.

"Well done, Hilga," Raph said.

Azdal and another soldier leaned out, one on each side of the window, and slapped something against the wall. Before Lessus could ask what was happening, Azdal slung him over his shoulder, like a porter carrying a sack of vegetables at the market.

"Hang on!" Azdal shouted exultantly.

The world tilted crazily. Lessus screamed as Azdal leapt off the balcony. Azdal's hands raced, one under the other, the second under the first again, while Lessus dug his hands into Azdal's flesh hard enough to draw blood. The ground rushed toward them, and as Lessus shut his eyes, expecting to become a smeared mess, they landed with a thud. A grinning Azdal dumped him on the ground. Another soldier, also grinning, dumped Raph. Raph looked as ill as Lessus felt.

Around them stood at least ten huge black shapes, Outsider shaped, but inhumanly still in the hailstorm gloom. Other Guards each carried a passenger, except for one who carried a child over each shoulder. The children shrieked with glee.

"Don't worry," Raph said, his voice still shaking. "The Soljas will escort us. They're not the brightest of our troops, but here we need strength, not intellect."

Only a few people had seen their escape, which was so quick, no one had reacted. As Felipe landed in the square formed by the Soljas, a few Jaya started shouting insults again.

The Soljas moved forward. Around and behind them, the giants kept a shuffling square pressing against the mob. Somehow, though Lessus hardly believed it, they pushed the crowd back. "They're trying to be as gentle as possible," Azdal explained. "The less who get hurt, the less trouble there'll be. Hopefully."

Lessus peered through momentary gaps in the shuffling crowd of giants. The mob shoved back against the Soljas. Several people were pushed up bodily, like corks on water, by the pressure of the crowd. One Jaya had a loudspeaker, keeping up a running commentary. "There is only the True Way. There is no other! To those who upset the balance of the True Way, Death! Death!"

"Death! Death!" The crowd roared back.

A man shouted, his face distended by rage, "They have the unbeliever!" He bellowed, "Look! They dress their lackeys in their uniforms!" He hurled fruit at Azdal, but missed. The crowd pushed back, redoubling their efforts.

"Don't worry," Raph said. "You'll be at the barracks soon."

"Where will I go from there?" Lessus asked. Raph didn't reply.

The man with the microphone fell silent. Lessus relaxed slightly. The non-stop blare had started to fray his nerves.

Lessus jumped up to see how the other group with the box was progressing. Both groups had pushed out through front gates designed for ceremonial processions. Fortunately, the path to the Eastgate was almost completely open, so at least they were safe from a rain of fruit and other missiles from the trees.

Around them, the shouts grew increasingly frantic, turning to screams. "Shit!" one of the Guards said. "The Soljas are treading on the crowd! There's gonna be nothing left of 'em."

"Keep your mouth shut!" Felipe barked. "Eyes open, and keep walking, nice and steady."

A few people were passed bodily over the heads of the mob to the front of the crowd. One Jaya was even thrown up into the air in an attempt to lob him into the square of soljas. To Lessus' relief, the man didn't clear them, but then another one was thrown higher. A huge black paw rose and swatted the man, smashing his skull like an over-ripe melon, flinging the broken-doll limp body back at the crowd.

Silence fell; then shots rang out. The roar that followed nearly split Lessus' eardrums. The phalanx rocked for a moment, but the Soljas linked arms, pushing forward again.

The rest of the journey to the Eastgate was a nightmare. Lessus dared not clap his hands over his ears or shut his eyes in case he fell. The sight of the crushed bodies and dead eyes would haunt him for the rest of his life.

At last they were outside the city walls into open space. Here the mob couldn't exert so much pressure.

Overhead hovered a great, distended black shape, too big to land on the narrow embassy roof; silent except for the whirr of engines whispering in the breeze.

"Almost there," Raph said.

Even Azdal flashed him a grin. Determined to crack his own shell of diffidence, Lessus asked, "You've kin here, Private?"

The Guard's smile faded, "No sir. My relatives are in the West." He paused, asked more from politeness than genuine interest, "You?"

Lessus shook his head. "All in the West." None of whom would want to know him, Lessus, the fool who had started a civil war. He hadn't seen them in years. Academics like Shortime were his family. He wondered if the Guards filled the same function for Azdal.

The aircraft lifted a net, with several guards and the box.

"It looks like I've fulfilled my function, Raph," Lessus said wearily.

Raph's grin faded. "What do you mean?"

"You only needed me as a distraction from the box. I overheard you and the sergeant talking. I speak Thal, but I thought it best not to let on. Please, shoot me first. They're so angry, they'll never notice they're only ripping a corpse apart."

"Sir, we should be going," Azdal said to Raph.

"It's a shame you're abandoning the best chance you have to understand that creature," Lessus said. "Who better to understand an outsider than another outside? You understand, if someone as shy as I am claims to be the best anthropologist there is, then I must be telling the truth?"

"Sir," Azdal urged Raph.

Lessus stared at Raph. To say anything else now would be futile.

"He comes with us," Raph squeezed his arm, and Lessus felt a surge of affection for a man who'd risk so much to help a semi-stranger. "Captain Prieto will burst a blood vessel, but I don't work for Military Intelligence."

A ladder swung over their heads. A Solja grasped Lessus round the waist, jumped, and they were reeled up. Lessus turned around in the doorway of the huge bay to look out. The mob stretched across the city. There seemed to be more of them than ever; even women and children spilled out of their houses to join the carnival of hate. The city burned in several places as the mob, furious at being deprived of their prey, had turned on their own.

Lessus helped Raph in.

"Thanks," Raph said. "I shan't miss this place." He stood in the open doorway, turning to look out. "I hope my next post is more peaceful." His smile turned to puzzlement, and he frowned. He coughed, and blood trickled from his mouth. He crumpled, as Azdal screamed "Medic!"

"Sniper!" someone yelled. "Get moving!"

The carrier wheeled ponderously. Azdal pulled Lessus further into the hold. "I hope you know what you've done." he snarled at Lessus, who stared back, unflinching.

"Azdal! Enough!" Felipe shouted.

"I know better than you realize." Lessus straightened his clothes and met Azdal's glare.

Raph lay, staring blindly, blood pooling beneath his prone body. *I would like to have known you better*, Lessus thought. *I'll pick that bastard in the box apart for you, never fear.*

The city, now burning furiously, fell away behind them.

CHAPTER TWELVE

Cassidy removed the headpiece, and put it carefully to one side.

"How do you feel?" Sophia stared anxiously at him, her face a chiaroscuro mask in the half-light.

"Fine!" he snapped, "You ask me that every time." He pressed a hand to his left eye and rubbed it, though it didn't ease the pain.

"And I will keep asking, as long as you keep overusing it!" Easing his hands away, she rubbed his forehead. It was probably only his imagination, but he felt momentarily better, as if her touch had eased his aches.

He nodded his acknowledgment. "I feel ravenous, to be honest. And a little wired."

"Wired? What's that?"

He laughed. "Your English is so good, I forget it isn't your native language. I feel," he groped for the right words, "like I haven't slept properly for several nights. Over sensitized, acutely aware of every noise, every touch." He yawned, and blinked his eyes.

"Starting to see a pattern?" Sophia nodded at the crystal.

"I think so," he said. "Interesting parallels to our own world." Without waiting for an answer, he stifled another yawn, and added, "You were building an empire." He smiled, but he could see from her troubled look that she'd seen through him.

Someone cleared his throat behind them. Cassidy looked around. "Davenport," he said, more emphatically than he had intended. "I hear you've had the men looking round?"

"Seemed like a good idea, sir," Davenport said, a little defensively.

"It was," Cassidy said. "Find anything interesting?"

"Apart from enough food to feed the Thals for months?" Davenport grinned. "Not much." His grin faded, leaving him with a worried look.

Cassidy drew the young man to one side. "Find a back door?"

Davenport shook his head. "Nothing. We're bottled up."

The lack of an alternative exit worried Cassidy. He changed the subject. "Who's on watch?"

"Two soldiers and Farooq at the near end of the tunnel." Davenport flashed another of his ephemeral grins. "Farooq isn't happy. Keeps making evil-eye gestures." He resumed his worried look. "Sir, what's going on?"

"I'm still working through these things," Cassidy showed him the crystals. "If they're genuine, these people are refugees, not invaders." He kept to himself the fact that in the last crystal he had seen an Empire being gradually accreted, as slowly as a pearl in a shell. He said, "Don't allow the men to let their guard down. We need to debrief the first patrol again, see if they've picked up anything that contradicts what the crystals are telling me." He should have already done so, but there were so many things to do, so many leads to follow.

He staggered, and Davenport said, "I'll debrief them, sir. You look like you need a break."

Cassidy clapped his arm, and Davenport stood ramrod straight. "Good man. Take charge."

***

Kaminski's breath steamed in the morning air. It was barely light enough to see, but the day would brighten quickly. In the west the sky was so dark it was black, but towards the east it was already turning gold.

His men were stretching in the gloom around him, a few muttering curses or laughing quietly at their colleague's jokes. Kaminski stood up, signaling that it was time to start the day's march.

They wolfed a quick breakfast of MRE's as they marched, climbing over the same steep paths as the British had only a day earlier. "We're gonna go through the food in about five days max at this rate," Adler murmured, "Four meals a day. The guys are burning the cals up. We can't expect them to carry these," he pointed to his hundred-and-thirty-pound backpack, "and not eat constantly. If only we could've had wheeled support."

"Sure limits the mission span," Kaminski said. "But the Brits are gonna have the same problem, unless they find a secret hoard of food." He grinned at the unlikelihood of that.

"Unless they live off the land." Adler chuckled grimly at the thought, nodding at the mountains around them.

This land is beautiful, but brutal, Kaminski thought. It wasn't for him, personally, but he could appreciate it in an abstract way. "It sure ain't California," he said, so quietly no one else could hear him. The thought of Barbara made him ache physically.

They lost the trail for a few moments and fanned out, half of them searching the ground methodically, the others guarding the searchers. Chao held his hand up, and Kaminski blew a short, two-fingered whistle. The others looked up, and regrouped around Chao. Raymund, their unlikely named Afghan guide, spoke urgently to Trooper Pontrescu, and then clambered up a steep slope.

Clearing the slope, they marched onwards. "Trail's fresh," Pontrescu whispered to Kaminski. "They came this way less than twenty-four hours ago."

In the wafer-thin air Kaminski's heart labored. It wasn't the only reason he felt light-headed. The fact that they were that close to the Brits made his head spin. Soon they would find out what had sent men scurrying across this wilderness, leaving their wounded to die.

***

By the time the Mawson Fly arrived, only the *Aurora Australis'* masts and superstructure poked above the waterline. The water still swirled and churned in the wake of the tsunami. "I guess the remnants of the bergs are holding her up," Turner said.

Nearby, the AA Fly hovered. Helicopters from Mawson had been and gone; fuel being insufficient to allow them to stay more than briefly. The pilot of the AA Fly confirmed that the few bodies they'd pulled from the water had been dead. "A body could probably survive less than ninety seconds before the cold stops its heart, cold weather gear or not," the pilot concluded.

"If I hadn't come with you, I'd be dead, too," Phyl said.

"We're not out of jail yet," Turner said. "AA Fly, can you spare some fuel?"

"Sorry, Mawson Fly, we've used too much. We're at the edge of our range."

"Could you take a passenger?"

"No!" Phyl plucked at his arm. "I'm not leaving you alone. We both go, or neither of us goes. Okay?"

"Don't be silly, woman, this is no time for heroics!"

"Don't you 'woman' me! I've got a name, remember?"

"Sorry, Phyl," he sighed. "But I might be able to get to Mawson, if I'm alone."

"Bullshit. My weight won't make that much difference."

Turner surrendered to her and turned the Mawson Fly towards the Chinese base at Zhong Shan. They flew south in silence. Forty minutes later came the moment that Turner had been dreading. With the Larsemann Hills separating them from safety, the Sikorsky's engines began misfiring. "So close," Turner said, "but we're on the red line already." He spoke into his radio.

"Mayday, mayday," he said. "This is the helicopter Mawson Fly, out of Mawson Base. We are losing altitude rapidly. Our position is," checking the GPS, he read out the co-ordinates. "Mayday, mayday," he repeated the message. There was no answer from the radio. He tried again, and again.

The engine was misfiring constantly. "I have to put her down," Turner said. "I'll try to get us as far as we can."

"We aren't going to glide?" Phyl asked. Turner was about to snap at her not to be so stupid when he looked up and saw her tremulous smile over the worry etched in her face.

"Nah," he said lightly. "This bird's got the aerodynamics of a house-brick. I'm putting her down. Brace yourself," he added grimly.

White snowfields loomed ever larger in their cockpit window, while to one side they could see the brown of exposed rocks. "There are rocks under the snow!" Phyl shouted.

"Bloody hell!" Turner quickly increased the power, but he had so little fuel that the Sikorsky barely changed her altitude, and he heard the shrill scream of metal ripping on rocks. The snowfield loomed even larger in the cockpit window. Then there was pain and darkness, and then nothing.

***

Cassidy struggled to make sense of his emotions. Why was he so uneasy? Sophia hadn't lied to him; she'd only withheld part of the information. He could hardly criticize her for it. He'd done it with his own men. It was exactly what every leader did, telling their people what they needed to know, and no more.

Was it that he didn't like being led? He'd never had a problem taking orders from women, far from it. An ex-lover had once snapped at him, "Your trouble is, Josh, you're so bloody laid back that at times you're comatose!"

Was it that he'd been too easily fooled? For years he'd queried the validity of every piece of information, the source and the motives for the source that provided it. Such cynicism had inevitably spilled into his private life, corroding every relationship he'd ever had.

Yet now he was taking everything at face value. Was his judgment impaired? Part of him said yes. He'd rarely felt so drawn to a woman, and that had to be tainting his perceptions. Or was he only looking for an excuse to run away from emotions that were starting to scare him?

***

"Up here!" one of the soldiers shouted and, scrambling up a path, disappeared into the side of the cliff.

I'll rip that guy a new mouth for yelling, Kaminski thought He realized with mounting excitement that it was the mouth of a cave. He felt light-headed, whether from the altitude, or from excitement, he wasn't sure. *No wonder the Brits tried to keep this quiet,* he thought. The public relations value of announcing a second Tora Bora would be incalculable. Of course, they'd want to check it out first.

He stopped for a moment as he entered the cave to let his eyes adjust. The difference in the light levels was slight, but it was enough that he needed a few seconds, and in those moments, as he stood on the cusp of the world inside and out, several things happened at once.

From out of the gloom, Kaminski heard raised voices, those of his men and voices with British accents. At that moment, Private Charles, the man at the back of the line said, "What the hell are those things with gray skin?" Kaminski halted. His eyes still trying to adjust to the dimmer light inside, he saw Charles' look of horror, as the trooper shouted, "What's that red dot? Oh shit, get inside, sir!"

Charles shoved his commander inside, even as his own body exploded, arms and legs cart wheeling away from the ruined torso. Kaminski was splattered with blood, gore and bits of uniform; something grazed his eyes. Blinded, he gasped with pain.

Adler grabbed Kaminski, yelling, "Come on! Get in here!"

***

Cassidy wasn't sure how far beneath the ground he was. The tunnels were all the same, carved out of rock, white walled, smooth sided, the surfaces of some dotted with storage cabinets, others by fire hydrants, cooling pipes, or ventilation ducts. Those made him stare upward, wondering if they could get out by climbing the ducts. He shook his head. They were too narrow.

All the tunnels were full of Thals. Some slept. One cried out in his sleep and was comforted by the woman next to him. Some crouched, watching him as he passed. Many coughed and sneezed, their noses running, their eyes red and rheumy. One child held out his hand as Cassidy passed, and as he reached out without thinking to take the boy's hand, the child's mother snatched him away and stared wildly at Cassidy as if he was a monster.

As he walked, Cassidy argued with himself in his mind. The Thals posed no threat, no military one, anyway. Whether this savaged, depleted country could stand an influx of hungry mouths was a different matter. He wondered why they'd stayed here and not moved on.

But that last crystal had showed an empire being built. His own ancestors hadn't started out wanting an empire. But trade eventually gave way to dominion, the initial motives irrelevant. He could not ignore that; above all, he had the security of his country and even that of the world to consider.

He could only get the answer he needed from the last crystal. He still had no idea how accurate the information was or how much he could even trust his own judgment, but his instincts told him that the crystal gave him the best chance of finding the answers he needed. He re-traced his steps, and, far sooner than he'd expected, he stood in front of Sophia. "You'd better give me the head-set," he said, avoiding her gaze.

CHAPTER THIRTEEN

Seven Years Before Present Day

"So many alternate Earths," Bel waved at the swarm, row upon row, rank upon myriad rank of marble-sized blue and green worlds hanging in mid-air in the middle of the lounge, swirling languidly round a fixed invisible core above the leather couch.

What are these? Cassidy wondered. *Holograms?*

Looking through Bel's eyes, he thought that the dark wood cabinets and bookcases around the room could have come from any room in the last three hundred years on Earth. *My Earth,* he corrected himself. So could the rugs and throws scattered about the open lounge. Their very familiarity was actually part of their strangeness. Bel resumed, "What was first the Centurium, then the Millennium, and as the numbers of alternates grew, became eventually the Multiplicium."

Fascinated by the word, Cassidy broke it down into its component syllables, rolling it round in his mind. He tried to get Bel to say the word again, without success. As his efforts overrode the crystal-viewer's normal restraints on its user, he thought he glimpsed Sophia talking to stupefied soldiers in American uniforms. The vision passed, as abruptly as it had come.

Cassidy flashed a mental apology to his host who seemed to be, from her voice and clothes, an adolescent girl. She no more noticed his apology than his television at home would have, instead saying, "As they were all variations of one world, we couldn't call each world Earth, or New Earth, or even New New Earth."

Bel's parents chuckled dutifully, and Bel bobbed her head. "So we number them, in order."

"And our world is?" Kazan sat, a gray grizzled monolith, in one of the chairs. Form fitting, leather covered, the chairs molded their shapes around their occupants. They had been moved to one side to give the feeling of an auditorium. Kazan obviously felt he should contribute something rather than sitting there like a trophy on the wall.

Kazan was hairier than the Thals in previous crystals, Cassidy noted. Then he realized that Kazan hadn't just shaved his body hair. The hair that was shaved was patterned into swirls, whorls and curlicues, as complex as any tattoo.

Bel frowned her disapproval at his interruption, "Sixty-eight twenty, Dad!"

Sarla said sharply, "Belapharus Kazansdottir, don't talk to your Papa like that! You mind your tongue, my girl! You're not too big to put across my knee!" Beneath the sound and fury, Bel saw a twinkle in her mother's eye, quickly suppressed.

"Sorree," Bel muttered, biting back the obvious retort that her mother only reached her shoulder. Bel had her father's height, if not his blocky physique, and her mother's exotic blue-green eyes. Cassidy felt another shock of recognition, he couldn't tell at what, along with her temper. Her stomach churned with anger, but she kept her mouth shut.

A burglar bee hummed serenely past on its way to pollinate one of the massed walls of night bloom plants glowing in the dusk outside the veranda. Its oversized antennae, which it used as crowbars to pry open the closed petals, were covered with sticky nectar. Its flight took it obliviously through one of Bel's alternate Earths, and she nudged with her mind so it changed course and covered her mouth with her hand to stifle a giggle.

"It's okay," Kazan's gentle voice recalled her to the task at hand. "We know finals are tough. I'll shut up. You were saying, Bel?"

Bel nodded, as if acknowledging him, but she was merely gathering her thoughts. Then she continued, "The Multiplicium is governed from Prime. The government sits on whichever world has been so designated. Actually, government is a misleading word. Prime tells the Multiplicium what they should do, and the Multiplicium mostly ignore them and do what they want. That's because actually governing so many worlds requires too many resources." She paused for breath and then resumed. "The current Prime has been occupied for three hundred and twelve years, ever since the Multiplicium last suffered a major Sauroid invasion."

She stopped for a moment, pondering, savoring the lemony tang of the night bloom plants that drifted through the air. "Although the worlds of the Multiplicium are autonomous, certain principles apply throughout. We don't settle worlds with primitive indigenous populations, in case we twist their development. We co-operate with aboriginal governments where they exist; we have no wish for Empire. Perhaps this is because for most of our history, others have sought to include us in their empires. We'd rather run than fight and only fight when cornered. Where it's possible for us to co-exist with indigenes, we try to do so on an equal footing. It isn't always possible. Memories of the long civil war on Jaya that we sparked still linger. Where we can't co-exist, we place those worlds off-limits." She paused and said, "That's the end of my presentation. Thank you." She waved a hand, and the miniature worlds vanished.

Her father's flat, percussive hand claps rang round the room like echoes of his antique fire-arm in the fields on spring mornings, drowning out her mother's gentler applause.

But when her mother said simply, "That was very good," Cassidy felt Bel's warm glow; a tiny gift from a miser is sometimes more appreciated than largesse from a spendthrift.

"What subjects are the others covering?" Kazan asked.

"Marram's presenting on the decline of Talents and the rise of mechanization. I don't know about the others."

"Oh?"

"Yes," Bel missed the frown that passed over her father's face at the mention of Marram Palosson, but Cassidy noticed and wondered at it. "He says that once upon a time everyone had Talents, and often people mastered several. Fire breathing, levitation, snake charming, plus the few that are left today."

"Well, that's a little exaggerated. The Talents are like your appendix. Once it was useful, but now we don't need it. Same with the Talents. Now we have machines, plants or animals to do things for us. We have poor night vision, so we gengineer burglar bees to pollinate the night bloom plants. Same as we have Portals, so we no longer need as many people who can Shift."

"You make it sound like we discovered Portals deliberately so we didn't need people with the ability to Shift. I think it's more that the portals saved us from the consequences of our fading ability to Shift." Bel's tousled hair fell over one eye. "Suppose the Sauroids attack again? We'll need everyone we can find with Talents then, won't we?"

"That won't happen!" Sarla cried. "We've had centuries of peace! Enough! Bedtime!" Seeing Bel's face fall, Sarla added, "It's the last time until school resumes in the New Year."

"Okay." Bel brightened. "Are we going away next week?"

"Maybe," Kazan grinned.

Bel grinned back. "If you only tell me we're going, it doesn't ruin the surprise. You can keep exactly where secret."

"Would you like to go off-world?" Kazan raised an eyebrow. "If we go, of course."

"Oh, yes!"

"Come on now, my girl," Sarla said repressively. "Bed!"

"Yes, Mama." Bel leant forward, pecked her mother's cheek. When she kissed her father she tugged at his beard, and he mock-wrestled her, growling like the scavenger bear that ransacked their rubbish-mound by the back door.

Strolling across the moss-grass carpet, she pulled the curtain closed behind her. The carpet muffled her footfalls, and her parent's voices kept her company as she climbed up the stairs. At the top of the stairs, she paused and looked out across the Naribor valley.

Downstairs, the visible light and tiny quantities of ultra-violet cast by the night blooms gave the illusion of a languid summer's evening. The heating was on full tonight, and it was already unseasonably warm, which only added to the illusion.

She watched the auroras' manic streamers dance across the night sky. Lights from the houses on either side of the valley were scattered like fireflies over the hills dark bulk. She opened the window a crack to release a little warmth and took a deep breath of the night air, savoring the night blooms' perfume and the tang of the pines that mantled the high ground away from the coastal lowlands. Nearby, owls exchanged territorial hoots, and in the distance a shriek shattered the quiet. A rhino-bird had caught its horn on something; the clumsy birds were prone to such disasters.

She became aware that her parent's voices had grown louder and sharper as they argued. Shutting the window gingerly, she crept back downstairs. She heard her mother first. "Surely there's nothing to worry about? We've had peace for so long!"

"I'm sure there isn't," Kazan soothed. He broke off. Bel could almost see her father shaking his head in exasperation. "But we're going on holiday anyway. Why not go off-world?"

Yes! Bel silently punched the air. Mother would grumble, and then plead, but Father would prevail, as he usually did.

Not like her classmates' parents. Most were ditherers like Bel's mother, or bullies – big and strong enough to impress their children- but when a couple had tried to cross Kazan, she'd seen what they were really like. They turned into whimperers when faced with someone who'd stand up to them.

She'd heard enough. She climbed the stairs again but this time almost skipped up them, not bothering to gaze out over the valley. *"We're going off-world!"* she sang to herself.

In her room, she flung herself onto the bed and gazed up at the ceiling, counting the lines of the ornate tracing she'd scrolled into the plaster under Kazan's guidance.

Her father could afford workmen to plaster the ceiling. He didn't need the nominal councilor's salary he received. But he genuinely enjoyed working with his hands at the end of long days of what he described as "Sitting, listening to people spend more time and energy explaining why they can't do things than it takes to actually do them." He'd carved the bed-head, which she patted as she rolled off and walked to the dressing table.

She removed traces of blusher from her face. Mother didn't like it but accepted that it hid the dark patches of skin. Her piebald appearance had made her different enough to get her bullied when she'd first gone to secondary school. Even now, some still occasionally called her "freak" and other insults.

With the presentation looming, sleep didn't come easily. Outside an owl hooted and was echoed by another. When at last she slept, her slumber was uneasy, haunted by dreams that she knew were prescient visions. Cassidy, sharing her dreams, was shocked by how powerful and how erotic those images were.

When she awoke, weak winter sunshine lit the wall under the curtains. She half-dozed, memories of **him** still fresh. He'd spoken a language she didn't know and called her by a name that wasn't her own, but somehow she knew he'd been talking to her.

He'd seemed strange when she first dreamed of him with his thin, sharp nose, over-developed chin, and high, flat forehead. When she'd seen him naked, he'd seemed thin and stringy compared to ordinary men. Now she accepted that there was no fat on him, and his alien features were so familiar she'd grown to like them.

When she'd first had the dreams, she'd struggled to remember anything definite. Now, after a month of nocturnal images, they were clearer when she awoke in the morning. Why the memories were growing stronger, she wasn't sure.

Her mother called, "You're going to be late for school!"

Muttering, she leapt from the bed and dived across the landing into the bathroom, pulling her nightgown over her head before she'd closed the door. Emerging from a quick dip in the bath, she toweled herself dry and shuffled back to her room. She sketched make-up over the dark parts of her face, and buttoned up her smock. Scuttling down the stairs, she skidded to a stop in the kitchen. She bit into an apple, cut a chunk from the cheese-wheel, and carved slices of bread off a loaf, threw them into her carryall, with a pair of quinces, and a small knife.

Her mother watched her with amusement while washing pans. Kazan would have left for his office at dawn, an hour before.

"What?" Bel snapped, the anger that lately was never far away suddenly flaring again. "Can't I even pack my lunch without you checking on me?"

"I was about to say," Sarla replied, "good luck with the presentation. Now I don't know if I should."

"Oh." Bel suddenly felt very small and very stupid, and it made her even angrier. She noticed for the first time how tired Sarla looked. She still looked white from when she'd been bedridden with the virus last spring. Bel wondered if the murmurs she'd heard between her parents the night before had been a dream. But if so, why had they talked so late? Was there a problem? "Mum? Is everything okay?" Suddenly worried, Bel threw her arms around Sarla, squeezed her in a bear hug, and kissed her cheek.

"Careful, you'll ruin my hair." Wrestling an arm free, her mother patted stray locks back into place but looked pleased.

Sarla said carefully, "I don't think Marram's preoccupation with the past is completely healthy, Bel."

"What do you mean?"

"Well, his carping about everyone having Talents. Those days are gone. You have to make the best of things as they are."

"I know!" Bel snapped, her good humor evaporating. Did her mother really think she was pining for a past where she'd be ordinary? She liked being different; she had never wanted to live four or five centuries earlier. It was Marram who pined for the glories linked with his name, Marram who would gladly have traded places with his great-great multi-great-grandfather.

Now that she was no longer bullied, she relished being the only one at the school who could push things, if only a little, with her mind. She was special, and everyone knew it, especially Marram. She shook her head. Parents! Didn't they know anything? She realized then that she'd had no flashes of the coming day, which was rare, but not unheard of.

She sighed. "Don't worry, Mum," and kissed Sarla's cheek again, inhaling the scent of her mother's powder.

Sarla pushed Bel away, smiling indulgently. "Get top marks, my girl, and that prize for outstanding student of the year."

Bel nodded. She didn't have the heart to tell Sarla that she and her friends didn't give a kiss for the prize. That was for Olders. Taking her fox-fur winter-cape from its peg in the foyer, she tried unsuccessfully to shoo out a burglar bee that had become confused and was repeatedly battering the window.

She made it out the gate just as the pachyderm-bus lumbered round the corner. He trumpeted a greeting when he saw her, and she scratched his hairy knee. He rumbled happily, an almost sub-sonic grumble, and she wrinkled her nose at the warm, damp fur smell. They'd been over-feeding him again; he always farted when they gave him too much grass. Everyone knew that, it seemed, except the beast's keepers. She wondered if that was the keepers' idea of a joke.

The bus knelt when the driver nudged him from where he perched, between, but just behind his ears. "Morning," Bel called as she clambered the rope ladder and into the howdah, her breath steaming in the cold, crisp morning air. Arnos grunted a reply; he was as miserable as the bus was friendly.

She'd seen pictures of a creature called a tapir on some worlds; the bus looked similar to it, albeit a hundred times bigger. She swayed from side to side down the aisle, in time with his strides and slid onto the bench on which Marram perched, her hip bumping his. "Morning, Palosson."

"Morning, Kazansdottir." Marram stifled a yawn. "I'll be glad when today's over, and I can sleep 'til midday."

"You should stop pulling it," she pointed to just below the belt of his kilt and answered his grimace by sticking her tongue out. "And tiring yourself out."

"If you'd pull it for me, I wouldn't have to," he said, but under the friendly smile he looked sad, and she mentally kicked herself. They'd stayed friends when they split up, but she wondered if it was because he hoped they'd get back together; perhaps her dreams were because she secretly wanted them back together. She decided that was unlikely unless frustration had led her to transmogrify Marram into the stranger.

They sat in companionable silence as the bus strolled down the broad, tree-lined avenue onto the main boulevard. They passed the spiral tower at the base of the Portal from which her father Shifted to the regional council world he served on each morning. Portals on most worlds were above ground; some were very high. The scouts sent to check new worlds had appalling mortality rates, and most of the early losses were due to them plummeting to their deaths after emerging in mid-air. Even after the scouts were issued with parachutes, sometimes the portals were just too low for them to be opened in time. Often many attempts were needed before a Portal could be found at ground level, if at all. Once survey teams had spread out, Portalfinders, the sensitives whose minds were attuned to the vibrations from the weak spots in the world, were dispatched to map out sites, and the teams built towers such as the one they'd just passed.

The bus stopped to let the next wave of passengers on.

"Morning, you twosome." Dalalla grinned, sliding into the bench in front of them. "You ready for today?"

"Oh, yes," Bel said. She wished the other girl would do her top button up so Marram wasn't constantly gazing down her front. Or put her damned cape on, not drape it over her shoulders like a cheap performer. It annoyed her almost as much as Dalalla's lion-mane of tawny gold hair and ornately waxed eyebrow ridge.

Bel dozed, rocked by the swaying of the bus. She awoke with a start, her heart racing, although she was unsure of why. She'd dozed only briefly, but the bus had walked down the length of Riverside Heights towards Fengelor City center. Pedicabs covered all five in-bound and all three outbound lanes of the Concourse like flies on a sugar-bowl, while freight-megalotheria lined the crawler lanes. The compact town cottages gave way to the high towers of local businesses and in the very center, the District Government. Her father had started there, trading imported exotics for local spices, building a fortune and reputation, until he walked away to serve on the Multiplicium Council as one of the facilitators who served as the link between their world and Prime.

Dalalla and Marram were arguing. Dalalla's voice had grown a little strident, and her face was flushed. "We have- I know it's a little conceited to say it- the greatest civilization in history. We've had peace and prosperity, and why should anyone want to wreck that?" There were rumors Dalalla sometimes fucked boys. Those she argued with, for example. Bel didn't want to follow the thought through to its nasty conclusion. *If you want to stop it, you only have to let Marram fuck you like he wanted to,* a treacherous inner voice urged.

"I'm not saying there's anything to worry about, Dalalla. There've been too many oddities lately, though. Kidnappings across the Mutliplicium this Prime Year are almost double over last year. Some are only local gangsters, but not all. We've had sightings of man-shaped creatures down by the coast." Marram's voice had that unsettling edge it took on when he was getting too intense. He saw Bel's eyes were open and said, "Hi. Awake then?" They quickly changed the subject to yard gossip. Bel wanted to tell them not to stop arguing on her account.

The bus swung to the left, taking his usual diversion to pick up the last of his passengers before turning back towards school.

"Are you still dreaming about **him**?" Dalalla's stage whisper cut through her reverie. Bel wished she hadn't told Dalalla about the dreams, but a week or two before, they'd almost become friends. Before Dalalla had started flashing that chest at Marram.

"Who?" Marram asked, and Bel felt her face burn. He stared at her, and she looked away.

"No one." When she continued, her answer sounded lame. "I have these weird dreams about this, I suppose you'd call him a man. He talks in a strange language, but every so often he'll say something I understand. It's really odd. He keeps calling me by someone else's name, but it's me he's talking to." She shrugged defiantly, unwilling to say any more. After an awkward silence, inspiration struck. "So what are you presenting on?"

"I thought I'd do Karina the Lost," Dalalla said.

"The one with the Jaya lover?" Bel enjoyed seeing Dalalla's discomfited look. *You didn't expect me to have heard of Karina*, she thought. Aloud, she said, "Didn't she spend her life looking for Lessus?"

"He wasn't her lover!" Dalalla said venomously. "Just because you've got sex on the brain!"

Before Bel could spit back a reply, the bus stopped at the school gates and sank to his knees.

She jumped up and pushed her way down the aisle, ignoring a younger boy's muttered, "Watch out!" She almost smacked his face, but it was Dalalla that she wanted to slap. How could she say Bel had sex on the brain? How dare she! Bel's head spun, and her heart pounded. She thought of her dream-lover again, and her face burnt some more.

She descended the ladder, absently patting the bus' flank.

At that moment, as she turned toward the school on a bright, mid-winter's morning, the world as she knew it ended.

An explosion ripped through the morning air, silencing the children spilling off the bus. Smoke rose from the far side of the school in a billowing cloud. Before anyone could react, there was a second explosion, this time from behind her. Someone screamed, and the mob of now terrified children surged, almost knocking her off her feet. They darted first one way, then another like a shoal of sardines fleeing marauding dolphins. Another explosion ripped the air.

Something flashed overhead, almost too fast to see, silent except for a whoosh that followed seconds later. Two black dots fell to the ground and before Bel could react, exploded nearby. The heat from the blast warmed her face like a slap, and she staggered backwards from the concussion, her ears ringing.

It seemed that every time the children caught their breath, another blast set them screaming again. Through the muffled ringing, the others' screams fuelled Bel's panic. She had a sudden, incongruous thought that her dreams about the strange man couldn't be foreshadows of her future, if she was going to die here.

She needed to get to safety. She ducked into the shelter of the low wall that ringed three sides of the schoolyard and tried to think of what to do, but it was so difficult when she couldn't breathe and her heart threatened to burst free of her chest.

In the shelter of the wall, sense crept back to her, as leisurely as a snail circling a flowerpot. Where were all the explosions coming from? Those black seeds dropping from sky could only account for a few of the blasts.

She glimpsed a flicker of the answer across the schoolyard, as she winced at a near miss, so close that her guts trembled with the vibration. When she opened her eyes, the Sauroids were gone. She'd never seen real ones, but she recognized them from pictures. Four of them had shuffled sideways round a corner, two carrying a stubby tube attached to a limp tripod, one in front and one behind swiveling backwards and forwards through a one-hundred-eighty degree arc, their rifle barrels swaying like metronomes.

Nearby, she saw a dazed-looking figure wandering like a sleepwalker. "Dalalla!" Bel shouted, waving at the other girl.

"Thank the Gods!" Dalalla threw herself into Bel's arms. Her eyes were red from weeping, her hair hung in a limp shroud to her shoulders, and mucus ran from her nose down to her mouth. Her tunic was torn, and she'd lost her cape. But just then, Bel thought her the most beautiful girl she'd ever seen. She almost kissed her. "Where's Marram?" she asked instead.

Dalalla shook her head. "Don't know." Her face crumpled like a used bag. "I'm so scared."

"So am I," Bel heard her own voice tremble. "We've got to get home. Our parents will know what to do."

Dalalla nodded.

"Come on," Bel took her hand, and they stood up. Dalalla flinched at another blast. "It's okay," Bel said, though deep inside she wanted to shriek for her mother at the top of her voice.

They scuttled, crab-like, across the road. The pachyderm-bus lay on his side, a man-sized metal shard sticking out from his flank, his screams adding to the din.

Two uniformed men rounded the corner, and Bel was about to call them when she saw that a pair of Sauroids accompanied them. The men each wore a strange metal headpiece that wound round their heads, down to one ear and to the jaw on the other side.

Bel slapped her hand over Dalalla's mouth before the other girl could shout out. "They're not our people," she hissed, and saw Dalalla's eyes widen. "They're with the enemy."

She took her hand away and pulled Dalalla into a crouch, so they were the same height as the younger children. They shuffled through the mob, using the youngsters as a screen.

"Come on kids," a turncoat said kindly, "we'll take care of you." He took a child by the hand, and Bel felt an overwhelming hatred. It was bad enough to be attacked by the enemy, but to find her own kind ranged against her was almost unbearable.

"Where are we going?" the child piped, voice shrill with fear.

"You're going to meet a real God," the enemy Thal said. "Bramaragh likes children," he added. The boy wailed like a siren. The traitor tried to calm the boy, but the child's panic was contagious, and another child began to cry.

Soon all semblance of kindness was dropped, and Bel could only watch in horror as the screaming children were rounded up, the smallest of them tossed like wriggling maggots into the arms of waiting Sauroids. "Why?" One of the older children cried, as one enemy tossed him to another.

"Because it's heresy that you worship false Gods when there's a real one waiting for you," the rogue Thal said in a flat, unemotional voice. "Bramaragh awaits you."

When each Sauroid had a child under each arm, the air around them squirmed, and they all vanished. A dull thud marked the filling of the sudden vacuum. A few couldn't Shift unaided and linked arms with a turncoat, an untidy process with their squirming, shrieking captives doing their best to get away.

Bel and Dalalla shuffled sideways behind a screen of milling children until they reached the corner of the yard where they took shelter by the fence. "Marram," Dalalla whispered, pointing.

Bel looked across the yard to where Marram swayed in the breeze like an old tree in a gale. His face was deathly white beneath the soot-stains, and one arm hung useless by his side.

"We've got to help him!"

Bel hugged Dalalla from behind to hold her back. "The best thing we can do," she hissed into Dalalla's ear, "is to get help. Two unarmed girls against those things? Come on Dalalla. Think!" Dalalla slumped, and Bel led the weeping girl away.

Bel never saw Marram again.

They ducked and fought their way through a hedge of water-reeds. "At least if it's hard for us, it should stop them from coming through," Dalalla said.

"Don't depend on it," Bel panted, hissing as a reed flicked back from Dalalla's push, catching her just below her eye.

They struggled out of the reeds to stand on the canal bank. They often used it as a short cut. Ethereal, otherworldly, it ran through the winter landscape, disappearing into the horizon. Even this morning, the sounds of battle were muted. They walked for twenty minutes before the canal swung to the right, away from their homes. The swirling water, swollen by winter rains from the mountains, was a muddy brown. Pieces of wood, cattle droppings, feathers and even dead birds and animals drifted past. Along each bank, with the man-high clumps of bamboo fringing the canal, banks of water reeds ran into the water, and great drooping willows overhung the banks, blocking any view of the outside world.

"Can't you use your Talents against these things?" Dalalla gasped between breaths. Bel always walked quickly, especially so this morning.

Bel laughed bitterly, "I can just about push a burglar bee off course. Not much use against our scaly friends, is it?"

"But even if you're say, one in a million," Dalalla panted as she tried to keep up with Bel, "there may be more like you. Adults, people who can fight them."

"Maybe," Bel conceded. She thought that it would take thousands of people like her, if what they had seen this morning was an example. Bel realized that she needed to be strong for both she and Dalalla. She didn't feel very strong, however. She felt tired and hungry. And she wanted her Mama and Papa to be safe. She looked back, saw Dalalla was about to say something, and speeded up. Dalalla took the hint, and stayed silent.

Just before they left the canal, a body drifted by, face down. Although they could see it was a Thal, they couldn't tell whether it was friend or foe. Bel shivered. They emerged from the reed-hedge onto the street with hearts in their mouths, but nobody noticed them in the confusion.

Forever afterwards, wherever she slept, whether beneath the open sky, in ruined buildings, or even sometimes in a bed, Bel's sleep was haunted by memories of that nightmare day.

The city was on fire all around them, but no one was there to fight the fires. Columns of smoke spiraled into the sky, and the smoke stung Bel's eyes until tears rolled down her cheeks. They would duck down when they heard gunshots and screams, until things quieted again. Sometimes they saw bodies, mostly of armed civilians who'd died fighting, but also those of Peacekeepers who'd risen that morning expecting only to direct traffic or to settle minor disturbances but who had died defending their people. They even saw a few Sauroid corpses, and once they saw the body of one of the traitors. Bel scurried across the road, ignoring Dalalla's warnings, wrenched the headset off the corpse and pried a hand-gun from fingers already stiffening with rigor. She thought for a moment, and then picked up the dead man's rifle, then put it down. *Too heavy,* she thought. They might need to run, and weight might be precious.

They saw the wreckage of the cable car to Caltren Mountain strewn across the road, the cables coiled serpent-like round the wreckage. As they zigzagged towards Dalalla's home, they smelled roasting meat everywhere. When they passed a sizzling carcass, they realized that the smell was burnt Thal. Leaning into a gutter, Bel was violently sick.

I can't do this, she thought. *I can't go on*. But her body obeyed, even when her mind wanted her to lay down and give up.

They finally stood on Prospect Street, a few houses away from Dalalla's, peering carefully each way before crossing the cobbles. The front door hung off its hinges, and someone lay face down on the path.

"Oh, Gods! Mama!" Dalalla ran forward and turned the body over. Even as Bel realized what the red snakes were that trickled out of the woman's stomach, Dalalla whispered, "It's not her. It's Sumi, two doors down. What's she doing here?" Before Bel could answer, Dalalla ran into the house.

Bel followed cautiously, checking for lurking Sauroids. The house was silent, the only noise a clock ticking in the hallway.

Dalalla's "Mama?" drifted down from the stairs, along with the sound of doors opening and slamming shut. Bel grabbed a handful of ghost crystals from a wooden bowl and studied the titles. *The Fall of Shalimar* nestled with *Palo's Journey* and *A Sea of Grass*. She didn't recognize *The Dreaming Tree* or *The Eastgate Siege* but guessed they'd be the same tawdry history romances as Dalalla usually watched. She was so intent on listening for intruders that she pocketed them without thinking.

"They're not here!" Dalalla appeared, shoulders slumped. Bel knew how much Dalalla had been relying on her parents to be home, as had she.

"Come home with me," Bel urged. "Our people will fight back. Dad will organize search parties."

"I'd rather wait here." Dalalla pushed her bottom lip out.

"What if they come?"

Dalalla shrugged.

"You can't stay here alone!" Bel wanted to shake her. Why was she so stupid? "Even if your parents return, do they have weapons?" When Dallala shook her head, Bel said, "Mine do. Come on! Come with me!"

For a moment Dalalla looked mulish, and Bel expected her to refuse again, but the other girl shrugged. "Okay."

On the way out, they stepped over Sumi's corpse, and Bel had to look away or be sick. *"I won't forget you,"* she promised Sumi grimly.

While they'd been indoors, clouds had bubbled up, and the wind swung round to the east, taking on a bitter chill that cut through Bel's cape. Dalalla had lost hers; she could only wrap her arms round herself.

As they walked away from the city the streets became eerily quiet, as if they walked through a ghost town. They were a block away from Bel's house when they rounded a corner and nearly ran into an enemy patrol. Bel shoved Dalalla over a low wall and dived behind her, landing on top of the other girl. Bel heard shouts and almost resigned herself to being captured.

Looking round, she saw inspiration in the house diagonally across the street. Concentrating, she stared intently, pushing with her mind. Nothing happened. Pushed again, shutting her eyes, pushing harder until spots danced in front of her eyes, pushing at the inside of the glass--

The window exploded outward, showering the garden below, shards spilling into the street. The enemy ran across the road to the house, across grass now strewn with blossoms of glass sparkling in the patchy sunlight. The soldiers behaved as if they were invincible. Bel would have loved to stick around and prove them wrong, but she wanted to see her Mama and Papa more. "Come on!" She tugged at Dalalla's tunic. "Let's go, while they're distracted." They sneaked past the enemy troops and arrived at Bel's house without further incident.

Bel pushed at the back door, but it stayed closed. She knocked. "Mama!" she called. "It's Bel! Are you there? Open up!"

She was about to break the glass when she saw someone move inside, and the bolts were shot back. Her mother pulled Bel through the doorway, sobbing. She cried, "Thank our Grandmothers you're safe! Dalalla! Hello! You're okay? Where are your parents, you poor girl?"

"Mama!" Bel said, "Where's Papa? Have you heard from him?"

Her mother blinked twice. "I don't know." Her eyes suddenly glistened. "He called me when the attacks started, to say he was safe and said he'd be home straight away. I haven't seen him since." She wilted as if realizing the implications of what she'd just said.

Sarla shot the bolts shut, picked up the long-barreled gun that Kazan used for hunting and led them into the lounge. For the next few minutes Bel told her mother about the attack, and their journey home.

When Dalalla mentioned the dead woman, and that she'd thought it was her mother, she broke down. "It's been awful," her voice quavered. "Kidnapping, shooting, killing. Why?" She slapped the hallway wall to punctuate the question as she followed Bel and her mother into the kitchen. "Why do they do this to us?" She looked away, wiping her nose roughly, as if she were angry at it.

"I don't know," Bel said. "Does it matter?"

The speaker on the wall buzzed; Sarla flicked a switch and a landscape ellipse appeared on the wall. In it was an image of a woman's head and shoulders and the room behind her. Kazan's secretary sat in front of a smashed window and a curtain-rail half-hanging off the wall. "I have Kazan Emrisson for you."

Kazan's head and shoulders replaced his secretary's image. The transmission was a variant on the portals, sending an image, not a person, over a short distance, rather than across worlds.

"Kazan?" Sarla cried, "Are you alright? You said you were coming home-"

"Easy, easy, my love," Kazan looked as if he wanted to climb right out of the unsteadily hovering bubble.

Bel felt like an eavesdropper and stepped back, but Kazan saw the movement and said sharply, "Sarla, who's that with you?"

"Bel and Dalalla."

Kazan's frown lifted. "Good," he dipped his head for a moment as someone spoke to him from off screen. He faced them again. "Darlings, the fighting's too fierce for us to be able to get through. Our people are holding on where they can, but our enemies are too many, their weapons are superior, and they had the element of surprise. We're losing," his face was as bleak as Bel could ever remember seeing it.

"They have spies, as well," Bel said, holding up the headgear. "I took this off a dead one."

"What?" Kazan leaned forward to peer at it. He sighed and said, "That explains how they know so much. They've turned us against ourselves. That explains the disappearances."

"They were taking everyone they could today," Bel said.

"Bel, my darling, you've been absolutely magnificent." Kazan leaned forward, and she could feel his pride in her. "I want you all to take the Portal and Shift-"

"No!" Bel and Sarla shouted together.

"You must," Kazan said. "Get that thing to Prime and tell them everything you've told me. We'll worry about meeting up afterwards. Anything that adds to our knowledge is vital."

The debate degenerated into everyone trying to out-shout the others, but Kazan was adamant. Bel was convinced it was simply an excuse to get her off world. What had seemed tempting twelve hours earlier was now the last thing she wanted if it meant leaving her family, which seemed to be their idea.

Dalalla's shriek interrupted the argument. "They're here!"

Something crashed through a window, and smoke filled the lounge. Sarla ran to the kitchen and smashed the window with the rifle-barrel. There was a bang! Part of the window-frame flew clear, scratching Bel's face, and she cried out.

"Get them away!" Kazan shouted.

"I can't!" Sarla shouted back. "I'm not leaving without you, so you decide! Who's going where?" Kazan hesitated, and Sarla shouted "Fine! I'll decide! You come here!" She snapped off the speaker and said, "Typical man. Brain turns to shit when you need him to think." Bel was shocked – she'd never heard her mother swear before. Sarla added, gently, "If you're ever to use those Talents, it's now, my girl. You have to Shift."

As Bel shook her head, she heard a shot. A puff of dust erupted by her head. She'd drifted too close to the window.

Sarla fired back with her rifle. They were only needle-darts, but they could still kill. "You must go! You heard your father! He has enough to worry about without an unruly daughter!"

Dalalla seized Bel's arm, "She's right."

Reluctantly, Bel gave in. She tried to think how Palo had done it in the crystal. She hoped it wasn't just a made-up story. "Think of where you want to go," Palo's uncle had said. "Fix it in your mind." Bel remembered the pictures she had seen of Prime. "Mother, I'm scared."

Sarla turned to face her, her face filthy with dirt and blood from glass splinters. "You'll be fine," she said and smiled proudly. She turned back, firing again at the shapes milling outside.

Gripping Dalalla, Bel willed herself to move. She looked out at the vestibule and before the world turned inside out, upside-down and sideways, saw the still small body of the burglar bee, in the bottom of the window frame, lying where it had battered itself senseless against the window.

CHAPTER FOURTEEN

Cassidy removed the headpiece and gazed at Sophia. He found it suddenly difficult to breathe. "What is it?" Sophia asked. He shook his head. "Tell me," she urged.

"I--" he struggled to regain composure. "That crystal, it affected me far more than any of the others." She watched him with a steady, unwavering gaze. "All those poor children!" Cassidy shook his head as if something was in his ear and continued. "I was fostered at birth." Seeing her blank look, he said, "My mother died giving birth to me. I never knew my father."

"Did your mother's family –"

"She had none," he said harshly. "I was raised by foster parents, one after the other, all unable to cope with me."

"You had no mother? No family?" Cassidy had never seen Sophia look so distressed.

His laugh was a humorless bark. "I was sly and disruptive, rather than obviously troublesome. But I was enough trouble that I looked bound for Borstal– that's a correctional facility."

"Something changed you? Or someone?"

Cassidy nodded. "When I turned thirteen, a very quiet, sad-faced woman took me in. Her name was Margaret. I think of her as my mother, if I think of anyone. She turned me from a sullen little hooligan into something resembling an ordinary teenager." He stopped, his jaw working.

"Please," Sophia said. "Go on."

"I stayed with her all the way up through high school. Then Margaret had a backache that wouldn't go away, so she went to our doctor. Within weeks she was dead from cancer."

"I'm sorry," Sophia whispered.

"I went off the rails," Cassidy said, as if he hadn't heard her. "I dumped my girlfriend. I drank myself stupid. Eventually the high school got me to see a shrink. Margaret had made me promise before she died that I wouldn't do anything silly. I finally realized I was going to let her down." He shrugged, and smiled. "But seeing all that-it just-I don't know."

"So you know how it is to lose someone special," she said.

"But not everything, not in one single day."

She watched him steadily through watering eyes and bit her lip. Cassidy looked around. They seemed to be alone, though they sat in the midst of a throng. *Life goes on,* Cassidy thought. But for these people, life was sitting around guttering fires. In the dim light, families carried on as near normal as possible, men and women mending clothes, eating, trying to control children with too much energy for these confined spaces, or trying to make sick ones stop crying. Despite their activity, they had the pitiable air of all refugees.

"So all these people," Cassidy said. "They're here because of this...this Bramaragh?" Sophia nodded. "You were Bel, weren't you?" It wasn't a question, although it had taken him a while to realize that he was her dream-lover.

When at last she spoke, her voice was husky with suppressed emotion. "It was so long ago. The person you saw in the crystal is someone else. Bel died that day, though her shell lived on. I took the name you gave me in my dreams, Sophia. I grew up awfully fast."

Sophia's lips quivered and her eyes were moist but her voice held steady. "We didn't get to Prime. When we Shifted to the next world, it seemed like the very sky was alight with fire. We got out of there so fast we barely had time to draw breath. The next world, we emerged next to a Portal; everyone was screaming, and pounding on the doors to be let in. The next world was little better. Every world we Shifted to was under attack. Eventually, we had to stop to rest. We slept for a few hours, though only lightly – we were convinced that we'd be attacked at any moment. We eventually found people from our timeline." She paused and ran her hands through her hair.

"The local Thals escorted us to a portal, where we moved on again, but even using a portal, Shifting is draining. We rattled through worlds as fast as if we were flicking through the pages of a book, but it took us weeks to get to a world not under attack. World Number Thirty-one ten. It fell eleven months later." She took a breath and stared into space, taking shallow breaths. "I've been running ever since," she said. "Ahead of endless waves of Sauroid attacks. They must have been preparing for one great all-out offensive for centuries. While we thought we had peace, we just had a lull while they readied themselves."

"What happened to Dalalla?" Cassidy said.

"She was pregnant. I was worried she and Marram might get together." She laughed, sadly. "They already had. Their baby was born eight months later. Dalalla was killed when he was a year old." She fiddled with a piece of rag. "I persuaded a family to look after him. I last saw Little Marram a year ago. He already looks like his father. I hope he's safe."

"And your parents?"

Sophia twisted and tugged the rag in her hands. "I haven't seen them since that day. I'm sure they're alive. I'd have known if they'd died." She looked at him. "I'm going to get them back, with or without you. Bel effectively died that day and so did my dreams, except from an occasional one every few weeks. They're all that's kept me going. But I'll fight on alone, if I have to, without you." She bowed her head.

He put his arms around her in a hug and felt her warmth. She started to shiver, sobs coming from deep within her, like miniature earthquakes shaking her whole body. He kissed and stroked her hair, trying to stay dispassionate.

Knowing he was lost.

***

"Cap'n needs medical attention!" Adler shouted. Adler could have been shouting for minutes or just seconds; in all the chaos, time seemed to have stopped. Adler poured water into Kaminski's eyes and wiped them clean, but Kaminski couldn't see properly and was nearly blind in one eye.

Garcia shouted nearby, though Kaminski couldn't make out what he said. Kaminski tried to see what was going on, but everything was hazy. "Jamie, what's happening?" He felt a huge sense of relief as the sergeant gripped his arm.

"It's okay, bud," Adler said. "A piece of Charles grazed your eye. Lucky it didn't take your head off. Hey Limey!" he shouted. "Where's your commander? We got casualties here!"

"Corporal Davenport's just coming sir." The Brit sounded like a nervous kid, Kaminski thought.

"Corporal? They've put a corporal in charge of you lot?" Adler shouted. "No wonder the situation's a shambles!"

"I'm Corporal Davenport, Sergeant." The Brit's voice was thin and reedy, and even with his impaired vision, Kaminski could tell he was no giant. *The Brits must have been desperate to have taken this guy,* Kaminski thought.

His men gripped Kaminski's arms. He made a mighty effort to lift his feet, but he couldn't get them working. The co-ordination wasn't there, so they dragged on the floor.

"What you clowns been doing?" Garcia snapped at Davenport. "Selling arms to the towel heads?"

"Where did the shots come from? None of our men fired," Davenport said. "This is the first sign of trouble we've seen since we've been down here." His voice turned harsh. "With respect sir, it's usually your men who shoot their allies. Blue on blue, I think you call it?"

"Easy, Corporal," Kaminski said. "No one's pointing fingers. Who saw anything?"

One of the men carrying Kaminski said, "I saw a laser dot on Charles' uniform."

"Not ours, sir." Davenport said. "We left no one outside."

"Apart from your wounded!" Garcia said.

"That'll do, Garcia!" Adler barked.

"Sorry, sir." Garcia added so softly Kaminski almost missed it, "Friendly fire, huh!"

"Corporal," Adler growled. "Keep that up, and you lose those stripes."

"Maybe we should have stationed men outside," Davenport said. "But we've been concentrating on finding the back door. Things have been quiet. Too quiet, with hindsight."

"Yeah," Adler said sourly, "ain't hindsight a wonderful thing. **Is** there a back door outta this place?"

"Haven't found it," Davenport said and added, "we're taking you to Major Cassidy. He'll explain things better."

"At last, an officer," Adler said.

"Jamie," Kaminski said quietly, but his warning was clear.

"Sorry, sir, but I think we got a right to be sore at these guys. A Major leaving a Corporal in charge?"

Someone shouted, "What was that?"

"Hold your fire!" Davenport shrieked. "Hold it!"

"Corporal," Adler's voice was so taut it chilled Kaminski's blood. "What scampered round that corner? A chimpanzee?"

"No, sir," Davenport said. "It was a young Homo Neanderthalis. Or Homo Sapiens Neanderthal." His giggle almost slid into hysteria, but when he continued, his voice was calm. "They've been sheltering in the caves. They're friendly. Major Cassidy's been talking with them. I'm sure he can explain everything," Davenport said, and Kaminski caught the anxiety in the corporal's voice and wondered what he had to be anxious about.

***

Sophia's storm of tears finally eased, and she wriggled to let Cassidy know that he should let her go. When he did, she didn't pull away completely, but instead leaned against him. She wiped her eyes with her piece of rag. "Thanks," she squeezed his arm, seemingly content to stand there.

He felt the weight of her dependence but said nothing of it, only, "If all these parallel worlds each split off from an event, why is there only one of me? Or are there infinite copies of me, talking to an infinite number of you?"

"Good question." Thinking about the answer seemed to ease her melancholy. "We don't know. One of our philosophers posited that our lives are like the threads on a rope. They can be unwound without changing the universe significantly. We're so insignificant that there's some elasticity. Whole worlds though, are different. When a world changes, things matter."

Tandala interrupted them. "Sir, there's something happening at the tunnel mouth."

Cassidy brushed the hair back from Sophia's harlequin face. "We'd better get back."

***

One by one the Neanderthal patrol had been picked off. *Surely, they won't fight to the last man,* Henry thought.

A harsh, strident voice called in Thal from the marsh to their right. From the Neanderthal's answering volley of shots, Henry guessed it had been a surrender demand. Their assailants' response was yet another burst of fire in turn, the woodpecker noises drifting across the ground.

Their assailants had prepared the ambush carefully. The firefight had been brutal, bloody and with the attackers having the advantage of surprise, one-sided. The Thals had lost men steadily. Their assailants could fire down from the surrounding knolls, even when the Thals tried to hide in the long grass.

The voice again echoed through a lull in the shooting, and the Fuhrer stood reluctantly, his hands by his head. Henry noticed his fists were still clenched and wondered at the rage and grief he must feel. One by one, the members of his troop followed his lead.

From the knolls, their enemy descended from all sides in the same manner of all soldiers emerging from cover, wary, crouched, their fingers no doubt half-squeezing their triggers.

As they came nearer, Henry drew in a sharp breath, and Esteban sketched a cross, muttering, "*Madre de Dios.*"

If the Neanderthals had been a shock, their attackers were like a walking nightmare. They were man-sized, man-shaped, and walked like men but had too many needle-like teeth to fit into a human mouth. They had skin of gray-green hide, and their eyes were inhumanly cold.

They circled around the Neanderthals and their captives, reminding Henry of sharks circling in the water. One of them saw Henry and called out in a voice that sounded like oil in a frying pan.

The Fuhrer replied in Thal, and the one who was clearly the Sauroid's leader walked over to him. The ensuing conversation didn't sound friendly.

The Fuhrer dropped something from each hand. In the split-second of panic, with everyone diving for cover or firing their weapons, Henry saw the Fuhrer's look of triumph and, wishing he had never named him that, realized the Thal had made one last, doomed gesture of defiance. The double flash blinded Henry, and a microsecond later, the blast knocked him off his feet and swatted him senseless.

***

"Good morning," Cassidy said.

"Don't know if I'd agree with you," the American officer said. He was wounded, one eye a gaping mess, the other almost covered in the same blood that smeared the rest of his face. He saluted, a little shakily. "Captain Stuart Kaminski, 504th Parachute Infantry Regiment."

Cassidy saluted back, deliberately sloppy, to show who was top dog. "Major Joshua Cassidy. 504th, eh? That's the 82nd Airborne Division?"

Kaminski blinked, surprised. "Yes...sir. You seem to know all about us."

"Except why you're in the British zone," Cassidy said.

"Sheltering from a hostile force sir," Kaminski said cagily. "Can you tell me who our attackers are?" As they fenced, the others caught the tension as each sought an advantage.

"Afraid not, Captain," Cassidy said. "I'd guess, but I could be wrong. Let's treat your wounds first." He said to Sophia, "Can you help?"

She nodded. "My men tell me two were killed and two injured." She pointed to Kaminski. "The healer says this one we can help. He may not be able to save the other."

"He's gonna die," a man wearing sergeant's chevrons interrupted. "That's the bottom line."

Another American voice asked, "Is there a back door, or do we have to fight our way through the cave mouth?"

"We've found no other exit," Davenport said. "And we've looked bloody hard."

"Captain, a word," Cassidy nudged Kaminski to one side. He pondered for a moment and made a decision. He had nothing to go on but a hunch, but his hunches had been more right more often than wrong, over the years. "You've been no more frank with us than we with you," he chuckled at the surprised look on Kaminski's face. "So, let's cut the crap. I'll tell you everything I know. You tell me what you're really doing here."

Kaminski smiled. "Looking for you, sir, if you're the guys who hiked up here a few days ago. Can Adler, my second in command, join the briefing?"

Cassidy considered it. Talking to Kaminski was a breach of security; telling his second in command compounded the breach. He blew out his cheeks. "Oh, hell," he said. "I may as well be hung for a sheep as a lamb. Davenport!" Cassidy called. "I'll bring you up to date as well." He glared at the young Hispanic corporal with Kaminski and Adler. "Give you Yanks an inch and you take a mile." He smiled to rob his words of their sting. "Who's this?"

"Corporal Garcia, sir," the newcomer saluted. "Temporary 2IC until the Captain can resume duty."

"Palace coup?" Cassidy raised an eyebrow at Kaminski.

Kaminski stared back with his good eye. "Like you say," Kaminski said, "you may as well be hung for a sheep as a lamb. Why not a whole flock?"

"Okay," Cassidy agreed. "Tandala, you're in the briefing too to keep the numbers even. Gather in twenty minutes."

"Sir!" Garcia said. "We gotta airlift out the wounded!"

"And in fighting our way out more men get wounded, right?" Garcia nodded. Cassidy continued, "We'll treat the lieutenant's wounds, and tell you what we think is going on. Clear?"

"Sir!" Garcia snapped a salute and turned to go.

Cassidy said, "Hold on," and said to Kaminski. "In our zone, under Coalition rules, as the ranking officer, I have command. Yes?"

Kaminski said, "Of course." Adler cleared his throat, and Kaminski smiled. "I think that our temporary commander feels that the question should have been directed to him."

Adler smiled, but without warmth. "As Temporary Commander, I agree, for the record. But with conditions."

"No conditions," Cassidy said, and stared Adler down. "You mounted an unauthorized incursion-" Adler, Garcia and Kaminski all began to gabble at once, and Cassidy bellowed, "BE QUIET!"

He continued. "You have mounted an incursion which, unless you can show in writing, **here and now**, is authorized I will take as illegal. So, either you are here under my jurisdiction, or it is a hostile act. Which, **gentlemen**, is it?"

The silence stretched into what seemed like an eternity. While they had been talking, the British forces had stood, with their weapons cocked. The Thals had also stood, and many of them seemed to have gained weapons from somewhere. Cassidy wasn't quite sure how the situation was going to go, but he felt, deep down inside that the Thals would back him. And he was prepared to bluff.

"Like that, is it?" Adler hissed.

"It's like that," Cassidy said grimly. "The next man who questions my orders, I will court-martial for insubordination. You know what that means?" Garcia swallowed. "Good." Cassidy dismissed the American soldier and bellowed, "Sophia!"

"Yes, sir?" she said, so humbly she had to be mocking him.

"Come with me."

***

Officer Habib was settling an argument between two youngsters when the monsoon came. The argument had already threatened to get out of hand, and Habib had no doubt it would resume as soon as his back was turned; clenched fists might give way to broken bottles, or if they possessed them, knives.

Habib had felt depressed and ashamed all day. He should have done something, he thought as he stared morosely into space. He had only Khan's word that the baby was already dead. Even if no crime was committed, then surely Khan had committed a public order offence. The simple truth was that he, Habib, had funked it. Even though letting Khan walk free had probably saved Habib from being torn apart by the mob, the fact that he had done so still left a foul taste in his mouth.

As he sent one of the youths in one direction while holding onto the other, something landed on his shoulder. He thought that one of the gulls that lived off the rubbish tips had shat on him, but no one laughed, which would have been the usual reaction to a good omen, nor was there any telltale white smear on his shoulder.

There was another thud on his left shoulder, leaving only a dark stain. Water? Another drop landed.

"It's raining!" he heard someone call.

He cried in reply, "The monsoon's here!" There was another splash, and another.

"It looks as if Khan has done the trick for us!" Amin, one of the stallholders called, with a flash of teeth.

Habib was dimly aware of a noise like a distant freight train as he reveled in the life-giving monsoon, tilting his face up into the downpour that had sneaked up on them. In months to come, he knew, when his feet were sodden from lugging sandbags for flood defenses, he would curse the rains. But just at that moment, as he wandered out of the square, into the next street, all he wanted to do was to luxuriate in rain. To strip off his uniform and spin round naked, washing away his cowardice.

"Habib!" Amitra waved to him from her balcony.

His landlady was a pretty woman, widowed while young, forced by straitened circumstances to send her young children to tend the market stalls, to take the village constable as her lodger, and to wash clothes for those elders who could no longer do their own laundry. Too shy, he'd kept his admiration for her quiet. But though they spoke only of small things he sensed she knew his feelings. In time he would ask her to marry him, which would still the wagging tongues.

He'd heard nothing said openly, but the looks from some people left no doubt in his mind. In Chittagong, they'd probably have been stoned for adultery, but the countryside was more relaxed. Still, his living in her house had scandalized some.

"Come on down, huh?" he called back, grinning. She hadn't attended the previous night's gathering – he'd looked for her, and she definitely hadn't been there- nor asked what it was about. It might as well never have happened, though he suspected she knew of it. Word spread quickly in small communities.

"No, come here! I can see something odd!" She hopped from foot to foot.

"Okay," he shook his head in amusement. *Probably a spider, or snake*. For such a brave, sensible woman, Amitra was frightened of a lot of things. He climbed the stairs, aware of a faint vibration and that rumble again, like a distant train.

On the balcony he followed Amitra's pointing finger. She said, "Birshawod has vanished. All you can see is that low cloud."

He squinted, and then gasped, "Oh merciful Allah! That's no cloud! That's a wall of water." Where water met shallows it had forced the crest up until it stood as high as the sky. He swallowed and said, "It's moving like the Chittagong Express."

"We should run!" Amitra said, but made no move when he put his arms around her.

Habib thought how comfortable she felt in his arms. He knew the truth. "There is nothing we can do. It's too big, too fast."

She gathered the children to her, shushing their cries.

The ground shook. They fled into the house, just before the balcony sheared off behind them. Habib shoved his bed into the doorway, blocking it. "I don't want to die never having kissed you." He put his arms around her and tried to shut out the fate that bore down on them, like the express from Dhaka to Chittagong. With one arm she gathered the children to her. Habib put one arm around Rena, Amitra's youngest daughter.

"Mummy, it hurts my ears!" Rena cried, and Habib squeezed her fiercely, as if to give her something else to think about.

Habib kissed Amitra again, and from the way she pressed against him, knew that she too was trying to blot everything else out.

Then the world went black, the pain grew almost unbearable, and ratcheted still higher. The last thing Habib heard was the children screaming before his eardrums punctured.

***

The Americans sat in a semi-circle around Cassidy. Adler waved a coffee cup, and Cassidy nodded. "How's your eye?" he asked.

"Fixed." Kaminski had the look of a man who'd seen a magic trick on stage and was trying to work out how it had been done. "This guy just stared at me, for maybe, ten minutes, mumbling all the time, and eventually I began to see out of it."

"Don't think it was easy," Sophia said. "Tisarias is our finest healer. Repairing the damage took all his skill, and he's had to go and rest. It'll be some time before he recovers."

Cassidy sat down cross-legged. When he had their attention he began, "This all started thirty-four thousand years ago..."

***

"I can't go any further," Phyl's teeth chattered. "I'm so tired. Let me sit and rest, Ethan. Just a few minutes."

"Come on, love," Ethan said. "You've done really well."

They'd made good time, despite the fact that they had both sustained injuries. Turner guessed they had mild concussions. He was covered with cuts and bruises. A piece of metal had embedded itself below Phyl's shoulder blade. Turner had stanched the wound and hoped there was no internal bleeding.

"We'll walk to Zhong Shan," Turner had said, bundling up as much as he could carry: medical kit, blankets, rations. "Even if they're looking for us, the Chinese are unlikely to find us. They never acknowledged our Mayday."

Their walk had been little more than a crawl. Turner helped Phyl, hearing her gasp with every step. The wind was slight, but for every mile an hour of wind speed, the temperature dropped another degree.

"Just let me sleep a little," Phyl begged.

Turner knew hypothermia stalked them; if Phyl slept, she would never awaken. "Phyl," he said. "There are penguins there. Emperors."

"Hhhmm?" she murmured, as he made her put one foot in front of the other.

It took ten minutes to reach the flock. The birds stood shoulder to shoulder in a huge clump, with stragglers on the sides. As winter strengthened her icy grip, the birds would huddle even more closely together for warmth. By mid-winter, they'd pack tightly so it would remain warm in the middle. Then the birds would revolve, each taking it in turn to stand on the fringes, and as they grew cold, others would take their place, and they'd move back toward the center.

Turner and Phyl sat down at the edge of the flock. The birds grumbled, but curiosity prevailed, as Turner had hoped, and they were soon surrounded and blissfully, incredibly, warm. "If we survive the night, we'll resume in the morning," he said.

"Mmm." Phyl nuzzled him. They slept then, and Turner dreamed of strange creatures, more lizard than man-like. They pulled Turner and Phyl from amongst the penguins, and there was warmth rather than a howling wind and bitter cold.

***

It took Cassidy an hour with clarifications from Sophia and interruptions from the Americans to tell the Thals' story.

"You're very quiet," he said to Davenport.

Davenport shrugged. "I tried out the headpiece, and watched the first two crystals while you slept. It wasn't a complete surprise." The Americans shook their heads, in disbelief, amazement- or both.

Sophia said, "Eighteen months ago, we heard rumors of a final onslaught. Even before that, we'd increased our efforts. We took MaryAnn and others and learned your language."

Cassidy had the feeling of standing on the edge of a precipice. He asked, "Do you know what Bramaragh's plans are?"

She looked at him steadily. "Nothing too colossal," she said dryly. "He only plans to dismantle the universe."

PART THREE

The Wounded Earth

CHAPTER FIFTEEN

Cassidy stared at Sophia. "What?" He laughed humorlessly. "Is this a joke?" Even he, who could stretch open-mindedness like a snake's jaws and take evolved Neanderthals in his stride, had reached the end of his credulity.

Garcia raised an eyebrow, Kaminski raised his brows, and Adler laughed an explosive, derisory bark. "Oh, man!"

Some of the troops had gathered around their officers, like moons orbiting the planets, which in turn orbited the double star of Sophia and Cassidy. *Well, it will save the trouble of briefing them,* Cassidy thought.

"When I say the universe, I mean ours. And all the others, except Bramaragh's timeline." Sophia looked at Cassidy. The other soldiers might as well not have been there. "That's what all the double moons are, two universes merging. It takes a second or two, even longer if they're truly divergent parallels. That's enough time for earthquakes, and huge tidal waves." She sighed. "That's just the 'normal' branches of our universe. There are others, some apparently so strange we can't even envisage them."

"The lightning," Tandala said. Cassidy stared at the quiet, intense man, his black skin and hair hinting at South Indian ancestry. He shrugged an explanation. "I wanted to do Physics at University, but my grades weren't good enough."

"You think this is possible?"

"I...think so," Tandala said. "For years physicists have been arguing about whether there are ten or eleven dimensions."

"They can't accept three like normal people?" Cassidy frowned. "I thought time was the fourth dimension?" Tandala opened his mouth, and to forestall a lecture Cassidy added quickly, "Ten or eleven. What's the difference?"

"To us, very little," Tandala said. "We'd never see them. One dimension is an infinitely long, but microscopically thin universe. Another is never ending sheets of lightning. Yes?" He grinned at Cassidy's 'o' of comprehension.

"So what we thought was simply bad weather might not just be normal thunderstorms?"

"You're absolutely right," Sophia said. "All these events are manifestations of Bramaragh's assault on the continuum. He wants just one universe. His."

"So who are these people who have turned up? Invaders? Refugees?" Kaminski asked.

"Both," Sophia said.

"Double talk!" Adler snapped.

Kaminski waved for silence. "Care to elaborate?" he said coolly.

"Some are refugees from the merging of worlds – which, where there are duplications, may be merging as well. *You* may even be merging as we speak. How would you know? There are also doppelgangers sufficiently unique for merging not to be possible. Some are members of Bramaragh's forces. They're the invaders. And us?" She looked at them. "We're the good guys."

"Yeah, right," Adler drawled. "You just turn up, flutter your eyelashes, and tell us what nice people you are."

"Two minutes ago," Cassidy said, "you didn't believe any of it. Look around you. Do these people look like Neanderthals? If something walks, barks, and sniffs like a dog, then it usually *is* a dog. If that part of their story's true, then why would they make the rest up?" He didn't completely believe everything, but it wasn't the first time he'd had to convince people that white was black while knowing that it wasn't. Hanging around politicians had that effect. He asked Kaminski, "If they're hostile, why would they fix your eye?"

"Okay," Kaminski agreed cautiously, clearly not entirely convinced. "What are your plans now?"

Cassidy waved the headpiece and crystals. "Your men will help mine get these back to Whitehall, while we go scouting."

Kaminski stared at Cassidy, his chiseled features creased in puzzlement, stubble made prominent by the harsh light in the cavern. "You're serious?"

Cassidy stared back and said levelly, "Captain, we're here with Neanderthals, who are supposed to have been extinct for thirty thousand years. We have volcanic eruptions and earthquakes in seismically stable areas, dinosaurs and aircraft unlike anything we've ever seen, two moons, and I wouldn't be too surprised if Elvis is around. You have a better way of finding out what's been going on?"

Kaminski said, "I guess not."

"What's next, sir?" Adler asked, looking uneasy.

"We'll split into three groups. Adler, you and Davenport get the crystals back to a British base." He added, "We need to get these people into sheltered, controlled conditions."

"Why?" Garcia asked. "They seem fine right here."

Garcia had a point, but he had ignored the politics of the situation. "So, allowing aliens to roam this powder keg of a country is acceptable?" Cassidy asked.

"What you gonna do? Put 'em in a camp?" Garcia said.

"Sabra, or Chatila?" Davenport's comparison to the infamous Beirut refugee camps in which thousands had died in 1982, left little doubt about his opinion.

Before he could say more, Cassidy interrupted, "There's a practical difficulty here. The enemy has us bottled up."

Sophia said, "I think we can help. We can use the portal we came through – it's one level below the cave entrance. We'll cross to a world where there isn't an ambush waiting for us."

"How do we know that they haven't sealed off the tunnels in the next worlds?" Cassidy asked. He did not like the possibility of emerging in mid-air, or in the middle of solid rock.

"We don't," Sophia said, "but isn't it better than staying here?"

Cassidy nodded and turned to Kaminski. "Adler can have a third of the men and Davenport as his 2IC, to take the head-piece and crystals back to base. I'll give Davenport the validation codes. Garcia will accompany me; we'll take another third of the men on reconnaissance, and leave you in charge of the rest. You'll guard the civilians." He smiled grimly. "Neither Afghans nor Sauroids, nor anyone else is going to massacre these people."

"Agreed," Kaminski said. He eyed Cassidy speculatively. "Big leap of faith, isn't it...Major? How do you know you can trust me? Especially after our little stand-off a while ago?"

Cassidy stared at him. "You ask straight questions, Captain. Let me give you a straight answer. I pride myself on being a good judge of character, and you don't seem the kind of bloke to reprise My Lai. And how many other options do I have?"

Kaminski let the silence hang, then just as it grew awkward said, "Thanks for the vote of confidence," and turned away.

Cassidy said to Sophia and Adler. "We move in ten minutes."

Sophia nodded, a ferocious grin splitting her face. "It'll be good to be doing something at last."

It was nearer twenty minutes than ten before they were ready to go. All the troops, human and Neanderthal alike, were heavily laden. The British and Americans packs rose high over their helmets, but the Thal's packs were lower and wider.

Sophia had changed into the baggy, mustard-colored coveralls worn by many Thals of both sexes. She introduced a man who was squat even for a Thal and whose left arm hung limp and withered. "This is Hethor Donektsson. He speaks English, so he'll be your interpreter, Captain Kaminski. Gavrel here," she introduced a whippet-thin young Thal, "will accompany Sergeant Adler."

Sophia briefed them on the procedure. Cassidy's group was comprised of four columns of ten marching into the tunnel leading to the portal. Immediately behind him, Adler commanded a similar number. The lights were brighter in the tunnel and threw the men into sharp relief. When they reached a certain point- to Cassidy it looked the same as the rest of the tunnel- Sophia called, "Wait!" They stopped, and, turning sideways, linked arms, the men at each end of the columns linking arms with their opposites, so everyone held onto two others, with the exception of one Thal, who stood apart. He seemed to rotate through ninety degrees, then vanished with a dull *whump!*

Sophia clapped for their attention. "Before he returns, I want to say a few words. You'll feel some odd sensations; don't be afraid, and whatever happens, don't break contact with your colleagues, or we'll be scattered, the Gods know where!"

A few minutes later, a shape appeared in the air where the Thal had left. It rotated, and expanded quickly. in moments it was man-sized, and the Thal solidified. He and Sophia exchanged a few words, and joined the chain.

"Ready?" Sophia called.

Cassidy felt the same sideways-turning sensation that he'd felt when immersed in the crystal-stories.

"Wow!" One American called, and another, "whoo-ee!" Several English voices shouted excitedly as well.

Adler's drawl echoed, "Quiet down, guys!"

"What happened?" Garcia said.

One of the English-speaking Thals answered, "See the change in light? We've Shifted to another cave identical to the last."

Cassidy wondered if they had doubles in this world.

"We must keep Shifting," Sophia called above the chatter, then implicitly answered his thought. "The enemy's camped outside. Iritka threw a rock out, and it was shot to pieces."

Iritka Shifted again and returned a few minutes later. The conversation with Sophia lasted longer before he linked arms with the end Thal, and they all Shifted.

From the muttering from the British and Americans troops, they were finding it hard to get used to Shifting. At least Cassidy had the benefit of having experienced the sensations in the crystals, which had proven astonishingly realistic.

"Iritka tells me this passage is blocked too," Sophia called. "He's going on."

They repeated the process six or seven times, until Cassidy lost count. Each time they Shifted it was to another cave, but the caves were all slightly different; in one the lights didn't work. In another there were signs of battle.

Another Thal took over. The replacement was also visibly tiring when he finally re-appeared and chattered excitedly with Sophia. Several other Thals called out.

Cassidy didn't need to speak Thal to guess the scout had found an unblocked, unguarded cave. "Let's go!" Sophia shouted.

They Shifted into a dark corridor. Cassidy shone a torch around. There were no lights on the walls, no sign of occupation. The squads separated, and they marched up the corridor, up the levels, until they reached the tunnel. The advance guards checked the exit before Cassidy led the others outside.

They looked out over hills and valleys even more ragged and torn than those they'd left, whole mountains split in half, rock slides everywhere, and in the distance, a smoking volcano. Cassidy wondered if men even lived on this Earth. The caves here opened out onto a rock ledge that they could use as a platform. The path down was also easier.

The sun was low in the sky. Cassidy guessed it was evening. He'd lost all track of how long they'd been Shifting. Checking his watch, he decided that six-thirty in the evening was about right. "The air smells like our Earth," he said.

"Things would need to be radically different for the air to be much altered." Sophia looked thoughtful and said after a few moments' silence, "The air smells a touch sulphurous, which could be due to volcanic activity. But it's breathable."

Cassidy asked Tandala, "What are you looking at?"

"The moon," Tandala said. "Moons, rather. Look!"

There were five, four, then three moons, touching, sliding into each other, until one overlaid another, as if badly piled coins had been tidied up. Then there was only one moon. Ragged edges smoothed, and the moon looked like that of their earth. Except, Cassidy decided, it no longer looked like a face.

"How does that happen?" Tandala breathed. His teak-colored features were lit up as if by an inner light, as though he were Paul on the Road to Damascus.

Sophia spoke, "We think that these are alternates which are not quite matched at first." Seeing their puzzled frowns, she explained, "Think of an infinite number of worlds. On one you ate lunch today, on a second, you didn't. As the Multiplicium and beyond merge, some of the worlds will be so alike that we won't notice it happening. The worlds we see are the ones so divergent that lunch wasn't invented, or they ate wood. Worlds where Sauroids or even stranger races evolved."

Sophia beckoned Davenport to them. She tapped a Thal on the shoulder. "Gavrel here is going to guide you to the next weak spot, to take you back to your world." The youth swung round and grimaced at them.

"Let's hope," Cassidy said, "that you don't pop up in the equivalent of Iran or somewhere equally unfriendly."

Davenport nodded to Gavrel, who bowed and said in accented English, "I happy to working with you."

Cassidy nudged Davenport away and said quietly, "Obey Adler's orders, as long as they don't conflict with getting the crystals back to base." He added, "Adler doesn't look too happy."

"I heard him say that the Thals may be the Devil's agents," Davenport replied. "He has a simple view of the world."

"Oh, joy," Cassidy muttered. Then repeated, "You're to take whatever action necessary to follow my instructions."

"You mean, I disobey his orders?" Davenport looked shocked.

In some ways that made Cassidy a little happier. "I mean if he does anything outside of my orders, you shoot him, and take over!"

"Seems a little harsh, sir," Davenport said.

Cassidy locked eyes with Davenport. "You work for me. Got it?"

"Sir," Davenport mumbled, and saluted.

"Until then, you obey him as if he were me." Taking a pen, Cassidy scribbled on a scrap of paper. "Learn these then destroy them. They're validation codes, and the names of who you report to, including the substitutes. Don't let any flunkey get in your way. If you really can't reach a British base, go to the Yanks." He slapped the worried-looking Davenport on the shoulder. "I've got total faith in you." He had little choice. *The kid's got the brains; it's whether he has the balls,* he thought. "Good luck." He saluted Adler, who'd joined them.

"You too, sir," Adler said, returning the salute smartly.

"Take care of the boys."

"They'll be okay," Adler said. "We'll see you back at base."

"Josh?" Sophia called from behind him, as he watched Adler lead the line of forty British and American soldiers, and Thals sliding down the trail. He turned to her, as she said, "We should move, as well. Do we take a different route?"

"Why not keep Shifting in the caves?"

Sophia shook her head as Garcia drifted over to join them. "The caves are safer, but it would be easy to get bottled up. We've been lucky so far – we haven't emerged into solid rock – but there's no guarantee that our luck will hold."

"Sounds sensible to me, sir," Garcia said.

Josh squinted into the sun. "You think we'd do better heading the other way?"

She nodded. "Finding the next portal won't be easy. Anything to improve our chances."

"Okay," Cassidy agreed. "Let's go!" he called.

They trudged down the trail, away from the other group.

***

Long after Cassidy and Adler had marched their teams out of the cavern, Kaminski stood lost in thought. Around him, the Thals talked in murmurs, as if their nomadic existence had leached all bravado from them.

The smell of cooking and smoke from their fires (a corner of his mind wondered how they'd avoided setting off the smoke alarms) was everywhere, along with the smell of too many bodies in a confined space. The odor was slightly off-key. *We probably smell strange to them,* he thought.

He fiddled with his helmet strap and scrubbed the corn-colored stubble atop his head. He fiddled with his pack, which lay propped to one side with the contents spread in piles; food, ammunition, bedding, and other necessities. He kicked a pebble and then paced around, before sitting down again. He fidgeted.

A woman's soft voice pierced the gloom. "I used to have an old sitting hen like you. Feeling left out?" Kaminski looked up.

A woman carrying a sleeping baby in a papoose studied him. She was obese. But she was human, and spoke with an American accent.

He shouldn't have thought of home. For a moment he ached to see Barbara and the children again and hold them in his arms. Such thoughts had no place here and now, so he stuffed them away in the mental drawer that all soldiers had.

He'd almost snapped an answer, but he forced himself to relax and smile. "A little," he said. "I've never liked sitting around." He stood up. "I suppose we could do something useful."

"Uh huh?" MaryAnn's grunt was question, not argument.

"Walk with me?" he asked. She was a civilian, but she had a chin and forehead and stood upright. That she was American was a bonus.

"Okay."

"I can't take to them as easy as Cassidy does," he nodded at a Thal family who sat together; the mother braiding her daughter's hair, her son playing with ten-sided dice.

"Well, don't expect no sympathy from me," MaryAnn showed him the baby. "His daddy's one of 'them.'"

"That's why I thought you could show me around." He was pleased to see the look of surprise cross her face. "You've had time to get used to them. I haven't." MaryAnn nodded slowly. "You must've been terrified when you first met one," he said.

"To be honest," MaryAnn's smile lit up her face. "I was a little, uh, distracted at the time, and it was a while before I gave it too much thought."

As they walked, she told him of her abduction. Her terror, then her slow-coming trust in Sophia and the other Thals. "Took me a little whiles," she said, "apart from Aulth. Him I trusted from the very start. In some ways he was like me. A bit slow, not good with people." When she finished, they walked through the tunnels in companionable silence.

Kaminski muttered something.

"What's up?" MaryAnn asked.

"Just thinking out loud," Kaminski said. He added, "Can we do a head count in each cavern?"

"Sure. Why?"

Kaminski pointed to a family huddled beneath a fire extinguisher on the wall. The woman, struggling to stop her baby's screams, wiped a hand across her own forehead, and slumped with exhaustion, hunger, or both.

"Look at them," he said. "Everywhere we've walked there've been people. I bet you no one knows how many there are." He continued. "They're eating the food they've brought with them, but what happens when it runs out? How long will the stores last?"

"Good questions, I guess." MaryAnn let out a gusty sigh.

"We need to list how much food we have, as well. If we're going to be kept here some time, we may have to ration it."

"Yuh know," MaryAnn grinned, "You ain't as stupid as I look. Hey, Hethor!" She waved at the Thal with the withered arm, who'd trailed them at a discreet distance.

Kaminski hadn't noticed him. "Getting sloppy," he muttered.

"What's that?" MaryAnn said.

"Nothing," he said and waited while MaryAnn briefed the Thal on the taking count of their food supplies and the people.

"It will be done," Hethor's voice was harsh, made stranger by his accent, which was much stronger than Sophia's.

"Sophia speaks good English," Kaminski commented.

"Don't she? She's bright that girl, and brave."

They walked in silence through a tunnel into the next cavern, which was more crowded. "These people have been running and running, until there ain't nothing left in them," MaryAnn said.

"What do the enemy do with the ones they take? Why do they take those? Why not other ones?"

"I don't know, I don't know, and I don't know," MaryAnn said. "The way they shoot most Thals as soon as look at 'em, I can't believe the ones they take are due for anything pleasant."

Kaminski sighed. "And now they're here." He looked at his watch. "I wonder if they've got out yet," he said, referring to Adler and Cassidy.

"Wish you was with them?"

"Yes," he admitted. "No. If anyone can get them out of there, it's Jamie Adler."

"You rate him?"

Kaminski nodded. "My first mission, he saved my life. He's a couple of years older than me, had just been made Corporal. I was a wet-behind-the-ears know-it-all Lieutenant. We were patrolling the so-called safe havens in Bosnia, when we were ambushed in Zagordze market. I froze. If he hadn't taken command for those few seconds, we'd have been massacred. I took a bullet to the shoulder. It knocked me to the ground and hurt like hell but brought me to my senses."

"He took over?"

"He called in air support and covered for me while they tended to me. He got us out alive. He wouldn't put it in the report. Said anyone was entitled to freeze on their first trip."

"Sounds like a good guy," MaryAnn agreed.

"He's my son's godfather," he replied. "I'm his youngest's in return. He's one of the most decent men I know. Brave, too."

Kaminski paused, and then continued, "We applied to the 504th at the same time. The 82nd Division, including the 504th, has so much history; Carenton; Arnhem; Bastogne. When I read some of the things they went through, so we'd be free... Those guys who fought in World War II," he searched for the right words, "it was easier, in some ways. They knew who the enemy was. Nowadays, al-Qaeda, Shining Path, Knights Templar, they don't wear uniforms. Half the time, they look like our next door neighbors." He shook his head. "Hell, half the time they are our next door neighbors."

"I know what you mean," MaryAnn said. Raul stirred, and gurgled. "Even without Raul, I'd still be with them. With the

Thals, it's clear-cut. They've been fighting for their lives for so long; they give it no more thought than breathing. But when you're fighting 'gainst the odds, fighting for your life, and your families' lives; that makes it right. Don't it?"

Kaminski smiled. "You said it much better than me." He exhaled. "Whatever Jamie's reservations, I'd give these guys the benefit of the doubt."

"That what this is?" MaryAnn said, as they entered another cavern. "Big poster campaign for the man, he might think you're the devil's own, but really he's an okay guy?"

"Give him a break," Kaminski laughed, "he's just had a bit of a shock. It's not every day you meet people who're extinct Suddenly Kaminski stiffened. "I heard gunshots," he muttered, and ran to the entrance to the tunnels.

***

Adler asked Davenport, "You sure you know what you're doing?"

"Well, sir," Davenport made himself sound cheerful, "if they wanted to harm us, they could have picked us off as we entered the caves."

"I guess so." Adler sighed. "It looks even more torn up than the Afghanistan I know. Are those elephants down there? They are!" He stopped dead, and the Thal behind almost slammed into him, but managed to stop in time.

"I guess things evolved differently round here," Davenport said. "Assuming we're still in Afghanistan, and not on the local African plains. I thought that when we Shifted we would end up at the same physical location as we started from. But there's no reason why that has to be the case."

There must have been fifty elephants marching in line, their trunks sweeping over the ground for foliage and other tidbits. They passed giant palms, bigger than anything Davenport had ever seen; looking closer, he realized they were Bromeliads, the huge ferns that had survived for millions of years. He wondered what other quirks this world had. It was a shame they wouldn't have time to find out.

"Sir!" Stetler called from the back. "There's a lot of volcanic activity that way." He pointed to their right, slightly ahead of them. From a small hillock, lava leaked from the ground in oozing, ropy coils. Every plant it touched sizzled and burst into flames. A plume of smoke and steam rose lazily into the air. "Should we make a detour?" Stetler asked.

Davenport looked at Adler, who nodded. Miming, they passed the message to the Thals, and the double line changed tack.

Davenport felt the ground shudder beneath his boots; it only lasted for a second but it was enough to make his stomach churn. There was something horribly wrong when supposedly solid ground moved so much. Another tremor, then another, and a hundred yards in front of them, a great yawning fissure opened. Streams of lava bubbled out of the crack. "Can we get round?" Davenport asked.

"We'll have to," Adler said grimly. "But not easily. Goes for at least four hundred yards." There was another tremor, and a cry from the men. Behind them was another fissure, longer and wider than the first, ending just short of the volcanic hill.

"Drat! We're cut off!" Adler said.

"We should go that way," Davenport said, "cut between the pimple," he nodded at the hill, "and the end of the fissure ahead."

Adler beckoned Gavrel forward. "Can we get to another world, the same way we got out of the caves?"

Gavrel shook his head. "Unless there's weakness between the worlds, probably only one or two of us can, and, I have no idea of where we'd end up..."

"Then let's make it three abreast," Adler snapped. "In case any more fissures open. At the double!"

Shouts in Thal echoed his orders, and the lines bunched. They were fit and, despite their heavily laden backpacks, moved quickly. The day was drawing to a close, and the wind had only a puppy's nip in it that should have cooled them. But Davenport had seen how fast the fissures had opened, and he doubted that shortening the line would save them if the ground opened nearby.

He knew he was blessed with too much imagination. It wasn't that he was a coward. When he could switch his brain off, he was as brave as anyone. But he kept thinking about falling into that crimson, coruscating lava. It'd be over before he felt anything, he told himself. Sweat trickled and pooled round his torso, filling the hollows.

He had worked in a bakery the previous summer. Standing parallel with the fissure's end fifty yards away was like standing by one of the industrial ovens. With the heat that prickled over his skin, each breath was harder to find. The air seared his throat with each breath. He accidentally burned his hand on a metal clip that had been superheated by the hot air.

To his right Gavrel panted in short, jerky breaths. Despite being in the line furthest from the fissure, his tongue hung halfway out of his mouth like a dog's. He flashed Davenport a grimace, either in sympathy for Davenport, or for himself.

To his left, Adler was the closest to the crack, but he seemed less bothered than anyone. He marched as if he were on a routine exercise, rather than racing for his life. "Not far now," he called, panting slightly. "You're doing well. Keep your head and we'll be fine." Davenport wondered if his anxiety had been so obvious. "Keep them going another four hundred yards, maybe further." Adler slowed and waved the troops past, patting each of them on the shoulder as they passed, human and Thal.

Davenport counted as a distraction. At six miles per hour, to cover four hundred yards, they needed to march for two to three minutes. *One thousand and one, two thousand and two.* It was easy when you narrowed it down to numbers how quickly time passed. As his count reached one hundred, his lungs felt as if lava from the crack had been poured down them. He glanced over his shoulder. Some of the Thals were struggling. A couple looked as though they were about to drop in their tracks. "Help those men!" he called, his voice little more than a croak. He almost stumbled, but managed to keep his feet as Gavrel shot out an arm to steady him. "Thanks," he gasped.

A half-mile to their right, another fissure opened. Davenport had lost count, so he started again. Erring on the side of caution, he counted past two minutes. His legs felt as if they'd turned to jelly, and he couldn't pull any more air into his lungs. He had a splitting headache, and his fatigue finally outran his terror. "Halt!" he gasped, bending double.

"Well done, men!" Adler was panting more now, but he still managed to stay upright, despite being several years older than Davenport. "Looks like we're far enough from that crack."

Swaying on his feet, Davenport braced his hands on his knees and hauled great, rasping lungfuls of air in. "I thought..." He couldn't finish the sentence.

"Get your breath back," Adler said.

"I thought..." Davenport nodded at the other chasm, "We should get further away from it." Around them men stood or sat; a few lay down, getting their wind back.

"Listen," Adler stood, head cocked.

"Can't..." Davenport found it easier, but breathing and talking were still hard, "...hear...anything."

"Exactly."

"The rumbling's stopped," another American said, white teeth grinning joyfully in a dark face.

As Davenport stared the earth yawned one last time. With a huge, splintering groan another chasm opened, running at right angles from the fissure they'd just passed, now a good half-mile behind, hurtling at them as fast as an express train. The yawning jaws stopped barely five yards short of the nearest man, who'd leapt back in panic.

"Let's get out of here," Adler said wearily.

***

Cassidy's men made good time. They skirted the crevasses that littered the landscape, a tortured ruin of bubbling lava pools, steaming springs and holes torn like open wounds in the earth, following the instincts of Taran, their portal-finder.

Though it shook beneath their feet with the chronic intensity of a malaria victim, the land was flat, unlike anything Cassidy had seen since landing at Kabul airport.

They'd seen elephants in the distance and, tearing across the flat scrubland, what Cassidy guessed were antelopes of some kind, though he was no zoologist.

After a couple of hours, the mountains to the west shielded the setting sun. Cassidy was considering stopping for the night, when Taran called out.

They often called him Sniffer, rather than the more polite "Finder." It was a good name for him, Cassidy thought. Taran was a weaselly little wiry man. He said little to the other Thals, and when he did, his high-pitched voice grated on the ear.

"He can feel it close by," Sophia interpreted.

Unlike most of the other Thals, Taran's beard was full, covering any facial tattoos he had. "He says he doesn't need them," Sophia had explained earlier. "He walks barefoot," she added, "to better feel the vibrations around a portal."

The man gave off an acrid, pungent body odor that had made Cassidy literally step back when the little Thal stood close to him. "Gland problem," Sophia had said, with a slight smile.

Few of the others seemed to more than tolerate him. Cassidy wondered how much of that was due to his body odor, and how much was due to his own introversion. Taran loped away swiftly with the men strung out behind him. "There's a ravine just there," one of the Americans said.

As suddenly as if someone had flicked a switch, Cassidy felt an agonizing pain behind his right eye, worse than any migraine he'd ever had. He doubled over.

"You okay?" Garcia asked.

"Yeah," Cassidy gasped, rubbing his right eye. Sophia called to the Thals ahead, and they paused. "Don't worry. Just a twinge." He straightened up. The pain was fading by the second;

it was now no more than a throb, then a dull ache. In a few minutes it would be completely gone. "Let's find this portal," he shouted.

They resumed their trek, the ground still trembling beneath their feet. About five minutes later, Taran slid through the jaws of a ravine.

Cassidy couldn't see properly in the thickening gloom, so he pulled his night-goggles down off the lip of his helmet. His squad sprang into sharp relief.

From ahead came a deep groan, like someone opening a colossal door whose hinges have never been oiled. The ground quivered again, and Cassidy heard a sharp, splintering crack, followed by a deep-throated roar ahead of them.

Cassidy saw one side of the ravine shear away. Before he could move out of the way, a semi-liquid wall of shale hurtled down onto his men, so quickly he could do nothing but watch as his squad was engulfed, their heat-signatures blotted out by the background white of the land.

"Jesus – Fucking – Christ," one of the soldiers said.

"Amen," said another.

Cassidy shook his head to clear it. "Sound off! We need a head count!"

Ten men were missing; two Americans, three English, five Thals. "Time to start digging!" he ordered.

"We need Taran, or we're stuck," Sophia said as she scrabbled at the rock pile.

He felt a surge of relief that she hadn't been caught in the slide. She sounded close to tears, and he wanted to put his arms round her and protect her, but there was no time." We need them all," he said. "Get some lights on." Immediately, a dozen torches and lamps shone against the pile of rocks. Those with shovels dug frenziedly, while others moved rocks with their bare hands. For a long time, Cassidy thought they would find no one. It seemed as though they'd been digging for hours, but a glance at his watch showed that it was only a few minutes. He wiped sweat from his forehead as it trickled into his eyes. His hands were torn and bleeding, but he'd blocked out the pain.

The men's breath steamed where they stood in the light. One of the Thals yelled, and someone called, "We got one!"

Cassidy watched them scrabbling at the rocks. They dug round the man who'd yelled, jostling one another, and he shouted, "Some of you men keep digging further over! We need teams spread across, rather than crowding one spot!"

Garcia nodded, and said, "This is the problem with having them all mixed in. We haven't trained together, so we don't know how to work together."

The diggers cleared an arm, then a head and then a torso. Minutes later, they'd pulled the gasping Thal clear. "Let's get the next one!" Cassidy called in answer to another shout. Almost before he'd finished the sentence, another man yelled elsewhere.

As Cassidy passed Garcia, the corporal said, "You're pretty keen to get these hombres out. How come you weren't so concerned for the guys in your own party that you left behind to die?"

Cassidy stopped. His reasonable tone belied his inner fury. "We know what the situation is now. We didn't then. Then the vital thing was speed; now we need men in numbers. The circumstances changed. If you make officer," he said as he turned away, "you'll find that you have to adapt."

They worked faster as the men established a routine, and the rescuers quickly cleared the victims. They finally pulled the last body clear. "Four dead," Garcia said. "One Brit, one American, two Thals. Six survivors."

"Let's cover the bodies," Cassidy said. "Keep the animals from picking the bones." His eyes felt gritty, and his arms and legs were so heavy, his clothes could have been lined with lead.

The sky to the east was smudged faintly with light when they finished. Too tired to talk, the men slept where they dropped. Two Thals stood guard.

"Shouldn't we Shift first, then sleep?" Sophia asked. "There might be other rock falls."

"There might," Cassidy said. "But it's quiet here, and we could Shift into a combat zone. The men need sleep now."

He climbed into his sleeping bag, and, drifting off, felt Sophia squeeze in, pressing against his back. "Must keep warm," she murmured.

"Mmm," he replied, too tired to argue.

The next morning, they ate a swift breakfast before they set off again to the portal. Several of the men shot Cassidy slyly amused glances.

Garcia pointed to the landslide, "You realize, if you hadn't got that pain in your eye and stopped, we'd all have been under it?"

"It did occur to me," Cassidy said. "Lucky escape, huh?"

"Weren't it just?" Garcia agreed, as they reached the portal. They linked arms and Shifted.

CHAPTER SIXTEEN

Heading toward the sound of gunfire, Kaminski rounded the corner and almost collided with one of his men. The mishmash of Thal, American and British troops had gathered in the outer cave. The mouth of the tunnel ahead was a faint disc of light. Sentries lay flat, peering over their barrels, waiting.

Several men were wounded, and their shouts and screams bounced off the cavern walls. Dust and ammunition hung heavy in the air, and Kaminski struggled not to sneeze.

A British soldier said hoarsely, "They started lobbing in shells at the mouth of the tunnel, but the trajectory's flatter and lower than any shell should be, sir. It's like they're firing horizontally, but unless the bastards are hovering in mid-air, they can't be. If they had choppers, we'd a heard 'em." He moved his arm and whimpered, a grimace racking his stubbled features. "We fell back. They ain't sent anyone in yet, but our guys will be waiting when they do."

"They have gun-platforms," MaryAnn panted from behind them. She'd followed Kaminski and caught up in time to hear the conversation. "They're almost silent."

Standard procedure, Kaminski thought. *Blast the shit out of your target, before launching the assault. But surely they don't think they can get through that bottleneck? Or maybe that isn't the target at all?* "MaryAnn, Adler and Cassidy's squads, they left through something called a portal, right?"

"Uh-huh," she agreed.

"Can they enter through it, as well?"

"Yeah, of course," she squinted; then her eyes widened. "Think the Sauroids will attack us that way?"

"It's what I'd do," he shook his head, disgusted with himself, and the others. He should've thought of that. "Kalinis, you and six others, come with me!" Kaminski tapped a Thal on the shoulder, beckoning him to follow.

MaryAnn said something, and the Thal overtook Kaminski and led him through tunnels filled with increasingly agitated on-lookers. Even those who hadn't heard the shooting knew something was up; word of the attack was filtering down. Kaminski was just starting to feel short of breath when they rounded a corner, and he heard a chuckling noise.

The Thal grunted, stopped in his tracks, and, toppling back into Kaminski's arms, unwittingly saved the American's life. Kaminski felt the impact of more slugs thudding into the Thal. The force was almost strong enough to knock him over. Staggering back around the corner, he shouted, "Ambush!"

He dropped the Thal and rolled him over, but it was clear the man was dead. Before falling back, he had seen enough to confirm his worst fears. A dozen Sauroids and a half-dozen rogue Thals were in the corridor, most carrying the equivalent of his men's semi-automatics, but four had bazooka-like weapons with barrels wide enough for his arm to fit through. In a last glance before falling back, Kaminski saw more Sauroids appear as if they'd just stepped round a corner, except the corridor was dead straight.

His men dropped to the ground, and two crawled snake-like on their bellies round the corner in the sudden silence. "Stop!" Kaminski hissed. "Are there any more coming through?"

"No, sir," one man whispered back. Then he said, "Four more just appeared carrying things. One of them's gone again."

"That'll be the one who opens the Portal." Hethor had appeared beside Kaminski.

"Wondered where you'd got to," Kaminski replied. "If we take him out, can we stop them coming through?"

"Until they find another Opener." Hethor's voice was bleak. "We don't know which alternate they're from. If they're from their prime, they'll have another one ready before you can say Sauroid."

"Cheer me up, why don't you?" Kaminski said. "We gotta try. How do we identify this Opener?"

"Let me." Hethor snake-walked on his stomach, joining the two scouts. He murmured, and Kaminski heard a snick of safety-catches being released. Hethor called so quietly Kaminski had to lean forward to hear. "He'll reappear in a moment."

Kaminski beckoned Kalinis, and hissed, "Get as many men around the far side as possible." He knew it would be next to impossible to pen the Sauroids in this labyrinth, but they had to try.

A single shot rang out, and he heard a harsh cry, cut off in a microsecond. Someone shouted, "Gotcha!"

The world went mad. The wall above the men's heads exploded and showered them with debris. There was a second blast. *That's a bazooka,* Kaminski thought. The clatter and chuckle of small-arms fire was now continuous. Men and Sauroids screamed and shouted. Kaminski's men switched to automatics and fired streams of bullets that glowed in the dark like jet-propelled bees.

A Thal stood by the edge of the tunnel holding a grenade. He pulled the pin out and, visibly counting, flung the grenade around the corner. Seconds later the dull crump was followed by clouds of debris and bits of arms and legs from enemy soldiers. A few seconds later, the Thal threw another. He kept going until he ran out of grenades. A Briton with a fresh supply took over.

One of the marksmen flung up his arms at an impossible angle and rolled over. "Next!" Kaminski waved a Thal forward, and the soldier snake-crawled like the others to join Hethor and the surviving sharpshooter.

"Hethor!" Kaminski beckoned the Thal.

Hethor crawled backwards. He said, "I've told your man to aim at the portal, and fire at any movement. I hope they don't guess our tactics and put troops between us and the portal."

"Are there any more portals in the caverns?" Kaminski had to shout. The fighting had become even more intense.

Hethor shook his head. "We never found any."

"So if we hold this," Kaminski mused, "we're safe. Can we close this portal down permanently?"

Hethor shook his head again. There was another loud blast, and a piece of wall exploded, showering them with debris. The marksmen fell silent. Before Kaminski could replace them, they'd shaken themselves free of the rubble and resumed firing. When one exhausted his ammo, he retreated while another wriggled forward to replace him.

Kaminski and Hethor backed far enough down the corridor to be able to speak, although Kaminski's ears still rang. "We'll station guards here," Kaminski wiped grit off his face and felt dampness on his hand. He stared at it and saw blood. "We'll see if we can outflank them and blast anything that appears in the other end of that tunnel."

"Your idea sounds good," Hethor agreed cautiously. "Whether it will be, I don't know."

"Yeah," Kaminski said sourly, "I figured it sounded easier than it would be." An idea came to him. "If we used this portal, could we go somewhere else rather than where these things have come from?"

Hethor said cautiously, "I think you could go elsewhere. You'd need an Opener, and they would need an idea of your destination, but there's more than one exit from most portals."

"Good!" Kaminski said. He tapped a British soldier on the shoulder and shouted, "I'm getting reinforcements down here.

You okay to take over?" The Brit nodded, and Kaminski said, "Good man. If the bastard's heads pop up, blow them to hell!"

***

"This looks more like our reality," Davenport said.

"Oh?" Adler grunted. "I can't see the difference."

Davenport was convinced the land was familiar, that it was the same scrubby mass of rocks and desiccated shrubs that they had marched through days before from opposite directions.

They'd crossed through two portals since their narrow escape from the fissure. They'd marched hard, making good progress, in what Davenport hoped was toward the caves. From there they'd head to the British sector.

"I recognize that mountain up there," Davenport said. "The one that looks like a lion's head. See it?"

"Yeah," Adler said, and was silent. He raised his hand, and the men stopped. Ahead of them the clatter of machine guns echoed. He summoned one of his men. "We'll take a look." He turned to Davenport, "Take over."

Before Davenport could stammer a protest, Adler and the other man scuttled up the scree to the ridge separating the valleys and then froze.

Davenport watched them, scouring his surroundings at the same time, the hairs on the back of his neck crawling.

Adler and the scout returned quickly. "Looks like they're attacking the cave we left. That's a mighty big coincidence."

Davenport said, "Must be Kaminski, and the others."

"The attackers are those lizard-looking critters," Adler shook his head, in dismay or disbelief, or both.

"Sauroids," Davenport corrected Adler without thinking, and winced at the glare he got for his pedantry. "Sorry." he added, "Can we attack them from behind?"

"No," Adler said. "We can't be sure it's Kaminski and the others inside the tunnel." He looked sour. "I hate doing it, but our priorities are clear. Our orders are to get these crystals back to Base. So that's what we're gonna do." Looking up at the path, he beckoned Gavrel and told them both, "If we take the right fork at the top of the ridge, we end up back at the tunnel. If we take the left we may just work our way round."

Gavrel passed the instructions to the other Thals. Some looked unhappy. It was obvious they wanted to help defend the caves, but they obeyed orders. The chuckling of the Sauroid's guns and the roar of the heavier weapons obviated the need for absolute silence, but they still tried to move quietly, climbing the path in single file and turning as they passed the ridge.

Davenport took over at point, shepherding the men at the fork and sneaking quick looks at the fight raging round the cliff. A machine like a flying bedstead hovered ten meters from and just above the tunnel mouth.

On the platform, two Sauroid gunners fired their heavy cannons alternately, firing a shot almost every other second into the cave, the blasts a deep, rhythmic thump.

Several minutes later, the firing paused, and a squad of Sauroid troops entered the tunnel, to be met by the clatter of the defender' machine guns. After a barely perceptible pause, the gunners on the platform poured more shells into the tunnel. The Sauroid's tactics made no sense, Davenport thought. They were losing troops as if their lives meant nothing

The last of their men were climbing the slope, and one stopped beside him to say, "I'll take up point, sir."

Davenport nodded his thanks and started down the other side. He reached a bend that would take him out of sight; the last man was still standing point at the fork. Suddenly he threw up his arms in a wave, spun untidily and fell.

"Shit!" Davenport lumbered to the body and felt for a pulse; the man was dead. He grabbed the man's ammo clips and tried to catch up with his group, who were lumbering up the path, the weight of their packs slowing their pace to a crawl.

Several minutes passed, during which Davenport constantly expected the hammer blow of a bullet between his shoulder blades at any moment. The squad used the precious time to get as far as possible from the attackers. Davenport was much fitter than when he'd joined the Territorials, but it was still grueling carrying such a heavy pack so quickly at this altitude. His lungs soon felt as if they were on fire. When he could go no further, he dived behind a rock that thrust half-out onto the path and shucked off the pack. Checking his gun, he gasped for breath.

The others lurked on either side of the path behind similar outcrops. An American whispered, "Where are they?"

"They're, coming," Davenport panted. Gradually he felt less light-headed. He munched a chocolate bar, shoving the wrapper into his pocket.

Seconds, then minutes, ticked by. The troops at the back ran past their colleagues, who covered them, before taking cover farther on. The leapfrogging continued until it was Davenport's turn. Adjusting his pack, he ran beside the American, while the others covered him. They rolled for cover, their packs taking the impact of the landing. Adler dived behind the rock next to Davenport's.

"Movement!" the American trooper hissed.

"Hold fire," Adler said. "Let's see how many there are."

The Sauroids ran from rock to rock, checking each one, oblivious to the danger. By the time six of them had rounded the corner, the leader was twenty meters down the path. It would only be a matter of time before it found them.

Davenport looked at Adler, who shouted, "Fire!"

The Sauroid leader staggered, jerked and writhed under the impact of the bullets, as if shaken in the jaws of an unseen beast; blood spurted from a multitude of wounds.

While Davenport and others shot the leader, his colleagues fired on the Sauroids behind him, resulting in three dead Sauroids and two more crawling for cover. One body jerked and lay still as bullets slammed into it. Puffs of dirt flew up around the other Sauroid, but it reached cover and returned fire from behind a rock. Flakes flew from the boulder behind Davenport and Adler.

"Staggered withdrawal!" Adler shouted. "Cover the four men nearest the enemy!" That included Adler himself. The others laid down covering fire, and they scuttled to safety. Then it was Davenport's turn. He, an American soldier and the two closest Thals scuttled for cover.

For the third time, the Sauroids waited out the covering fire and unleashed a volley of shots. One of the Thals screamed and fell, clutching his leg. The Sauroids' response was withering, but, firing from a second position, the wounded Sauroid joined the firefight. More Sauroids appeared; many fell to the gunfire from the Thals and Sapiens.

"Some of our men have rounded the next bend!" Adler called. "If we keep covering them, we can buy them time!"

Davenport ducked as something whizzed by, "And they may think that we're the defenders, escaped from the caves, so they may think that we're the only ones to escape."

"You may be right," Adler conceded.

"I – oh, shit," Davenport groaned.

The gun platform hovered on the lip of the hill.

***

Whenever they'd stopped in the last two days, Cassidy had tried to teach some basic English commands to the Thals and to learn some Thal in return. It was starting to pay off; while still imperfect, communication between them was slowly improving.

It was a risk, for any noise could reveal their position to an enemy lurking in ambush. But it was less of a risk than trying to fight alongside allies they could barely understand.

It was yet another frustrating aspect to a mission that was almost unworkable, had he stopped to think about it. Cassidy was used to dealing with an enemy who, if his motives and thoughts were unclear, was at least physically familiar to him. Numbers, dispositions, what they looked like, all this was usually known before he started a mission. Things might immediately descend into chaos, but at least they were clear, in theory, at the start. Not this time. The enemy was nebulous, numbers unknown, motives hazy; the only sure thing was that they were hostile.

Cassidy's men stood in a temperate savannah surrounded by open spaces, so they could see if the enemy approached, but still with enough cover to hide from Sauroid patrols. The grasses swayed to the rhythm of a gentle northerly, which blew down from distant towering mountains that stabbed the white clouds. Were it not for them and the constant tremors, Cassidy could have thought they were in an English meadow.

Sophia raised her eyebrows in an unspoken question, but didn't break the tense silence that now lay between them. She clearly hadn't completely forgiven him. His face burned at the memory of their conversation earlier that day. *"I think that we should put some physical and emotional distance between us," he'd said.*

"What does that mean, exactly?" She'd said in a low voice, and he saw from the look in her eyes that she knew exactly what he meant, so he ignored the question.

"I'm not happy at the looks, the sniggers, and the double entendres that I'm getting from the men."

"What, are the boys teasing 'oo?" She asked in a fake maternal voice, as if talking to a toddler. "Poor 'ittle baby." And with that, she'd stalked away and not spoken to him for hours. When she had, the frost in her voice could have chilled a drink.

He pressed the heel of his hand against his forehead.

"So what's wrong?"

He said, "Nothing I can put my finger on." It was an excuse, but at least they were talking now, however stilted the conversation. So to stretch it out, he added, "I feel tired, achy and just generally blah."

"You're overtired. We don't normally Shift so often."

Cassidy could tell that many of his men felt the same as he did. He was quietly impressed at his men's commitment. Though he'd primarily worked on Intel missions rather than in the field, he was still fairly experienced. Most of the soldiers he'd worked with had been tough and dedicated, but they were feeble compared to the quiet determination of the Thals.

"We'll stop here," Cassidy said. It was heaven compared to their previous stop, where they'd had to push through a tropical rainforest under sideways drifting sheets of rain that plastered their fatigues to their skin. Carrying the backpacks was hard enough without the rubbing of sodden clothes.

Cassidy felt the prickling sensation at the back of his skull again and shivered. The feeling had been more frequent since the rockslide. He dropped his backpack and unrolled his sleeping bag away from the others; the others all camped together, especially the Thals, who huddled like a flock of sheep on winter uplands.

He wondered where Sophia was sleeping. Or with whom. He was shocked by the bitterness of his thought. What was the matter with him? He was acting like a jealous school-kid.

He sat with the others and opened an MRE. He gave the chemicals around it time to heat the meal through, then chewed the tasteless lasagna mechanically. Afterwards, he crawled into his sleeping bag, cursing himself for a fool. Every time he heard a noise, he wondered if it was her. If he had any sense, he'd find her, and sort things out. But he didn't want to be the one to make the first move.

Finally he fell into a troubled sleep. It was if a dying elephant lay on top of him, suffocating him. Dread and despair suffused every nerve, every fiber and every tendon of his being. He'd never felt such a yawning blackness.

Then, in the ebbing tide of despair, he felt a presence. He couldn't tell what it was, but with the logic of the dreamer, he knew it was the source of his despair and that it was looking for him. He didn't want it to find him. He wouldn't like the result if it did.

Later, in the darkness, he saw big orange eyes. Whatever they belonged to was old and huge, and the emotions that emanated from it were deeply unpleasant.

In his dream Cassidy tried to hide, but the very act drew its malevolent attention. It moved ponderously toward him with almost geological slowness. Every heartbeat seemed to take an hour, every blink of an eye, a day. It breathed like a geyser, Sequoia slowly, but regular.

It was coming for him, and he knew that there was no hiding. He swam away through clouds, but the creature swam after him, gaining by only fractions of millimeters with each stroke, but that didn't matter. It had all eternity to hunt him down.

His dream seemed to last forever, or perhaps time jumped, for he felt the heat of its breath, and a fetid stench. It inched closer. He felt its jaws open wide to bite...

He woke up. For a moment the creature was still there. Then he awoke fully. He was drenched in sweat, and for a moment he wanted to cackle hysterically. *If the rain doesn't soak your uniform, then your dreams will,* he thought.

Gasping with relief at finding that it had only been a dream, he crawled out of his sleeping bag and bumped into something. His nerves were so tightly strung he almost shouted, but a hand covered his mouth, and Sophia hissed, "It's me!"

He almost broke down, so great was his release of tension. She must have felt it, for she held him and murmured something meaningless in Thal. He was achingly aware of her body. But he was too tired, too shaken to do any more than lie in her arms, and perhaps she felt the same, for she simply held him until it was light, when they rolled apart, both hollow-eyed with fatigue, before the others awoke.

CHAPTER SEVENTEEN

The incessant din of shouting and bullets cracking off walls had left Kaminski's ears ringing. It was several minutes before his hearing returned to normal.

Tunnels that had seemed so roomy when nearly empty were suddenly congested with Thals milling in near panic. It wouldn't take much for them to go completely ballistic, Kaminski thought. Already, some small children had been trodden on; mothers cried, babies screamed, and the men shouted angrily to vent their frustration.

Kaminski shouted, "Corporal Branch!"

"Sir?"

"We're counter-attacking. We'll work our way around. Grab ten men from the outside tunnel. We can only station so many men there, and it isn't the main objective."

They moved quickly but cautiously through the maze of tunnels, stopping in their tracks at the sound of a harsh gobbling, mixed with what sounded like a cat spitting. The Sauroids passed, deep in conversation. Kaminski breathed again.

"I think I recognize this," Branch pointed to symbols graffiti'd on the walls.

Kaminski nodded. "I think the portal's in the next tunnel over. Can't be sure, though." He paused, holding his hand high, and they heard more of the dissonant Sauroid speech. "Let's go!"

Two of Kaminski's men ducked round the corner, and sprayed the tunnel with bullets. One of them was caught by enemy fire, and spun to the ground, but the other kept firing.

At his signal, Kaminski waved his men forward. Two peered round the corner, and jumped into the corridor, showering the Sauroids with an absolute blizzard of bullets. One of the men fell, clutching his stomach, but reinforcements fired round the corner at the Sauroids. Three others threw grenades into the corridor, while two more crawled across the tunnel floor. The crawling soldiers pulled in their heads like turtles as the grenades detonated. The blast sent the standing soldier spinning back. Kaminski shouted, "What's happening?"

Before anyone replied, gunfire from the Sauroids spattered the corridor walls. One of the men lying prone shrieked.

Kaminski shouted. "Grenades!" The three grenadiers flung more around the corner.

Four more times they attacked. Kaminski peeked, ducking back as enemy fire scoured the wall behind where his head had been. He'd seen a barricade of Sauroid bodies piled high, from behind which the survivors fired. "Let's change tack," he said. "Two of you crawl to the barrier." He mimed the action of tossing grenades up, and Sapiens and Thal snake-crawled beneath the gunfire until they were beside the wall of bodies.

"There must be loads of them behind that pile," Branch said. "Unless they're getting out at the other end. Ev'ry time I look, I see that shimmer and more come through."

"They don't seem worried about how many of them die," Kaminski said sourly. "We don't know if they're still bottled up. They may have beaten back our guys at the other end, so when they come through the Portal, they can sneak round and outflank us." His head spun from trying to work out the tunnel's topography. "Enough chattering. Hit them NOW!"

They unleashed streams of bullets, while at the base of the wall of bodies, his men wriggled to their knees. Still kneeling, they tossed up a grenade from each hand in high, looping arcs that cleared the pile.

Seconds later came four consecutive blasts. Kaminski shouted, "Cease fire!"

Incredibly, there was silence.

Kaminski stared round the corner. The barricade had been blown apart, and his men were wriggling clear of the bloody mess of severed limbs, blood and intestines that had buried them. Behind him, his troops whooped with joy.

There was a shimmering at the portal, and at the same time, a Sauroid at the bottom of the pile fired a salvo that scythed the grenade throwers to the ground.

The two sides swapped fire for the next ten or fifteen minutes until they were like two punch-drunk boxers, too tired, or too brainwashed to stop trading blows. One by one Kaminski's men fell, last of all Branch, who took a headshot that left a dark trickle of blood running down over sightless eyes. "Fall back!" Kaminski shouted to the last four Thals. They had been so close, he thought, but that wasn't good enough. The sheer weight of numbers of Sauroids and their complete disregard for casualties had driven the humans and Thals back.

For hours firefights ebbed and flowed, raging throughout the tunnels. Incredibly, Kaminski napped, and snatched a bite to eat. He exchanged a few words with a wounded Brit, the man surprising him with an unexpected perspective. "If you were a fly on the wall, this battle would look like oil and water, swirling and dancing mixing in a tank." Seeing Kaminski's surprised look, he added, half-defensively, half wryly amused, "I'm a photographer in me day job, and take arty pictures in the evenings."

"Your imaginary fly would need a good vantage point," Kaminski mumbled, tearing off great bites of jumbo sausage roll, chewing and swallowing almost in one motion.

"Need to be a bloody brainy fly, as well," the squaddie said, and they cackled, their laughter tinged with hysteria.

Kaminski waved the now empty wrapper, and said, "Thanks for the eats. You fit enough to go back to the fighting?"

The squaddie nodded.

"Good man. Gotta get going."

Hours later, when Kaminski stepped over a body in one of the tunnels, he knew who it was, though he had barely registered the man's face. He had no time to mourn. He was too busy dodging bullets.

For all that day, if it was actually day- he had no way of knowing without checking his watch, and he had no time for that- fights and conversations took place in a series of blurred cameos. By contrast, the rare quiet moments seemed to stretch forever. The biggest problem Kaminski had was that encountered by every soldier in battle, other than staying alive, trying to work out what was going on and whether they were winning.

There were moments of elation when they drove the Sauroids back. But overall, he knew that they were failing to stop them from spilling out. As the day wore on he saw the same faces – Hethor, MaryAnn and others, increasingly often. In the end, they were crammed into only a few tunnels. "No doubting it," Kaminski said to Hethor, "they've got us penned in."

"What do we do?" Hethor's look of despair showed he already knew the answer.

Kaminski tied a piece of white rag around the end of his rifle butt and, praying the Sauroids understood, waved it around a corner, shouting, "We surrender!"

The firing faded away. A voice that sounded as if it came from a mouth filled with too many teeth boomed, "Lay your guns on the ground! Step away! There will be no second chance!"

They laid down their weapons. MaryAnn wept softly in the corner, clutching her baby, who'd screamed incessantly for hours. Kalinis stood silently, head bowed. Hethor wiped an eye surreptitiously. "We gave it our best shot," Kaminski said.

A dozen Sauroids stepped round the corner, followed by two Thals wearing headpieces. Their expressions were dull, their eyes glazed. The Sauroid leader gazed at Kaminski and Kalinis.

"Hyoo. Mann." It stared at Hethor; drew back the baby's blanket over MaryAnn's protests. It spoke to an aide in its sizzling language and then said, "Come," to Kaminski.

"Where?" Kaminski said and asked, "Why have you attacked us?"

The creature stared at Kaminski. "You worship false Gods," it said. They led Kaminski and MaryAnn away, leaving Kalinis and Hethor where they were. From behind him, Kaminski heard shots, and a choked-off scream.

"Why?" he gasped.

"They are not needed," the Sauroid said. Then Kaminski felt a wrenching dislocation as they took him through the portal.

***

"We gotta nail that platform," Adler said to Davenport. "If it pins us down any longer, they'll have time to move reinforcements up and finish us. That thing's too far away for grenade throwers. You!" he called to a Brit who hefted a missile launcher. "What's its range?" He told himself that he should know the answer, that if it were an American ATML, he would.

The soldier squinted. "We need to get closer, sir. If we can get within five hundred meters, we'll be right on the limit, but we'll be within a shout."

Adler converted it to yards; five hundred meters was no worse than the American SMAW or CMS systems, but he still felt an irrational niggle of irritation that they'd have to risk their necks by moving a few feet closer. "Okay. We'll lay down covering fire." He looked across, and beckoned Davenport. "Take two men," Adler instructed. "You pick them. Get the headpiece, crystals, and tape back to base."

"Judging by all this activity, sir," Davenport waved his arms, "Base'll know something's happening. There's no point-"

"Davenport! Two men! Take them! Go!" Adler shook Davenport's shoulders. "Direct order. Got it?" He pressed a pair of night-goggles and a radio the size of a brick into the corporal's hand. "You'll need these. The range of this radio is about ten miles on a good day, down to almost nothing in this area. Terrain interferes with it."

"Sir," Davenport looked close to tears, but saluted. "You'll be okay?" he asked. It was a foolish question, but Adler understood why he asked it. "I mean, you won't be able-"

"We'll manage," Adler said. "Good luck, Corporal. We'll hold them as long as we can."

Davenport led two others in a crab-wise scuttle from rock to rock, edging their way toward the lip of the valley and comparative safety.

"Hold your fire," Adler shouted to his men, "until they're almost on us." Davenport's team would need a few more minutes to get over the brow, and then every subsequent minute they could buy them was equivalent to roughly another hundred yards. *Every minute,* he thought, *is a victory. We'll buy you as much time as we can,"* he promised Davenport underneath his breath.

On Adler's signal, the men at the front popped up, squirting short bursts of gunfire that raked the Sauroid troops, ducking back before the platform could react, in a deadly game of Russian roulette that left them scratched and bleeding from rock shards. The two men with the ATML zigzagged from boulder to boulder, narrowly escaping both enemy and friendly fire. At last they were in position.

Adler could barely breathe; such was his expectancy. Meanwhile the enemy platform, unable to make out their ducking, darting enemies in the lengthening shadows of late afternoon, reverted to their earlier tactics, unleashing a rain of cannon shells that indiscriminately carpeted the valley floor and walls, injuring and killing their own in the process, but by the law of averages, Adler's casualties mounted too.

The men fired the missile. Adler watched it cut through the air. It started to wobble as it reached the limit of its range, and as the platform moved effortlessly sideways, it fell. "It woulda hit," Adler had never wanted to swear more than he did at that point. *You will not take the Lord's name in vain,* he reminded himself.

In answer, the platform unleashed another rain of shells, rock shards flying in all directions. A few almost hit the spot from which Adler's missile-men had moved.

Calmly, they re-loaded the launcher and took careful aim at the platform, which was weaving closer and closer to them. *It should be well within range now,* the watching Adler thought. He prayed silently for his men.

They fired again, and the second missile sped toward the platform, then wobbled, as Adler felt an invisible giant on his shoulders. It was only a moment before the weight vanished as suddenly as it appeared, but the missile shot upwards, then exploded in a bright orange ball of flame.

"What the-?" Adler had no time to think, as the ground started to buck and heave, in easily the worst quake they'd felt yet. He leapt to a new vantage point.

Quickly, but with a hint of panic- Adler saw the second man fumble the re-load- the missile-men loaded a third time, while the platform homed in. The blast from the platform quartered the men instantly, arms and legs spinning end over end in all directions in a gout of blood, the launcher now bent into an unrecognizable tangle.

"Shoot!" Adler spat. "Gavrel!" The Thal scrambled round, as low as he could, through the flying splinters of rock. Like the others, the Thal's face was a crisscrossed mess of red.

Adler said, "We must buy Davenport time, any way we can."

Gavrel nodded. "Did you feel a sudden weight just now?" he asked and beckoned a skinny young Thal Adler had barely noticed before. The lad scrambled between rocks and crossfire to join them.

"Yeah," Adler replied. "So?" He looks barely strong enough to lift his pack, he thought as he looked at the young Thal.

Gavrel said, "I think it was two parallel worlds so close together that we felt the gravity of both."

"So?" Adler said. "We aren't going to be around to worry about it, if we can't take that platform out. Any ideas?"

Gavrel said cautiously, "I have one." He jabbered at the youth, who crouched, white-faced and trembling, beside him.

"This is Nasitra," Gavrel said. "He is a Talent. His kind are almost extinct now, and he's young, and raw, and we hesitate to rely on him, but we must do something."

The youth shut his eyes, scrunched his forehead and muttered, faster and faster. He stopped, shaking his head and spoke anxiously to Gavrel, who replied soothingly. Nasitra shut his eyes and muttered again.

Gavrel said, "They have replaced liquid-fuel platforms with crystal ones; we can't ignite them with friction as we used to."

"Huh?" Adler said.

The platform veered toward the other side of the valley, so it could fire on them. "Watch," Gavrel said.

Nasitra muttered again, and the platform suddenly swerved, as if shoved by a giant hand. It scraped along a rock and then climbed vertically. Nasitra slumped, gasping. His face was beet-red, with broken capillaries in his cheeks.

"One more try," Gavrel said and spoke again to Nasitra in Thal, clearly encouraging him. Gavrel wrapped Adler's fingers round a pair of binoculars.

The youth muttered frantically, and Adler saw the pilot stiffen, clawing at his chest. The gunners lunged for the controls ,but the pilot blocked them by slumping over his console. The platform plunged onto the rocks below, crumpling in a screech of torn metal. Then it exploded.

"The ammunition," Gavrel explained as he hauled Nasitra to his feet. "We should get out of here!" An eerie hush fell on the valley. The Sauroids had stopped firing, and the allies re-loaded. Then an inhuman ululation split the air.

"They've realized we have a Talent," Gavrel half-pulled, half-pushed the exhausted Nasitra. "If you thought it was bad before, now it'll be ten times worse."

"Why?" Adler put his arm under Nasitra's other shoulder.

"What little we've learned includes the fact that they hate us because of our Talents. They consider them blasphemous aberrations, usurping their God's powers."

He broke off as the Sauroids resumed firing, puffs of dust kicking up all round them, adding, "The lad will be useless for hours. Until then, he's a passenger."

"But he's bought us time," Adler panted, exultant. "So we owe him."

Yard by yard the Allies fell back, fighting for every bit of ground. Retreating as slowly as possible, to buy Davenport time. They were within fifty yards of the ridge separating their valley from the next. A colossal explosion that flattened several men was followed by the shriek of a low flying jet. When Adler saw the delta-winged craft his heart sank. Picking himself up, ears still ringing, he dusted his clothes down and saw yet another man wounded.

Another platform broached the valley rim behind them. "They've called up reinforcements," Adler said.

Gavrel said, "They won't rest now, until they've killed us. That's why we always hesitate to use what Talents we have left."

"So they're dictating your tactics," Adler said. "You are doing exactly what they want you to." Reaching the ridge, he counted heads. Nine men; four were wounded or incapacitated. The rest were dead, or left behind, cut off, or too wounded to move. "We'll fall back slowly," Adler said. "Gavrel and four others in the next valley," he nodded at the wounded. "Three to stay here with me." He looked over the next valley, which was less than a mile long. There was no sign of Davenport or the others. They must've made it to the next valley. Adler searched for spots from which to ambush the Sauroids. There were a few, and he nodded with grim satisfaction as he checked his watch. *Thirty minutes have elapsed,* he thought. Every minute they could buy meant another few yards for Davenport. So far, they'd bought about two miles.

By the time the nearest gun platform was so close Adler could see the dents in it, he had only three men left, all wounded. Adler was wounded too. His left arm hung limp from a bullet in his shoulder, and with only one hand, he could only use his pistol.

Though they'd killed hundreds of Sauroids, Nasitra had died from shots from another gun platform, but not before, with one last effort, he'd caused the delta wing to explode, raining fire down on the Sauroids.

Adler sneaked a glance at his watch. *Seventeen minutes,* he thought. That had to be good for another mile or two for Davenport. These things might not even know Davenport had skedaddled.

He felt a moment of intense pain in his side and looked down at the blood pumping from a gaping hole. As the darkness closed in, his life ebbing away, he cried, "Oh Pen," and wished he could see his wife and children one last time.

***

Cassidy had fallen back to sleep and awoke stiff and aching, after the others were awake. It may have been his imagination, but as he looked around, several men looked away rather than catch his eye, and he was sure he saw several of them smirking. He felt his temper rising like boiling water in a pan and only put a lid on it with an effort.

Sexual relations in the British Army were a court-martial offence if the parties were more than two ranks apart, but he wasn't sure what rules applied to troops and civilians, or if Sophia even counted as a civilian. Not knowing only added to his irritation.

As he eased himself out of the sleeping bag, he saw Sophia smiling down at him. "Good morning."

"Morning," he muttered.

"What's wrong?"

"Nothing." He was aware that he sounded like a sulky child but was unable to get past his irritation.

"Breakfast?" She tossed him a ration pack, which he made no effort to catch. "Maybe later," Cassidy said, walking away.

He toured the camp, learning a few more words of Thal, in turn teaching the Thals a few more words of English. After they broke camp he walked apart from Sophia, talking to Garcia and the men.

All day they saw no other signs of life, except once, in the distance, a cloud of dust. When Cassidy trained his binoculars on it, he saw hundreds, perhaps thousands of antelopes chased by something vaguely lion-shaped.

The day was still and overcast. Taran made constant minute adjustments to their course through the endless savannah. In the enervating heat, Cassidy's thoughts kept drifting back to his nightmare; he'd never dreamed so intensely, or had one so horribly realistic. He shuddered at the memory. Even now, he still felt as if something watched him.

"You fallen out with the chica?" Garcia's question broke his reverie.

"No," Cassidy said, more sharply than he intended. He tried to apologize by making conversation but could think of nothing to say. It was as if the thing in his dream still stalked him.

A cry went up ahead, and Cassidy trotted to the front. The Thal leading the column pointed. Cassidy trained his glasses.

It was a small, ruined house that looked like a face, black holes where the windows should have been for eyes, a doorway for a mouth and an aperture above the door, its nose. One of the walls had half-fallen in, and the roof was missing. In the courtyard at the front was a dried-up fountain half-overgrown with weeds. Cassidy shivered and cursed himself for a fool for being spooked.

"First sign of civilization that we've seen," one of the Americans said.

"Probably a farmstead," Garcia replied.

With each minute that passed, they came a little closer to the ruined house. Even if their course hadn't taken them past it, they'd have detoured to take a look. It was so different from its surroundings. Farmstead, Cassidy wondered. Or caravanserai? Each minute that passed, he became jumpier.

Sophia spoke to a Thal, and then to one of the British troops. *If I was a sniper*, Cassidy thought – and he couldn't say why it occurred to him- *she'd be a clear target. It looks as if she's in charge.* He yelled, "Sophia, get down!"

She turned and looked at him, puzzled, and at that moment, there was a flash from one of the windows, which streaked toward Sophia at light-speed.

There's no time to get to her no time I can't catch her OhmiGod she's going to die!

Cassidy wished- urged her to fling herself to the ground.

And it was as if something swatted her, so she landed several meters away.

The world returned to normal time; as the flash ploughed into the ground the explosion threw up a fountain of earth, the blast flattening the men nearest it. An arm sailed over Cassidy's head. As the others flung themselves to the ground, a maniacal chuckle came from the house. Puffs of dirt kicked up. Another explosion followed.

Three of his men set up a mortar and two others a bazooka. The house took two direct hits, and the building imploded, walls cascading inwards, leaving only rubble. The whole incident took less than a minute.

Cassidy remembered to breathe. "Send a patrol," he told Garcia. "I want any survivors taken prisoner." Then he ran to Sophia.

She sat up, squeezing her shoulder, arm, and back where the invisible blow had landed. She winced.

"You okay?" Cassidy framed her face with his hands. He could feel the men looking on and grinning. "Boss is back with his squeeze," he heard an American say, and he would have bitten the man's head off, but fought the urge. *Ignore him*, he told himself.

"I'm fine," Sophia said, wincing as he helped her up. She looked around, her hand to her mouth. "McKibben must have pushed me." She clutched Cassidy's arm, digging her fingers in. "It must have been the last thing he did." Blinking back tears, she gazed at the ruin of the British soldier she'd been talking to. McKibben's face was untouched, but little was left of his lower torso. "He saved my life." She stroked McKibben's face.

Cassidy detailed men to bury the three dead. He turned to the building. Several men pulled away rubble, the rest watching, weapons cocked.

Someone shouted; two men pulled away rubble, others hauled upright the struggling shape of a Sauroid. They each gripped an arm, but it still fought, so one Thal grabbed it by the legs. When the Sauroid continued squirming, the Thal yanked its legs apart. The captive squalled and stopped struggling.

They carried it to Cassidy. "How many of you are there here?" Cassidy asked. A Thal translated into its language, all spits and hisses.

It yowled and lunged at Cassidy. Surprising the soldier holding its arm, it managed to break free and raking its claws, scoured the air in front of Cassidy who stepped back as the Sauroid lunged again. When the soldier tried to grab its arm, it turned and bit his face. The soldier screamed, clutching at the gushing hole where his nose had been.

Cassidy shot the Sauroid in the chest. Then shot it twice more, just to make sure. "Let's look at that wound," he said.

The soldier pulled his hand away, and blood poured down his face.

Cassidy felt sick. "We'll do what we can," he said.

The medic, who'd already joined them, clapped a handkerchief over the wound, trying to staunch the flow of blood. He shook his head sadly at Cassidy. "He's inoculated against tetanus, though that doesn't preclude septicemia. But when shock sets in..." He sighed heavily. "We'll do what we can," he echoed Cassidy's promise.

Behind them, the search party shouted as they found another survivor. At the chuckle of a Sauroid weapon, another Thal fell, clutching his chest. The others fired their machine-guns; then silence.

A soldier shook his head in disbelief. "Even when we tried to rescue him, the fucker only had one thought, to kill as many of us as he could. What drives these things, sir?"

"Don't know," Cassidy said. "But we'll find out, even if it means killing every one of them."

"Josh," Sophia plucked at his sleeve.

"What is it?" A thought popped into his head, "Do you think they're native to this world?"

Sophia shook her head. "They were just using the local terrain."

The Thal-Sauroid translator tugged at her sleeve. He spoke quickly, urgently, and when he had finished, Sophia turned to Cassidy, her face troubled. "The Sauroids hate us," she said, "because of our Talents. Just as the Sapiens on our first Prime loathed us, so do the Sauroids. They say we usurp a God's power."

"We've had lots of wars over religion," Cassidy said.

"Vagiskar says that the Sauroid was trying to get to you," Sophia said. "It said that it watched you; that it was a," she clicked her fingers, suddenly struggling for a word, "sensitive. It felt you push. It saw me fall down as if knocked down by an invisible hand. You were yards away-" She broke off, her face working through a whole spectrum of emotions, the implications sinking in. "It said that you were the opposite of a God. What do you call that?"

"A devil?" Cassidy feigned indifference, but inside, he felt a chill.

"More specific," Sophia waved her hands. "The arch, the counter-God."

The Antichrist?" Cassidy laughed.

"The Anti-God. That's it!"

Cassidy turned away. He didn't believe what she was saying, not for one minute, but when he thought of Sophia flattened, swatted to the ground, he felt sick with fear.

They marched on until late. As night fell like a curtain of darkness, they found the portal, and Taran Shifted them again.

CHAPTER EIGHTEEN

That night Cassidy was again haunted by vague, disquieting dreams. While there had been a sense of specific menace the previous night, tonight's nightmare was ill defined.

All Cassidy could remember the next morning was a fleeting contact with something so alien he couldn't begin to imagine what it was. The contact was lightning-brief, there and gone in a second, and the disorientation he felt was so overwhelming, it was like touching madness and would have overwhelmed him had it lasted longer.

Whether because he hadn't cried out or because she'd taken the hints he'd dropped throughout the previous day, Sophia wasn't there to comfort him this morning but kept her distance.

Thick fog covered the fifty yards from riverbank to camp. Visibility was so limited they could barely see two hundred yards the other way, to the wall of jungle at their backs. From the jungle peeked a derelict stone temple, covered with dragon carvings, which disturbed Cassidy as much as the way the fog made grotesque silhouettes out of his men. They drifted in and out of focus as the fog clutched and then released them, and more than once Cassidy almost shouted an alarm before realizing it was one of his own men, distorted in the fog.

They ate a frugal breakfast of crackers, local fruits and purified river water, in tense silence. Cassidy tried to avoid looking at her, but Sophia drew his gaze as if he were a meteor snared by a planet's gravitational pull.

She stared back steadily, until a flush rose like bruising on the paler parts of her patchwork face. When they finished eating, he rose and, as if his feet were possessed, walked over to her. He cleared his throat several times. "Everyone seems tense this morning," his voice sounded cracked and brittle.

"They say groups take their mood from their leader," Sophia wiped her fringe clear of her eyes and added, "They're probably just tired. Maybe we're getting close to the enemy's lair-"

Yes, he thought, feeling a tingle of anticipatory fear, *that's it*. A part of him wanted to run back to base, though he had already learned a lot, but another, stubborn part of him felt that there was yet more – that he was on the verge of stumbling into the solution to a much larger mystery than just how powerful the enemy was; the answer to why. He realized Sophia was still talking. "- something probing. The other psychics feel it, too."

"What was that?" he blurted.

"What was what?" She sounded both annoyed and puzzled.

"About something probing?"

"In my dreams," she said with exaggerated patience, "as I was saying. I've dreamed constantly for the last few nights. Usually nothing specific, but often pursuit dreams, sometimes a huge eye looking for me. Why? Josh, are you okay? You look like you've seen a ghost."

"No, I'm okay." He tried to shake off memories of a huge eye in his dreams. He clapped his hands. "Come on, you lazy lot!"

The men were lethargic, testy, with all the signs of a hangover – except that they'd had neither late night nor any other drink. It took them longer than their usual ten minutes to muster, but they were finally ready, and moved out.

***

"Pen! Over here!" Acutely aware of how precarious her high-heeled pumps were, Barbara half jumped and waved at her friend. Her feeble hop at least put her momentarily on level with the taller people in the crowd. *Why'd these bozos all have to be so tall,* she wondered.

The arrivals halls at LAX were always busy, but today was awful. She'd overheard someone say that the French Air Traffic Controllers were on strike and that everything out of Europe was delayed. Even where flights hadn't waited for the in-bound passengers, those who'd missed their flights had tried to get on the next one, and the chaos had spread. It looked as if even flights from North Carolina were affected, she thought wryly.

"Penny Adler!" Barbara waved wildly at a tousled blonde mane, ignoring the man who snarled at her as she inadvertently jostled him.

"Barbara Kaminski! Look at you!" Penny dropped her wheelie-case, flung her arms wide and almost smothered her petite friend in a hug.

"No, just look at you! Pregnancy becomes you! Hello Dylan! How're you, honey? Got a kiss for me?"

"'Lo, Auntie Barb'ra!" Dylan was flushed with excitement.

"How long to go?" Barbara patted Pen's bulging stomach.

"Four months. You?"

"Six lo-o-ong weeks." As they barged their way to the exit, Barbara laughed to show she didn't mean it. Well not completely anyway. But it would be nice to wear normal clothes again, even if maternity wear was halfway stylish nowadays.

As if reading her mind, Penny said, "Bet you can't wait to get your figure back?" Pen would never be a "clothes-horse," as she'd once laughingly called it.

"But it's such hard work, existing on a lettuce leaf and one cup of water a day. While I'm pregnant I get to eat like a horse. Like you always do!" Barbara stuck her tongue out at the face her friend pulled and then said, "Oh, crap! It's raining!"

"Ah California," Penny sighed, and they roared with laughter.

"Okay," Barbara said, "I'll waddle to the car park and pick you up here. We'll throw your bags into the back and get away."

"Wouldn't it be better if we all went together? You might get a ticket while we're loading up."

"It isn't safe crossing with Dylan, hon," Barbara said. "When the rain comes, local drivers check their brains into storage."

"Meow," Pen clawed at the air with her free hand.

"Huh!" Barbara grinned. "You wait 'til you see 'em park their hoods in the trunk in front or fishtail or aquaplane." She winced. "It is not a pretty sight."

"You know, Mrs. Kaminski," Pen said mock-severely. "You really must do something about your army brat attitude."

Barbara blew a raspberry. "Someone told me once that I was a typical expat; wherever I was, the last place I'd been was always better." She paused for effect, "So I fired her."

They both chuckled.

"I think it's easing off," Barbara said. "I'll be five minutes. Here I go!" She quacked like a duck.

Pen waited until Barbara's SUV pulled up. She threw her bags in the back, then strapped Dylan into the car seat even though the child squirmed and protested. "Come on!" Barbara called. "There's an attendant coming, and he'll ticket us if we don't get going!" Pen clambered into the front passenger seat with only moments to spare. "Woo-hoo!" she shrieked as they set off.

"Belt up!" Barbara said.

"Hey, there's no need to be rude!" Pen grinned as she grabbed the belt.

"I can just see Stu clap his hands over his ears, and moan that we've exceeded our bad joke limit!" Barbara laughed.

"Have you heard from him?" Pen said.

For the first time they were quiet. "Nuttin. How 'bout you?"

"Not for a week now. Jamie rang last week, said they were going on a short hike, and they'd be back in a few days." Pen frowned. "You know what the Army's like. They're probably lost, and no one's willing to admit it." They laughed again, but now it sounded forced. "I wondered if I ought to cancel my visit."

"I'm glad you didn't," Barbara said. "They'll turn up." As the traffic eased, Barbara gunned the engine. "Come on, we'll drive through Hollywood, and you can see the transvestite hookers!"

Dylan asked, "Mommy, what's a trasbestite?"

Pen bared her teeth in a rictus of mock-horror, and rolled her eyes. "Nothing you need worry about, darlin'." She added in a whisper, "We'd better watch our little Gauleiter here doesn't say something when Jamie comes back. Jamie's already convinced that you live in Sodom and Gomorrah all rolled into one."

"Well, he's right!" Barbara said, laughing, "He's still Mister Enlightened, then?"

"Oh, yes. You know my big cup cake."

"I surely do." Barbara's eyes twinkled. "You've forgotten it was through me dating his cousin that you met him?"

"Oh no, I haven't forgotten," Pen said, mock-threateningly.

"Well, don't worry, it'll only be a glass of sacramental wine passing your lips tonight."

"That's a dirty laugh you've got there, missy." Pen put her hand on her heart and parodied their old teacher's southern drawl, "Ah can't think why you should consider mah need for refreshment so amusing." She chuckled, "Can you imagine if you'd married Cousin LeVine?"

Barbara pulled a horror-stricken face; "Oh, puh-lease."

"No, come on," Penny protested. "Remember-" She glanced around at Dylan "—what an unlikely partner I thought Jamie was at first. But he grew on me."

"Yeah. But Cousin Le-vine," Barbara intoned the name in a monotone, "had none of Jamie's good points and all his bad ones. The only way he'd have grown on me would'a been like a fungus."

"Yeah," Barbara said. "I couldn't see him accepting you moving out here. He'd want you back with the rest of us. Stuart really doesn't mind?"

"Pen," Barbara said, "I earn much more than Stuart. He'd be a fool to mind. And he may be many things, but he's no fool."

Penny whistled. "Advertising really pays that well? Enough to keep that hair so very black?"

"It does if you're good," Barbara said, eyes narrowed above her grin. "And I'm good enough to sell sand to the Arabs and rice to the Chinese. That may sound smug, but false modesty's worse, and I'm through apologizing for being good at my job." She tensed. "Here's the 405. In rush hour this is more like Armageddon than Sodom."

Twenty minutes later, Barbara said, "It's been smoother than I expected. Maybe a little slow."

"At least it's moving," Pen said, "What the-? That car's lifted right up in the air! Oh my! It's turned end over end!"

"Earthquake." Barbara slammed on the brakes muttering, "Hope no one's tailgating us." Their car shuddered, and Dylan began to cry. The car suddenly tilted almost thirty degrees, and Barbara looked down at her now white-faced friend. "Don't worry, we get earthquakes all the time out here." She hoped she didn't sound as frightened as she felt. *This is worse than any of the usual little quakes*, she thought. All around them car horns hooted, and people shouted and shrieked. She glanced ahead, saw the hood of the car in front lift in the air, as the ground beneath it rose. A crack opened in the highway, and it toppled down into the gap. Like an animal's jaws, the crack closed on the hood, and they heard the sound of screeching, crunching metal.

"Let's get off this road!" Barbara muttered, slamming the car into reverse, weaving around the car behind them, and waving at the irate Asian driver who shook his fist at them.

"Mommy, I'm scared!" Dylan said.

"It's okay, Dylan," Pen said, shooting Barbara panicky glances as she reached in the back to smooth his forehead.

"We're almost there now!" Barbara's SUV had two wheels on the raised verge to offset the road's sudden tilt. "Ohmigod!"

"What!" Pen asked, trying to stay calm.

"The Simi Valley – it's gone!" Shaken, Barbara managed to reverse onto the access road, which had ground to a standstill as many drivers got out to gawp at the desolation. She stared at the scenes of chaos, dimly aware of Pen sitting open-mouthed.

Where there had been apartment-covered hillsides, now there was only a cloud of dust, through which she glimpsed a churning mass of water. The edge of the landslide was a sheer slope of mud and rock dropping down into the murk. Another row of toy houses that a whimpering part of her mind recognized as a street, slid gracelessly down the hill, disappearing into the cloud, which swirled higher, bulking out on another addition. "It's getting worse, it's headed this way," Pen said.

"It's headed southeast," Barbara said, half to herself, "So we need to head down Van Nuys and see if we can out-run it."

"How far will the quake hit?" Pen said.

"No idea."

"Should I turn on the radio?" Penny didn't wait for an answer. Most of the stations were only static, but finally they found a news station. "West LA has fallen into the Pacific! We're flying over what was Sherman Oaks, now no more than a sheer cliff of mud-"

"Pointless going home," Barbara grunted.

"— devastation extends as far east as Garnsey," the reporter jabbered. "All police and fire personnel have been called in to duty. We have reports that the Air Force has mustered jets-

"Wait! The jet is swinging around and firing at something on the ground!

"We can see the aircraft from the station here. It's turning around!" the announcer cried. "It's firing at us!" There was silence, then only the crackle of static.

"Oh, shit," Penny whispered.

"Mommy shouldn't swear," Dylan said sleepily.

"You're right, Little Man," Penny blinked back tears. "You'd better tell Daddy next time you see him." She had been punching numbers into her cell phone ever since switching the radio on, but shook her head. "The cell phone isn't working. I think the network's simply jammed."

"I thought they'd beefed up the emergency networks," Barbara said, and tossed her phone at Pen. "Try my Treo." Penny kept punching numbers in, but after several tries, shook her head in disgust. "I'll keep trying," she said, "but it doesn't look good."

"Let's head east." Barbara leaned out of the window to see around the car in front of her. Glancing at Pen she said, "Probably a good thing that your Mom's looking after Emmy and Tanya- not that there's anything to worry about," she added. She shrieked as she weaved through the packed road, "Come on asshole, move that pile of junk!" and added, "I gotta a woman in labor in here!"

"Barbara Kaminski!" Pen laughed as her petite friend offered to punch someone's lights out.

"Sorry, I'm a tourist!" Barbara called to someone else. She pulled her head in, speeded up slightly, and said sourly, "Wow, we're doing almost twenty miles an hour." Puffing her cheeks out she wiped her forehead, leaving a dark smudge.

"Why, my dear," Pen had regained some of her natural good humor. "You're positively glowing!"

Barbara nodded. "Nothing like a good, healthy dose of terror for getting the blood pumping." She swore under her breath as they slowed to a stop. Ahead, a fallen building had blocked the road. "Um," Barbara said, thinking furiously.

"Can you back up to the last turn?"

"Good thinking, Catwoman. Let's try it." She did so, and swung the car around. "Aagh! One way! Oh, hell!" She drove down the street while muttering, "I hope no one's coming."

She swung right and then swore. "This one's blocked, too." They spent a dispiriting ten minutes trying to find a route that was not blocked.

"Mommy, what's that?" Dylan cried.

Pen twisted round to see what he was pointing at. "Barbara, we need to get a move on," she said, so levelly that Barbara shot her a look and stared in the mirror.

"That looks like water," Barbara said with a frown. "But the ocean's at least ten miles away." Gunning the engine she swerved around another car, up onto the pavement, nearly running over a woman pushing a stroller, who shouted obscenities at them.

Even Dylan grew silent, as if realizing that Barbara needed to concentrate. She weaved through honking traffic, cyclists who swerved without warning and jaywalkers- all of whom seemed to be trying to get home, or anywhere else that wasn't where they were now- without hitting anyone, until Pen nearly lost count of the number of near misses. Even so, they barely managed to get above walking speed, and Penny found her eyes repeatedly drawn to the mirror. Each time another section of the hill behind them seemed to have slipped into the muddy spume. She could feel the tension crackle in the air.

"Are you stamping on a phantom brake pedal?" Barbara asked in the half-distant tone of someone concentrating.

"How'd you know?"

"Because I hear you hiss occasionally, usually about the time you think I'm about to knock someone into the next world."

"Sorry," Penny said.

"It's okay. I'd be doing the same if you were driving." Barbara paused, weaving around a Corvette, abandoned in the middle of the road, its doors wide open, then resumed, still absently, "You know what? This is getting scary. There's more and more abandoned cars."

"Are we there?" Dylan stirred from his nap.

Barbara said, "The road blocks are getting worse." She bit her lip. "We can't drive much further."

"What now?" Penny gulped and took deep breaths. Barbara could almost hear her thinking, *I've gotta stay calm for Dylan.*

"We walk."

"Where will we go?"

"We'll go as far as we can," Barbara squeezed her arm. "Then we'll bum a lift or steal a car. Something, anything!" She added fiercely, "We'll be okay!"

They clambered out of the SUV, taking a few moments to look down the street to where the wounded earth groaned and cracked. Slowly, almost imperceptibly, but relentlessly the slide was gaining on them. "You know how you often tease Jamie about his Bible-Belt fundamentalism?" Barbara said with a gulp.

"Yeah," Pen replied quietly.

"Well," Barbara said, looking down on fires flickering from ruptured gas pipes, and a pall of smoke hanging over what resembled a medieval painting of Hell. "Maybe he's right." *The screams and shouts from the survivors are like the cries of the damned,* she thought.

She said, "Hold onto Dylan!" and pulled the stroller out of the back of the car. "It'll save carrying him," she said. They strapped the protesting Dylan in, and wheeled the carriage around stones and potholes. "I've almost managed to screen the quakes out," Penny said. "They come just one after another so regularly that it gets sort of constant."

"Yeah," Barbara said. "It's a bit like sleeping by a busy road. After a while, you don't hear the traffic. And they're quite low-level." She added, "You won't believe this, but we've been quite lucky."

"Lucky!" Penny almost sobbed the word. "You've been out here too long, honey!"

The grumbling grew suddenly worse, and the pavement shook. Masonry showered them, and Dylan screamed. "Get into the road!" Barbara cried. "In the middle, as far from the buildings as we can!"

Penny wished she were anywhere else but there. She was scared and tired, and her feet hurt. It seemed like a lifetime since she'd left Fort Bragg.

Only yards behind them, the ground tilted, and rows of shops collapsed in an eruption of dust, sliding down into the maelstrom. "Run!" Penny screamed, pushing the stroller.

From a side road ahead came a burst of machine-gun fire, and another noise, like a mechanical chuckle, but impossibly fast. "Is that the police?" Penny asked. "Why would they be shooting?"

Barbara shrieked, but Penny was dodging a lump that another micro-quake had suddenly pushed up in the road and didn't look back immediately. When she did, Barbara was limping badly, leaving a trail of blood behind her.

"Turn down the side-street!" Barbara screamed. "The road ahead is blocked!"

Penny steered the stroller round the corner on two wheels.

Barbara rounded the corner and heard the strange chuckling sound again. She saw with a clarity she knew she'd never recapture puffs of dust kick up, the stroller leap and twist in the air. She heard Dylan's screams cut short and then heard Penny scream too. Saw her friend buckle, then collapse like a ruptured plastic bag leaking water.

She froze. Out of the corner of one eye, she saw the buildings to her left fold in on themselves. To her right, figures ran, pausing to fire across the street. She felt something grasp her arm. She looked into a face with green skin, too many teeth, and feathers on its head.

Then everything went dark.

***

All day Cassidy had sensed the tension among the men. They were like springs, wound so tightly they might snap at any additional pressure. Several times Sapiens and Thals squared up against one another and only backed down just before they came to blows.

Perhaps they too felt constantly watched by unseen eyes in the impenetrable wall of jungle, which was half-hidden by the fog. Cassidy had been in the African and South American rain forests; they had been filled with creatures that hooted, shrieked, howled and screeched, quiet only when predators stalked them. This jungle was silent and still.

All day the squad trudged through the muddy margins between the wall of jungle and the great river, whose thick brown water was so thick and viscous it oozed, rather than flowed.

Cassidy had now mastered enough Thal for basic conversation, and throughout the day he repeatedly asked Taran how far it was to the next Portal.

Taran's answers grew more brusque, until he lost patience with Cassidy. His short, sharp monologue was said so quickly that it was almost incomprehensible, but his tone left no doubt in Cassidy's mind about what he had said.

It was late in the afternoon when tension spilled over into violence. Cassidy didn't know how it started. He was watching a log, wondering if it was a crocodile, when he heard shouting from behind. One of the shouts turned into a gurgling scream, then stopped like a turned off light switch. The men's shouts were echoed by the sound of flapping wings as birds and bats flew from the treetops.

A Thal lay on the ground, his eyes open, but lifeless. Blood stained his uniform so dark it was almost black. Several Sapiens held one of their comrades, while other Sapiens and Thals were held back by an untidy mixture of the races.

"QUIET!" Cassidy was relieved that the tumult died abruptly. At least they still accepted authority. But for how long? "Who saw what happened?" he barked. Several voices shouted at once, and he bawled again for quiet. "Who actually saw what happened?"

Sophia translated into Thal, and one of the Thals answered, hesitantly at first, then with increasing conviction. "Chantay says," Sophia said, "that they were shouting at one another. That he," she pointed to the Sapiens, "stabbed Ercol."

"He asked for it!" The Sapiens, Farmer, was a Territorial. Cassidy wondered when he'd stopped identifying with his own kind, and started to think of his men as "Sapiens and Thals", not "them and us."

"Is this true?" Cassidy asked the other Territorials one by one.

One of them, Sands, nodded. "It's true."

"You weasel!" Farmer shouted. "You can't trust them fucking apes, nor their ape-lover mate!"

"Enough!" Cassidy roared. He pointed to an American, "You," he said, then to a Thal, "You," in Thal then in English, "Hold his arms." He nodded to Garcia, who returned the nod, and beckoned Farmer's colleagues away from the rest. He said, "Can any of you add anything to Sands' statement?"

One of them mumbled, "There's been niggles all day, sir. Insults, pushing, almost fights-"

"And that justifies murder?" He stared at the young man, barely more than a boy. He didn't even know his name – he was one of the first patrol. *Some leader you are, Cassidy,* he thought grimly.

The young man stared at the ground.

Cassidy gazed at each of the others, who shook their heads or shuffled their feet. One scratched his crotch. They clearly thought they were letting Farmer down, but no one was prepared to lie for him. Cassidy's feet felt like lead, his guts hollow, as he led the men back to the others. "Corporal Garcia!"

"Sir!" The American stood ramrod-straight.

"Are your men aware of the gravity of the offence?"

"They know the regulations...sir." Before Cassidy could go on, he said, "I've spoken to the men. They confirm that it was Farmer, sir. And they'll follow your orders to the letter."

"Very well." Cassidy swallowed, once, twice and, pitching his voice as low as possible, said, "Bind the prisoner's hands."

Farmer's normally ruddy face was white, and he seemed unable to take his eyes off Cassidy. "Private Farmer," Cassidy said. "In normal circumstances, you would be formally charged with murder. These are not normal circumstances. We're in a combat situation, where there's no room for niceties, or debating your actions. We have given every opportunity for your comrades to offer mitigation. None have done so." He was making it up as he went along. He'd never attended a court martial, so had no idea if what he was saying was accurate, but he had to make it sound quasi-legal, as much for the men who were left as for Farmer.

"I didn't mean to kill him! He shoved me, and I snapped!" Farmer wailed.

"Private Farmer, this tribunal finds you guilty of murder. It is the sentence of this tribunal that you be executed by firing squad."

Four Americans picked by Garcia led the struggling, shouting man away, tying him to a tree at the edge of the jungle.

"You! And you!" Cassidy picked out two Territorials and two Thals. Two more Americans stepped forward at his command and followed him to a spot ten yards from the tree. Hysteria had rendered Farmer almost incoherent, as they raised their weapons.

"Ready!" Garcia shouted. "Fire!"

After the shots, Garcia checked Farmer's pulse, though he was clearly dead. At Garcia's command, the firing squad cut the ropes that bound the corpse to the tree, and it flopped to the ground.

They buried the two bodies side by side, and Cassidy said a few words, before concluding with, "Garcia, the men can rest for ten minutes. But I think the sooner we move on, the better."

He stood behind a tree and was violently sick, bile bitter in his mouth. The pain was a huge lump in his throat. He felt soft arms wrap round him. "Please don't send me away," Sophia whispered. "You shouldn't go through this alone."

He wiped his eyes, his mouth and nose, then wiped his sticky hands on the grass, smearing them with mud. "I've killed men before," he said woodenly, "but always in combat. I've never had someone cold-bloodedly executed before." He laughed bitterly. "Executed. What a nice word for legitimized murder."

"Shh," she put her fingers to his lips.

The words poured from him. "What else could I do? If I'd let him live they'd have been at each other's throats again by morning. I did do the right thing, didn't I? Could I have done anything else?"

"No," she said. "You did what was necessary."

Eventually re-joined the squad, and when they moved out, Sophia stayed beside Cassidy. But it was Farmer's eyes that Cassidy constantly saw, staring at him when they'd placed him against the tree, full of fear and accusation.

CHAPTER NINETEEN

"What the-?" Davenport stared down at the base. Beneath the searing Afghan sun a long line of humvees, jeeps, trucks and tanks rolled out from the base toward the border with Pakistan, churning up a cloud of dust that almost hid them. Above the din of revving engines and shouts from the soldiers on traffic duty, helicopters whined, and a low-flying jet screamed overhead.

"Looks like your folks are moving out," Schmitt observed from around the inevitable chewing gum, his oversized adam's apple bouncing up and down. He was one of the men Davenport had picked. He'd picked well. Schmitt's good-humored bitching about their situation had often been a welcome distraction. "Looks like you were right about it being our world, anyways," he added.

"Or as near it as makes no difference," Davenport said.

They'd all noticed how much busier the skies had become, but were unprepared for this fury of activity. Afghans stood around watching. One of them was one-eyed, already growing stubble, as if unsure whether his allegiance was to the bearded Mujahadeen, or the clean-shaven forces of the Northern Alliance. He shuffled toward them, his gun pointed nervously at Eiles, the Thal who made up the trio, clearly unsure if Eiles was their captive.

Schmitt snapped his own gun up. "He's with us," he growled.

Davenport pushed Schmitt's gun barrel down. "I'm looking for Lieutenant Urquhart," he said with all the authority he could muster. He jumped as a motorcycle roared by.

"Who?" The guard spat on the ground and glared at them, but pointed his gun downwards. Like all the other Afghans Davenport had seen, he wore a *chapan*- a long, thick quilted coat worn like a cape, the arms hanging down empty.

"Lieutenant Urquhart," Davenport said. "You know where he is?" Cassidy had been adamant that the information be given to no one else, but he'd never have expected such an exodus.

The Afghan turned away and shouted at a countryman. A furious argument erupted, the two men shouting, waving and gesticulating, even poking each other in the chest. "He," the first Afghan broke off the argument, "take you to man in charge."

Davenport wanted to ask what was going on, but the first Afghan stalked off to harangue another of his countrymen.

The second Afghan set off without waiting to see if they followed and stomped through the line of vehicles, narrowly missed by a humvee whose driver didn't see him. He stopped and turned, shouting "Burru!" *Hurry*. It was an order, not a request.

Davenport and the others followed circumspectly. They passed through gates once guarded by British troops, now by Afghans.

They weaved through chaos, their guide leading them to a harassed-looking adjutant. "Who are you?" His red face was almost claret-colored though he paled at the sight of the American and the Thal.

Davenport saluted and ran through the litany of name, rank and unit, until the adjutant interrupted, "Your lot flew out yesterday!" Then comprehension dawned; "Were you one of them sent into the mountains with some fookin' spook? Is that where you dug up these two?"

"One of these two," Schmitt drawled, "speaks English." He paused just long enough for emphasis, before adding, "Sir."

Davenport interrupted, "Where's everyone gone?"

"Oman." The adjutant added, "While you've been on your fookin' holidays we've been recalled. The whole fookin' world's under attack. We lost radio contact with London. The Russians have uprisings all over the place; the Yanks are in even worse shape. They've millions dead and even more homeless. There are flying saucers shooting everyone up. The Indians say they're Pakistanis, the Pakis say they're Indian; the Chinese say it's an American plot. The whole place is going to hell in a handcart."

"Sir," Davenport interrupted. "It's imperative that we report to Lieutenant Urquhart, or his replacement!"

The adjutant waved a summons. "Lieutenant Shah!" he shouted.

The lieutenant came forward and held out his hand. "Mark Shah." He had the look of a Bollywood star, but his flat vowels and nasal whine came from Birmingham. "Why haven't you shipped out, Corporal?"

Davenport asked again for Urquhart, adding "I've been told by Major Cassidy to report only to him."

Shah straightened to his considerable full height. "Urquhart thought Cassidy had been killed. Why didn't you use the radio?"

Davenport said, "We were told by Major Cassidy to observe strict radio silence, sir. We didn't know the situation had changed."

Shah looked skeptical. "You'll know the authorization codes?" He recited his set of alpha-numerics. "Your turn."

Davenport took a deep breath, hoping he had them right. When he finished, Shah recited his response.

"This is for Urquhart." Davenport passed the padded envelope containing the crystals and headpiece to Shah. "And take these guys with you."

"I'd like you to come as well," Shah said.

Davenport shook his head. "Cassidy's orders were clear," he lied. "My squad's still out there." He was tacitly disobeying Cassidy's order, but the situation seemed to have changed out of all recognition. He wasn't even sure if there was anyone to send the information to.

"These men will present to Urquhart." Davenport had briefed them thoroughly on the way back, in case anything happened to him. They had the headpiece, the crystals, and Cassidy's hastily scrawled, but signed testimony to verify the information. "Would you leave your mates for dead?" Davenport had to stand on tiptoe to eyeball the adjutant, but it seemed to work.

Normally he'd have been charged with insubordination, but there was nothing normal about this situation; his countrymen were desperately trying to pretend the withdrawal was an orderly one, but it had the air of a rout.

"Your look-out," the adjutant shrugged, waving the others toward a Lynx that sat on the tarmac, blades spinning, his mind already clearly elsewhere. There was a gleam in his eye, as he added, "Now fook off, sonny, before I put you on a charge!"

"You got any dollars?" Davenport asked.

Schmitt rummaged in his pockets and waved a wad of bills. "Take 'em," he said.

"Give me ammunition!" Davenport plucked at Eiles's sleeve. They passed him two clips each.

"Good luck, Bud!" Schmitt shook his hand, and the Thal pounded him fiercely on the back, almost knocking the wind from him. "Kill a few freaking lizards, huh?" Schmitt growled,. Then they were gone, and Davenport was alone.

For a moment he wished he'd gone with them, but the moment passed. He ran back through the line of vehicles to the man with the *chapan*. He felt curiously exhilarated, the way he'd felt on the last afternoon of school, as if all cares had fallen from his shoulders. He should be retreating with the others. He had a girl and a sprog, he reminded himself sternly, no matter how much he blathered on about rescuing his colleagues. It didn't matter. The world had changed beyond recognition, and he felt that only those who could change with it would survive.

Haggling with the Afghani, he bought the *chapan* for fifteen dollars, ignoring the smirk on the man's face. The man thought he had ripped Davenport off, but the soldier knew that the *chapan* would be warmer than a sleeping bag. "I need ammo," he said, but the Afghan shook his head and turned away.

Davenport checked through his possessions. Besides what the others had given him, he had five clips of ammunition for his pistol and three for his rifle. He hefted the radio and decided to hang onto it.

He headed back the way he had come, away from the vehicles, toward the mountains. He walked until after nightfall, until putting one foot in front of the other was too much effort.

When he awoke the next morning the sky was a blue he'd never seen before. Whatever Earth he walked on now, he knew it wasn't the one he'd fallen asleep on. Somehow, without even trying he'd Shifted across worlds. Or they'd Shifted around him.

***

Cassidy awoke like a drowning man surfacing. He stared at the gray sky, taking a few moments to orient himself. His hand was snared in a rope by the side of his sleeping bag, but that wasn't the cause of the nightmare; he knew that much. He was drenched in sweat but shivered, despite the warmth of the morning.

"Shh," Sophia leaned against him, stroking his forearm.

Cassidy gulped; he wondered if he'd been screaming before he awoke. "I'm okay," his voice was tremulous in his own ears, and gave the lie to his words.

"Was it the suffocation dream?" She ran her hand beneath his opened shirt over his still-damp chest, and he saw her moue of distaste.

His mood swung like a compass needle. Her expression annoyed him; no one was making her touch him. "No," he lied. Even talking about it obliquely brought the crushing weight back down onto his chest. "Why do you think that?"

"Because I've dreamed exactly the same dream for the last four nights. So have some of the men. I can't believe you've been having different nightmares, while everyone but you shares the same dreams."

He nodded. "How many of the men have had these dreams?"

"About a dozen," Sophia said. "All the Sensitives. The more talented they are, the worse they seem to suffer."

To fill the suddenly stretching silence he said, "Always the same dreams?"

"Either nightmares about being suffocated," she said. "Or about being chased by something unseen; occasional visions of a huge eye, or breath on the back of our necks- Josh, are you okay?"

"Yeah, I'm fine." *Don't think about that thing stalking you,* he told himself. He shivered again.

"You know what this means, don't you?"

"No." Cassidy struggled free.

As he climbed to his feet Sophia said, "Everyone of us who's had these dreams has Talents. Latent Talents often emerge after Shifting a few times. No one knows quite why."

Cassidy understood her implication. "That's false logic," he said. He paused. "Everyone who has the dreams has been a Thal, apart from me, correct?"

"Ye-es," Sophia said.

"Well," Cassidy said as she climbed to her feet as well, "The simple explanation is that I've heard them talking but not consciously thought about it, so it's manifested itself through dreams!"

She shrugged. "Believe what you want, Josh."

As he warmed up in the morning sunshine, he asked himself why it would matter if he had some of their precious Talents.

It would matter, of course. Any government would sell its collective soul for the chance of controlling the powers he'd seen on the crystals: teleportation, clairvoyance, psychokinesis and telepathy. Pity the unfortunate who developed them. They'd have a one-way ticket to a research establishment when, or if things returned to normal. The very thought of being tested like a lab rat terrified him. He'd spent his whole life being anonymous. There'd be no room for anonymity anymore.

The day before, they'd Shifted onto a pleasant greensward, and camped in a meadow that was more like an English pastoral scene than had been found anywhere in Britain since the eighteenth century. Around him, the troops were warming up as well. The stayabeds were rousted, much to their colleague's amusement.

"Morning," a Thal said and followed with his own greeting.

"Good morning," Cassidy replied in both Thal and English. Cassidy was rapidly mastering Thal. Learning had been made much more interesting by his insisting on having as many

English and Thal swearwords in the lessons as possible. It had also shown some odd cultural quirks.

The worst Thal swearwords involved sodomy. They hated it far more than the most reactionary Sapiens culture. "A Thal might as well get caught with an animal as another man; both reduce the potential gene pool," Sophia had explained with a grin. "Swearwords based on sex? 'Fuck' is just a verb to us."

A Thal had taken Cassidy to one side the night before. With pidgin-English-Thal and by pantomime, the Thal asked if he could bed Sophia. Cassidy had marched Sophia away from the squad. "What am I, your pimp or something?"

"No, just my man." She looked him straight in the eye, then burst into laughter. "Everyone but you seems to think so." Without warning she suddenly flared. "Even if you aren't, it's courtesy to his commander!"

"Pardon?" The conversation was getting weirder by the second.

"You clearly don't have women troops," Sophia said.

"Not many in the front lines. You do?" He let his surprise show.

"Of course," she said. "Or do you think I'm just a token? We just haven't brought any others on this trip. There have been enough confusions already, haven't there?"

"Um," he admitted with a rueful grin. She was right. God only knew what would have happened if they'd had more women with them.

"So," she said, like a mother reasoning with a stubborn child, "Mashneyk was being courteous to his commander, whether that commander was male or female. And asking your permission to screw one of the women troops. Me, that is," she added with a grin, "as they don't know if you're interested in me, or not."

"Oh." Then Cassidy asked, "Doesn't it lead to discipline problems?"

She shrugged. "We've got by so far."

After a long pause, he said, "If I'm your man, do I have to ask anyone else if I can take you to bed?"

Tilting her face up, she kissed him. "Only me," she said when they parted, "and you already know how I feel, don't you?"

"Not sure," he said. "Can we check again?"

After all the confusions, the false starts, the pavane of missteps in the last few days, it really had been that simple. He smiled at the memory, his flash of temper forgotten.

"Morning, Major," Vagiskar yanked Cassidy's thoughts back to the present.

Vagiskar was proud of his English, although he was an unlikely-looking scholar. A tall man by Thal standards, his beard was sparsely trimmed, but ornate; his face was almost bare of tattoos, but every inch of his body was covered. Some were familiar designs; hearts, lions, even a dragon that sent shivers of premonition down Cassidy's spine.

"He's one of only a few captives ever to escape from the Sauroids," Sophia had once said. "He's near fluent in their language."

A bird screeched, and Vagiskar flinched. He was constantly nervous, Cassidy noted. It was another legacy of his time with the Sauroids.

"Morning, Vagiskar," Cassidy replied in Thal, as he carried on with his exercises. He felt a hand on his back and turned.

"You look happy," Sophia said.

"Mmm, daydreaming." He sobered, and she noticed instantly.

"What?" she said.

"It feels obscene to be enjoying a lovely morning less than thirty-six hours after I was responsible for a man's death."

"Farmer was responsible for Farmer's death." She stared into his eyes. "Put it behind you," and reached up to kiss him. After a moment's hesitation, he kissed her back. And almost broke away laughing at the cheer that went up around them. When they finished, he looked around. "What are you lot staring at?"

They snatched a quick breakfast; then Cassidy summoned Garcia, Sophia, and Taran to a meeting. "If we're getting close to the Sauroid Home, how come we haven't seen more of them?" Garcia asked.

"The theory we have is that they've already absorbed the worlds close to their own," Sophia said. "One day we'll simply arrive in their world, or one very close to it. You asked about your world merging with others, and I said that only those creatures and places that were unique would be left? I think that's what's happening here."

"So how would that turn out? You mean we're gonna disappear, like a puff of smoke?" Garcia's teeth flashed white.

"Wouldn't it be more like essence of Garcia?" Cassidy said, adding, "now **there's** a frightening thought- pure, unadulterated Jose Enrique Garcia!" He chortled.

Garcia lifted an eyebrow. "I don't think the chicas could take it, my man. Too much in one body for any one woman."

Sophia, said, struggling not to laugh, "We think it's more like a compromise of Garcias."

"Wow!" Cassidy said. "So we could be changing all the time; one day there might be a manic-depressive Cassidy, the next day one who's stable?"

"Who's gonna notice?" Garcia said, deadpan.

"You probably wouldn't," Sophia agreed. "There might be, for example, mood swings. But we think that most changes would be too small for us to notice. So you might be clean-shaven one day and bearded the next. But this is only theory."

Cassidy shuddered, stroking his beard; he had no more than a vague feeling that if he'd not been clean-shaven, he'd had no more than stubble. What other changes were going on, he wondered. "That doesn't answer the question of what's causing this? How does it tie in with Bramaragh's plans?"

Shouts and shots from nearby interrupted them. Cassidy grabbed his semi as two sentries hauled a squirming Sauroid between them. One of the sentries, a Thal said, "Two dead lizards. One captured."

"What are they doing here?" Cassidy asked.

Vagiskar translated into what sounded like a series of hisses and fizzes. The prisoner answered, via Vagiskar. "Reconnaissance."

"Can he lead us to his home world?" Cassidy asked, again via Vagiskar.

Vagiskar answered, "He says he'll be glad to help us die."

"Friendly, isn't he?" Cassidy said. "Tie his hands together, and we'll move in five, after the men have tidied up." He said to Sophia, who was tidying things into her backpack, "A three-man squad?"

Sophia nodded. "It's unusual for them to have such a small patrol. This is too easy."

Cassidy nodded. He thought so, too. The patrol buried their waste, removed as many traces of their presence as possible, and moved out. They marched for an hour through spring sunshine, before reaching the portal.

***

Sophia jerked her thumb at the Sauroid. "It says there are two more portals to cross through to reach its home world."

"Let's take a break," Cassidy said. "What do you think?" he asked Sophia. "One-meter eighty? Weighs about sixty kilos? Its cranial feathers are mangy, but its claws are well developed." It glared at him, then yawned, stretching its jaws wide, giving him a view of teeth-like miniature steak knives.

Sophia said, "I think it's a young one, but I'm not an expert. It's not as big or heavy as most."

"What's your name?" Cassidy asked, and Vagiskar translated again into the hissing, spitting Sauroid language.

It spat back, and the Thal said, "Blue."

"Blue what?"

"Just Blue." Vagiskar added, "Their names aggregate with age. When they're young, their society seems to consider them barely worth naming at all."

"How old are you?"

Spit. Fizz. The Thal mumbled, and Cassidy said, "What?"

Sophia interrupted, "Blue said, 'Old enough to kill you'. With lots of descriptions," she said dryly.

"Am I re-inventing the wheel?" Cassidy said.

"I don't know," Sophia said, "which wheel?"

"The wheel of torture." He grinned. "Meaning, am I asking stupid questions?"

"I don't want to criticize." Sophia smiled openly now.

"But..."

She moved her head from side to side, trying not to laugh. "But we've asked these questions before."

"So I should just give up?"

"Did I say that?" Sophia said innocently.

"You didn't need to," he grumbled.

"They're usually neither friendly, nor helpful," Sophia said, "which is why I'm so suspicious of this creature."

"Do you think we shouldn't go?"

Cassidy had already made up his mind, so he was pleased when she replied, "No, I think we should go with it. We gain nothing from not going, and it could all be a huge double bluff."

He stood up and called to the men, "Let's move on!"

As usual, Taran the Opener led a small advance party of four. He returned after ten minutes, reporting no dangers.

The Shift into a desert world, where by the position of the hot, fierce sun it was mid-afternoon, was uneventful. The Thals suffered in heat, so they kept going through the night, trudging beneath the stars over mile after mile of shifting sand.

They stopped at daybreak and rested uneasily through the next day, making tents from their uniforms by draping them over frames made from their packs.

This time it was Sophia's turn to cry out in her sleep, and he held her gently, shushing her when she half-awoke. "It's okay," he said, stroking her forehead.

He didn't want to sleep. Their conversation in the meadow had scared him more than he had admitted. If he slept, would he change? He might awake and find Sophia was gone, or that she was with someone else. Despite his trying to keep his distance, she'd become so close to him that he was vulnerable.

Still, he eventually dozed and awoke with a start, his heart pumping. In his dreams he'd fled down endless corridors from something vast and unspeakable. For a moment, he couldn't remember who or where he was. Sophia whispered, "Sleep well?" She ran her fingers down his day old growth of stubble.

"I'd better get shaved," he said, kissing her back.

They set out when the sun hung low on the horizon, late enough that they could march without getting too hot.

"This isn't only a desert world, it's a deserted world," Cassidy said, as the night closed in, the moonlight adding a ghostly cast to their surroundings.

"We only see a small part of these worlds," Sophia said. "Would you judge your whole world by the land around the caves where we sheltered?"

"True," he conceded.

"A lot of these places are deserted, though," Garcia said. "Seems life isn't that commonplace."

"Or maybe whatever was here was wiped out by our lizard friend," Cassidy said.

They marched through the night without stopping, desperate to avoid the heat of another day. As they neared the portal in the last few minutes before sunrise, the young Sauroid grew agitated. Cassidy convened a council of war and jerked his thumb at it. "It feels like we're marching into a trap," he said without preamble.

"Is there another way through?" Garcia asked the same question Cassidy had been about to.

The Thals muttered, and Sophia said, "Kesack says there's a secondary Portal a way further. It will probably take us another day, and we don't know if that Portal is right to take us where we want to go."

"Let's try it," Cassidy said.

So they stopped at dawn; they resumed their march that evening, moving past the Portal. The young Sauroid writhed against the cuffs holding him, snapping, biting and scratching. They dragged him until Cassidy threatened to leave him where he lay.

They had run out of water the day before, but still they marched on and on, despite their aching legs, despite their thirst. They marched on past dawn, almost to midday, when they reached the second Portal. "We're here," Sophia panted, as Taran stopped, quivering with suppressed excitement.

They linked arms, a Thal holding the Sauroid's chain. The world turned upside-down and inside-out; they'd Shifted.

Sophia hugged him. "We've done it!"

They fell on a freshwater brook like birds of prey onto a kill. Cassidy surveyed a landscape of desolation beneath a sullen, brooding sky, before going to quench his own thirst.

PART FOUR

In The Shadow of the Dragon

CHAPTER TWENTY

"I thought you'd given them up, David," The Foreign Secretary eyed the Home Secretary's cigarette with disdain. "Considering you were talking about banning them recently."

David drew one last, deep drag, flicked the cigarette to the ground and stamped on it. His gaze raked the walled courtyard that passed as a back garden, and nailed the armed policeman at the gate. "That was then, Stephen, this is now. And anything that brings me a little pleasure at the moment is not to be mocked." He laughed bitterly. "Fat chance of banning them, anyway. They've almost completely funded the Health Service for the last few years. Now we don't need to ban them; the black market's pushed the price through the roof."

"Things still bad?"

Stephen was so solicitous; David's metaphorical antennae twitched. What did he know? Then he brushed the paranoia away. "What do you think? We've got mountains springing up overnight in Norfolk. We've had to pull the troops back from the Middle East to quell the mobs; if they're not fighting with each other, they're stockpiling for the next change. And here we are, stuck in the PM's bunker."

"Hardly a bunker," Stephen's gaze wandered along the new snow-capped mountains north of London. "It's quite a nice house. Richmond's not exactly a ghetto. You can hardly blame our leader for wanting 24-hour access to his Cabinet. Nor for thinking that having our families around would help us sleep easier."

"You can talk. France being buried beneath lava is the extent of your problems." David sighed. "The Channel Tunnel's disappearance at least makes defending ourselves easier."

"Not when these Sauroids can pop up at any minute," the Foreign Secretary said with obvious satisfaction.

"Sauroids?" David said. *Go on,* he urged silently. *You know you're dying to tell me about it.*

Instead, the Foreign Secretary smiled. "Briefing in ten minutes, David. Josh Cassidy sent a messenger and some devices that may shed some light on things. If they are reliable, of course."

"Cassidy's all right?" David said. He hadn't realized what a good operator he'd inherited until Cassidy was moved to the Foreign Office.

"I'm sure he is," Stephen stroked his chin, already blue with his perpetual five o'clock shadow. "At least I would be sure, if I knew where he was."

Was Stephen dropping a few preparatory hints that Cassidy was AWOL? Was he setting the operator up as the scapegoat? David felt a wave of loathing, which quickly passed, leaving him feeling nearly washed out. "I'll be there in ten minutes, Stephen. I wouldn't miss this for anything."

***

"Well that was a bloody waste of time," Cassidy wiped his hands on the grass. "Literally so," he laughed bitterly, looking away from Blue's corpse. "It took us twenty minutes to kill him, and I can count on one hand the number of useful things we learned."

It hadn't taken long for their euphoria at reaching Sauroid Prime to evaporate. That was partly due to their surroundings, which were as grim as any industrial wasteland. Then a couple of hours of hard marching to a high ridge had revealed an unlikely sight in the next valley.

As they marched down into it, Cassidy kept feeling as though they were walking through an illusion. There was something slightly off-kilter about everything. The setting was too perfect to be so close to the slag-tip wastelands. Birds sang around them, and the scent of flowers wafted on a warm breeze. When the sun ventured out from behind black clouds, the sky became an almost eyeball-melting blue. Those without shades had to squint and shield their eyes. So when storm clouds brewed later with frightening speed, they were equally intense, but their gray color, shot with sizzling copper greens and inky blues, was also slightly off kilter.

A high, thin waterfall cascaded down a hillside into a pool. Small deer and other animals lapped shyly from the water, then exploded into a frenzy of legs at any unexpected sound. The air was still, but the very stillness hummed with expectancy.

The quiet had ended violently. Blue had lunged at an American, the soldier just barely managing to evade its snapping jaws. The others clubbed the Sauroid into submission, but even as it fell to the ground, it still hissed defiance.

Vagiskar kicked it. "It called us Food That Moves." He breathed through his nostrils, like an angry buffalo, about to charge. "You can guess what their main use for us is."

"Let's see what else he has to say for himself," Cassidy said grimly. "Strip him!"

Sophia said, "If you want to torture him, I've got a few suggestions."

"Ok-a-ay," Cassidy breathed, not knowing quite what to say.

"We have a little more history to avenge than you have," Sophia said coolly.

"And all we know," Cassidy muttered now. "Is that he thought we were to the south of the main city." They headed north. Cassidy muttered, "We won't get the answers we need in the middle of a wildlife park."

***

Water seeping into his boots awoke Davenport. The impossibility of that snapped him alert. When he'd fallen asleep the night before, he'd been a thousand miles from the sea.

He lay on a beach. On one side of the bay thick fog cloaked both sea and sand. Looking the other way, he saw sheer cliffs rising from the beach. They were so high that he got a crick in his neck from staring up at them. Fluffy white clouds drifted over the tops of the cliffs, which formed a line in the sunshine all the way to the mouth of a fjord. Then they resumed, until they reached another fjord. The sand didn't reach that far, petering out a half a mile away.

Before the sand finished, there was a row of statues, the bodies those of dogs sitting on their haunches. The heads however, which stared out to sea in a uniform row as if standing sentry, were those of eagles. Davenport hefted his pack, and tried the radio, but unsurprisingly there was no signal. He walked up the beach toward the nearest statue.

It was a far longer walk than he'd expected, and he revised the scale; the beach must be miles long, and the cliffs over a mile high, far taller than anything on his Earth. The statues were about fifty yards apart and almost as tall as that. They seemed to be made of weathered granite, and were covered with bird droppings.

He shivered. A chill wind danced across his forearms, raising goose bumps. He kept walking, his feet sinking into the sand. To his right, the tide licked at the feet of the last statue.

Eventually, he reached the base of the cliff and walked parallel to its base. It was cold here in the cliff's perpetual shadow, but he was able to make better time over the rocks toward the fjord's mouth. He couldn't have explained why he was walking in this direction. It seemed to him that it was as good as any other way. He'd marched for so long, first with Cassidy, then with Adler and now on his own, that he had no idea of what else to do.

At last both beach and rocks ended. Ahead of him, he saw only spray, spitting into the air as the waves lashed the cliffs. Shrugging, he sat. When he'd eaten an MRE, he rested for a while and then began slowly, steadily climbing the cliff. There were plenty of handholds and a few ledges. When night fell, he slept on one of the ledges.

***

Cassidy's men emerged from the undergrowth, staring bemusedly at the earthen road that stretched in either direction. They'd worn themselves out hacking their way through the undergrowth. The Thals all had short swords, little more than long knives, with which they nicked themselves with depressing regularity. The Sapiens didn't even have knives; they'd prepared for Afghanistan, not the jungle, and had to push their way through the ferns, ignoring the blood streaming down their arms from a plethora of scratches and cuts. Despite the potential danger of being in the open, the road was a welcome relief from hacking through the foliage.

"Which way now?" Garcia asked.

"Hold on," Cassidy said. He felt a powerful urge to go left, as if something were tugging at him. He resisted the idea that something was tugging at his mind. "These trails are used for...?"

Garcia shrugged. "Transportation, I guess."

"They have flyers," Cassidy said. "Though it's a useful back-up. Moving troops is what they're used for," he grinned wolfishly, "So let's move our troops along them! We go this way." They set off in the direction opposite to that in which he'd felt pulled. They made quick time along the road for the next hour, but Cassidy's nerves jangled. He expected to meet a Sauroid patrol around a corner at any moment.

So it was almost a relief when one of the Thals on point held his hand up. They fell silent. From around the corner they heard hissing, spitting and caterwauling. They barely had time to dive off the path and back into the undergrowth, before a Sauroid patrol marched round the corner.

A dozen Sauroids marched in parade ground formation, in front of and behind a ragbag collection of captives. The prisoners- humans and Thals- were linked by lightweight chains that looped around their wrists to the captive in front and to the one behind. A similar chain linked each prisoner's right ankle. The line could march but would find it difficult to run, particularly if one of them fell.

"Garcia," Cassidy murmured. "Tell each man to line up a target."

Garcia hissed to each of their snipers; at this close range, any soldier with a rifle qualified as a sniper.

"Hold fire, until they're almost past," Cassidy muttered. "Now!"

A blizzard of bullets raked through the Sauroid's ranks. In seconds, only the captives remained standing. One Sauroid had returned fire, but he hadn't hit anyone.

The captives were in a piteous state, semi-naked, their ribs prominent from malnutrition. There were two Thals, one of each sex, and five Sapiens; two men and three women, of varied races. Most were middle-aged, or younger; it was an elderly black man who stepped forward. "Thank you, whoever you are."

"Where did you come from?"

"As far as we can gather," the old man said, "we're all from different places." His face clouded over, "I'm Henry Obanga. I'm the only survivor of my group. They've been marching us for days. Anyone who couldn't keep up was executed." One of the Thal soldiers moved, and Henry started.

"What's wrong?" Cassidy asked.

"We were originally captured by...people like these," Henry said, looking suspiciously at the soldier.

"Any ideas who they could have been?" Cassidy asked Sophia.

She shook her head. "We've settled thousands of worlds. It could have been our people, panicking or thinking Henry was an enemy. Or they could have been collaborators."

A young Asian said, "My name is Stephen Lo, from Singapore. I was going to the Foreign Affairs Ministry to discuss ways of lifting the Filipino Empire's blockade, when these things came from nowhere," he shrugged. "We haven't been allowed to talk much." He nodded at Henry. "We barely know each other's names."

"I'm Cassidy," Josh pointed to himself, and one by one the captives gave their names. Cassidy pointed at himself again and said, "English," in as many languages as he could.

Cassidy had two soldiers tend each of the captives, one to debrief, while another tended the sores, blisters and bruises that were a legacy of their captivity. The rest of the squad hid the corpses in the undergrowth, while trying to remove all traces of the ambush. Cassidy ensured everyonc was fed.

Besides Henry and Stephen, the other five came from a variety of countries and worlds. Most of them spoke little, if any English. Enrique was Venezuelan. Judith was from Ghana, and Natalya was either Russian or Ukrainian; Cassidy couldn't quite establish which. She was terrified and spoke so quickly she was unintelligible. Cassidy suspected she'd say whatever she thought would keep her alive, including changing her name and nationality with bewildering regularity.

When he said so afterwards, Sophia said, "She might come from an Earth where the countries as we know them don't exist. Maybe she was trying to tell you the nearest country she could to where she came from. Her name might change, depending on who she's talking to, in her society."

"Trust you to make me feel like a cynic," he grumbled, and she pecked his cheek.

The male Thal was called Gralinte. He was barely past adolescence and was probably in the best shape of any of the captives. Noor was older. She looked badly beaten, and Sophia eventually drew out of her that she'd been liberated from Sapiens slavers. She was even more scared than Natalya and spoke so quietly that Sophia had to make her repeat herself.

"Those things you killed," Henry pointed at a Sauroid. "They weren't actively brutal. We simply didn't exist as people. If we weren't fast enough, they executed the slowest to speed us up. Believe me," he chuckled grimly, "once you've seen someone shot and left to die, you get the idea very quickly."

"You're in pretty good shape, considering," Cassidy said. "How old are you?"

"As old as my tongue and older than my teeth," Henry's eyes crinkled with amusement. "I keep fairly fit. And as I said, Mr. Cassidy, the wish to stay alive is very good motivation."

"Call me Josh, Henry. Where are you from?" Cassidy asked.

"Cape Town. You know it?"

"Uh-huh," Cassidy nodded. "Why didn't they just shoot you? They don't seem to value human life."

Henry shrugged, "I can't explain it. Maybe their orders changed. Or they found they had more captives than they could handle, after they found us."

"Were you in the ANC?"

Henry nodded.

Josh said, "Then you appreciate my dilemma."

Henry chuckled. "I wasn't in the front line. My role was the provision of safe houses, with an occasional hike, carrying heavy packs. Not very glamorous, but I had family to raise."

Cassidy guessed Henry had seen active service, despite his claims to the contrary. The man would have endured much, including fearing for the lives of his family members. "What do we do with the liberated civilians? Do we leave you to take your chances?"

Henry snorted. "We'd be re-captured in thirty seconds."

"I agree. But we can't leave anyone to look after you."

"You have my sympathy," Henry said dryly. "Can I suggest that those of us who want to join you, and can be of use, do so? Those who don't, can defend themselves with the Sauroid weapons." Before Cassidy could object, he added, "You've said I'm fit. I know which end of a gun to hold." Cassidy didn't like the idea. *But he might be useful,* he thought. Of the rest, only Stephen wanted to come with them. The others wanted to try to get home.

"I suspect," Sophia said, "that for many of them, home no longer exists."

Cassidy asked Stephen, "Where were they taking you?"

Stephen shrugged. "Who knows?"

Cassidy pondered, then said to the others; "We'll follow the road. We're not going to learn anything by wandering in the countryside. If we find a town we might be able to learn more."

Sophia said, "I have an idea." She crouched over a Sauroid corpse. "What's our main problem going to be?"

Cassidy turned and looked at her. "Go on."

"Camouflage!" Sophia triumphantly held up a severed Sauroid head. "We could use these!" Cassidy looked doubtful, and Sophia urged, "Let's try it! We have twelve bodies; we should get a few usable masks. We'll dress our men in the uniforms."

"Why not skin the entire body?" he mocked.

Sophia's eyes lit up, and she grinned ferociously. "Why not?" she breathed, dancing a little jig of excitement.

So the Thals went to work, two skinning each corpse. One Thal used the knife, the other held the skin taut. *Every time I think I know her, she surprises me,* Cassidy thought. Catching Henry's eye, he said lamely, "I guess they've never lost the art of skinning animals."

"It's a great idea," Henry said, "though I won't be volunteering to wear one. Far too hot."

"If they get all the blood off." Cassidy was torn between watching, captive to a horrified fascination, and wanting to look away. The Thals took special care around the ears, eyelids, fingers and toes. Despite the horror of what they were doing, he had to concede they did an effective job. He shuddered; skinning a sentient being was revolting.

When Sophia stood up after an hour, she shoved her hand into the small of her back, pushed and grimaced. Her hands were covered with blue-green Sauroid blood; wiping her face absent-mindedly, she smeared it across her cheek.

"You've got blood on your face," Cassidy licked his fingers to wipe it off, but she held his hand.

She smeared a daub across his forehead, and down his nose. She said in Thal, repeating in English, "May you be able to smell the enemy, and take his knowledge." With her cleaner hand, she unbuttoned his shirt, over his protests. "May you have the heart to take his heart and his blood." Then she pulled him back into the bushes, unfastening his trousers. "May you take his balls," she whispered huskily.

"That isn't my balls." He could hardly speak. He stiffened under her stroking.

"No." she smiled. "Now you must do the same. Wipe the blood from my hand. Now, on my forehead."

Part of him rebelled, but another, atavistic part exulted. "May you be able to smell the enemy and take his knowledge," he said. She stroked him, more slowly. "May you have the heart to take his heart, and his blood." Now he clumsily unfastened her trousers, and she stepped out of them. "May you take his balls." He gasped at how wet she was.

She wiped his lips with her still-bloody hand, leaned against a tree, and lifted one leg. He plunged into her. This wasn't the previous night's tender lovemaking. This was fierce, brutal, as if he were bayoneting the enemy.

She didn't cry out. Instead, she stretched up and bit his mouth, until their blood mingled with the Sauroid's. He came in only seconds; so did she, tremors racking her body. When they were both spent, they slumped.

"That was a very old ceremony," she kissed his chin, with a hint of a smile, her touch as light as a dandelion seed.

"What happens if there aren't any women about?" he joked.

"The first part was the ceremony," she said, mock-sternly, but smiling.

"Ah," he smiled back.

She looked up at him. "We should rejoin the others."

"We should," he nodded. He redid his clothing.

When they rejoined the group the Sapiens studiously looked away. The Thals by contrast, grinned openly. "You got some blood on you," Henry said, "while you were helping skin the creature." He was so deadpan, Cassidy couldn't tell if he was serious.

"You want us to wear these?" Vagiskar held up a skin.

Cassidy nodded. "Any volunteers?" he called out.

"I'll take one, sir," Stokes, one of the Americans said. He was a bull-necked, red-faced cheery looking man.

Stokes picked the biggest Sauroid skin, which looked as if it might burst, but he squeezed into it. The Thals also put the skins on. They needed to swap them around, but most finally fitted reasonably well. Then they put the Sauroid's uniforms on. "This'll never work," Cassidy said gloomily.

"Don't be too sure," Sophia replied. "Their eyesight isn't as good as ours."

They set out in the gathering gloom, returning the way they'd come. Cassidy had night gasses, as did the Thal on point, who wore a Sauroid costume. "The man at the back had better wear a costume, as well," one of the Sapiens suggested.

"Good idea," Cassidy agreed.

They marched at a steady pace. Fortunately the night was clear, and the half-moon shone so brightly even those without night gasses could see somewhat. The road was smooth, so falls were kept to a minimum, though a few still stumbled over an occasional rut.

When the Thal's masks were pulled down, their voices were muffled beyond recognition. Soon, only those at the front and back walked with theirs down- the rest pushed theirs up, like visors on a medieval knight's helmet, ready to close them at the first sign of trouble.

It was almost midnight when Cassidy saw that most of the captive's heads were drooping. Some of the Thals in skins had stumbled as well. "Let's stop for the night!" Cassidy called, to a small cheer from someone.

"Off the road!" Garcia said. "We'll use the trees as cover."

They unrolled sleeping bags. "Take my bag," Cassidy said to Henry. "We'll use the spare blankets."

"You take mine," Vagiskar said to Stephen. "I'll take the first watch, and we'll swap with the watch."

They sat and ate silently, Sophia leaning against Cassidy. He felt spent and embarrassed after their earlier sex. Although the Thal's customs were different, he was Homo Sapiens, not a Thal, and a professional. His men must have known what was going on, and he wasn't setting a good example. Fortunately, Sophia picked up on his mood, or she was as tired as he. She curled against him and was asleep within minutes.

The night was quiet. He hadn't noticed while they'd been moving, but there were fewer calling creatures here than in other forests. So he lay listening, occasionally leaning on one elbow to look for the sentries at each corner of the camp.

Eventually he drifted off to sleep; for a time he dreamed that he was still awake, and he could feel a vast, cold presence. Then he dreamed properly.

The presence was already old when the meteor struck with the force of a trillion Hiroshimas. The great slow things had ruled their world for hundreds of millions of years. In most realities, the dinosaurs were brute behemoths, but in a few worlds they evolved rudimentary intelligence.

He snapped awake; his heart raced, and he felt for his gun. As he woke, he calmed. There was nothing there. He slept again. If he dreamed again, he didn't remember it in the morning.

CHAPTER TWENTY-ONE

On this, Davenport's second morning alone, the sheer gradient had eased slightly, so that it was as if he was walking up a steep hill rather than rock-climbing. He was so high that he shuddered at even the thought of looking down. He wasn't normally acrophobic, but every time the wind blew, he felt in imminent danger of falling.

The alternative was looking out. Then he seemed to be staring into infinity. A gull danced past on the wind, then with wings folded, dropped. Apart from occasional scurries in the grass on the cliff-face, it was the first life he'd seen.

His imagination wouldn't rest. Over and over again his mind conjured images of him toppling into a flailing, screaming drop, to smash on the rocks below. He'd spent an uneasy night perched on a ledge, his dreams haunted by those thoughts. He was so self-absorbed that he almost fell over a bundle of feathers.

The bundle suddenly reared up and cawed at him. Although visibly a mammalian female, she was covered in brown feathers. She stood about one meter fifty, but probably weighed only half his eighty kilos. She had wings in place of arms, while her delicately boned, twig-thin legs were more like feathered human arms, complete with elbow joints. Her bare feet were like hands, even to the opposable thumb. Her feather-covered face was humanoid above a savage beak, which thrust out from where a nose and mouth should have been.

She looked as stunned as he felt. The look in her fierce, glinting eye showed her intelligence. He was sure he detected language amongst her caws and cries.

Her wing was caught in a tangle of roots just out of reach. She was clearly in pain, and panting with exhaustion. She might be able to free herself, but in the process of doing so, she might cripple her delicate wing. "If I'm to help you, you mustn't hurt me," he said quietly, gently, as if reassuring an injured chick, though she was clearly an adult. The beak that snapped at him could rip his throat out. "Let me touch this," he pointed to her trapped wing. Expecting to feel that savage beak on the back of his neck at any moment, he tensed as he crouched down, but no bite came.

He worked methodically, cursing his clumsy fingers, sweat pooling in every hollow. Once he must have hurt her, for she cried out. He said gently, "Sorry! Sorry!" and stroked eider-soft feathers.

At last he worked the delicate wings free of the tangle, and stood clear. She stretched her wings, wincing slightly, and stepped toward him. He stepped back, but unsure of his footing, and not wanting to roll end over end down that long, long hill, he stopped. She bent her head, but instead of the bite he expected, she blew through the huge nostril nearest to him and then, turning her head, blew through the other. She wiped her beak on his face, one side then the other. Was this a kiss? Was she marking him? Was he her possession or her friend?

She cooed once. Then she stretched and threw herself off the cliff. He watched her circle, beating her great long wings. She swooped, chattered something, and was gone.

He returned to his lonely climb.

When he finally reached the top of the cliff, it was several seconds before he realized it. On either side of him, a path followed the cliff edge. Shading his eyes against the bright sunlight, he looked out to sea. There was no sign of ships in any direction. More out of habit than hope he checked the radio, but heard only the crackle of static.

In the distance, he saw a flock of birds. When he squinted, he saw that their legs hung down in the same way that her legs had dangled when she flew.

The flock flew away from him, their great wings beating slowly, regularly. He watched them until they were too small to see. Suddenly lonely, he turned and studied the paths laid out in front of him. He was unsure of which one to follow. He stared inland. The terrain was flat, rising gradually to low rolling hills. On an impulse, he decided to head inland, toward the nearest hill.

***

Cassidy awoke at the feeling of something moving. He reached for his gun, but it was only Sophia, sliding back under the blanket. "I needed to piss." The hands she thrust under his shirt were like blocks of ice.

"If you're going to torture me," he threw back the blanket, "then I'm getting up."

Their breath steamed in the morning air as they stretched, soon warming up enough to be comfortable. Cassidy felt a twinge of sympathy for those who would have to spend the day inside the Sauroid skins.

After a snatched breakfast of fruit plucked from trees to supplement the rapidly dwindling supply of MRE's, they set off.

It was near noon when the mock-Sauroids at the front rounded a corner and stopped so abruptly that the men behind banged into them. They waved those behind them back. Cassidy sneaked to the front and peered around.

Ahead of them, the road abruptly metamorphosed into a brick-paved path leading to a town, which was surrounded by a tall stone wall. A set of black, iron gates was the only break in the wall. "They're unguarded," Cassidy whispered. *Either they're supremely confident they won't be attacked, or they're unbelievably complacent,* he thought.

On one side of the path rose a sheer earthen bank, twice the height of a man. From its flat top sprouted a ragged profusion of untended cedars and beeches, of all sizes, from saplings to fully-grown trees. On the more open ground on the other side of the path, plants shaped like huge bone teeth covered by mosses and lichens, sprouted at forty-five degree angles. There were thousands of them occupying the area from the path to the woods a hundred yards beyond.

Scattered among the cedars were strange looking triangles, their tops curling over toward the compound, casting shadows on the walls. Cassidy decided they were trees, with the triangles being their trunks. Leaves covered their triangular bodies.

The whole area stank of damp, of mulch and leaf mold. There was another smell too, the stink of carrion. It blew from the town, on the breeze. Cassidy thought he heard faint screams. Was it a bird? He listened carefully and heard someone shriek.

The wall surrounding the town was almost three feet thick. Its smooth face was broken only by the huge black gates, which were only half the height of the wall, but were three times as tall as a man. The gates were festooned with dragon shaped-designs. Stones shaped like the tooth-like plants lined the top of the wall.

Within the walls rose a higgledy-piggledy concatenation of ziggurats, pagodas and columnar statues; on top of the columns, stone figures of dragons rested, pounced, or flew. The mess of buildings almost reached to the walls, but there was a slight gap through which two Sauroids strolled and disappeared into the silence. Apart from sounds within the compound, the air was oppressively still.

"What do you think?" Cassidy asked the others. "Do we go through it or around it?"

"I say we head around it," Garcia said. "We can't take on a town, especially a walled one."

Sophia said, "We won't learn anything wandering round the countryside. But if we can get in-" She was interrupted by the sound of a woman screaming from behind the wall, "For God's sake, no!" The woman's shout broke off.

Silence returned.

"We're going in," Cassidy said. "Volunteers?" Repeating the question in Thal, he picked two of each group. Sophia looked mutinous when he didn't pick her, but kept quiet.

"Psst!" a Thal hissed. "Someone's coming along the trail!"

They scattered for cover, some diving for the near side, Cassidy, Garcia and Vagiskar leaping across for the other, where the tooth-shaped plants were. Diving beyond, into the undergrowth. Cassidy patted a tooth-shaped plant in passing. It felt like rock.

A Sauroid patrol marched past, oblivious to their presence. "They could be out for a Sunday morning stroll," Garcia breathed in disbelief.

Vagiskar said, "Blue told us they leave their young out in the wild to survive, each year. The ones that survive are rounded up and returned. This could be such a group."

Cassidy nodded, "In our history the people of Sparta did the same." A head popped up from the undergrowth on the other side. Cassidy waved it back.

The Sauroid patrol's leader pressed its hand to a plate on the wall. The gates swung open. They marched in, the youngsters hissing, spitting and caterwauling excitedly.

The allies watched for several minutes, but the area was silent, so they scuttled back to rejoin the main group. "Nothing," Garcia's voice quivered with amazement. "No guards; No security. They just walk in."

"That plate probably works on palm recognition," Cassidy said. "Vagiskar, let's test it out. You're taking some more prisoners in. Porter, with me. Garcia, you've got command!"

Several of the others muttered protests. Cassidy stared at them until they fell silent.

"Take the hand-held," Garcia urged, pressing a small radio onto Cassidy.

Cassidy checked to make sure it was switched off and pocketed it.

The volunteers climbed out of the undergrowth, and silently formed up, two fake Sauroids each at front and back, Stephen, Cassidy, Porter and a couple of Thals shuffling forlornly, their heads bowed as prisoners, in the middle. Their weapons were hidden. They wouldn't stand a body search, but then Cassidy knew no Sauroid would need to get close enough to try. He had no illusions about the disguises; while they could probably pass inspection from a distance, anything more than the most cursory examination would expose them immediately.

When they reached the gates, Vagiskar slapped his Sauroid-skin covered hand against the panel. Cassidy suddenly found it hard to breathe. His heart was beating so loudly, he was convinced they would hear it inside the town.

The gates opened slowly, like a cheap horror film. Vagiskar sizzled in Sauroid and waved them forward. *Don't over-act,* the shuffling Cassidy thought.

"We're in!" Cassidy breathed. "There's no one here to greet us!" Then he did a double take at the Thal who marched, head bowed at the back of the line. "What are you doing here?"

"I replaced Surius," Sophia said.

"I'll talk to you later." Cassidy looked away, furious and anxious. He stared at the narrow alley dividing the wall from the buildings. A similar human town would probably have held ten or twenty thousand people, Cassidy guessed, but he didn't know if such comparisons were valid. Holding his breath, he was aware of every noise: birds chattering outside the walls, shouted commands in Sauroid, a scream, more shouts. He had a horrible feeling that in rushing in, he'd led them into a trap. "Vagiskar. How long do you think you could pass as a Sauroid?"

"About two seconds." Vagiskar lifted his mask to breathe fresh air.

"It's either that, or we stay in this alley all day."

"Then let's go." Vagiskar slapped the visor back down. "The layout of what we've seen so far seems similar to the town where they took me prisoner. We'll head for the central square."

They marched through narrow, high-walled alleys only two or three meters wide. They reminded Cassidy of Mediterranean towns, although no town in the Med was ever this quiet. He noticed what looked like drainage channels running down each side of the alley.

Pointing at it, Porter hissed, "That looks like blood!"

Cassidy knelt and dipped his finger in it. "It is blood." They stiffened at the sound of Sauroids, and the "prisoners" slouched into their characteristic shuffling poses. Two youngsters swung around a corner behind them.

Vagiskar sizzled at one of the other fakes and jerked the prisoners' chains. The group stepped to one side, to allow the Sauroids to pass. If they were discovered now, they were dead. One of the youngsters spoke to Vagsikar, who spluttered and sizzled in reply. Another youngster glanced at the "prisoners," and for a moment, time stood still. Cassidy tensed, ready to grab his hidden pistol, but the youngster looked away after a minute. It crackled a comment to the first youngster, and the two Sauroids cackled together. Then they rounded the corner and were gone. Cassidy breathed again. "What did they say?"

"That you were poor specimens," Vagiskar said. "I said you dragged your feet all the way home, but it seemed a shame to shoot you. She suggested we throw you in a burial pit instead."

"Where were they going?" Sophia said.

"There's a feast in the Town Square," Vagiskar said. "Some youngsters are joining God. She said that we're near the jail."

"It might be worth peering through the bars," Cassidy said. "See who else there is there."

***

The jail was on the far side of the town square, which was jammed with pushing, shoving Sauroids. The square made Cassidy think of those of the former Soviet Bloc; it seemed to have no purpose other than parades, or other official functions. The Sauroid's universal uniform of functional coveralls heightened the resemblance to Red and Tiananmen Square.

Five-story houses packed together surrounded the square.

Black beams crisscrossed their white painted faces, giving them a faux-Tudor look. Alleyways radiating from the square separated them into blocks of nine. Cassidy guessed that this was an indigenous town that had been occupied by the Sauroids. The houses didn't fit with the Sauroid uniforms.

Another Sauroid passed them in the alleyway, and Vagiskar grunted. It hissed at him, and when Vagiskar didn't reply, the creature spoke. Cassidy tensed and gripped his weapon, but Vagiskar grunted again, and the creature pointed to the other side of the square.

"What was that about?" Cassidy said.

"Directions to the jail," Vagiskar said. "We have to cross the square."

Cassidy said, "I can't believe we've got this far."

Vagiskar shrugged, "They see what they expect to see."

"They seem incredibly complacent," Cassidy's voice trailed off.

Vagiskar shoved, elbowed and jostled his way through the throng. The Sauroids were so intent on what was happening in the square that no one paid them any attention. Some of the youngsters had climbed tall, thin structures that Cassidy thought looked like gallows. Despite the crowd's drabness, a few shuffling hops gave the impression of an almost carnival atmosphere.

The crowd parted, and they had a clear view of the tableau.

Ropes separated the throng from about a dozen barber's chairs. An adolescent Sauroid reclined in each chair, with an apron draped over its shoulders. Next to each youngster stood an adult. On the far side of the group, an ornately dressed Sauroid intoned something, although it was hard to tell what when everything they said sounded like a cross between a boiling kettle and a catfight. There was a specific, regular cadence to the Sauroid's speech that implied a recitation of some sort. Cassidy caught his breath as an adult sliced open a youngster's skull. The youth whimpered, and the adult hissed angrily.

"The kid asked for some relief from the pain," Vagiskar whispered to Cassidy. "The adult accused it of sacrilege."

Several Sauroids had now had their heads sliced open. One had its wound stitched closed while the others. Cassidy stood on tiptoe and felt a weight land on his shoulder.

Something hissed behind him, and he felt hot, stinking breath on the back of his neck. Turning round, he was confronted by an adult Sauroid. One that looked very unhappy.

Vagiskar yanked the chain, and Cassidy almost fainted at the fiery pains that shot down his arms. Another fake Sauroid cuffed the back of his head, and Vagiskar hissed at him. The real Sauroid yowled and raked Cassidy with its claws, but his 'captors' yanked his chain again, and the claws whirled past millimeters from his face.

They beat a hasty retreat, praying that the enraged Sauroid wasn't following them, and edged away from the tableau, toward the jail. Now they were pushing against the tide of Sauroids still shoving toward the ceremony.

It seemed to take hours to work their way to the far side of the throng, although if Cassidy had glanced at his watch, it would probably only have been minutes.

They finally reached the edge of the Square. Vagiskar tapped a youth who was straining to see and grunted a question. Without taking his eyes off the ceremony, the young Sauroid pointed to the next alleyway.

When they reached the deserted alley, Cassidy asked Vagiskar, "What were they doing in the square? Was it some kind of religious ceremony? It looked more like torture."

Sophia mocked, "You mean your religious ceremonies all involve exchanging flowers?" She wilted under his gaze. "Sorry."

"It was a religious ceremony," Vagiskar said, "but also surgery. There's a part of their brain that creates a telepathic link with Bramaragh. They were cutting the part that inhibits the link."

"So if we'd been seen, Bramaragh would have known?" Cassidy was horrified.

"I don't know if it's full telepathy," Vagiskar said, "It may be limited, like our mindspeakers were, as you saw in the crystal. Not all of our people could talk to one another, and lots of things limited those who could."

Cassidy fretted. He couldn't let an ability the Sauroids may or may not have had decide his actions. They slumped again, shuffling toward the far end of the alley. A pair of Sauroids appeared and, walking to where the alleyway forked, stopped at the door to a grim-looking brick building, so dirty it was almost black, its windows barred.

"Looks like the local jail," Sophia said quietly.

"I guess," Porter said. "One jail looks like another."

Vagiskar strode up as if he owned the jail and pushed the doors open. A shot echoed out, and the others ran in. The last man shut the door behind him, and they all stood packed like sardines in a cramped vestibule. A Sauroid lay face down, blood pooling by its head.

Vagiskar pushed up his mask. "He said he was the only one here! The others are watching the celebrations, or on patrol."

"Okay," Cassidy said grimly. "Let's see what or who, they've got."

"Downstairs," Vagiskar said, "if this is designed the same as the place where they held me."

"How'd you get away?" Cassidy said.

"They spent a week marching me to where a flyer picked me up," Vagiskar said. "Within a day a Thal patrol shot it down."

"Odd they should bother flying you back," Cassidy said, "Given how they treated Henry, and the others."

"Maybe there were less prisoners to be transported then," Vagiskar said.

Cassidy, thinking of the Nazi's increasing brutality as the number of Jews they had to kill grew, nodded. "They're so alien, who knows how they think? You two," he ordered two of the fake Sauroids, "Stay here and keep watch. You two, up the stairs; see if anything's on the roof."

He led the rest across to a heavy door. Pulling it open, they descended wide, steep stairs to dimly lit corridors. Cassidy pulled his hand away from a damp patch on the wall and looked at the blood on his hand. He guessed that many of the older stains were dried blood. At the end of the corridor was another door. "Locked," he spat the word.

"I got the keys," one of the Thals held up thin, glowing metal strips. After two or three attempts the door swung open.

Realizing he was holding his breath, Cassidy exhaled.

The cells inside the door were like any cells on earth. Those nearest the door were empty. The next held a stupefied group: Thals, Sapiens, and a Jaya who sat staring dully at a pile of corpses sharing their cell. The next held more corpses. Each further cell contained fewer live and more dead prisoners. Many were mutilated, missing limbs, eyes and one, her cheek. At the far end of the corridor, the last cell was packed with the dead, like cattle in an abattoir. Cassidy liked to consider himself hardened, but this carnage made him sick. "What monsters treat people this way?" His voice was raw.

"You said yourself." Sophia's pale face and glinting eyes hinted that she felt the same revulsion. "Monsters."

"Sir!" Porter called. "More stairs!"

They descended in silence, nerves twitching, ready to shoot anything that moved. A low moan drifted up. They stopped, but no one appeared. At the foot of the stairs a Thal checked the area. "All clear."

The cells upstairs had been a charnel house, but these were worse. Men and women alike were jammed into one giant barred cell. Many of the occupants were covered with blood and feces, where they'd fouled themselves before they died. Some corpses were almost dismembered. Incredibly, one was still alive. He opened his eyes, croaked, "Please."

In another part of the cell, someone else moaned. "Get them out," Cassidy said. "If we have to blow the whole place apart, get them out of there!"

The man was an elderly Asian man. "Hang on," Cassidy told the man, who nodded weakly. "I need information, if we're to beat these things," he told the old man. "Can you answer some questions?"

The old man nodded again.

"Why'd they bring you down here?" Cassidy asked.

"We were no use to them," the old man spoke so quietly Cassidy had to strain to hear him. "We failed the tests."

"What tests?"

"To see if they could control us. They can use some of us, like puppets." The old man said. Then he sighed, his eyelids fluttered, and the breath rattled in his throat.

Cassidy felt for a pulse. "Nothing." He straightened. "Is there anyone else alive in there?" he called. A muffled moan came from somewhere in the cell. He thought frantically; *picking the lock would take too long – it looks complicated.* He fired several shots at the lock, but though pieces of metal flew off, it remained stubbornly intact.

At Cassidy's signal, one of the Thals used a cloth to tie a grenade to the lock, leaving only the pin exposed. Cassidy waved the squad up the stairs.

"We can't risk it!" Sophia said. "If they hear the grenade go off, we're dead. Come on, we must leave them; there's nothing we can do!"

"We're probably dead anyway," A wild elation seized him. "What are the odds against us getting out of this? They must be astronomical." He pulled the pin and pushed her up the stairs.

The blast shook the building, and Cassidy was sure the bang must have been heard outside. He coughed at the thick, choking dust billowing up the stairs. His ears rang.

The door to the cell hung open. Several bodies had spilled out into the corridor. "They must have had to really stuff these people in," Sophia said. "It just doesn't make sense."

"Efficiency," Cassidy said, turning body after body over.

"But it isn't efficient, is it?" Sophia shook her head. She let a head drop against the paving with a dull clunk.

"Depends on your priorities."

"Sir!" A Thal called. "One here alive. Just about." He bent over an elderly black woman. Her breath rasped, and her eyelids fluttered.

"Another one here!" A second Thal called.

The second survivor was a youngish woman, barely semi-conscious, who was covered with bite marks.

Cassidy strained to make out her mutterings.

"Sounds like 'stew'. What does that mean?" a Thal said.

"Food." Cassidy said grimly. "Maybe she means they were using her for food. Might be what the teeth marks are."

"Josh, she's pregnant," Sophia said. "It looks as if they were trying to get at the baby."

Cassidy cursed. "'Food that moves', they call us. These are not nice people."

"Sir!" Porter said. "Look at this!"

'This' was a lone Sauroid, even younger than Blue, trapped amongst the mammalian mass. It recoiled and hissed. "Cuff it," Cassidy said. "Bring it with us. If it resists, knock it out. Don't hurt it more than necessary." Seeing Porter's puzzled look, Cassidy said, "My enemy's enemy is my friend." He turned to the others. "Any more?" He was answered with shaking heads.

Climbing the stairs, they heard the sound of gunfire.

"Oh, crap!" Cassidy muttered. "You were right about calling attention to ourselves."

Sophia gave him a twisted smile. "We'd never have got across the square again. What you did was a fine act."

"I'm getting soft," his laugh was a humorless bark. "In my dotage."

On the next floor they paused to blow the doors on the cells. "Come on!" Cassidy yelled, but only four of the prisoners moved, most simply staring dully at him, as if unable to comprehend the idea of escape. Cassidy shrugged. "I can't make them want to leave."

"We have other things to worry about," Sophia said.

In the lobby, a Thal was firing into the street through a crack in the doors with short raking bursts, while others fired from either side of the windows. One of the men sent to check on the roof re-appeared. "We've found a flier up there."

"Good!" Cassidy said. He tapped a fake Sauroid's shoulder. "Get up on the roof and spray the street! Don't take any unnecessary risks, but make sure they see you if you can. We want these bastards as confused as possible!" He prayed the local Sauroids hadn't already put snipers on the nearby roofs. He turned to the Thal who'd found the flier, "Show me."

The flier was a square platform a little larger than a humvee. At each corner was a wheel, kept in place by a wooden block. The flier dominated the flat roof; there was only about five feet of space on any side. The machine was predominantly a featureless square ringed by a bench that was fenced off by a metal rail about a foot above the edge, with a small helicopter-type engine at each corner. The only other feature was a small seat at the front, with a joystick and horizontal lever. It was, Cassidy decided, the ugliest craft he'd ever seen. "This'll do!"

"Sir?" The lead Thal said.

"Nothing that ugly could be fragile!" He clapped his hands. "Look at the thing! It's a flying truck! All we have to do," he said more confidently than he felt, "is start her up!" And hope the Sauroids don't have ground-to-air missiles, or other aircraft, he thought to himself.

It took several attempts, but they finally worked out how to start the engines. All of the time Cassidy's scalp crawled; he expected to take a bullet from another roof at any moment.

"Easy!" The Thal who'd volunteered to fly the craft crowed. He moved the joystick forward, and the flier lurched against one of the chocks. "Careful!" Cassidy said. The Thal gingerly lifted the horizontal lever, and one corner of the flier lifted.

Cassidy dashed downstairs. "We need to buy time for our people to get onto the roof. Give me something to jam these doors with!" He and Sophia looked at one another; both cried, "Bodies!" at the same time.

They carried corpses, one of them lifting arms, the other the legs, piling them against the doors.

"You!" Cassidy shouted at a Thal. "Get the wounded up to the roof. Make sure you take the Sauroid." He said to Sophia, "I want him. He's the first clue we've had that hints at any kind of bumps in this perfectly uniform society."

Two more Thals grabbed a corpse, and four freed prisoners from the upper cells joined them. One was a blonde-haired woman, whose hair hung down over her face, almost hiding her tears. "It's okay," Sophia said. "We'll be out of here soon. "The woman shook her head and carried on weeping. Sophia lifted the legs of another corpse, while a male prisoner took the arms.

When the pile completely blocked the doors, Cassidy called, "Enough!" He waved the prisoners upstairs and said to the Thals, "Keep firing through the window for two minutes. Then run like hell upstairs."

Cassidy ran up, threw himself into the flier and turned the radio on. It took three attempts before the radio crackled.

"This is Garcia, Major. How you doing?"

A bullet thudded into the metal beside Cassidy. Puffs of dust flew up onto the walls. The Thals laid down covering fire around them, onto the other roofs and into the alleys below.

"We've got transport," Cassidy said cheerfully. "Look for the biggest, ugliest flying flatbed you've ever seen, with an engine on each corner; that'll be us. You okay down there?"

"Yeah," Garcia said dryly. "Been a picnic. We heard some noise and shots from the town. We were thinking of coming to give you a hand when you called."

"No need," Cassidy said. "See you in a few minutes. Out." As the roof fell away below them, the Thals stripped off their masks, whooping with excitement. "We're not out of danger yet," Cassidy said to Sophia. "They may have surface-to-air missiles." He peered over the rail. The town seethed like an anthill poked with a stick. A few Sauroids pointed up, some fired handguns, but as they flew over the town, they encountered little resistance. It was as though the idea of somebody raiding the town had never occurred to them.

They sailed over the town at what Cassidy guessed was about seventy miles an hour. "Can you go faster?" Cassidy shouted. They accelerated, but the craft began to wobble. The pilot slowed down and shook his head.

Cassidy tapped his teeth and thumbed the radio. "Garcia, I want no slip-ups. I think we know where you are, but just to be sure, have one of the men stand in the open with a flare."

"Will do."

The town fell behind, and they saw a patch of open ground, where Garcia and the men waited for them. As they landed, the rest of the squad leapt in.

"Nice work, Sir," Garcia smiled.

"How'd you know it wasn't a trap?"

Garcia's smile faded, and he pondered the question. "How'd you know you weren't flying into one?"

"I didn't," Cassidy said. "But we were more likely to be turned. Next time keep your men hidden, as I ordered. Got it?"

"Sir," Garcia snapped.

The flier took off, keeping to just above the trees. "Where to, Major?" an American soldier asked. He had taken over as pilot when they landed.

Where indeed? Cassidy felt the momentary tug that happened whenever he was faced with the question. He distrusted it on principle, just as he'd distrusted his attraction to Sophia. "Why don't we fly round the town, and keep the same heading as before?" It was an order posing as a question, to which the pilot nodded and adjusted their course. Cassidy estimated their speed at about fifty miles an hour. "Can you give me any more?"

"Not with this load," the pilot said. "We've spread the men around, but this craft isn't easy to fly."

"Can you fly in the dark?"

The pilot shook his head, "I wouldn't risk it, sir." He nodded at the sparse instrument display. "However, the good news is the Thals say the power crystal gives us almost unlimited range."

"Major, I know this woman!" one of the Americans called. "This is Barbara Kaminski, the Captain's wife!"

"Oh, Jesus," Garcia breathed.

"You're sure?"

In sunlight, the woman from the lower cells looked deathly pale, her breaths rasping, labored. "Positive," the American, said. "I've seen her picture in the Captain's wallet. Mighty proud of her, he was. Is," he corrected himself.

A Thal Healer ran his hands over the woman's abdomen; he shook his head and moved out of the way so a medic could dress her wounds and set up a makeshift IV. "Her chances are poor," the medic murmured, "I shouldn't even bother treating her. But I'm damned," his voice thickened, "if I'm going to lose her."

"What's Kaminski's first name?" Cassidy said.

"Stuart," Garcia said.

"Stu," Cassidy said, "that was what she said in the cell." He said to the medic, "I really need to talk to this woman." The medic shook his head, and Cassidy leaned closer. "I'll shoot you if I have to," he never took his eyes from the medic's, "then she'll die anyway."

The medic looked away. "You bastard," he muttered.

This is the hardest part, Cassidy thought. To interrogate an enemy was one thing, but to question his own kind, especially when they're injured-he hoped he could sleep tonight. Cassidy knelt by her. "Barbara," he said. "Ms. Kaminski?"

"Stuart?" Barbara breathed, barely a sigh. "Where's Stu?"

"How did you get here, Barbara?" Cassidy stroked her head.

"Meeting Penny," Barbara whispered.

"Penny Adler?" Garcia blurted.

"Barbara? Where's Penny? Is she here as well?" Cassidy asked gently. Barbara licked her lips feebly. Cassidy moistened a cloth with water from a canteen and dabbed her lips with it.

"'Ank you," she breathed. She had paled further. Her flesh was almost translucent now, the color of flour.

"She's lost so much blood," Cassidy whispered to the medic, who nodded.

Garcia said, "I saw chunks missing out of her side and her legs..." He shook his head and cursed in machine-gun Spanish.

"Barbara?" Cassidy whispered and thought what a fine looking woman she must have been, before pain carved those lines on her face. "What about Penny? What's happening at home?"

"Dead," Barbara whispered. "All dead," she nodded weakly. "LA fell into the sea." Her eyelids fluttered, and she spasmed.

"She's gone into shock!" Cassidy yelled. "Medic! Healer!"

She was instantly surrounded. The Healer beat at her chest and blew into her mouth. The medic shouted, "Give me the adrenaline! No you fool, not that one, that needle, that's it! Quickly! Quickly!" He injected her. Listened to her heart. He listened again and then shook his head.

"Gone," he grated. "'Less we coulda got her to hospital, she was dead anyway."

Cassidy was almost overwhelmed by what she had said. Los Angeles had fallen into the sea? Everyone dead? He glanced up at Garcia, who was hunched over Barbara, gazing down at her as if he could learn something, just by looking at her and willing her to speak.

"Let's talk to our Sauroid," Cassidy said grimly, tapping Garcia on the arm.

"What about them?" Garcia nodded at the other prisoners.

"Henry or someone else can debrief them." Cassidy crawled across the crowded, swaying platform to where the Sauroid sat bound and glaring in a corner. It tried to squeeze back further into the corner at their approach.

"I've dressed what wounds there were," the Healer said, "The main problem was extreme malnutrition."

"We got anything we can feed it?" Cassidy asked.

The Thal said, "Vagiskar tells me they only eat fresh meat. Some of your packet soup?" He produced an MRE with a flourish.

Cassidy read the label. "Oxtail soup. No meat in that." He grinned back.

"So much the better." The Healer ripped the top from the packet, and the chemicals began cooking the soup within the inner foil pouch.

After a couple of minutes the soup was steaming. Tipping it into a tin mug, Cassidy beckoned Vagiskar, who crawled over on all fours. "I need your language skills," Cassidy said. "Tell him this is meat. Presumably they don't always eat live flesh?"

"Not on campaign," Vagiskar said. "They eat dried food."

The Sauroid sniffed at the soup and made a mewling noise like a gull, stretching its head back.

"I'll force feed it, if necessary," Cassidy said bleakly. "Tell it the soup will be all it gets to eat."

"It knows there's no meat in it," Vagiskar said.

"I don't care whether it lives or dies," Cassidy said, "If it doesn't tell me what I want to know, I will hurt it. Tell it that it has no idea of how much I can hurt it." He wasn't bluffing. Although he had never known Barbara, her death had brought him to boiling point.

Another hissing, sizzling conversation followed. The young Sauroid pointed to a festering wound, running from back to front of its hairless head. "It says that nothing you can do will match the pain it has already endured," Vagiskar translated.

With fore and little fingers in his mouth, Cassidy whistled and beckoned to the American medic. "Can you treat this?" He pointed to its head and then said to Vagiskar, "Tell it we're going to treat its wound."

As the medic approached, the Sauroid reared back, then slumped when it saw it could back away no further. "I've got no anesthetic," the medic said.

Vagiskar gabbled at it, fell silent, then gabbled again. He shook his head, "I don't have the words. I don't know the words for healing, or sickness."

Cassidy sat on his haunches and waited. The medic stitched the long, ragged wound. The Sauroid mewled once or twice, but sat remarkably still, only crying out when the flyer hit an air current, causing the needle to dig more deeply into its head.

While the medic worked, Vagiskar quizzed the Sauroid. "Here's what I've learned so far," the Thal said. He took a deep breath. "It has no name. They're only named on becoming adults ,and those are only descriptions. So the other one was named Blue, after its coloring. Also, they only become male and female on reaching adulthood. This is why I've struggled with the language. They have an extra gender."

"Some of our languages do too," Cassidy said, "German has male, female and neuter." He added, "Sorry, I interrupted."

Vagiskar nodded terse acknowledgement. "This language has **four** genders; male, female, child, and thing; what you call neuter," he said. "When they're 'Joined to God', and their telepathic sense is enhanced, that's when they're named. And Bramaragh chooses their sex." At Cassidy's surprised look, he said, "When they link to Bramaragh, it triggers hormonal surges. They change from child to male, female or neuter." He paused, took a breath and resumed. "This one failed the ceremony, and at that point it ceased to be a person, both in its own eyes and those of its society. It became an object, to be thrown out with the refuse."

"What if the operation had worked?" Cassidy said.

Vagiskar wagged his head, "It would've joined the community of minds. If I understand it, Bramaragh isn't just a single mind; it's a collection of minds, but thinking as one, influenced, rather than controlled by a dominant personality."

"Gestalt," Cassidy breathed softly, stunned by the implications. What does that do to its societal development, he wondered.

"Because it was discarded, it couldn't understand that we would treat its wound. It believes absolutely in its own worthlessness. That's why they have no words for healing, or sickness. If you're not fit, you're dead."

Cassidy said, "We can't call it 'hey you', can we? We'll call it Nemo. It means 'no-one' in one of our languages."

Vagiskar said "Nemo", and pointed at the Sauroid.

It stared back.

CHAPTER TWENTY-TWO

The sun was a muddy orange ball hanging low in the sunset when they parked the flyer in a clearing. The men spilled out. Most rested against its sides, a few stayed inside the rail. Those who were fit tended to the wounded.

"You okay?" Sophia asked Cassidy. "You seem troubled."

Cassidy shook his head. "I need to take a walk, to clear my head. I won't be long."

"Don't go alone!" Sophia said. "You might run into an enemy patrol."

"I'll shoot them," he said flatly. "I need some time alone."

"If I promise to be quiet, will you let me accompany you?"

Cassidy nodded reluctantly.

Chest high saplings lined the path. There were no signs of cultivation, but the scrubby branches were easy to push through. They walked along suspiciously regular pathways. It was as if something had blunted Nature's teeth on this world.

Cassidy needed solitude to sort out his thoughts. He couldn't think straight; his thoughts circled round and round, over and over again, as if he were trying to simultaneously watch TV and listen to a radio, all while reading a book.

He tried to ignore Sophia's silent presence, but finally he said to her, "Ever since we arrived, I've felt an overwhelming-" he stopped and took a deep breath.

"Take your time," Sophia took his arm.

"But that's just it!" Cassidy shook her off, groping for words. "We haven't got time! Ever since we arrived, I've felt such an overwhelming compulsion to go in one particular direction. I fought it at first, then I turned around and rationalized why I gave into it." Sophia raised an eyebrow. "The compulsion is leading me- leading us toward Bramaragh's lair," Cassidy continued. "I've been trying to figure out how to sort the contradictory possibilities into some kind of order."

"Hush," Sophia put her finger to his lips. When he had quieted, almost like a nervous horse settling, she said, "I think you're over analyzing all this."

"It's what I do," he said. "I analyze, decide and act."

"But you risk paralyzing us by doing so."

She's right, he thought. In Military Intelligence, they called it paralysis by analysis.

"We came here to learn about Bramaragh. Yes?" Sophia said.

"Yeah," he said, "But on our terms, not his."

"So, we keep going, and when we get close to the lair, we do something unexpected. Until then, follow your instincts."

"You make it sound so simple," he said.

"It will be simple," Sophia said. "We will make it so." She looked around at the gathering darkness. "We need to get back."

They rejoined the group. Four men had dug a grave. They lowered Barbara Kaminski into it. *We seem to do nothing but eat, sleep and bury people,* Cassidy thought. Garcia raised his eyebrows in question. Cassidy nodded, and Garcia removed his helmet. "I didn't know Barbara Kaminski," he said, fiddling with the strap. "But the Captain made her his wife." He stopped, shooting a sheepish look at Sophia, "Or she made him her husband. They was going to have a baby soon." There was an intake of breath from some of the men. "But that isn't going to happen. We gotta find the Cap and let him know what happened." Garcia fiddled some more with the strap. "This isn't coming out the way I intended," he cocked his head to one side. "I guess that's why we have preachers, so they can sum up people's lives and say what good folks they were, all nice and neat and tidy." He laughed edgily. "I'm not likely to make much of a preacher. I'm trying to say that she must have been a damn fine woman, for her and the Cap to be a couple, and she deserved better than this. We owe her something, to make sure she didn't die for nothing."

The Sapiens nodded grimly, while the freed prisoners sat listlessly, as if drained by their ordeal. The Thals looked on impassively. Cassidy had noticed how stoic they were. Was that because of the war, or was that how they had always been, he wondered. Did they think Sapiens were all hysterics, because they didn't simply leave their fallen where they lie? Archeologists had always said Neanderthals mourned their dead. So it must have been war's brutalizing effect. Or the archaeologists had been as wrong about that as they had been wrong about everything else.

Cassidy recited a short prayer, and the squad dispersed, to sit round the flier, which had become like a campfire, for them to huddle around. They opened MRE's, grumbling as usual about them. The Thals were already wolfing theirs down although they were only half-cooked.

Cassidy ignored the other low-level grumbling and instead said, "We've been through a lot the last few days. So I'm going to tell you something of our mission." He summarized recent events, omitting anything that might make them doubtful. Doubt was contagious, corrosive.

When he outlined the disaster in California, the men were stunned. Finally Tandala spoke. "What else is happening back home, sir?"

"I don't know anything, other than what I've told you."

An American asked, "Why don't we go home, sir? Help with the relief effort."

Another said, "Why we wastin' time here, anyway? We should be back home, lookin' after *our* people, not pissin' round on Mars or wherever we are."

Garcia was ready to interrupt, but Cassidy waved at him to be quiet. "Hard though it is to accept, the attacks start here," Cassidy said. "Our best opportunity to help our Earth is here." Then he said quietly to the freed captives, "I'm afraid that tomorrow we'll have to leave you behind."

Stephen Lo protested, "These people are in no condition to look after themselves! Look at the state of them! Do you think they'll last a day before they're recaptured?"

"We've no choice," Cassidy said. "We're not a Red Cross mission. We are a military operation. If we take them with us, at the very best, they will slow us down. At the worst, they will get all of us injured or killed." Cassidy added coldly, "Feel free to stay and look after them, Stephen. We'll leave whatever supplies we can."

When they turned in, Cassidy wriggled on the unyielding ground to get comfortable. When Sophia ran her fingers down his chest, he whispered, "Go to sleep."

"Not sleepy," she murmured, hooking her leg over him.

They made love quietly. At last, spent, he slept. Dreamed.

Of a huge fireball that tore a ragged trail across the heavens. It landed a thousand times on different versions of the Earth and ended the dinosaurs' rule ten thousand times, perhaps even more. The dreaming Cassidy had no way to count the never-ending kaleidoscope of impact, column of fire, the shattering effects of the fall-out and then the long descent into night. Such were the almost infinite permutations possible that maybe the thousand-and-first, or millionth-and-first time, something survived. Even then, a thousand times more, the lizards faded in the face of competition from the mammals, or intelligent avians. So the odds were a million, ten, even a hundred million to one. Until in one world, things were different. The meteor came in obliquely, skidding off the troposphere. Neither birds nor mammals had evolved here, so they posed no challenge to the thunder-lizards. Crucially, the dinosaurs had developed rudimentary intellect. Given enough spins of the roulette wheel of life, even the longest odds eventually deliver a win.

Cassidy saw through the eyes of a fledgling gestalt. They /it watched the flame in the sky. One lizard on its own could not have thought through the implications. But this was a mass of ant-like intelligences, their minds acting as refractive lenses for each of the others.

They /it sensed danger. Could even see into the nearby alternaties. Saw their kind slowly fail in a never-ending winter beneath a rain of sulphuric acid, when life both on land and in the sea perished en masse from three years of perpetual night.

"Ugh," Cassidy grunted as Sophia shook him awake.

"You were mumbling in your sleep," she said. "Another dream?"

"Nothing much," Cassidy said, wondering guiltily why he didn't tell her the truth. He patted her hip. "Go back to sleep." He wrapped his arm round her. "It'll be light soon."

***

Davenport had spent a miserable night in a tree, trying to stay dry from the rain. It was driven by gusting eddies of wind that never blew from the same direction, and whichever way he lay, he got wet. The day before, he'd walked all day, barely reaching the first of the low hills in the distance. They were sparsely covered with grass, and dotted with a few trees. He was lucky to have found a tree that he could climb. He sneezed, and shivered. The rain had stopped. It was time to get moving. There was little point staying where he was.

As the morning wore on, the cloud gradually lifted, and as the sun emerged, so his spirits rose. He switched the radio on. *There can't be much power left,* he thought, as the now-familiar static greeted him. Part of him wanted to abandon it, but he had a superstitious dread that if he did, he might miss his one chance of finding friendly faces.

It was mid-morning when he reached the top of the next hill. He sat on a rock, sunning himself and saw movement from the corner of his eye, some kind of low, slow-flying aircraft. Rolling off the rock, he ducked for cover. The radio crackled to life. He grabbed it, and a moment later, the rock exploded into fragments. Shards shrapneled through his uniform, and he yelled. Still clutching the radio, he rolled, hearing shouts and the coughing chuckle of Sauroid weapons a hairs-breadth behind him. "My name's Davenport!" he yelled into the radio, forgetting protocol, more concerned with dodging the bullets kicking up dust all around.

"Where are you?" An American's voice squawked from the radio. There was another burst of gunfire. Davenport thumbed the transmit button. "I don't bloody know! My compass is spinning like a weathercock in a thunderstorm! I am under fire. Repeat, under fire!"

He dived behind a tree to avoid the next burst, praying that he hadn't dived into the firing line. The radio crackled, but he couldn't hear what the voice said. He thumbed the transmit button. "I'm on top of a hill. Can't you triangulate on the signal? Quickly! The battery's failing!"

"Roger that." The American's voice was already fading. "Keep the signal open."

"Hurry up, for Christ's sake," Davenport prayed. He would be dead if they didn't get to him soon. Wherever the Yanks were, they must have been close, within five clicks at the most, or the radio wouldn't have worked.

The tree trunk behind him exploded, and he felt thuds into his backpack. He hoped it was bits from the tree, rather than the explosive bullets the Sauroids tended to use. Silence fell like a dropped cloak. "It's okay to come out!" someone with an Australian accent shouted.

Giddy with relief, Davenport was about to stand up when a woman, also Australian, shrieked, "Don't! It's a trap!" Her shout turned into a scream. Davenport slumped. Gunfire erupted, and the trees around him spewed fragments.

To his horror, a flier rose over the trees, and although he took aim at the Sauroid standing in the front, it had passed him before he could move, the look-out beckoning to the Sauroids who'd ambushed him. Then, to Davenport's amazement, it fired down into the trees. Explosions showered smoke and debris.

The radio crackled. "Can you stand up?" Cautiously, Davenport slid upright, using the trunk at his back as a lever.

"Hold your fire, we're turning round," the radio said, and Davenport realized that the whip he could see poking up over the rail was a radio antenna.

"Bugger me," Davenport muttered in astonishment. The flier settled on the ground, and Sapiens, Thals and Sauroids spilled out of it, laying down a hail of covering fire. One of the Sauroids spun around, wounded; Davenport glimpsed the baggy fit of the skin, and saw the Thal inside the Sauroid skin.

"Get aboard, hombre!" Garcia roared, grinning broadly.

The few feet to the flier felt like miles; Davenport ran, bent beneath the weight of his pack and lurched at the rail. Hands hauled him over, and he landed in the bottom of the flyer, staring at a pair of feet.

"Nice to see you, Mr. Davenport," a familiar voice said.

"Nice to be back, Major Cassidy," he croaked and buried his face in his hands with relief.

"Easy, tiger," Porter patted his shoulder. "Have some water." It tasted better than any he'd ever had. He goggled at the Sauroid, sitting handcuffed in the corner.

"Come on," Cassidy snapped. "Let's nail these buggers."

"Sir," Davenport croaked. "They're using humans as decoys. Australians." He described the attempted trap.

Cassidy swore, slowly, precisely and viciously. He thought for a moment and then said, "Okay, this is what we do." He barked a series of instructions to the soldiers and said to Sophia. "Debrief him, will you?" Davenport watched them climb out and lost sight of them as they disappeared into the trees.

Sophia sat beside him. "Oh, for a scanner," she sighed.

"A what?" Davenport said. He was exhausted and felt he had little to tell her that was of interest.

"Scanner," Sophia said and added, "What we view the crystals with." He inched away from her shark-like grin. "We've adapted them for interrogations. So, what's happened since we last met?"

Davenport realized that had only been a few days ago! His tale was straightforward, until he came to his meeting on the cliff with the avian. For some reason, he didn't want to talk about it. He felt he should have tried to find out more about her before he had let her go.

"After all our efforts to get here," Sophia sighed. "You just go for a stroll and end up on the same world."

Davenport shrugged. "It wasn't planned. Shame your famous foresight isn't working."

"Isn't it?" Sophia said, grinning.

The flier shook as the returning squad climbed in. They lifted a red-haired woman into the flier and then threw in a semi-conscious handcuffed man, who groaned.

Nemo squalled. Vagiskar shushed Nemo, tied a blindfold around the man's eyes and covered his ears.

"What's that for?" Davenport asked.

"When he comes round, whatever is possessing him may be able to see through him," Cassidy said grimly. He half-smiled at Davenport's raised eyebrow. "I meant 'possessed' literally. We jumped him from behind and clubbed him hard enough to kill a normal man, but he still fought us as though he were bewitched. I don't think he realized he was fighting humans," he added, more hopefully than sure.

They were silent. A Thal carefully lifted the man's earmuffs to get at the headpiece the man wore. The Thal replaced the muffs and examined the headpiece gingerly before passing it to Sophia.

"It's the same thing I saw the traitors wearing when Home fell," she said. "It doesn't fit perfectly; it was designed for a Thal's skull, not a Sapiens."

"Is he still under Bramaragh's control?" Cassidy asked.

"Don't know," Sophia said.

"What's his name?" Cassidy asked the red-haired woman, who sat, watching them warily. Her eyes flicked from the prisoner, to Nemo and back again. When she picked at a fingernail, her hands shook. One eye was closed and puffy, and her face was covered with bruises, cuts and mud. Sophia reached out with a damp cloth, and she flinched.

It had been she who had yelled, Davenport realized. She had saved his life.

"His name's Ethan Turner," the woman said, her voice trembling with suppressed emotion. "I'm Phyl. I thought we'd died and gone to Hell," her voice shook, and she paused. "They injected us when they caught us and fitted these things to us; suddenly there was this great big voice in my head, as big as the world. I managed to ignore it, but it was then that Ethan turned on me."

"That wasn't Ethan," Sophia said. "But a shell. When the Multiplicium fell, I saw people do terrible things. It took me a long time to accept that they weren't my people any more." When Sophia brushed her leg, Phyl cried out. "Let's see," Sophia said gently. Seeing Phyl glance at the men, Sophia added gently, "Look away, please, gentles? Allow us some privacy."

Phyl whimpered, and Davenport heard Sophia's in-drawn breath. "That's a bite mark. Sauroid. And that one?"

"Human." Phyl's whimper stretched it to 'hee-oo-man'.

"Was it Ethan?" Sophia's voice was gentle, but insistent, "Was it?"

Phyl said, "Yes," but it was barely a sigh. She broke down, and wept, while Sophia made cooing noises.

Davenport looked away, unable to bear watching such naked agony. He glanced at Cassidy and noticed the dark, puffy rings beneath his eyes, visible even through his tan. Dirt smeared the man's face. There was something else; at first Davenport couldn't quite work it out. It slowly dawned on him. The Cassidy who had left the caves had had authority. This Cassidy had **presence**. Thals and Sapiens alike looked to him for leadership.

Catching his gaze, Cassidy said, "How are you? All right?"

"I'm okay," Davenport said. "But things are really crappy back at home."

"I think the phrase is gone to hell," Cassidy said. At his signal the pilot started the engines, and the flier lifted off.

Sophia said, "Phyl's sleeping. She's exhausted." She kicked Turner, not hard enough to hurt, but like kicking over a rock to see what lay beneath. "What do we do about this?"

Cassidy peered at the man's skull. "There's a wound here," he said. "It looks as though he's had amateur surgery." He beckoned the medic. "Which part of the brain is this?" He pointed to the wound.

The medic grimaced. "It looks like a lobotomy scar," he finally admitted. "They used to do them to pacify violent cases."

"Makes sense," Cassidy said. "Remove volition, and you're half-way to mind control, in a crude sort of way."

"Sir, where are we going?" Davenport said.

Cassidy brought him up to date. When he described the town, Davenport said, "So much for a living God."

"Maybe," Cassidy said. "We're used to a benevolent God, or in the Old Testament, an angry one. A god who cares, not one who simply isn't concerned what suffering his people endure. If he even notices." He stared at Davenport. "Do you care about the fate of one of your toenails?"

"Only if losing it hurts," Davenport said.

"Exactly!" Cassidy clapped his hands.

Davenport thought, *How do we beat a god?*

***

The flier flew north. Cassidy dozed, watching Davenport through half-narrowed lids. Cassidy hadn't realized how much he missed having the younger man around to bounce ideas off of. Sophia was bright, but Davenport had a way of looking at things differently. He'd seen how Davenport had watched Phyl earlier, sideways on, so she wouldn't notice, but intently. That was the closest thing to emotion that Davenport had shown.

Rather than doze in the sunshine, as most of the troops did, Davenport peered over the rail at the ground below. "The land looks increasingly heavily populated," he said aloud.

"Maybe we're approaching civilization," Henry's tone gave no clue as to what he thought of that civilization, but Cassidy could guess. He noticed that lately he seemed to have a lot more insight into people than he ever had before. He shied away from following that thought.

He dreamed again. With the logic of dreams, years passed in only seconds, yet time flowed as normal. It was as if he lived another's life, remembering what happened, but, as with memories, only selectively.

Bramaragh killed off the other gestalt-intellects in battles to extinction as catastrophic as the meteor impact had been. The victors enslaved and ate the surviving losers. In time, the gestalt attained a veneer of civilization. Survival depended on absolute obedience, in deed, word and thought. After several million years they died off; the same happened with another gestalt. When they, too, failed to survive, Bramaragh allowed a race to evolve, upright, bipedal, but yet still clearly Saurian. They were allowed slightly more freedom, although it would have seemed insignificant to an outsider, for they were still slaves worshipping a living, breathing god that dwelt amongst them. The experiment appeared to succeed.

Millennia trickled by. The Bramaragh gestalt began to think beyond mere survival, to think in three, and even four dimensions, to wonder what the strange shadow worlds were that were so similar, yet so different from its own. Bramaragh saw only the directly convergent alternates, not most of the near-infinite possibilities. Yet it/ they pondered the scheme of things, slowly, glacially, worrying at the puzzle. Bramaragh was absolutely alone. With solipsistic faux-logic, it wondered if the alternates were mistakes, made by a defective cosmos. Eons passed, and as Bramaragh aged, its/ their mental arteries hardened. Theories became certainties, facts, and finally dogma. In a world where the only voice and thoughts were Bramaragh's, there was no one to debate the point. The universe was guilty of heresy. The errors must be corrected.

Bramaragh was as immortal as any creature could be. In time, if it waited long enough, it would be able to conquer, even destroy. It could wait, until the day when it had gathered enough workers, when it was strong enough to punch holes in the barriers between alternate realities, and could rip down the barriers that separated perfection from error.

One day it needed to wait no longer. Its time had come.

Cassidy awoke abruptly in fading light. A massive cloudbank hid the sun. For a few moments, he saw Sapiens and Thals through alien eyes; was appalled by their hairiness, their strangeness. He licked his lips, gradually returning to normal. He looked up, to see Sophia studying him intently. "You were muttering in Sauroid," she said. "Have you been taking lessons off Nemo?" Her tone was light, but her eyes were worried.

"Well, you know the saying," Cassidy joked. "Know your enemy." He changed the subject. "How are we doing?"

"Quiet," Sophia said. "Too quiet."

"You think it's a trap?" Cassidy sat up straight. What if he had shared his dreams with Bramaragh? What if he knew exactly what their plans were?

"Could be," Sophia agreed cautiously, watching him. "You see how many more towns there are below? I'm surprised no one has shot at us."

"We can turn back, if you want."

She shook her head. "We've had this conversation before."

Cassidy sat back and sipped at a water bottle. They purified the water every night, but he wondered how difficult it'd be to drug the water supply and induce paranoia, or hallucinations.

Sophia gasped, and Cassidy leaned forward, but she waved him away. "For an instant, I felt something really, really strange, but then it was gone again."

"Bramaragh," Cassidy said.

"I don't know," Sophia said and fell quiet, thinking.

Cassidy caught Nemo watching him. He stared at the Sauroid, willing it to look away, but it never wavered, and eventually, it was Cassidy who looked away.

***

Davenport said to Phyl, "You should eat." He leaned forward, stopping as she flinched. "I won't hurt you," he said. "I know you've had a terrible time."

"Oh?" Phyl said flatly. "Do you know what I experienced?"

Davenport tried to speak, but stopped, flustered, his face brick red. "No," he finally admitted.

"Show me your teeth," Phyl said.

"What?"

"Show me your teeth," Phyl repeated.

Davenport bared them self-consciously.

"Every time someone smiles at me," Phyl said, "I think of them," she glared at Nemo, "talking to the man who was my lover. I think of Ethan looking at me like I was a piece of meat," she choked the words. "Sinking his teeth into my leg. The same teeth that he smiled at me with, a few days ago. So don't tell me that you understand!"

She ran down like a clockwork toy.

Their fellow Sapiens pointedly looked elsewhere, but the Thals stared, openly curious. "I'm sorry," Davenport said, lamely.

Phyl shrugged.

Sick with congealed rage and shame that someone could turn on one of his own, especially a lover, Cassidy kicked Ethan's prone body as he crawled past, drawing a groan from the man. Cassidy kept going, pushing his way past the others until he crouched, facing Nemo, who sat propped up in a corner.

"Careful!" one of the Americans said. "It'll have your nose off as soon as look at you!"

Cassidy beckoned Vagiskar, who crawled through the forest of legs. "We need more," Cassidy said. "Wring it dry."

"What do you want to know?"

Cassidy leaned back and crouched on his haunches. "How many young Sauroids are unable to talk to God? Are they born with the potential to link to Bramaragh; does it develop as they mature, or is it only the result of this butchering that we saw in the square? Are there others like Bramaragh? Are there any Sauroid communities outside the gestalt?"

"Wait!" Vagiskar said, "One question at a time!" A long conversation followed between Vagiskar and the Sauroid, the Thal nodding as Nemo answered his questions. Sometimes Vagiskar stopped the youngster, to ask for clarification. The Thal looked troubled, although Cassidy was unsure whether he was misreading Vagiskar's expression. At the end, the Thal puffed out his cheeks. "I think I got everything. But it's not an easy language. I may have misunderstood."

"Go on," Cassidy prompted.

"There is nothing, no life, no existence for adults, except Bramaragh. That may be because even the possibilities of such things are taboo. Apparently, Nemo is one in a generation." Vagiskar sipped at a water bottle and resumed, "All Sauroids are born with some empathic ability. My assumption would be that it's probably been bred into them over the ages, except Nemo was born without the ability. It only became clear how different he was when they tried to join him to God." Vagiskar's voice thickened. "They wouldn't even waste a bullet, or rope on him."

Cassidy shared his anger, but could see the remorseless logic of the Sauroids. "You wouldn't shoot your table, would you? We're no more than furniture to them," he said to himself, remembering his dreams. The implications of the logistics of 'processing' the parallel Earths were staggering, frightening in their immensity.

Cassidy noticed how they had all fallen into the habit of referring to Nemo as "he" even though the Sauroid was actually a "thing." Cassidy decided that it was their way of trying to relate to Nemo. Until they needed to dehumanize him, when his usefulness was over, and it was time to use a bullet. Turning away, he noticed that Turner was stirring and mumbling.

"What do we do about him?" Garcia asked. "Shoot him?"

"Seems a waste, now we've got him." Cassidy scratched his stubble.

"Trouble is," Garcia said, "if we interrogate him, and he's linked to this Bramaragh like you say, he'll know about us."

Sophia interrupted, "Not if we get a Sauroid to question him. And we all keep out of sight." she added.

"Damn me," Garcia breathed, a gleeful grin slowly spreading across his face, "you are one sneaky woman."

"I do my best," she said, with patently false modesty.

"It could work," Cassidy agreed.

"If nothing else," Garcia said, "it may make Bramaragh think there's organized resistance. If there is already, he'll think they're part of it. If there isn't, it'll really light a fire under the *hijo de puta*. Make him think he's got enemies amongst his own kind, that Nemo ain't an isolated example."

They positioned the fake Sauroids into the front, ushering Nemo there as well. The pilot also swapped with one of the fake-Sauroids, and the craft wobbled while they changed over, but the new pilot quickly corrected it. "We may want to let the blind accidentally slip so he sees Nemo," Cassidy told Vagiskar, "The others won't stand close scrutiny. Try to learn what you can about Bramaragh's location, without revealing our own ignorance. For all we know, every Sauroid that ever lived knows where he is. Anything you learn will be useful. If we have been able to break the link, I guess you'll know. I don't think acting is a Sauroid strength. Make sure Nemo knows what he has to do, okay?"

"I'll try," Vagiskar said, none too confidently.

One of the fake Sauroids removed Turner's earmuffs, while another threw water over him. The effect was electric. Turner spat, sizzled, yowled and howled constantly in Sauroid, while writhing and kicking against his bonds so ferociously that Cassidy thought he would break his back. Out the corner of his eye, Cassidy saw an ashen-faced Phyl shrink back into the far edge of the craft, as if to push herself through the metal.

Vagiskar shouted at Turner in Sauroid, but the prisoner just shouted back; they were having two completely separate yet simultaneous conversations. Everything Turner said was in Sauroid. It was clear that now the link to Bramaragh was established it, no longer needed the headpiece to continue.

Vagiskar looked directly at Cassidy and gave a shake of the head to signal the interview was going nowhere.

Cassidy mimed replacing the earmuffs and gave a thumbs down to signal that Nemo was to dislodge the blindfold.

As soon as the youngster had done so, Turner redoubled his spastic writhing and tried to bite Nemo, shouting and screaming so ferociously that the young Sauroid scuttled back, mewing and whining piteously.

Before Turner could writhe free, another 'Sauroid' grabbed Turner from behind and roughly replaced the blindfold. Another put the earmuffs back. Turner kept screaming and howling. Cassidy said disgustedly, "Gag him as well. Did you learn anything?"

"I think you could tell that he's still linked," Vagiskar said. "And the idea of renegade Thals almost sent him insane."

"What do we do with him?" Davenport said. "We can't leave him like this."

Cassidy said, "Maybe, when we land, we'll just drop him off."

"What?" Vagiskar shouted. "Let him loose?"

Before Cassidy could reply, Sophia spoke in machine-gun Thal. Two men grabbed Turner and tossed him over the side. Cassidy watched in horror as the wriggling man shrank until he became only a dot.

Phyl stared open-mouthed, relief and horror on her face.

Cassidy turned to Sophia, who looked at him innocently. "You said drop him off. So I had the men do it for you."

"You didn't, hear me say anything else, like 'when we land?'" he asked, shaking with anger.

"Did you?" Her eyes widened. "I'm sorry, I didn't hear you." She added, "I thought you were being oddly pragmatic."

Cassidy leaned over and whispered, "Let's see if you hear this: If you ever, ever pull a stunt like that again, I'll shoot you myself. There'll be no trial, just a bullet to your head." He leaned back, pleased to see that the lighter patches on her face had paled, and the black ones were now a dark gray. "Is that completely, absolutely, one hundred per cent clear?"

Gulping, she nodded.

"Don't think that because we share a bed, that allows you to interfere. If we continue to share a bed."

"Josh, I'm sorry." Sophia's bottom lip quivered, and her eyes filled. "I know you don't like to mistreat people, but that was no longer a man."

Cassidy shook his head. "I don't believe you thought at all." He turned away, scared at how angry he'd allowed himself to become. That's what he got for mixing business and pleasure.

Something flashed past, then banked. Cassidy's jaw dropped as he recognized US Air Force markings. "That's an F-15!" Garcia yelled. The troops let out whoops of joy. It was pursued by a half dozen or more unmarked gunmetal gray aircraft. Cassidy caught a glimpse of a Sauroid pilot.

The F-15 was in trouble. Its missile racks were empty, so it was reduced to using its cannon. The Sauroid planes, whatever their individual capability, were mobbing it like crows mob a hawk. They showed no fear, flying straight at the F-15, which barely managed to jink out of the way each time. Finally, the F-15 was unable to flick over in time, and the planes collided in a bright orange flower of flame. The explosion was followed a second later by a boom.

"Sir, in the distance!" Hatcher pointed. Cassidy took the field glasses from him, and swept the horizon.

"Skyscrapers!" Cassidy breathed. "Looks like a big, big city." He said, "Get Nemo over here." Nemo joined him, and he passed the glasses to the Sauroid. "Is that Bramaragh's lair?"

"That's Godshome," Vagiskar translated, in answer.

"Hardly original," Cassidy muttered and called, "swing her through ninety degrees, and we'll circle the edge."

"How close do you want to get?" Sophia appeared beside him, as if their quarrel had never happened.

Cassidy admired that toughness. "I don't know," he said. "Let's nudge round the outskirts, see if there's some place where we can park the old bus."

Whatever plans he had in mind were swept aside in the next moment, as Garcia called, "Sir, Captain Kaminski! On the radio!"

CHAPTER TWENTY-THREE

Sullen storm clouds licked the horizon; they were so thick that even at mid-morning, the land lay in shadow as dark as night. To the east, where the docks had burned in the Blitz, London burned again.

What's left of London, the Prime Minister thought. Where the London Eye had stood, a volcano belched lava into the Thames; steam covered the surrounding buildings in an eerie cape. To the southeast, huge pagoda-like structures had appeared. To the west, foothills were carpeted by green trees that had grown overnight.

No wonder they had become introverts, he thought, when what had been familiar vanished overnight. Friends weren't there any more, or had turned into strangers. Cassidy's crystals explained a little, but they made it no easier to accept the changes.

"Prime Minister, they're ready for you," Clarke said. He studied the man. "Are you all right, sir?"

"Just tired," the Prime Minister forced a smile, though it made his face ache. His reflection in the window looked like a death's head. Still, he bounded in, somehow dredging up the energy to look cheerful, and boomed, "Morning everyone." Each Cabinet member intoned a greeting. "What's the latest situation?" he asked. They had been here barely three hours earlier, and the news had been bad enough then.o

"Parts of Germany are now under water, Prime Minister," The Foreign Secretary said, "following the rise in sea level that swamped the Netherlands."

The Prime Minister turned to the next Cabinet member. "David, domestic situation?" The Home Secretary looked even worse than the Prime Minister felt.

The Home Secretary rubbed his eyes. "We're drowning in refugees. People are fleeing the lower ground. The sheer weight of numbers is pushing them through the Lake District into Scotland. We've regained contact with Fairford but lost it with Fylde."

"Call Fairford," the Prime Minister said. "Find out if the Yanks have pulled their B-52's back." The United States was in even worse shape than Britain. The President had been acting very strange lately, edgy, trigger-happy, even paranoid at times. The Prime Minister wondered if he even was the President or an unstable doppelganger from an alternate universe. He'd wondered that a lot lately. The United States had closed its borders a few days earlier and lashed out at any countries it suspected of having any sympathies toward the Sauroids.

"How about food stocks?" The Prime Minister asked. The Home Secretary's head dropped. The others looked away. "David?" The Prime Minister hadn't meant to sound so sharp. "Are we okay for food?"

"Even with rationing, we only have about a week's worth, Prime Minister," The Home Secretary's voice was so low the Prime Minister had to strain to hear it. "After that, we will need assistance from the Red Cross."

There was a collective gasp. *My God,* the Prime Minister thought. *We've become a 3rd world country in need of famine relief.* Was he the only one who wondered where that assistance would come from? He turned to Defense. "Jilly, what about the rest of the Coalition?"

Jilly shook her head. "We're receiving only intermittent transmissions from the U.S., Prime Minister. There are worrying developments to the east." At his raised eyebrow, she continued,

"A nation calling itself the Holy Mongol Empire has replaced India. Our remaining orbital satellite has taken photographs and listened in on telecommunications, such as they are." Not for the first time, the Prime Minister wondered where their hardware was vanishing to and why some returned later. "It appears," Jilly continued, "that they're as disturbed as everyone else by the current developments."

"Maybe we could contact them," the Chancellor said.

"We have more immediate concerns," Jilly continued, her tone repressive. "One of our Nimrod reconnaissance aircraft, while on long-range patrol, has photographed a city on a flood plain where the Alps were."

"Go on," the Prime Minister said cautiously. Jilly motioned to an aide, and the room darkened. She clicked on a screen.

"It's like something off the cover of a sci-fi book," someone said. "Is that a monorail?"

"What are those tubes?" another asked. "They look like something from a chem-lab, to connect the liquid flasks. What's that green liquid?"

If that is a monorail, then that city is colossal, the Prime Minister thought, trying to get an idea of scale. Jilly cleared her throat loudly and used a laser pointer. "If you look at these enlargements," she said, "you'll see the presence of Sauroids here, here, and here in large numbers. There are humans here. They appear to be prisoners. There are Neanderthals, apparently captive as well, and other beings, here, and here."

"Can we help free them?" the Home Secretary asked.

"We must be careful," the Prime Minister warned. "Even if their presence here is illegal, that doesn't automatically justify our breaching international law." No one had to be reminded of what had happened the last time they'd gone in with all guns blazing.

"Can we get the Nimrod in any closer?" someone asked.

"I'm afraid not," the Defense Secretary answered. "The Nimrod was attacked by what the crew identified as Sauroid aircraft before we lost contact."

"I'd say," The Prime Minister stood as the lights went up, "That if this isn't the Sauroid home city, it's certainly a major center. The question is what do we do about it?"

"Launch a preemptive strike!" the Foreign Secretary said.

"Rubbish!" the Chancellor, a long-standing adversary, was guaranteed to take the opposite view. "We have no proof that this hasn't all been a huge misunderstanding. And we're not in the habit of re-enacting Pearl Harbor, or the Twin Towers."

"We should send another patrol," the Home Secretary said. "But keep as far as possible from the city. The last thing we want is to provoke them."

The meeting soon slipped into a chorus of opposing views, each trying to win by shouting down the others.

The Prime Minister let them argue for five minutes, then stood, arms folded, waiting for them to be quiet. "I agree with David," he nodded to the Home Secretary, who smiled his thanks, "That we need to find out how we suddenly have an alien, probably enemy city within a thousand miles of us. But the last thing we need is to create further tension. Jilly, how soon can we change the flight path of our nearest satellite?"

The Defense Secretary pulled a face, thinking. "I'll need to check how long it will take for the orbital changes to take effect. It could be a while," she said. "You want me to arrange it?"

The Prime Minister checked his watch and said, "Yes. Let's reconvene at," he thought, "five o'clock. Meanwhile," he told Jilly, "Arrange a high altitude fly-by."

The Defense Secretary said, "I'll get on it straight away."

The Home Secretary looked out at the sky. "It's even darker than it was earlier," he said to no one in particular.

"There's a storm coming," someone said.

***

The pilot landed the flyer in a clearing outside Godshome. Cassidy swept the area with field glasses. *It looks positively bucolic,* he thought. Close up, the area wasn't quite so pristine. The fields were like a rubbish dump, with twisted metal, wood, and clothing scattered throughout the trees. A turgid stream, froth-covered and streaked with an evilly-glinting orange oil roiled sluggishly beside the clearing.

"I don't like the look of those clouds," Garcia murmured. He shivered in the freshening wind. "They remind me of the way the sky looks when twisters is building."

The breeze carried the stink of a nearby chemical works; Cassidy couldn't see any telltale steam columns, but he'd tasted that metallic tang before, during a visit to the Ruhr valley. "Emission levels mean nothing," a green activist had told him once. "Your nose and throat tell you what's being chucked into the air." Cassidy had dismissed that as propaganda. Now he wasn't so sure.

"Come on, where are you?" he muttered through gritted teeth. He realized he couldn't hear any birdsong. The silence was uncanny, as if the city had scared them off. He shivered.

"Cold?" Sophia said beside him.

"No, just something walking over my grave." He chuckled grimly at her horrified look. "Just a saying. Don't panic."

They were silent for a few moments, Sophia hopping from foot to foot, hugging herself. "I still can't believe that Kaminski and MaryAnn got away."

"Vagiskar managed it," Cassidy said. "I guess they were lucky, as well."

In the distance, an explosion lit the gathering dusk, illuminating an oddly familiar skyline. One after the other, from left to right, skyscrapers lit up, rising like giant phalluses penetrating the heavens. Lines of circuitry connected them to one another, and behind the buildings what looked like a giant CD rose hundreds of feet into the air.

"What was that?" Stephen Lo asked. He added, "It seemed like there was fighting round the city limits."

"Had to happen sooner or later that someone would object violently to Bramaragh's plans." Cassidy said.

"Sir, Captain Kaminski tells me that they've run into hostiles," Garcia called. "They're just working their way through the trees."

"Shit!" Cassidy slammed his hand on the metal surface. "If they don't get here soon, we'll have to take off. We were lucky to find somewhere quiet, so near the city. I'm half-expecting a Sauroid to fall over us any minute now."

"Their hard luck," Garcia grunted.

"I've no qualms about killing them." Cassidy's grin was vulpine. "I'm more worried about them getting away to raise the alarm." He stiffened at the chuckle of Sauroid small arms fire.

"Sir, I see them!" a Thal called.

So could Cassidy. The gloom had thickened quickly, and weapons flashes lit it up like dancing fireflies. The skyline burned to one side, and detonations rumbled through the evening in low, rolling waves.

A shape ran through the trees; Cassidy almost sprayed it with gunfire before he realized it was a woman. "MaryAnn!" he whooped as she reached the flier. "Where's the baby?" he asked. MaryAnn ignored the question, and gazed at him glassily. One of the men shook his head, and tapped his temple with his forefinger. Before turning back to the firefight, Cassidy said, "Lift her in!" They hauled her in like a sack of potatoes, and Cassidy left them. He'd worry about MaryAnn later. All of his instincts screamed at him to take off, before it was too late.

Cassidy vaulted over the rail. "Davenport, Hatcher, Tandala, Garcia and Lo! With me!" he said. "You others, wait here!"

They scuttled through the long grass. It was hard trying to keep low, while still staying high enough to see. It was a perfect place for an ambush, Cassidy thought. Of course, that worked both ways.

The firing was nearer now. He watched the tracer. "The bigger, thicker flashes are Sauroid. Listen to the noise, and watch the flashes."

"And they travel faster," Lo said. "Look at their speed."

"Stephen, make sure we know where the flier is at all times," Cassidy said, "I don't want us missing the damn thing, or having to stop and work out where it is."

"Understood."

They watched the nearest group of Sauroids come between them and Kaminski's group. Cassidy called, "Wait for them to get closer; watch the tracer. Wait, wait for it...wait for it...NOW!!"

They raked the enemy, cutting into them with long bursts that threatened to empty their clips, but Cassidy didn't care. All the frustration and hatred that had accumulated over the last few days was channeled through their weapons.

Davenport tapped his shoulder, pointed to their right, and mouthed, "British and Americans!"

Cassidy ceased fire and waved, then ducked as enemy, and perhaps friendly, fire flew toward him. He didn't blame them. Their nerves were probably stretched to breaking.

"Cover us!" Kaminski signaled.

The next few minutes were chaotic; shots, yells and screams echoed in all directions. It was impossible to be sure which blur, which shadow was friend and which was enemy, and where each was at any given moment.

Kaminski and a dozen Sapiens and Thals finally linked up with Cassidy's squad. Someone in the flier had run up a flag of Sauroid skin and lit it up in the gloom with a torch. As they fell back toward it, occasionally firing, Lo ensured they didn't wander off course, tugging back any man who looked like he was straying.

"There are more over there," Kaminski said in one of the lulls. He sounded exhausted. "They've got a few civs with them that we liberated when we escaped."

"Good job you've got your weapons," Cassidy said. "How'd you manage it?"

"When the Sauroids who took them were caught in a Thal ambush, we took them back," Kaminski said.

"Quiet!" Hatcher hissed, pointed to several shapes crossing their path. Cassidy held his breath; Tandala and Hatcher fired a half-second burst. They all sprinted the last hundred yards, then collapsed, panting, against the side of the flier. The shooting stopped momentarily.

"Tell your men to get in," Kaminski's voice was still a monotone, "We need to take off quickly."

"No, get yours in," Cassidy said. "If they sound like you do, they're all in."

"Hey, Kaminski!" Sophia jumped down from the flier. "What happened? MaryAnn's lying there, what's the word, trance-like?"

"Her partner's dead." Kaminski said, and something about the statement rang alarm bells in Cassidy's mind, but he had no time to ponder it. Kaminski said to his men, "Get in, while I wait with the Major."

"What about her baby?" Sophia cried.

"Dead," Kaminski said in the same dull tone.

To one side, tracer fire lit the air with glowing lines of death. Cassidy almost fired at a Sauroid, but when the face flipped up, there were Sapiens with it. "Hold it!" Cassidy pushed Tandala's barrel down. "It's Vagiskar and the others."

"Dressed as Sauroids?" Kaminski asked.

"Yeah."

"So that's how you did it," Kaminski said. Cassidy, distracted by another firefight, replied, "Hmm?"

"Stole the craft."

"Oh. Yeah." Cassidy fired off a burst. "I'll explain later," he knelt and fired again. "Where's that covering fire?" he bawled back at the flier, wondering why there weren't streams of bullets flying over his head. *Worry about that later,* he thought as he fired again and hastily changed clips. At that moment, he added, "I guess it was obvious that Aulth or whatever MaryAnn's partner is dead? He's been taken how long?"

Kaminski didn't answer. Instead he said, "The others are here," and for the first time, his voice was tinged with an emotion; satisfaction. "Here's someone you know." He shone a light on one member of his group.

"Hello Josh," Caitlin said.

***

The Home Secretary made himself snap to attention. "You know damn well that if you sleep, you'll only dream again," he told himself. For several nights he'd dreamed that a huge, invisible weight was pressing on his chest, forcing the air out of his lungs. But if he could sleep, he wouldn't feel quite so thickheaded, and the pain would lessen its vice-like grip from around his forehead.

He looked up at the smashed windows, at the wall where the plaster had come adrift and was streaked with rainwater tracks. Everyone was especially jittery. No one knew if the explosion two hours before had been from an enemy bomb, or simply something like a gas leak.

He realized that the Prime Minister was staring at him, clearly waiting for an answer. The man looked haggard himself, like an over-worn sweater that had started to fray at the seams.

"I'm sorry," he stammered, despising himself for showing weakness in front of the others. "Woolgathering."

The Prime Minister looked annoyed. "I asked, David," his lips were pressed so thin that they had almost disappeared. "Whether we've choked off the enemy advance from the Chilterns."

The Chilterns. Those hills hadn't existed for days. A huge lake now covered the area, but still they used the old familiar names, as if they might be able to conjure the hills back.

"There don't seem to be any more Sauroids coming out. I think we've closed the portal, and we've mopped up the rest."

"Could there be any more of these Portals?" the Air Vice Marshall asked.

David shrugged. "I'm sure if there were, the enemy would have popped up by now." He wanted a cigarette, the way he had wanted a girl called Mandy Dickinson when he was fifteen; aching, longing, with every nerve, cell and fiber. "Over the last twenty-four hours things seem to have, I hesitate to use the words 'settled down,' but compared to the last few days, when we had mountains, lakes, rivers and God knows what popping out of nowhere, they seem to have stabilized."

"Will they return to normal?" The Prime Minister fired the question, desperate for reassurance.

"I don't bloody know!" David wanted to shout back, but he took a deep breath, said, "I have no idea, Prime Minister."

"We need to have an idea, David." The Prime Minister paused as an aide entered and passed him a slip of paper. "Things are moving faster and faster." He removed his glasses, and rubbed at the bridge of his nose. He turned to the Defense Secretary. "Did you find out who was behind that attack on Saur City?"

When Defense shook her head, the Prime Minister looked disgusted. He read the piece of paper, the color draining from his face, leaving him like an old white shirt that needed washing. He said, his voice shaking, "The Americans are scrambling their B-52's from Fairford. They've given us no information, in contravention to the agreement covering their presence. They're headed east, directly toward the Sauroid City."

***

It was as if Cassidy stood at one end of a tunnel, with Caitlin at the other. The firefight, the flier, even Sophia had receded.

Caitlin was almost unrecognizable. Her blonde cap of hair hung in lank strands. Her face was pale, scratched and dirty, her eyelids puffy. She wore functional jeans and a baggy sweatshirt, instead of the tailored suits she normally wore. It was the first time he'd ever seen her in anything without a designer label. She said neutrally as if unsure of his reactions, "How are you?"

He wasn't sure what he felt. Relief that she was okay. Shame, that he hadn't thought of her since shredding her photograph. Annoyance that she should turn up now, of all times. Disbelief that she'd run into Kaminski, of all people.

"Josh," Sophia said, "Who is this?"

"Yes," Caitlin said, "Who is this, Josh?" Her voice was studiedly neutral, but he thought he caught a hint of malice.

There's something very wrong here, he thought. To buy time, he said, "Caitlin, meet Sophia. Sophia, this is Caitlin." He turned to Kaminski and ordered, "Get in the flier."

"Got most of them back, Major," The pilot said. "Except for Garcia and Davenport." A beam of torchlight caught his face, as he scowled at the city. "We should go, before it's too late."

Cassidy nodded, trying not to think of the men they would be leaving behind. "You're right," he said. An idea struck him, and he turned to Kaminski. "Captain," he said "I'm sorry but we've got bad news for you."

"Not now," Sophia touched his arm.

Cassidy shook her off. "I regret to inform you, Captain, that your wife has been killed," he said, "We freed her from captivity yesterday, but she died of her wounds. I am truly, deeply sorry."

For a moment Cassidy thought Kaminski hadn't understood, then the captain nodded. He said woodenly, "That's very sad."

Kaminski's bizarre response turned Cassidy's doubts to certainties, but before he could react, he heard a safety catch snick off, felt the coldness of a gun press into the back of his neck and heard MaryAnn say, "Don't move, Major."

***

He wasn't quite sure how, but Davenport had drifted away from the main group. In the gloom beneath the storm clouds, he'd overshot the flier, and when he'd tried to back up, he'd almost run into a Sauroid patrol. He'd stopped just in time. It was his lucky day; the firefight distracted the Sauroid. It stood still, its attention elsewhere.

Davenport worked his way, slowly, quietly, inching away from the Sauroid in a great circle around the flier and almost bumped into someone coming the other way. He jerked his gun up, heard the other's safety click off and to buy himself an extra second hissed, "Don't shoot! I surrender!"

He was about to fire when the shadow hissed back, "Davenport? It's me, Garcia!"

"Oh, thank God," Davenport almost slumped to the ground. He crouched, trying to calm down, and clicked the safety back on.

"There's reptiles between us and the flier. We'll have to shoot our way back," Garcia said.

There was a noise behind them up in the tree.

Davenport spun round. For the second time, he wasn't ready to fire, and for the second time in as many minutes, he just managed not to shoot someone he belatedly recognized. "Hello there," he said to the familiar shape perched up on the branch, hoping that his eyes didn't deceive him, that it really was her.

***

The Prime Minister was on the phone. He tried again to interrupt but got no further than "Yes," before he was cut short.

The Home Secretary watched with a certain amusement as the Prime Minister blew out his cheeks, opened his mouth again and then snapped it shut, unable to stem the one-sided conversation. Holding the phone to his ear with his left hand, he removed his glasses with his right and rubbed at his eyes, then the bridge of his nose.

"I understand, Mr. President." Frowning, he stared at the phone and muttered incredulously, "He hung up on me."

It was Defense who shattered the fragile silence. "You couldn't persuade him to turn the B-52's back?" It was typical that she would be the one to open her mouth, the Home Secretary thought. He liked her, but she was not the most tactful person.

"No I couldn't!" The Prime Minister slammed his hand on the table. "The man's panicked!"

"We'll get another Nimrod into position," Defense soothed, "Keep an eye on things."

***

"What the-?" Garcia snarled, as Davenport pushed his barrel down.

"We must stop meeting like this," Davenport quavered. What if it wasn't her?

The winged woman hopped off the branch, spreading her wings to slow her descent and stood in front of him. Unlike the last time, when they'd stood on the cliff, the wind wasn't strong enough to blow her odor away, and he was close enough to catch her stench, a mixture of sweat, fish and something indefinable.

She leaned over, and bent her head, smelling him. Breathed through her huge nostril on the near side. Turned her beak and breathed through the other. She wiped her beak on his face, one side, then the other. "Hello," he repeated, now sure it was her.

"Hey, this is no time for a lover's reunion-" Garcia said, but Davenport hushed him.

When she brushed against his legs, Davenport felt something solid. He touched a belt, containing what could have been a half-dozen giant eggs. Not quite solid, they gave slightly to the pressure of his hands. She chittered and pushed his hand away, her tone gently scolding. "Something dangerous?" Davenport shone the torch on eggs the size of ostrich's, but containing an evil blue fluid, with a stopper at the top. There were six in her belt.

Then he noticed the others behind her; he hoped they weren't Sauroids allies; somehow he doubted that they were. The Sauroids didn't strike Davenport as being the type to have allies, only subjects.

Another burst of fire came from near the flier. "I hate to break up your party bud, but there's trouble," Garcia said.

"No, wait." Davenport put his hand on Garcia's shoulder, looked her in the eye and said, "Friend." He pointed to her and said, "Friend," equally clearly.

"This is a waste of time," Garcia's voice dripped disgust.

"Hren," she tapped Davenport's shoulder with her beak.

Davenport pointed to the other avians and said, "Friend." He pointed to the flier. "Friend." Waving at the Sauroid city, he put all the disgust he could into his voice. "Bad." He hoped that even if she didn't understand a word, she grasped his tone.

"Hren," she said and, stretching her wings, took off toward the main Sauroid patrol. One by one, the others followed her.

"While you been kissing your lady friend," Garcia said, passing his night goggles to Davenport. "Some really weird shit's been going down at the flier."

Davenport watched MaryAnn put her gun to Cassidy's head. With mounting horror he saw Kaminski and his men force the troops out of the flier, then gun them down. Then, he saw winged shapes sweeping through the sky toward a copse.

***

"Why?" Cassidy gasped, as the last lifeless body flopped onto the grass. Kaminski's men had killed their former colleagues with as much emotion as if they were posting letters. To a stranger, they'd have seemed normal, but there was something not quite right with them, perhaps a fractional delay in answering a question, a blankness behind the eyes.

"The flier won't take us all," Kaminski said. Only Cassidy, Sophia, Vagiskar, Tandala and Henry lived. MaryAnn had stabbed three men in the flier, while their attention was diverted by the firefight. When Cassidy and the others had laid down their weapons and instructed the men to do the same, Cassidy's troops had clambered out of the flier. To Cassidy's horror, Kaminski had shot his own medic.

Caitlin shot the pilot, and so they died, one by one. Phyl, Stephen Lo, Porter, Surius, Taran, Mashneyk, the freed prisoners. The last one to take a bullet to the head had been Nemo, squalling and hissing in furious defiance. *Funny how, at the end, we all want to live,* Cassidy thought.

"Get in," Caitlin waved a rifle barrel at the flier.

Cassidy hesitated. When her gun pressed into his neck, he made himself relax.

"Get in," she repeated.

"So how come you don't need a headpiece like the other stooges?" When Caitlin didn't answer, he said, determined to goad her, "Did you turn traitor willingly?"

Caitlin said calmly, "As we've grown stronger, we no longer need tools to bend them to our will. If it consoles you, your Caitlin fought like a tigress, if only for a few seconds. You won't even last that long. With each passing day, as we add drone by drone, we grow stronger still."

"Yeah," Cassidy said wryly. "Very Nuremburg, Caitlin."

Behind her, there was a blue flash, and an explosion split the night. Sauroid gunfire chuckled through the sudden quiet. Another explosion followed, and a Sauroid screamed and rolled on the grass, to douse the flames consuming its body.

Then there were explosions all round them. Cassidy heard Garcia yell, "Run for it, Major!"

Garcia lived! Cassidy hid a grin.

"Get in, now, or we'll kill you," Caitlin said flatly. He had no doubt that she would carry out the threat.

He climbed in, and the others followed.

***

Davenport and Garcia stared at the disappearing flier. "Shit," Garcia said. "We shoulda gone in."

Davenport watched the avians land. They were all shorter than him and Garcia. He beckoned 'Hren,' as he'd named her and reached for her now empty belt. As he studied it, she twittered nervously. He tried several times to undo it, before finally succeeding. "Goes together like this," he muttered, "and there's a loop here." He struggled to fit it round his narrow waist, still far bigger than any avian's. "Hey!" He beckoned to another avian.

The male avian stepped forward reluctantly, and Davenport reached for him. When the avian stepped back, Hren cawed at him, and he stood still, trembling slightly. "If I loop this through his belt like so," Davenport said, "then I need- you! Come here!" He beckoned to another flier. Davenport wore a manic grin, and between talking, he poked his tongue out as he thought. "Ah, hah!" he crowed. "Here we are!" His harness now linked to two others, like a paper chain.

"What you doin', man?" Garcia shook his head.

"It's okay, I haven't lost my marbles," Davenport said, undoing another wingman's harness. He put it on Garcia. "We need the two biggest avians here 'cause I reckon you weigh more than me." He joined Garcia's harness to two of the biggest wingmen. "You empty your pack. No food, no water- take nothing but ammo and your chute. And can I have your spare? If it doesn't work you won't need it anyway; we'll be dead."

"Okay, brains." Garcia emptied his pack. "What's the plan?"

Hren cawed, and the two biggest wingmen stepped forward, clipping their harnesses to the back of Davenport's.

Davenport mimed flying to the winged men, and they lifted him into the air. "Simple," he said. "We're going after them."

***

Cassidy crouched in the flier, trying not to look at the blood pooling in the corner. "Is there anything of Caitlin left?"

Again that blank gaze was turned on him. "Of course, Josh," she said calmly. That was what was wrong. There was no emotion at all. Caitlin would never have gone this long without raising hell about him dumping her on the motorway.

"So, why?" he said. "What the hell's the point of all this?" Deep inside, he knew why. He'd dreamed it. The universe didn't fit Bramaragh's beliefs. So the universe must be corrected.

"It's simple," Caitlin said in that reasonable, utterly un-Caitlin-like tone. "Our savants have been working toward this, channeling their energies, training and practicing, year after year, collecting talent after talent. That's why we took prisoners, why we need all these-" she paused, "you can call them slaves, acolytes or converts. With them, we can systematically, one by one, tear down the walls separating the false worlds. Ours will be the only world left in the end."

"Where do we fit in?" Sophia said.

Caitlin turned on Sophia a look of raw hatred. Cassidy guessed that her instinct had identified her successor with unerring accuracy. Then the shutters came down, and Caitlin was again not-Caitlin. Cassidy's heart lifted. There was a weakness there. If she could look like that once, it could happen again. If he could only find the key.

The prisoners hunkered down under the gun barrels. Caitlin said, as calmly as if discussing make-up or nail polish, "Who says you will? You'll meet with God soon. If we have a use for you, you live. If not, you die."

She turned to look at Cassidy, and he felt a cold chill run down his back as the flyer lifted off and flew toward Godshome. "We'll find a use for you, Josh."

CHAPTER TWENTY-FOUR

Below the rain-battered flyer, Godshome was a hodge-podge of organic and inanimate. Buildings rose on thick, columnar legs, thousands of feet high.

They were all soaked to the skin. Cassidy, despite his exhaustion, couldn't help staring at the city. The others also craned their necks. It was, after all, their objective.

Below them, at street level, banks of crystalline steps rose in sweeping arcs; from the topmost steps, a pair of eyes set in the stone watched them carefully. And everywhere in the city as they flew past there were row upon row of stone dragons, on columns, on the roofs, seeming to watch them.

In the midst of grandeur was squalor. People and creatures slept beneath bridges and archways. Some had lit a sputtering fire into which they shoveled scraps of paper snatched from the breeze, broken bits of wood and anything else they could find.

Lightning licked with flickering tongues at the tallest of the twisting towers. One bolt narrowly missed the flyer as it docked, searing the side of the tower, scorching the white-painted metal into a two-foot-wide burning, bubbling pool. They stood and were marched across the swaying gangway, each captive chained to a giant Sauroid. "This way." Kaminski had taken charge. Whatever was left of Kaminski. Cassidy wasn't sure that Bramaragh wasn't playing a game, using a different person as a mouthpiece in any given situation. Or how much of what was said came from the person's residual personality.

He hoped for an opportunity to test his theory, but he knew faint hopes were all they had left. His head felt gripped in a vise, which squeezed out all thought. He almost wanted to die, to just lift the blanket of despair from his mind. He wiped his hands on his trousers, to dry the sweat from them; his guts roiled; pain stabbed at his stomach. His mouth felt dry as parchment.

Cassidy glanced across at Vagiskar. Sweat shone on his forehead. The Thal's eyes darted first this way, then that, and his tongue flicked his lips to moisten them.

Tandala looked calm, but his wet-clay complexion belied it.

Sophia did too, until Cassidy saw the nervous tic below her jaw. His heart lurched at the thought that all the things he'd left unsaid would now stay that way.

Only Henry seemed genuinely untroubled by the situation. He winked at Cassidy and surveyed their surroundings. "They like dragons," he observed. The stenciled shadows of tiny lizards froze in mid-scuttle on walls. Statues of every sort, from Chinese mythology to thunder-lizards, guarded the doors.

"Bramaragh honors our ancestors," MaryAnn intoned. "They're from our ostentatious period."

MaryAnn's voice was the least normal of them, Cassidy thought. There was a distinct gap between Henry's words, and her reply. Did it take so long for Bramaragh to think of an answer? Or did it take that long for the signal to travel from her brain to her mouth? Maybe she was damaged? He wondered if she was fighting Bramaragh. He filed it for future use and looked around as they were led deeper into the lair.

The decorations grew more sparse, the walls more plain, as they went deeper into the labyrinth, until there was only bare white plaster, suffused with a leaden battleship-gray fungus and shot through with pulsing veins of pink and dingy green. Kaminski said, "We're here," and the handcuffs were removed.

A pair of double doors swung slowly open.

***

"Birdcage, this is Blue Jay. Redwing is nearing the cuckoo's nest," DiMacchi said into the mike. He glanced at his copilot. Stone slumped in his seat. Almost eight miles below, the Sauroid City stretched to the horizon. DiMacchi looked left, then right. The eight B-52's had been in perfect formation, but as they neared the target and spread out, the flight lost pattern.

"Damned if I can work out how they picked the target," Stone's voice was metallic from behind his mask. "One bit of this city looks like another."

"They probably picked the city center," DiMacchi said into his mike. "Ours is not to reason why, as I learned at school."

"Only thing I learned at school was if you pick a fight, hit him so hard he stays down, or run like fuck," Stone said.

"Blue Jay, this is Birdcage, you're go to lay eggs," OPCOM's voice crackled in their headphones. As it relayed the codes, DiMacchi shivered. No one had ever done this before. The next few minutes would determine whether his name would become as infamous as those who had bombed Nagasaki and Hiroshima. "Jesus, lookit that storm up ahead," Stone muttered.

Perhaps fifty miles away, dozens of white cauliflower florets of superheated steam rose on a storm front. "We'll have time to get in and out," DiMacchi said. "But only just, and if the edge catches us, it's going to be a rough, rough ride." One they might not survive. "Redwing," he called to the rest of the flight. "We're go to clear the cuckoo's nest." He recited his codes, and Stone added his. "Let's do this," DiMacchi said, "and get the hell outta here."

***

The Prime Minister sat with his face in his hands. He no longer watched the wall screen showing the B-52's from the shadowing Nimrod. When he lifted his face, worry had added twenty years to his age.

He looks all in, the Home Secretary thought. He looked across the table at the Foreign Secretary and thought he noticed it too. Almost unconsciously, his politician's instincts took over. He wondered who, if they got out of this mess, he would need to cultivate, to ignore and to whisper about, to ensure that if he didn't succeed the Prime Minister, then that smarmy two-faced bastard across the table, wouldn't either. He nodded to the Foreign Secretary, who nodded back.

"If we survive this," the Prime Minister snarled, "I want them off our soil."

And undo a century of the Special Relationship? The Home Secretary said nothing. There was no one here to debate the Prime Minister's comment, and security was so tight now that government was as it had been a century before, when plumbing, not the ship of state sprang leaks. Anyone who repeated such an outburst would be a life-long pariah. At least for the political life of the current Prime Minister, the little voice whispered in his head. A new Prime Minister might forgive that leak. He looked around, to see who might fill that need.

The Prime Minister was simply getting it off his chest. He knew there was nothing they could do. The enemy's weight of numbers and their disregard for casualties had swamped Britain's conventional attacks. The Yanks had simply been pragmatic and thought the unthinkable. "Anyone know what they're carrying?" the Home Secretary asked. They shook their heads.

"If they're not standard Tomahawks, how did they get them into the country?" the Chancellor asked. The Foreign and Home Secretaries exchanged amused glances that asked how had he risen so high, while staying so innocent.

"Is that a storm ahead?" Defense asked. "That lightning almost hit them! And what are those shapes?"

"It looks like a giant doughnut," someone said. "

"It's a toroid." Health said and added defensively, "I did physics at University. I knew it'd be useful eventually."

***

The great hall was filled with Sauroids, other reptiles, Thals, Sapiens and even a Jaya. Liana-like creepers circling the room linked them all. In places it was hard to tell to which individual particular limbs belonged. Most had pressure sores from not moving. Flies were everywhere, buzzing from surface to surface, dining on a rank diet of crumbs, drink and bodily secretions.

The pain in Cassidy's head, which had grown throughout the day, increased sharply. He nearly blacked out; only the smell, a mix of sickly-sweet and ammonia so strong it pierced his fugue, saved him.

"What's that smell?" Henry gasped.

"Sauroids have a poor sense of smell," Caitlin said. "The room's cleaned regularly, but some things get missed."

Sophia looked ill. An impish part of Cassidy's mind thought, *Sophia, who has the Talents.* Blackness swamped him again, as if it were screaming in his face to stop him from thinking. He never knew what random combination of thoughts made a line from an old song pop into his head. As the words to *I Can't Get You Out of my Head* echoed in his mind, the blackness lifted slightly, no more than easing the pressure on a man's windpipe allows a gasp of air, but enough.

Then, as if it had just been changing position, ready to settle, its weight came crashing back down on his mind. He nearly blacked out. It stopped him from thinking, sapped his will, nearly stopped his breathing. He saw a ribcage poking out from underneath one somnolent lizard. "This is it?" he gasped. "THIS is Bramaragh?"

"The body is irrelevant," Caitlin said. "When we commune, we achieve a state of semi-grace. When that happens, it doesn't matter if the flesh rots. Thoughts and memories stay forever."

"So why does he need you?" Henry asked.

"We need mobile servants as well," Caitlin said. "Serving us, but without-" she stopped as if someone had turned her off.

Sophia turned and gazed at him, tears streaming down her face. "It hurts so much," she sobbed.

"Do you feel it as well?" Cassidy gasped at Henry.

"I thought I'd developed a sinus problem," Henry said. "Unpleasant, but nothing like what you seem to be suffering."

"It's...blocking...us," Cassidy somehow dredged out the words, from deep down inside of him. "It's stopping you from using your talents," he said.

Sophia nodded. "So. Why do you suffer?" she licked her lips and stared at him. "The av-a-lanche," she gasped. "Remember it? You said you've always been lucky. You made the right guesses." She insisted, "Talents."

He shook his head. "Just lucky," he said.

Their captors nudged them forward. Amongst the twisted, nightmare nest of creatures, one lizard was bigger than the rest. *Alpha lizard,* Cassidy thought; he couldn't tear his eyes away from it.

"We don't need to be joined when we're this close," MaryAnn said. "You'll be a useful addition monkey-who-would-be-Anti-God."

Cassidy thrashed against his chains until his wrists and mind were scraped raw. He drowned in despair and blackness, and as it closed over him, he said, "I never wanted to be anything but ordinary. I never wanted to be part of her bloody prophecy."

All that followed happened in a nano-second: He was drowning; the tumult was everywhere, frying his brain, scrambling his thoughts. Amongst them, brushing his mind like gossamer, was a familiar- not voice- but thought.

*"What, *who* are you?"* He already knew the answer. It was him; as if in a crowd, he saw his twin. Closer even than a twin. He reached out, a drowning man seeking safety. Like bubbles in boiling water, the alternate Cassidys merged into one another; this one was a priest. This one a psychiatrist, this one another soldier, this one, this one, this one...

"Where are you physically?"

"Moldering in the ground," came the mordant reply. *"Dead and gone to dust, brother."* This from priest-Cassidy.

"How?"

"We're the specks of dirt caught in the corners of the strands of Bramaragh's net of minds." He could sense that they couldn't lie to him, that they were open books. He sensed their thoughts, swirling round his own, fireflies on a summer's night.

"Bramaragh absorbs minds like a computer downloads programs. It's the nearest to immortality that he can imagine. For a nanosecond, he sees the seductive charm of living forever. For a while, anyway, until we're eventually absorbed. It wouldn't be life. We'll just become a part of this vast, soulless, organic machine."

One after another, they merged. "*Try not to think, to let the Bramaragh-mind know of the enemy within its own thoughts. Keep your mind blank,*" they urged.

All of them loners; none had families, or long-lasting relationships. All had latent Talents, some more developed than others, but none had realized their powers as fully as Cassidy; he'd hidden them from himself in a vain attempt at normality but couldn't do it any longer.

"*When all things are possible, and any alternatives are removed, then the sum of experience is what's left,*" the philosopher Cassidy thought. These were the Cassidys who took on Bramaragh and failed, now subsumed into the gestalt. While their Talents were not as developed as his, they were tenacious enough to preserve mental identity.

Bramaragh exterminated all alternates, before re-raveling the disparate skeins of probability. It/they was a gestalt, but a gestalt comprising others forcibly absorbed. Like anything else forced together, that left weaknesses. Bramaragh had no idea that as the timelines had collapsed, so the possible Cassidys had waited as potentialities. There was a chance- if only Cassidy could survive absorption.

The microsecond ended. The onslaught began.

***

Lightning flashed in the distance, and as he hung, suspended between the two winged men, Davenport prayed, "Please God, don't let it hit me." At least it was a change from "Please God, don't let me fall," which he'd mouthed constantly since they had taken off. His guts felt as if they would empty at any moment, and all he wanted was to land, anywhere. For all his confident claims, Davenport wasn't sure the harness would hold. He had little faith in Garcia's spare parachute saving him. If the harness failed, he would suffer the most horrible death imaginable.

His momentary flash of heroism had long passed, and he cursed himself for a fool. The city lay below like a psychedelic poster from his father's collection, futuristic spires, monorails, and transparent tubes, all rusted, decaying and run down, as if their makers had lost interest in their designs. Or maybe the occupiers weren't the makers.

He looked behind, at the solid black wall of cloud that rose, from almost ground level sheer into the troposphere, threatening at any time to topple over, like a breaking wave striking a reef. A solid black wall shot through with flashes, which boiled and roiled like something alive, rushing ever nearer.

The lightning flashed again, and Garcia hollered over the wind, "Why are these guys doing this? What do they get out of carting weirdoes like us around?"

Davenport yelled back. "Dunno. Maybe they know the Sauroids are villains. Maybe they've suffered as much as us. Who cares, anyway?"

"I guess. You got something going with the chica?" Before Davenport could reply, Garcia yelled "The flier! Over there!"

Davenport saw it, tethered about a hundred feet below the top of a domed building towering over the rest. "It looks," his shout emerged as a squeak. He cleared his throat and tried again. "It looks like there's a window on the dome. Shall we take a look?"

"Yeah." Garcia was already tugging and pointing out the roof to the winged men. As they wheeled, Davenport gritted his teeth and prayed silently.

***

Pain. Cassidy's universe shrank to an electric, bubbling raw overload. He felt the pain of the Sauroids whose heads were cut open, air scorching their exposed neural tissue as if a blowtorch had been turned on them. He felt taste, heard smells, smelled colors, all the colors of the spectrum and beyond. They battered him like an overwhelming tide, locking his thoughts into stasis, the pressure crushing the life out of him, squeezing his chest, so he couldn't breathe. The other Cassidys linked, trying to drive the gestalt back. But no amount of will power could make up for his being raw, untrained and not capable of forcing away an intellect that devoured minds like a glutton downs oysters.

Gulp! Another one gone; Henry's individuality was snuffed out like a moth too close to a flame. All the years of fighting for freedom, wiped out. *I'll mourn you later, friend.*

"*Why?*" Composite-Cassidy shrieked defiance at the wall of pressure. "*What about invention? Development? Progress?*"

[No need] the roaring torrent answered.

"*But without progress, there's only stasis; the universe cannot accept stagnation. You bring about your own death.*"

[Lies!] Another mind flickered and faded. Vagiskar.

***

The B-52 shook, as DiMacchi said, "Bird cage, this is Blue Jay, we've encountered severe, repeat, severe weather."

"Blue Jay, this is Bird Cage, you must lay your eggs. It's imperative that you reach the cuckoo's nest. Do you copy?"

"Got that, Bird Cage. We're seeing some really strange stuff ahead. We'll feed through the camera footage."

"Roger that, Blue Jay."

***

Cassidy was momentarily a teenager again, reading an old paperback, on its cover a man with raised fist, standing beneath a moon. In the book a rogue telepath had sung songs to jam the mind-readers attempts. With one of those intuitive leaps that had made his teachers despair of him, he thought of a song, and hurled the line at Bramaragh. *"I can't get you out of my head."* The pressure lifted fractionally, as the irritating song-loop ran repeatedly through his thoughts.

After a dozen practice runs, Cassidy felt enough confidence that the song-loop would hold Bramaragh, that he could think beyond defense. He drew his other selves together, like wagons circling for the night.

Composite-Cassidy stretched his mind, found a familiar set of thoughts. Sophia. He tasted/smelt/saw terror, fury, hatred of Bramaragh and, underpinning it all, love for a Sapiens male, for all that his moods and sudden changes of mind, baffled and infuriated her.

"Sophia, hum!" He fired the thought at her and felt her confusion. *"The more mindless the song, the more it'll block Bramaragh."*

"Nah, nah, nah," he sang aloud and, physically reaching across, touched Sophia's shoulder. "Sing, girl,- nah, nah, nah, NAH, nah, nah, nah." With his mind he flashed the same instructions to Tandala.

A fresh onslaught came, and physical Cassidy winced at the agony in his sinuses. Several of him splintered away from the composite, and for a moment it wavered, until he remembered the tactics in the Warriors crystal. *"Use me like a lens,"* he urged. *"Channel your efforts through me!"* None of the other Cassidys were as talented as he, and he alone couldn't hold Bramaragh. But together...

***

"Prime Minister, this is Professor Leys," the Defense Secretary introduced a stocky, bald man who wrung his hands constantly. "The Professor worked on quantum mechanics at both Princeton and M.I.T," she said. "He has some interesting ideas on the shapes."

Leys surveyed the room, and cleared his throat. "Imagine," he said portentously, "that our universe is one of many that float like bubbles. Some are exactly like ours; some so wildly different as to be almost unimaginable. Some will be our size, some much smaller, some bigger; the biggest will in effect, be beyond our comprehension. What we're probably seeing here," he pointed to the shapes on a monitor, "and here, are the visible parts of these particular universes." He stared at those who had started to fidget. "If this is unclear, please ask questions."

His hand wringing was forgotten as he warmed to his topic. "These shapes are alternate universes that are smaller than ours," Leys said, provoking skeptical muttering from several Cabinet members. As the hubbub died away, Leys pointed at the monitor. "You see here, sheets of energy; there, cylindrical and looped membranes. Here we have a whole universe of electrons and electricity, of lightening bolts and neutrinos."

He paused for effect. "Until now what we've seen have been manifestations of parallel universes re-integrating with ours. They are comparatively similar. These here are the first traces of universes so different that we can't co-exist."

"You're saying they're dangerous?" the Foreign Secretary's scorn rang round the room. "Those things are just clouds." The Foreign Secretary pointed to the screen. "Look at them!"

A lesser man would have quailed, but Leys was in his element. He stared straight back at the Foreign Secretary. "They're not dangerous in themselves," Leys said, "But..."

"Explain," the Prime Minister snapped.

"I'm trying to." Leys sipped a glass of water. "This is about our universe, and all the others; call it the multiverse." He paused, "I spoke of universes of lightning bolts, of neutrinos, and unstable matter. And gravity. It's one force we think of as comparatively weak."

He looked around. "Anyone have a magnet? No? Okay, think about this. An entire planet is pulling you down, yet you can move freely. Reach seven miles per second, less than a twenty-five thousandth of light-speed, and you escape this planet."

He paused as if for questions. No one spoke. "Gravity is weak. One reason is that we believe it's diluted throughout the other dimensions. It leaks into our universe, so all we experience is the residue of a much stronger force. Remove the barriers, and even if we survive the radiation, how do we withstand a colossal increase in gravity? I believe all life on Earth faces extinction."

There was silence. They stared at one another in disbelief.

At last the Prime Minister said, "Is there anything we can do?"

Leys pointed to the B-52's on the screen. They flew ahead of the Nimrod, into a stroboscopic sky, full of flickering lightning. "Pray that they find the source of the problem and that they get to it before it's too late," he said bleakly.

***

Composite-Cassidy felt the flicker of intelligence. Inhuman, cold, more alien than even Bramaragh. It was what he'd sensed in his dreams; and just as in his dreams, it was there and gone instantly. It flashed again. Composite-Cassidy realized that this was nothing to with the gestalt. Thunder rumbled overhead.

"*Feel that?*" Cassidy flashed the thought at Sophia.

"*I've never encountered anything like this before.*"

Lightning flashed again. "*There!*" he almost shouted out loud.

Lightning flashed, and he felt the alien. It was impossible to draw precise parallels, but he got the impression that if it had emotions, they were feelings of anger, fear, even grief.

He wondered how he could possibly communicate with it.

***

Davenport's foot slipped; he gripped a crenellated ridge so tightly his fingers bled. They'd managed to alight on the sloping roof of the cupola, the wind tugging at them with demented little fingers.

He peered through a huge window in the dome's upper quarter. Below him, Cassidy writhed as if in a fit, watched by the other survivors, all surrounded by Kaminski, Mary Ann, a woman Davenport didn't recognize and a lot of Sauroids.

"If we crash through the glass, we could land on that lot," Garcia pointed to a mass of reptiles on the other side, so twisted that it was hard to tell where one began and another ended.

"How many grenades we got? I have six." Davenport said.

"Ten," Garcia said, passing two over. "Evens us up."

"It'd be better if we stay here, until they find a way of attacking us. THEN we jump into the nest, if we have to. Yeah?"

"Sounds okay. Not as sexy as jumping in," Garcia flashed a grin, "But what the hey."

"We need something to break this glass," Davenport said. He clambered gingerly round the window, found two big masonry slabs. "These will do," he hefted one of them. Garcia grabbed the other and staggered with it to the far side.

"On three," Davenport said. "One, two-"

"Been an honor, Bunny," Garcia said. "-Three!"

They heaved the slabs, and as the windows collapsed into millions of shards, each pulled a pin from their first grenade and tossed them through, while reaching for their second.

***

"Bird Cage, this is Blue Jay. Red Wing Five's been hit by lightning. They're down. Do you copy?"

"Blue Jay, this is Bird Cage. We copy. Keep going. It's imperative that you lay your eggs."

"Roger that, Bird Cage. We're taking heavy punishment as well. Several bolts have hit the fuselage. Our EWO is dead."

***

"Change the tune," Physical-Cassidy warned Sophia, "Or Bramaragh may break through." He licked at lips dry from hours without a drink. "How do we communicate with intelligent lightning?" he asked, echoing composite-Cassidy's question.

"How can it be intelligent?" Sophia asked. "How can something that's only intermittently alive be conscious?"

"Well, how intelligent are you when you're asleep?" Cassidy said. "We're only intermittently conscious." He added, "If neutrinos and energy are all there is, how else can intelligence evolve? Some universes must have completely different laws of physics to ours."

"Hey guys," Tandala struggled with a Sauroid, "when you've finished theorizing, the snakes are getting restive." A Sauroid gun-barrel hit his head, and he grunted, collapsing in a heap.

Uh-oh, Cassidy thought. If they were unconscious, how could they defend themselves?

While Physical-Cassidy grabbed Caitlin for use as a shield, Composite-Cassidy tried to communicate with the Lightning. Among the flickering thoughts, Composite-Cassidy made out a question-image; searching for what had brought it here. This alien place, with its hellish qualities, was slowly killing it.

Sophia was clubbed unconscious, and Caitlin crooned, "It's useless, Josh. They'll go through me if they have to. My death is trivial."

The lightning flashed, and Composite-Cassidy flung an image of Bramaragh at it; he/they had no idea if it would understand. "So you don't mind dying?" Physical-Cassidy moved Caitlin one way, then the other.

"My essence," Caitlin said, "will live on."

There was a crash, the clanging tinkle of raining glass, and a stunned silence. Seconds later, explosions ripped the Sauroids in one corner apart.

A Sauroid smashed a gun-barrel into Cassidy's head.

***

"The last tea-party of the socially bereft," The Home Secretary said with a tired smile. All but four of them had gone. "Spend what time is left with your families," the Prime Minister had said. Only the Foreign Secretary, with his capacious appetite for socializing, and the Home Secretary, who hadn't told anyone that his wife had left him, had stayed with the Prime Minister, whose wife was in the North with her invalid mother, and Leys, who was divorced.

"How did this all happen?" the Home Secretary asked Leys.

"Whatever started the collapse of the singularity wave would be responsible."

"So if someone were trying to change history," the Prime Minister's mind was clearly on what they had been told of Bramaragh, "this could be a result of trying to merge probabilities."

"And the result of not understanding physics," Leys said.

The Foreign Secretary said, "The B-52's are dropping their bombs."

***

Davenport and Garcia compromised between speed and precision, throwing all the grenades within two minutes, dropping half with pinpoint accuracy into the nest and half into the Sauroid troops, who were spraying the ceiling with gunfire.

Davenport glanced up. To the south, the sun moved back and forth. Mountains appeared, were nibbled away and replaced by wooded hills, in only seconds. The sky flickered between blue and gray and black. Cities came and went, probabilities absorbed into Bramaragh's reality, almost faster than Davenport could watch. "End game," he whispered. It was like watching the last of the bathwater whirling down the plughole.

"Those are B-52's!" Garcia pointed in another direction.

Out of the corner of his eye, Davenport saw familiar shapes. "Hren!" he yelled with glee.

She'd been back to her base. Davenport fired his machine-gun down into the nest, as the avians hovered over the shattered window and dropped more eggs. Gouts of blue fire burst amongst the packed enemy.

***

Nighttime in Godshome. A Sauroid looked up as the first bomb detonated. Its eyeballs were fused, and its agony rocked Bramaragh, easing the pressure on Composite-Cassidy. It gouged a crater two hundred fifty feet deep, a quarter of a mile across, the temperature touching a million degrees Celsius. Two and a quarter square miles of Godshome were leveled, only three miles away from Bramaragh.

***

The composite-Cassidy drew together, shielding their last live aspect's consciousness from the relentless, inexorable mental pressure. Corporeal-Cassidy realized that he was managing to perform the telepathic equivalent of sleepwalking. He waited for the next flicker of lightning-thought, felt a mental scream from Bramaragh as blue flames licked over the nest.

He felt the earth-shaking concussion of the first H-bomb. The next bomb detonated five seconds later, then another, so close that the blast blew out the remaining windows. Cassidy felt Bramaragh's torment, its already vast power sapped by the grenades dropped into the nest, further weakened from the excruciating pain of losing hundreds of thousands of its selves.

He felt Sophia's groggy thoughts, gathered them in, even as Corporeal-Cassidy, sleepily hugged her. "Sophia!" he whispered, "Push with your mind!" He felt the doubt within her.

"I NEED YOU!! I can't do this alone!" He would have to let her closer than he'd ever allowed anyone, mentally and emotionally, as well as physically. He felt her love for him, realized that he'd been wrong to doubt her and that such knowledge was too little, too late.

They crawled across and pulled Tandala to them. "Davenport! Garcia! Down here!" Composite-Cassidy reached for their minds; he felt the agony of Garcia's landing. Even cushioned by Sauroid flesh, the impact winded him. Before the enemy could react, he crawled toward the others, shooting at any Sauroid that moved.

Davenport pointed down, and wrapping his arms round Hren's waist, they dropped through a gap. She cawed a summons to her flock who followed her down. "This is Hren!" Davenport yelled at anyone who'd listen. "She's on our side!"

"The more the better," Composite-Cassidy thought back. *We need each other.* As they huddled together, Composite-Cassidy even enfolded Kaminski, feeling the man's shame and anguish that he had only been able to maintain his will for more than a second before losing control to Bramaragh. Composite-Cassidy pulled in Caitlin and MaryAnn, who felt the same, along with MaryAnn's added grief of Raul and Aulth's deaths and her inability to mourn them. He urged them to drag their minds free of the crumbling Bramaragh, pulling them into a new gestalt. A human gestalt. *"A temporary one,"* Cassidy promised.

"I'm scared," Garcia admitted.

"So am I!"

"God help us," Garcia thought.

"If there is a God," Cassidy thought, *"and I've never believed in one, then he's left us here to fight this alone. No Gods, no supermen will rescue us. Just us, together!"*

He sensed the rallying Bramaragh's fury as it/they realized his plan. The weight of Bramaragh's million minds settled, an elephant kneeling on a mouse. If he could have screamed he would have, but the weight drove the air from his lungs. Ice-cold talons of black depression and pain dug deep into his/their mind, needle-sharp claws tearing, rending, beating him down, but somehow, the new gestalt held out.

"Hold on!" he cried, and at the same moment, as the lightning flashed, with one last mighty effort, Cassidy-gestalt reached out, and, groping for the next falling bomb, pushed and pulled at the fabric of space.

The lightning struck at the same moment as they Shifted the remaining twenty-six two-megaton H-Bombs into Bramaragh's chamber. For a nanosecond, Cassidy felt the pressure recede, as Bramaragh with a howling death-scream was vaporized, and the chamber was torn apart in an inferno of heat and noise.

There was white, white light and unendurable pain.

Then there was nothing-

CHAPTER TWENTY-FIVE

- nothing at all.

At the same moment as the nuclear detonations destroyed both Bramaragh and its enemies, the last alternate universes merged. There was now only one universe. One set of Laws of Physics.

Those laws meant that the universe was in an unsustainable state. Matter and anti-matter cannot exist together.

The resultant explosion, Big Bang Two, drove temperature and pressure to a million times that of the sun's core, to such a level that protons and neutrons were ripped asunder.

Quarks, charmed, strange, and otherwise that constitute ordinary matter were released from their sub-atomic captivity to roam a thick, super-incandescent soup of quarks and gluons, whose charge had previously bonded matter.

The proto-creative soup that was the quark-gluon plasma held for a microsecond. For that moment, the fate of the universe hung in the balance.

Then the fireball expanded in all directions, including time. Its impetus took most of the energy surging forward, onward from the moment of destruction. New, strange universes began to form from the super-hot, slowly cooling gases. In billions of years, life might begin to form, but it would be unknown to, and unknowing of, humanity.

A tiny part of the energy flowed

Drawkcab <-- > backward.

Briefly,

Inconsistently,

but

enough

to

re-splinter

the

single

timeline.

Timelines Fractured

again into shards. Each

event, no matter how tiny, created two outcomes:

Plus or minus. Life or death.

The odds were billions to one that humanity could re-occur. But with billions of trillions of possibilities, such odds meant that there were still a trillion chances that in some battered, fractured timelines, something, or someone survived...

CHAPTER TWENTY-SIX

In each of myriad universes, the room was a jumbled ruin of plaster, wood, metal and flesh. Uneven plains of masonry separated mounds of rubble and a few uncovered bodies. Dust hung in a haze. The coppery tang of blood and intestinal matter permeated everything. The room was utterly silent; the only noise came through gaping holes in the walls. Outside, the storms had given way to blue skies, and the birds sang to celebrate a new spring.

One side of the room was covered by a great, gray-green decaying mass, the physical aspect of the Bramaragh-gestalt.

In many universes a mound quivered, and bits of lath and plaster fell to the floor in an avalanche. Sunlight dappled the thick dust. A figure emerged from a mini-eruption, crawling out of the mound, white from head to toe, front and back. It coughed, its tongue a pink speck in the whitescape:

<table>
<tr>
<td>Garcia's sneezes snapped in the quiet. He wiped his nose. "So who else made it?"

He picked up a gun, blew dust from the barrel, and checked the magazine.</td>
<td>Davenport rummaged in his pockets, and produced a wad of tissues. Blowing his nose in a series of honks, he cleaned his glasses, and wiped his face clean.</td>
<td>Something coughed, opened its eyes, and gazed round the room. It stood and removed its baggy overall, to reveal a woman in panties and T-shirt.</td>
<td>Sophia sat up, and abruptly, without warning, was violently sick. She hadn't allowed herself the luxury of such self-indulgence before.</td>
<td>Cassidy lay prone, his heart rattling. His head suddenly felt very empty and silent. He licked dry lips, breathed deep and climbed to his feet.</td>
</tr>
<tr>
<td>He poked Bramaragh's vast corpse</td>
<td>Searching for survivors,</td>
<td>She shook out the overalls.</td>
<td>She checked each of the bodies, then</td>
<td>He checked the room. “Hello?” His</td>
</tr>
</table>

with his pistol, and kicked it hard. Now, sure that it was dead, he rolled the bodies over.

his growing frustration mirrored Garcia's. "Come on," he croaked. "Some of you must've pulled through."

Coughed. Muttered, "I could murder for a drink." She added, "and a smoke."

dug until she found who she was looking for.

voice was cracked and thin. “Anybody else make it?”

He picked over the last body. "Guess it's time to start digging," he gasped, between fresh bouts of coughing.

Davenport found Hren's broken body and held her for a while in an act of mourning, before resuming the search.

Caitlin's search was purposeful; she checked each of the bodies on the floor, then, she dug; at last taking the broken body in her arms.

She kissed the face of the dead man. "I won't let them forget you, or what you did," she whispered and then fell silent for a while.

Nothing. He felt with his mind, trying to remember how he'd done it when he was part of the gestalt.

For the next few hours, Garcia pulled at the debris until his hands bled from cuts.

When he finished, he checked another room, then another.

He never doubted that he'd find other survivors.

In time, she cried, giving herself over completely to her grief, until she had emptied herself.

"Well baby, time to move on," she said, wiping away her tears, and holding her stomach.

It had already begun to feel like a dream, full of half-remembered images that had made sense at the time.

When he was

Davenport

"Oh, Josh,"

Sophia

Beating the

sure there was no one else alive, Garcia pushed open the door, and checked the next room, and then heard voices. He ran to see if they were friend or enemy.

was going home. Maybe his family had lived. If not, he would manage. He had always been a survivor.

she wiped dust from her dead lover's face, and kissed it. "What am I going to do?" She finally slept, still holding his lifeless body.

pressed her lips a last time to the cold face, climbed to her feet, and left.

wall in frustration he muttered, “No use, it’s gone and marched from the room.

CHAPTER TWENTY-SEVEN

The room was a jumbled ruin of plaster, wood, metal and other, less clearly defined organic substance, all competing for every available inch of floor space. Mounds of rubble were separated by uneven plains of masonry and an occasional uncovered body.

The great, gray-green lumpy mass that had been Bramaragh lay silent and unmoving. Until, on one of the smaller heads, an eye opened, slowly, as if the effort was almost too much for it.

One of the drones still lived. Effectively, it was still Bramaragh, for it possessed all of Bramaragh's memories. It could no longer sense the alternate worlds, but that no longer mattered; it knew the heretics were finished. It had all the time in its one world to rebuild its empire.

CHAPTER TWENTY-EIGHT

Amidst the jumbled ruin of plaster, wood, metal and flesh, a figure sat and coughed, until it retched fluid onto the floor. It felt around for something, squatted and then patted the ground, until it found what it was looking for. It put a pair of glasses on, but they were so badly broken, that they were useless. "Bloody load of crap!" he muttered.

"Hello?" a woman's voice said, voice tremulous. "Who's that?"

"My name's Corporal Davenport, Miss. You are?"

"My name's Caitlin," she said, coughing again. "The last thing I remember is these things bringing me in here. Then they made me look into that thing's eyes..." she trailed off, and let out a deep shuddering sigh.

She doesn't sound like a threat, Davenport thought. He checked his gun, just to be sure. The barrel was so blocked that if he fired it, it would explode. He shrugged.

They checked for other survivors. Finally, Davenport said, "It looks like no one else was as lucky as us."

"No," Caitlin said bleakly. She touched his arm gently. He had noticed that she did that a lot. He didn't mind. He'd been alone too long. "What's your first name, Corporal?" she asked.

He thought about saying "Bunny," and decided against it. "You can call me Nick," he said with a grin. "It's a nickname."

She groaned dutifully and took his arm, "Okay, Nick, let's get out of here."

CHAPTER TWENTY-NINE

In the jumbled ruins, Cassidy awoke with a start. He lay still, his heart hammering. Swallowing, he licked his lips and, taking a deep breath, rolled across the room, wincing as rubble poked him in the back. When he was in a corner, he climbed to his feet. He thought he had seen movement. He kicked at the things that had been Bramaragh and hopped, cursing, just as Garcia had done in another timeline.

"Josh?" Sophia's voice was soft, but in the near-silence of the room, it seemed to echo and reverberate.

He turned to face her, a huge smile spreading. "Hello." The single, innocuous word was weighted with emotion.

"We made it then?" She wiped dust from her face and broke into a fit of coughing.

"It looks that way."

There were so many things he wanted to say to her, but he couldn't find the words. Instead he clambered gingerly through the rubble to check for other survivors.

It took them an hour of lifting and digging with their hands. By the end, the blood oozed from scores of nicks and cuts, making the dust sticky. "No one," he sighed.

"At least," she said with an attempt at brightness that faltered, "That thing hasn't survived, either." She tore a strip of cloth from her overalls, licked it, and gently wiped away the soot, and dust and blood from his face. He stood with his head bowed to the level of her face while she cleaned him.

He sensed there were many things she wanted to say. "My turn," he said, tearing a strip of cloth from his own uniform. He licked it and wiped her face. "The dust must be thicker on you." He found a water canteen lying to one side, and tipping a little onto the cloth, he wiped her face clean and on an impulse, kissed the tip of her nose. "Better?"

"Mmm-hunh," she nodded, smiled and wrinkled the end of her nose. "I can feel your contentment," she said. "Sort of like a warm glow."

"Me too," he said and added, "I mean, I can feel your emotions, at least on a superficial level."

"I sense worry, too."

"There may be alternates where Bramaragh survived."

"Does it matter?" she said.

"Not for the moment. If we've rid this world of the shadow of the dragon, then that's a beginning. I don't know if there's much more we can do. Don't know if we can Shift to alternate realities, if we even have Talents left."

"Do you want to Shift?" she asked.

"NO!" He took a deep breath and added more calmly, "At the moment, we don't know how things have changed- we might Shift and not be able to return." *We don't know how things have changed.* They had changed. He could feel the afterimages of the other Cassidys' thoughts receding like the tide. They were almost over the horizon now, out of sight, but he could still feel them.

Little by little, though, they were leaving him empty. The vacuum needed filling, and microns at a time, his 'normal' self was expanding to fill the void. He wondered if the loneliness would ever go away completely. He reached out for Sophia.

She gazed at him, and moments later, he felt invisible hands clamp his ankles and lift him a few inches into the air.

She looked down at the ground, at a bee crawling through the dust. "It's dying," she whispered, crouching down to look at it. "It's used its sting, and now it's fading away like the sunset." Her forehead wrinkled, as she whispered, "I don't know if I can do this." She smiled. "That's the sting repaired!" She straightened up, and the bee toppled into the air.

"Sophia," he whispered, bending down to kiss her. She put a finger to his lips. She sighed and said, "Let's go outside, into the clean air." They walked away, and Cassidy saw in the broken mirrors, their reflections; an infinity of Cassidys and Sophias walk away, down their halls of mirrors.

The bee flew out through a gap in a window.

CHAPTER THIRTY

The lightning flickered. In the moments of its existence, it remembered its friend Cassidy, and experienced an emotion whose closest analogy was contentment.

ABOUT THE AUTHOR

Colin Harvey's short fiction has appeared in Peridot Books, The Pedestal Magazine, and Flash Me! His first novel, *Vengeance*, was published in 2001, and reprinted as a trade paperback by The Winterborn Press in 2005.

His fiction can be found at www.geocities.com/colin_harvey

He is working on a fantasy novel, *The Silk Palace*.

Printed in the United Kingdom
by Lightning Source UK Ltd.
113635UKS00001B/450